PRAISE FOR JODI TAY
THE CHRONICLES OF ST. M. ... ᴊᴇʀɪᴇs

"A carnival ride through laughter and tears with a bit of time travel thrown in for spice . . . readers will be impatient for later installments."

—*Publishers Weekly*, starred review

"What a mess. A *glorious, glorious* mess. Let no one ever say that *Just One Damned Thing After Another* is a book that fails to live up to its title . . . . These books are so perfectly bingeable."

—*B&N Sci-fi Blog*

"Taylor does a great job of setting up an appealing cast of characters in this new series opener, most especially the intrepid Max. There is plenty of humor, lots of action, and even a touch of romance."

—*Library Journal*

"Taylor has written a madcap and very funny hodgepodge of a novel whose pacing and humor is reminiscent of a Simon Pegg–Edgar Wright film."

—*Booklist*

"Max is a thoroughly hilarious and confident narrator and the sense of real danger, interspersed with copious amounts of tea, pervades the story. This is the kind of book that you walk away from believing in time travel."

—*Manhattan Book Review*

"Danger, romance, history, financial and academic politics, hidden agendas, dangerous assignments, characters you care about, and the feeling that more is going on than you're actually reading about. I can hardly wait for book two. *Just One Damned Thing After Another* is a true page-turner."

—SFRevu

"*Just One Damned Thing After Another* is a novel that wastes no time getting to the good stuff . . . if character-driven stories are your cup of tea, then you'll find plenty to like. Max is hilarious, and I love her spirited and crafty nature."

—The Bibliosanctum

"If you're a fan of time travel, or if you're a fan of madcap British comedies, or better yet if you're a fan of both, then you'll want to check out *The Chronicles of St. Mary's.*"

—Adventures Fantastic

"The book can't be put down, and I loved every minute. I look forward to reading them all."

—YA Lit Ramblings

"The writing was witty and fun, and kept making me smile page after page. . . . Max is a brilliant character, the kind of character you root for, faults and all."

—All Things Urban Fantasy

A TRAIL THROUGH TIME

A TRAIL THROUGH TIME

THE CHRONICLES OF ST. MARY'S **BOOK FOUR**

JODI TAYLOR

Night Shade Books
New York

First Night Shade Books edition published 2016

Night Shade books may be purchased in bulk at special discounts for sales promotion, corporate gifts, fund-raising, or educational purposes. Special editions can also be created to specifications. For details, contact the Special Sales Department, Night Shade Books, 307 West 36th Street, 11th Floor, New York, NY 10018 or info'skyhorsepublishing.com.

Night Shade Books™ is a trademark of Skyhorse Publishing, Inc.®, a Delaware corporation.

Visit our website at www.nightshadebooks.com.

10 9 8 7 6 5 4

Library of Congress Cataloging-in-Publication Data

Names: Taylor, Jodi, author.
Title: A trail through time / Jodi Taylor.
Description: First Night Shade Books edition. | New York: Night Shade Books, 2016. | Series: The Chronicles of St. Mary's; Book 4
Identifiers: LCCN 2016012892 | ISBN 9781597808712 (paperback: alk. paper)
Subjects: LCSH: Time travel—Fiction. | BISAC: FICTION / Science Fiction / Adventure. | FICTION / Science Fiction / General. | FICTION / Fantasy / General. | GSAFD: Science fiction.
Classification: LCC PR6120.A937 T73 2016 | DDC 823/.92—dc23
LC record available at https://lccn.loc.gov/2016012892

Print ISBN: 978-1-59780-871-2

Printed in the United States of America

This book is dedicated to all the staff—past and present—of North Yorkshire Library Service. Thank you for your patience and your friendship during all those long dark years of fear and toil.

DRAMATIS THINGUMMY

Dr. Edward Bairstow   Director of St. Mary's.

Miss Rosie Lee   His PA. A nightmare.

TECHNICIANS

Dieter   Chief Technical Officer.

HISTORIANS

Tim Peterson   Chief Operations Officer.

Kalinda Black   Liaison Officer at Thirsk University.

Mary Schiller   Historian.

Greta Van Owen   Historian.

Mr. Clerk   Historian.

Paula Prentiss   Historian.

IT

Isabella Barclay   Head of IT.

Polly Perkins   IT Technician.

SECURITY

Major Ian Guthrie   Head of Security.

Mr. Markham   Security guard.

Mr. Randall   Security guard.

Mr. Evans   Security guard.

Research & Development

Professor Andrew Rapson	Head of R&D. Crumpet igniter.
Doctor Octavius Dowson	Librarian and Archivist.
Mrs. Theresa Mack	Kitchen Supremo revisiting her urban guerrilla skills.
Mrs. Mavis Enderby	Head of Wardrobe. Ditto with the skills.
Mrs. Shaw	Another one not to be trusted with a loaded condom.

Sick Bay

Doctor Helen Foster	Does not play well with Others.
Nurse Diane Hunter	The object of Markham's affections.
Turk	Officially a horse.
Maxwell	Refugee. Lost. Bewildered.
Chief Leon Farrell	Former Chief Technical Officer. Warrior. Hero.
Mrs. Partridge	Kleio, Muse of History. Former PA to Dr. Bairstow. Where is she?
Madam President	Judge, jury, and if things go badly, executioner.

Villains

Colonel Albay	Head of the Time Police
The Time Police	Bad news. For everyone.

PROLOGUE

*A*ND ONCE AGAIN, I was running.
I was always bloody running.
Over the years, I've run from Jack the Ripper; blood-crazed dinosaurs; a crowd of Cambridge citizenry hell-bent on indicting me for mirror-theft and witchcraft; Assyrian soldiers; you name it, I've scampered away from it. With varying degrees of success.

But—the point I'm trying to make here—is that I've always known what I was running from. I rarely knew what I was running to—I'm an historian and we don't always plan that far ahead—but I usually knew what I was running from.

Sadly, not in this case. In this case, I was running for my life and I didn't have a bloody clue why.

THIS NEXT BIT IS difficult. We all need to pay attention, because I'm not sure I understand it myself.

I'm Madeleine Maxwell, an historian. I work for the St. Mary's Institute of Historical Research. We investigate major historical events in contemporary time. It's time travel, OK. Using small, apparently stone-built shacks known as pods, we jump to whichever time period we've been assigned; we observe, document, record, do our best to stay out of trouble, and return to St. Mary's in triumph. Our pods are small, cramped, frequently squalid, and the toilet never works properly. For some reason, they always smell of cabbage, but they're our pods and we love them.

Following the death of Leon Farrell, I accepted the position of Deputy Director of St. Mary's and put in for my last jump. For sentimental reasons, I chose France, 1415, the Battle of Agincourt. As usual, we—my colleague, Peterson, and I—pushed our luck and this time we really pushed it too far.

Peterson was badly injured in the attack on the baggage train. In an effort to draw our pursuers away, I hit him over the head with a rock (unconventional treatment, true, but I was trying to save his life at the time), rolled him under a bush where the rescue party would be sure to find him, and ran like hell in the opposite direction. As far and as fast as I could, until someone stabbed me through the heart. A fatal wound.

I gave it all up without too much regret and commended my soul to the god of historians, who, as usual, wasn't concentrating, because I fell forwards, not into oblivion as expected, but onto someone's hairy Axminster carpet instead.

Still with me so far?

Mrs. Partridge, PA to the Director of St. Mary's, and, in her spare time the Muse of History, snatched me from my world and dumped me, confused and in pain, into a different one. This one. Pausing long enough to inform me I had a job to do and to get on with it—she departed. Because God forbid she should ever make things easy for me. I thought I'd been saved. And yes, I had, but only in the way that turkeys are saved for Christmas.

In this new world, it was me who had died and Leon who had lived. He had not handled my death well. I thought she'd brought me here for him. To save him. To comfort him. I got that wrong.

Leon and I had a painful and confused reunion during which I slugged him with a blue plastic dustpan. Long story.

Anyway, the upshot was that I was here now, living in this new world which closely resembled my own. Although not in every way, as I would soon discover.

Leon and I, strangers to each other, and scared to death of making a mess of our second chance, agreed to take things slowly. We would start a new life together in Rushford, away from St. Mary's, and see what happened.

What happened was more pain, more confusion, and a very great deal of running away.

Now that I've written all that down, I'm not sure I believe it myself.

The point is, though, that I thought I was safe. That, finally, I'd come to rest. The phrase, *and she lived happily ever after*, comes to mind. Although in my case, *and she lived*, is the important bit. The other part, *happily ever after*, is always a bit of an optional extra for me. But my plan was that I would live quietly with Leon. I'd paint, he'd invent things, and we would finally have a peaceful life together.

We had one day. Not even that. We didn't even make it to lunchtime.

ONE

THE FIRST MORNING OF my new life.

I'd had a good night's sleep, a very long, hot bath, and several mugs of tea. Thus fortified, and in the full glory of yellow-and-white-spotted pyjamas, I was now feeling very much more on top of things and ready to get to grips with this new life.

In an effort to overcome the slight social awkwardness occasioned by the two of us not knowing where to begin, he was fussing around doing tea and toast, and I was busy at the kitchen table.

"What are you doing?" he asked, plonking a mug of steaming tea in front of me.

"Writing my obituary."

"What on earth for?"

"Well, you can't do it, can you? I never met you before yesterday."

"My surprise was based less on the fact that we've hardly met, but more because you're not actually dead."

"No, but I was. Nearly. Maybe I'm a zombie. Do you have any brains?"

"No brains," he said, putting a jar on the table. "Will Marmite do?"

"A very acceptable alternative."

There was a slight pause. I wondered if perhaps his Max hadn't liked Marmite. Was this how it was always going to be? Each of us silently comparing this new version of ourselves to the old one? I liked Marmite—maybe his Max hadn't. I don't like milk—maybe his Max had bathed in the stuff. Suppose now . . . suppose we weren't . . .

I curled my hands around my steaming mug. It was so hard to see how this could work. Things had not gone that well for us the first time round, and then he'd died, and then I'd died—well, I would have if Mrs. Partridge hadn't brought me here. Both of us had so much history. . . . If anything went wrong—and it would—I wasn't sure I could survive losing him again. And then I remembered that wonderful, heart-bursting, soul-lifting moment in his workshop when I saw him again, and I knew that, between the two of us, anything and everything was possible.

I looked up and he was watching me, following my every thought. That hadn't changed, anyway.

"It's not going to be a problem," he said softly. "We don't have to rush anything. We have our whole lives ahead of us and we'll just take each day as it comes. The first priority is to get you fit and well again. I don't like women running around the flat with big holes in their chests. It makes the place look untidy."

"All closed up now," I said, squinting down at my yellow-and-white-spotted chest. "It just hurts a bit every now and then."

Actually, it still hurt a lot. Mrs. Partridge had closed the wound but not healed it. Initially, I'd been annoyed, but she knew what she was doing. I had no choice but to remain there and take things slowly. For a week, at least. A lot can happen in a week.

And it was about to.

The telephone rang.

Busy buttering toast, Leon ignored it and the machine cut in.

I heard his voice. "Please leave a message."

Dr. Bairstow, his voice harsh with urgency said, "Leon. Get out. They're here. Run!"

The line went dead.

He dropped the butter knife. I watched it leave a long, greasy smear across the floor. He never even looked at it.

"You have thirty seconds. Grab anything valuable to you. Move."

I didn't bother with questions. He wouldn't have bothered answering them.

I lurched into the living room and grabbed the model of the Trojan Horse he'd once made for me. Looking around, I also snatched up my little book on Agincourt—the only thing left over from my childhood—and my one photo of him and me. I draped my red snake around my neck—I'd made it in hospital while recovering from Jack the Ripper and there was no way I was leaving it behind—and presented myself at the back door with seconds to spare.

He eyed the snake. "One day, we must take a moment to discuss your skewed priorities." He hustled me out of the back door, down the steps, and into the garden.

I could hear sounds on the other side of the garden wall. "Aren't you going to lock up?"

"Won't do the slightest bit of good. Get into the pod. Hurry."

His pod nestled in a corner of the tiny garden, disguised as an anonymous garden shed. I called for the door to open as he ripped away the clothesline and kicked the water butt aside.

I had just time to inhale the familiar pod smell of overloaded electrics, stale people, damp carpet, and cabbage, before he piled in after me and slapped the door control.

"Don't worry," he said, calmly. "We'll be quite safe in here. I'm activating the camouflage system. We'll just wait here quietly. With a bit of luck they'll fail to find us and go away again."

I should be asking—who were *they*? Why wouldn't we be safe? Or the all-encompassing—what the bloody hell is going on here?

But I didn't. For one thing, all his attention was focused on the screen, watching for any movement. He probably wouldn't even have heard me. I stood, festooned with books, photos, and snakes, and felt my chest throb. And I still hadn't had breakfast.

"Here." He swivelled the seat. I was glad to sit down. I wasn't anything like as fit as I thought I was.

We waited in silence. But not for long.

They came right through the gate and they didn't stop to open it first. It exploded off its hinges and cartwheeled away. They poured across the little yard and fanned out. About six of them, as far as I could see, although there would be two or more outside, securing the entrance. They were frighteningly quick, quiet, and professional.

Two raced up the steps, kicked the back door open, and disappeared into the flat.

The rest made straight for us. Straight into the garden. Straight towards the pod.

They couldn't possibly see us. There was nothing to see. We were camouflaged. With a background of a simple stone wall, we were invisible.

I felt a twist of fear. They knew we were here. They might not be able to see us, whoever they were, but they knew we were here somewhere.

My first impression was that they were military. They wore full body armour. Black-visored helmets gave them a sinister look and they carried some very serious weaponry. Not rifles, but rifle-shaped. With an underslung something-or-other. They moved smoothly, efficiently, and as a unit. We were definitely in some deep shit here.

Leon swore softly.

They dropped to the ground, weapons covering every inch of the small garden. How could they know we were here? What was going on?

With every angle covered, the soldier at the back raised something that looked, to my non-technical eyes, like a hair dryer.

Was that an EMP device? An electro-magnetic pulse would disable the pod and render us helpless.

Now Leon really swore, swept me from my seat and onto the floor, at the same time shouting, "Computer! Initiate jump."

"Jump initiated."

The world went white.

WE LANDED WITHOUT EVEN a tremor. He scanned the console, flicking switches and shutting things down. His hands danced over the controls in the way that was so familiar to me. Since he was busy, I lay quietly on the floor where he'd dumped me, stared up at the ceiling, and had a bit of a think.

They were obviously looking either for him or for me. And since he'd been in Rushford for some time now, presumably living a blameless life, and I was a recently arrived alien intruder in this world, it seemed likely that it was me they wanted.

That they were connected in some way with St. Mary's, I had no doubt. They'd been carrying some really cool kit. Besides, there was Dr. Bairstow's warning call. They'd hit St. Mary's and Rushford almost simultaneously. Something serious had occurred and it was almost certain to be me. How had they found me so quickly? And if they caught me—what would they do with me?

As if I didn't know the answer to that one.

Thanks very much, Mrs. Partridge. She'd snatched me out of my own world and dropped me into this one. From the frying pan into the furnace, you could say. Without warning. Without breakfast. And now something was after me. Something serious. What is it with me and a quiet life?

Leon came to sit beside me on the floor. "Thank you for not bombarding me with questions."

"A temporary respite. Make the most of it."

"Did I hurt you?"

"On the contrary, I've never been hurled to the floor with such style. A five point nine score for that one."

"Up you get, then."

I sat in the seat and stared at the screen and the familiar coordinates. I knew where we were.

My Leon and I had a special place and time. A small island in the eastern Mediterranean, thousands of years ago, before people turned up. I loved St. Mary's dearly, but, sometimes, you really want to be alone and so we would come here, to this special place, to spend some special time together. Best of all, absolutely no one knew about it. Sometimes it shows on an ancient map as the island of Skaxos, but mostly it's too small even to appear, let alone be named. We would be quite safe here.

He finished at the console. "It's still dark outside. Shall we take a moment to catch our breath?"

"Good idea. And you can tell me what this is all about."

He got up and put the kettle on. The traditional St. Mary's method of dealing with a crisis.

I'VE ALREADY SAID MY name is Madeleine Maxwell. Chief Operations Officer at the St. Mary's Institute of Historical Research. Or rather, I was. Since I was never confirmed as Deputy Director, I wasn't sure what I was now. Apart from short, ginger, and bewildered, of course, but that's pretty much my default state, so don't pay too much attention to that.

A week ago, I'd been in the Cretaceous period, fighting off a hungry Deinonychus with a fire extinguisher and some harsh words. This time yesterday, I had been at Agincourt, staring at a sword in my chest, just before being transported to another world. I'd just had time for a bath and now, here I was, being thrown around the timeline—in my pyjamas. Someone owed me an explanation. And breakfast.

He draped my dressing gown around my shoulders.

"Thank you," I said in surprise.

"Well, some of us were a little more focused when grabbing important equipment to see us through our current crisis."

I smiled sadly at my little pile of possessions. "This is all I have in the world. You can't blame me."

"I keep telling you—half of everything is yours. You left me everything in your will."

We all make out wills. With our lifestyle, it's compulsory. They're all lodged with Dr. Bairstow. In my world, I'd left everything to Leon and then when he died, I'd divided it between close friends: Markham, Peterson, and Kal. In addition, I'd made provision for putting a bit behind the bar as well. Without a doubt, back at my St. Mary's they were all having a world-class piss-up at this very moment. It's always good to know you can be a disruptive influence, even after death. A posthumous pain in the management arse.

"So, who are they, Leon? And what do they want?"

"They're the Time Police."

That meant nothing to me. I must have looked bewildered.

"You didn't have them in your world?"

"No."

"Well—hope you never do."

Silence. He made the tea.

"All right. Here goes. A long time ago, I told my Max that Dr. Bairstow and I were from the future."

I nodded. "You told me you'd been sent back to protect St. Mary's. That we were—would be—under threat."

"Well, it looks as if that time has come."

"Hold on. Wasn't that Clive Ronan?"

"Yes—in his own way. But the real threat to St. Mary's here is the Time Police. Sometime in the future—nothing to do with St. Mary's, thank God—several countries almost simultaneously discover how to travel in time. Suddenly, everyone wants it because everyone thinks they'll be able to change their past and they all want to be first. An attempt is made to reach an international agreement that would allow limited and strictly controlled time travel, while still protecting the timeline. It holds for a while. A very little while—but the temptation to go back and re-fight old wars, this time with hindsight, is too great."

He looked at me. "You can imagine?"

I nodded. I could indeed.

I've never had a high opinion of the human race and I'm not wrong. Just look at us. We've been given this gift. This wonderful gift. Alone of every species on the planet, we're able to see our own past. To build on our triumphs. To learn from our mistakes. To discover at first hand, exactly how we arrived where we are today. And instead of regarding it as the wonderful gift it is, we'd tried to use it for nothing more productive than rehashing old conflicts.

I personally think humans have gotten about as far as we can go. We're wrecking the planet. We're never short of good reasons to massacre each other. Wrong god. Wrong race. Wrong colour. Wrong sex. I'm actually quite surprised a thoroughly pissed-off History hasn't waved a flaming sword and we're all back in caves in the snow, chewing on half-cooked mammoth. And even that's more than we deserve.

No wonder we still can't get to Mars. I suspect the Universe is making damned sure we don't get the chance to contaminate other planets with our stupidity. It's keeping us on this one where the only thing we can damage is each other.

He sipped his tea and continued. "Imagine what could have happened, Max. Nations would flicker briefly—then disappear. People would live, then die, then live again. Events would happen. Then wouldn't have happened. And then might happen again, but differently. Maybe some vital events wouldn't have happened at all. History could be changed and re-written so many times that it could be completely overwhelmed. It could have been the end of everything."

I felt a cold shudder run through me.

"But—that didn't happen? Did it?"

"No, it didn't happen. With the threat of everything falling apart, the Time Police were formed. To get everything back on track. They were drawn from the military, the police, and a few from St. Mary's personnel. Their remit was far-reaching. Some say too far-reaching. They had just one aim. Whatever it took—by whatever means necessary—to sort out the timeline. And they do. They do an excellent job. But when I say they do whatever it takes to get the job done, you understand, don't you?"

I did understand. Their job was to annihilate anything that could threaten the timeline. And I was, if not a threat, at the very least, an anomaly. And they knew I was here. They wouldn't rest until they found me.

He continued. "Nations are—induced—to give up time travel. No one wants it any longer, anyway. By now, they've all discovered that time travel is like holding a snake because, sooner or later, it always twists in your hand and bites you. And they've discovered they can't pillage the past, so there's all that expenditure and no return on it. And the possible consequences of their actions have been brought home to them in no uncertain terms. Of course, none of them wants to be the first to give it up, but the Time Police broker international

agreements and after a lot of pushing and shoving, things settle back down again.

"As I said, this is all in the future. St. Mary's, who have
kept their heads well down during all of this, are allowed to
remain in existence, but subject to strict controls. The Time
Police move up and down the timeline, monitoring all incarnations of St. Mary's, past, present, and future. All jumps must
be approved. We have to submit about a ton of paperwork;
risk assessments, perceived benefits, methodology, personnel
involved, aims and objectives—the works. We have to get permission for every jump and not much is permitted."

"Who gives this permission?"

"The initial application goes through our employers—
Thirsk University. And then Thirsk forwards the application to
the Time Police with their recommendations."

He paused to drink his tea again and I had a bit of a think.

"So what goes wrong?"

"From monitoring, it's only a small step to complete control. Which is what they wanted all along. Complete control
over all incarnations of St. Mary's. And largely they've succeeded. Can you imagine the power that gives them? A few
isolated pockets of independence still exist. Our St. Mary's is
one of them."

"Is that why they were after us?"

"No. I think they've been alerted to your presence. At best,
they'll want you for questioning. At worst . . ."

We fell silent, each staring into our empty mug.

"Come on," he said, with decision, pulling me to my feet.
"It's getting light. We'll check through our supplies and then
go outside and set up camp."

We let ourselves out of the pod just as the early morning
sunshine swept across the landscape, bringing life and colour
back into the world. I stood for a moment, just breathing in
the peace. I hadn't been here for a long time. The last time had

been just before Troy. After Troy, my Leon and I weren't even speaking to each other, let alone indulging in any romantic moments. Everything was as I remembered it and yet I'd never been here before. This was not my world.

A great wave of grief came out of nowhere. Grief for my St. Mary's that I would never see again. For Tim, lying injured and sad. For Kalinda, my friend. For Markham and Guthrie. For the Boss. Even for Mrs. Partridge. I remembered the smell of breakfast in the mornings, the clatter of feet on ancient wooden floors, the sound of furious argument—or scholarly debate as they insisted it be called—between Dr. Dowson and Professor Rapson. I remembered the click of the Boss's stick on stone floors. And it was all gone. Forever.

The grief subsided to be replaced by fear. I was alone in a familiar but strange world and now it seemed I was a fugitive as well. I'd jumped into this pod without a second thought and it struck me now (too late) that this might not have been the wisest move.

On the other hand, I'm an historian. I work for St. Mary's. I wouldn't know a wise move if it tried to hump my left leg.

Leon interrupted these less-than-useful thoughts. "Shall we sit down?"

He spread a blanket and we leaned against a rock in the sun. Just as I always used to with my Leon.

I closed my eyes and struggled a little.

"Are you in pain? Does your chest hurt?"

What to say? How to convey the sudden, almost overwhelming feelings of panic, of isolation, of fear?

I kept my eyes closed. He didn't speak, which I appreciated.

Eventually, I said, "Sorry. Just a bit of a moment there. All gone now."

"What would you like me to do? Leave you for a moment? Talk about something else? Fetch you another interminable cup of tea?"

I drew a deep breath. "Actually, what I want . . . what I really, really want . . . is just to sit here for a moment."

He made a move to get up but I pulled him down again. "No, it's all right. Please stay. Perhaps now . . . now is the moment to . . . to . . ."

He sat again, picked up a stick, and began to draw patterns in the dust as the two most emotionally inarticulate people on the planet circled warily around . . . feelings.

I said, "This must be difficult for you, as well."

He hesitated. "It is, but I think I'm a winner in all this. I've not lost anything—I've gained. Gained you. But you've lost everything and all you've gained is me. And I'm not the right me."

He did understand. I should have more faith.

I smiled. "I don't consider myself a loser at all. And let's face it, at the moment, neither of us has anything more than each other. And fugitive status, of course."

"Yes, that was effortless, wasn't it? One moment I'm a respectable small-business owner in one of the most sedate market-towns in England, then you turn up and unleash the Forces of Darkness, and now we're hiding on a small island, five thousand years ago."

"With no breakfast," I said, highlighting the main issue. "I bet you didn't think to bring my toast with you?"

He sighed. "Nothing but complaints."

"Would it have killed you to have grabbed a slice on the way out? I bet these Time Police people are scoffing my breakfast even as we speak."

We sat for a while, as the world got brighter and warmer.

He shifted his position. "I was going to ask, but you don't have to talk about it if you don't want to. How did you get here?"

"You mean here, in this world?"

"Yes. What happened at Agincourt?"

I started slowly. "It was my last jump. Tim Peterson and me. I was going to be Deputy Director, you know."

"I can only assume that Dr. Bairstow had suffered some sort of neural event. Did you manage to get yourself stabbed during the battle? Did you get too close?"

"Well, of course we got too close. We were right up there with the archers. But no, it happened when we went to check out the baggage train at the rear."

I closed my eyes and it all sprang to life in front of me.

"The baggage train was behind the battle. As were the hundreds of French prisoners. We wanted to see if Henry's order to kill them was justified. And if it was carried out at all. Just as we arrived, a bunch of French peasants came out of nowhere. They weren't fighting in the battle; they'd come to scavenge, rob the dead and wounded, steal the horses—that sort of thing.

"I know what you're going to say, but we were actually retreating. We were on our way back to the pod. There was fighting all around us. The bastards were killing the wounded, the priests, and the young boys, everyone they could. One came out of nowhere and nearly took Peterson's arm off."

I stopped and swallowed, reliving that moment.

"He was . . . so brave. I got him away and tied up the wound. He was conscious, but barely. The pod wasn't far away but he wasn't going to make it. I'd lost you. I couldn't lose him as well."

I stopped.

"What did you do?"

"I pushed him into a hollow, hit him over the head with a rock, buried him under the leaves, and left him."

"Good job he was a friend of yours. What do you do to people you don't like?"

I choked out a laugh.

He rubbed my arm. "That's better. Then what?"

"I took off. I ran and ran. Through the wet woods. Making as much noise as I could. They followed me. One was ahead of me. I ran slap into him. While I was dealing with him, someone ran me through with a sword. I never knew anything about it."

I stopped. He was still drawing triangles in the dirt. I took a deep breath and lived it all again. "Everything went very quiet and still. I looked up at the black branches and the white sky. Nothing moved."

I was talking to myself, now.

"I didn't feel the need to breathe. Everything had ended. Everything was over. I felt no regret. I'd given Tim a fighting chance. I fell forwards. Onto your carpet. Which I've bled all over and probably lost you your cleaning deposit. Sorry about that."

"And that's what happened?"

I nodded. What I'd told him was the truth. Just not all of it. I hadn't mentioned Mrs. Partridge's part in all this. I mean, what do you say? "Oh, I was dying in the 15th century and then the Muse of History plucked me out of my world and dropped me into yours—to fulfil some task she wouldn't tell me about?"

I don't know why I was so wary of mentioning Mrs. Partridge. It's not as if her role makes the story any more weird, any less believable, or any more impossible. Nothing could. The whole thing is completely weird, unbelievable, and impossible. On the other hand, I travel through time for a living, so don't talk to me about weird, unbelievable, or impossible. Really, I suppose, instead of jumping backwards or forwards, I'd just gone—sideways.

Please do not repeat that theory to any reputable physicist. I don't want to be spat on in the streets.

I LEFT LEON SETTING up camp and wandered slowly through the trees for a first glimpse of the glittering, turquoise sea, listening to the birds greeting the new day, hearing the distant crash of surf and the sound of the wind sighing in the pine trees. This was always a special moment for me. I sat on a rock and relived some happy memories.

Trees marched down to the shore, their acid-green foliage contrasting sharply with the rust-red soil and rocks. All the colours were sharp and fresh. The sun shone from a cloudless, blue, blue sky. It would be hot later on. Everything was still and peaceful. This had always been a little piece of heaven. Nothing bad ever happened here.

Not that I ever got to enjoy it for long. As usual, I was chief wood-gatherer and water-fetcher. I would have been the designated heavy-load carrier as well, but, fortunately, I had a fatal chest wound to recover from, so I was, to some extent, excused boots. And cooking. Actually, I'm not so much excused cooking as banned from approaching any food preparation area over three continents. Which is not the harsh punishment it might seem.

Leon busied himself lighting the fire, and I set off on the perpetual search for firewood. I'd kicked off my slippers and dressing gown and wandered along familiar paths, feeling the soft carpet of pine needles under my feet, inhaling the scents of pine and sea, and listening to the seabirds crying as they circled the rocky shore. Nothing had changed. Seasons came and went but nothing ever changed here. It would be thousands of years before people arrived on this little island.

There was plenty of wood around and I strolled slowly through the trees, bending painfully to pick up the smaller pieces.

And then, somewhere behind me, a bird called a harsh warning and erupted into the air, wings beating hard as it sought for height.

Instinct cut in. I drew back behind a tree and stood stock-still. Waiting.

I saw the movement several seconds before I realised what I was looking at. And there. And over there as well.

A line of familiar black-clad soldiers was moving slowly uphill. They weren't charging. There was a deliberation about their movements. They kept in strict formation. They weren't charging—they were beating. They were making sure nothing could slip past them.

Shit! How could they possibly have found us?

There was no time for finesse. They would see me as soon as I moved. There is no environment in the world in which yellow-and-white PJs can fade quietly into the background.

I dropped the wood, shouted a warning to Leon, and set off, running uphill as best I could, my chest straining with the effort. It was far too soon after my recent death for all this exertion.

Behind me, someone shouted an order. They'd seen me.

I half expected a hail of bullets but it didn't happen. Maybe they couldn't get a clear shot at me amongst the trees.

Leon was hurling our stuff back into the pod.

I risked a look back over my shoulder and two of them were pointing the hair-dryer things again.

If they were EMPs then they didn't need to shoot us. They could just disable the pod and then pick us up at their leisure. It was a small island. We wouldn't be able to avoid them for long.

I was struggling uphill. My chest hurt. I couldn't catch my breath. This time yesterday, I'd been dead. What did people expect from me?

I shouted to Leon. "Go! Get away!"

He ignored me. He ran towards me, seized an arm, and literally towed me into the pod. As we crashed through the door, he shouted, "Computer. Emergency extraction. Now."

I braced myself because I knew this would hurt.

And it did.

The world went black.

TWO

LAY ON MY BACK amid a clutter of stuff and stared up at the ceiling.

Bloody hell, not again.

Emergency extraction is—not surprisingly—for emergencies. When getting out quickly is more important than getting out safely. Because it hurts. You declare an emergency and the pod hurls you away from the current catastrophe at nose-bleeding speed. Shortly followed by bone-breaking impact. Believe it or not, there's the odd historian who's never, ever, had to call for emergency extraction. I, on the other hand, am losing count of the number of times it has happened to me. And they never get any easier.

I turned my head. Leon was slowly lifting himself off the floor.

"Stay where you are, Max."

As if I had any choice.

"We need to check whether they've followed us again. Just lie still. I'll get to you in a minute."

I was glad to see he didn't let personal concerns affect his priorities. There was no point in him bending anxiously over me as the Time Police crashed through the door.

He heaved himself up and dropped heavily into the seat, flexing his shoulder painfully. There's no such thing as a painless extraction. I had no difficulty in obeying his instructions to stay put.

"Well," he said, eventually. "It's the 17th century. London, I think, and it's cold. Actually, it's very cold."

Yes, it would be. Britain suffered the Little Ice Age between the 14th and 19th centuries. I groaned to myself. Lacking any return coordinates, the computer had randomly selected a time and place. Its priority was to safeguard pod and crew. Probably in that order. Since fifty per cent of the crew were still in their pyjamas, somewhere a little warmer would have been appreciated.

"I think," he said, thoughtfully, "we've landed on the River Thames. That doesn't seem right."

He began scrolling through screens.

"No," I said. "I think it is. I think you'll find the Thames is frozen over. Will it hold our weight?

He was peering at the screen. "It seems to be holding everyone's weight. There's a small town out there. Booths, tents, stalls, people, bonfires, roasting animals and . . . I think . . . yes, a bear. I don't think one small pod is going to make much difference."

"Are you sure? We came down with a bit of a bang."

"I know," he said, rubbing his elbow, "but there are no signs of splintering ice. And we're camouflaged, so there's no screaming and no panic. Which is remarkable when you think there's been an historian on site now for nearly five minutes. Is it possible you've lost your touch?"

"Yes, very funny," I said, clambering to my feet. "Personally, I always say that any landing you can walk away from has been a good one. Even with a techie driving."

"That was your definition of a good landing, was it?"

"Well, as you say—no external panic and no internal injuries. A huge success by St. Mary's standards."

I joined him at the screen. "Oh, cool. It's a Frost Fair."

"A what?"

"Don't you know about the Frost Fairs?"

"I'm a technician. I have different priorities."

"And yet, here's the historian once again saving the day with vital information the techie needs to know."

"In less than two hundred words, if you can possibly manage that."

"OK. Listen up. In the old days, the Thames was much shallower and wider than it is today. No embankment. All the debris and rubbish would pile up around the narrow piers on London Bridge and almost bring the river to a standstill. So it would freeze over. The weather was much colder then, too. So cold that birds fell dead from the air. Deer died in the parks. People died in the streets and public subscriptions were taken up to provide the poor with fuel to help them survive. Come on."

"You're not going out there?"

"I'm not missing this."

"Are you insane?"

"Leon, I must see this. It's my only chance. I'll never be able to come back."

"If it's so cold that birds are dropping from the skies, do you really want to be out there in your pyjamas?"

I pulled open locker doors. "There must be something."

Reluctantly, he pulled out a jumble of miscellaneous clothing. I saw sweatshirts, socks, gloves. I knew he'd have something. This was his own personal pod. He'd had it for years. In addition to his own cold and wet-weather gear, there was no way he wouldn't have accumulated all sorts of useful stuff.

I scrambled into as many garments as I could get on, tucking my jammy bottoms into several pairs of old socks. He picked up a blanket and cut a slit for my head and I wore it Clint Eastwood style over my dressing gown. And yes, he was right, I did look very odd, especially clumping around in his

outsized wellies with three pairs of socks, but everyone outside
was almost certainly wearing every single item of clothing they
possessed, and possibly their bedding as well, so, as I pointed
out, I fit right in.

He said nothing in a very meaningful way.

We stepped outside. He was absolutely right. It was cold.

Bloody hell, it was cold.

Oh God, it was cold.

Only pride stopped me bolting back into the pod. I felt the
hairs in my nostrils freeze. He wound a scarf around my head
and face.

"Told you."

I glared at him over the scarf.

He smiled. "You have snow in your eyelashes."

Before I could work out what to say to that, he said, "Breathe
through the scarf and don't cough, whatever you do, because
you'll never stop."

I could feel the chill striking up through the rubber soles
and three pairs of socks. My feet instantly turned into blocks
of ice. There was little wind, but the cold passed effortlessly
through my layers of clothing and froze the marrow in my
bones. My heart went out to the poor, huddled together in their
draughty hovels. Some without a proper roof and some probably without proper walls, either. Trying to stay warm. Trying to
stay alive.

"Come on," he said. "Keep moving or go back inside."

We turned back to familiarise ourselves with the pod's location because, sometimes, it's quite tricky finding something
you can't see. We were next to a red-and-white striped booth and
opposite a grubby white canvas awning with looped-up sides,
underneath which quantities of ale were being distributed.

There was plenty of dirty snow on the ice to give us a good
grip, so we were able to stride out quite briskly. He pulled my
arm through his.

"All right?"

I nodded so he wouldn't hear my teeth chattering.

I judged it to be late afternoon. The sun was already setting. Faint stars appeared above us. The odd snowflake drifted down. More people were appearing on the ice, calling to one another and laughing.

They say, "If life gives you lemons, make lemonade." For Londoners, if life gives you a frozen Thames and bitter temperatures then hold a Frost Fair and make some money. They were turning a fight for survival into an entertainment opportunity.

Smoke from thousands of chimneys streamed horizontally in the cold air and choked the city. The last streaks of colour left the sky. I felt even colder, if possible.

However, this was Restoration London in 1683 and it was impossible not to be excited. This was England under that Merry Monarch, Charles Stuart.

No sooner had the less-than-jolly Olly Cromwell died, than the English heaved a huge sigh of relief, resolved never to do that again, and restored the monarchy in the person of that astute party-animal, Charles II. Charles was famous for his mistresses, spaniels, the Great Plague, the Dutch War, the Great Fire of London (when he fought the fire alongside his fellow Londoners), the Royal Society, and at least fourteen illegitimate children. He packed a lot into his twenty-five-year reign.

England threw aside the social and religious restrictions of Cromwell's Commonwealth rule, drew a deep breath—and partied. Necklines and morals plummeted. Skirts, on the other hand, were raised on every conceivable occasion. The country erupted in an outpouring of promiscuity and riotous behaviour. The religiously rigorous departed for America in disgust.

The normal procedure on any assignment should be for us to note our surroundings and check for possible hazards. That's always good fun on a battlefield. Then study the people, behaviour, and clothing, and finally, record and document whatever's happening at the time.

In these conditions, however, there wasn't much chance of any of that. Everything was covered in snow. Huge long icicles hung from booths and nearby buildings as temperatures rose slightly during the day and then dropped again at night. Vertical surfaces glittered under a coating of ice. Everyone was swathed in great bundles of clothing so there was no chance of observing the fashions of the time. Well, we'd just have to do the best we could.

"Look," said Leon, pointing. People had tied animal bones to their feet and were propelling themselves with sticks and poles. There was a lot of shouting and laughing. And falling over.

Despite the cold and the anxiety, I felt my heart lift. I'm an historian. This was what I was born to do. I couldn't help a little skip of excitement.

Here and there, animals were being roasted on spits. Scruffy dogs and even scruffier children hung around, hoping for scraps. I didn't blame them. The smell was tempting. Again, I regretted my missed toast.

Pie men wandered around with trays around their necks, bawling their wares on the ice. Better than the other way around, I supposed.

All around us, I could see stilt-walkers and jugglers. Apprentices played football with enthusiasm and little skill. Giggling ladies with powdered hair and muffled in furs played very well-mannered skittles. Musicians marched up and down the ice, red-cheeked with cold. No one could afford to stand still for very long. Not in these temperatures.

Bloody hell, it was cold. I could feel ice forming on my eyelashes.

We should keep moving. Apart from small, warm pockets around individual braziers, the air was freezing. A few more snowflakes drifted down, mingling with the ash from the fires. Taking gentle, shallow breaths through my scarf seemed the best way to avoid coughing up a lung or two. I had long since ceased to feel my feet. I remembered that, in the past, the temperature of my feet and the interesting places I found to keep them warm had formed the basis of many a vigorous discussion.

However, everyone seemed to be having a wonderful time. Those purveying strong drinks were doing a roaring trade. People called to each other, greeting friends, drawing attention to some strange sight or other. Loud music was everywhere. It was all a bit like Glastonbury with ice and snow instead of mud. And even fewer toilets.

Now that dusk had set in, stallholders were lighting their lanterns around the ice and bonfires blazed higher against the stars. An air of excitement was abroad. People were obviously determined to enjoy themselves. In these temperatures, this time tomorrow, they could well be dead.

As could we.

I pushed that thought aside. While it was just vaguely possible the Time Police somehow knew of the existence of Skaxos and had followed us there, we had been able to leave them behind. With all of History out there, there was no way they'd ever be able to find us here.

I was happily watching two enterprising young men attempt to impress a group of girls with their skating prowess when we heard a commotion coming from what would have been downriver had we not been standing on solid ice.

People were shouting—and not in a good way. Dogs barked. Around us, people craned their necks, trying to see what was happening. Had someone fallen through the ice? I stood on tiptoe, trying to peer through the crowds. Maybe someone had caught a pickpocket.

Leon took my arm and saying quietly, "This way," drew me away from the excitement.

"What's happening?"

"They're here."

"What? How? How could they have found us?"

"We'll work that out later. Don't hurry. Don't look behind you. Just walk slowly back towards the pod."

We were a hundred yards away from the pod and the commotion behind was drawing ever closer.

"Don't look back," he said again. "This is a common technique. They start a disturbance behind us and as we run away, the majority of them are ahead of us, waiting for us to run blindly into their arms."

"Any helpful thoughts?"

"Let's get off the river. Too exposed. We'll lose ourselves in the streets and find our way back later."

"Suppose they find the pod?"

He stopped.

"Good thought."

It was. I do have them occasionally. If they found the pod and disabled it, we would be helpless. In fact, that was all they would have to do. In these temperatures, unable to gain access, we could be dead in hours. Maybe not even that long. Once again, I felt a little tickle of fear. I've said this before. It's not easy living out of your own time. Everyone has a place in society and without the backing of family, friends, a guild, a tribe, a village, we were officially non-persons. Scratching a living by stealing is no fun. And, it seemed, wherever we went, these people were only a few hours behind us. We could be in big trouble.

He looked down at me. "Can you run?"

I opened my mouth to say yes, but it came out as no. Sometimes prudence overcomes stupidity. Even for me.

We turned casually aside off the river, crunched over the snow, climbed a few icy steps, and scrambled over a low wall.

"Don't look back and don't run. Steady, now."

Walking slowly, we entered a warren of small lanes, fronted by narrow wooden houses leaning unsteadily over the street. Nearly twenty years after the Great Fire, the streets of London were still cramped and noisome. I knew there had been ambitious plans for a modern city with boulevards and avenues, but the common people, afraid of having their tiny plots of land absorbed into these new schemes, had started to rebuild even before the ashes cooled. The result was that, in parts, the new London wasn't that much different from the old one.

Away from the lights and fires of the fair, everything seemed dark and shadowed. And much, much colder. What snow remained was black and filthy. The few people on the streets were staggering home, clutching as much wood as they had been able to find. Tiny windows were heavily shuttered against the cold and any gaps stuffed with frozen rags. Few lights showed. The air was heavy with smoke and caught at my throat. I tried not to cough.

We wandered through the maze. The deserted streets contrasted strangely with the lights and bustle of the fair only a hundred yards away. I shivered under my layers of eccentric clothing. Snowflakes fell silently out of the dark sky. We were now the only people around.

The silence was actually a little worrying. Where were the feral dogs, cats, rats, and prostitutes who would normally be scavenging in these dark places?

Staying out of the cold was the answer to that one. Dogs, cats, rats, and prostitutes obviously had a lot more sense than we did. Not difficult.

"No prostitutes," I said.

"Of course not. Only a madman would get his todger out on a night like this. It would snap off in his hand."

We crept a little further. More flakes drifted down. The cold was almost unbearable.

"We're on our way back to the pod," he said in an undertone, breath billowing around his head. "We're walking parallel with the river, now. If we take the next turning left, we should come out somewhere nearby."

We flitted quietly from shadow to shadow. "Nearly there," he said, and barely had the words left his mouth than three or four dark figures appeared at the end of the street, fortunately, not looking our way. Yet.

"Down here," he said, and we wheeled left down an alley so narrow we had to turn sideways in places.

The good news was that overhanging roofs had kept this narrow space comparatively snow free. The bad news was that this place could accurately be called Bodyfluids Alley. The stink was bad enough but we were also slipping in pools of frozen urine. Icy turds crunched underfoot. One day, surely, I would find myself some place where I wasn't up to my knees in effluent. Just one day, please.

Leon stopped dead and I walked into the back of him. Slowly, he drew me aside, behind a broken barrel. I crouched, painfully. We both breathed into our sleeves so our frosted breath wouldn't give us away. In half an hour, we'd be well camouflaged. And frozen stiff, of course.

Voices sounded at the entrance. A bright, white, non-17th-century searchlight flashed past us, giving me a wonderful opportunity to see what I was crouching in. Appropriately, we froze.

Several endless seconds passed and then they moved away. Neither of us attempted to move. We were far too old to fall for that trick.

Time ticked by, as it tends to do when you're slowly dying of exposure in a frozen, piss-filled alleyway in the late 17th century. I decided our next jump would be to some fragrant tropical island. Still we crouched there. We passed the point where I would be able to move. When the time came, Leon would have to crack my joints to stand me up.

I felt him stand, slowly and cautiously. It took two goes for me to stand upright. We inched our way along the icy wall. At the end of the alley, Leon crouched and cautiously eased his head around the wall. He straightened and turned to me. "They're here. I know they are, but we have to get back. We're going to freeze if we stay out here much longer. We can't risk them finding the pod, but as soon as we're out in the open, they'll spot us. I'm going to run and you're going to get yourself back to the pod. Wait for me as long as you can, but don't risk yourself or the pod. You can always come back for me. Understood?"

I opened my mouth to protest.

"Understood?"

I nodded.

"It's not far. Across this lane and back over the wall. Turn right. The pod's opposite the beer stall, next to the red-and-white booth. OK?"

I nodded.

He turned and ran back down the alley, slipping and sliding in the ice. He kicked over a pile of something that made a satisfying clatter and launched himself into the street.

I heard a shout. Then another. Keeping to the wall, I stepped into the lane and looked left and right. There was no one in sight. All I had to do was nip across the wall, back on to the river, and lose myself in the crowds. Except I was nearly frozen solid and nipping anywhere was about as likely as finding a politician who works selflessly for the public good.

I shuffled across the lane, sat on the wall, and tried to swing my legs over. Eventually, I had to pick them up one at a time and lift them over manually. By now, I was chilled to the bone, shivering uncontrollably, and worried that my fingers and toes would just crack off in the cold.

I dropped back down on the riverside, skidded, and fell painfully onto the frozen snow. As I hit the ground, I heard a shout.

Oh, great!

Finally, the weather worked in our favour. As I struggled to my feet, the snow started properly. Swaying lanterns blew out and only the bonfires showed in the sudden darkness.

People laughed, cursed, and generally milled around and I milled right along with them. The crowds were thick and I stayed in the middle, allowing myself to be carried along. I knew I couldn't miss the beer tent. The crowds outside wouldn't let a little thing like a snowstorm divert them from their sworn purpose of knocking back as much ale as they could possibly manage.

They had braziers going outside. I stood with a family group and warmed my hands. Worryingly, I could barely feel the heat.

Across from me, I could see the red-and-white booth through the snow, and next to it, the darker patch of shadow that was our camouflaged pod.

Warmth. Light. Safety.

Despite the fast falling snow, the crowd was still good-natured. Alcohol helped.

I inched my way through the people, laughing and smiling at complete strangers. Fitting in. It was vitally important not to hurry. Not to disturb the flow of people as they streamed past.

Then, just as I thought I'd made it—just as I drew level with the booth, some instinct kicked in. Something about the way the crowd was moving . . .

I heard a cry of protest as a woman was shoved roughly aside and her escort shouted angrily. Risking a glance behind me, I could see two or three men, wearing all enveloping, black cloaks, which was surprising. Black was a rare and expensive dye before modern times. I suppose it enabled easy identification. Or intimidation, more like. One held something in the palm of his hand. Faintly, I caught an electronic beep. They'd found the pod. They were shouldering their way roughly through the crowd. You could tell they weren't historians—they didn't care about careful concealment. Their job was something else entirely.

The crowd liked being shoved about as much as crowds usually do. There's always someone who's had that bit too much to drink and whose temper is, consequently, that bit easier to lose. In this case, there was a whole gang of them. Young men—apprentices probably—out for some fun, noisy and belligerent.

I eased away from the shouting. Thoughtful family men were ushering wives and children out of harm's way. I ushered myself along with them.

A group of roughly dressed men issued from the beer tent; some to see what was going on and others to take a more participatory role.

Sadly, I was even further from the pod than when I'd started. The huge press of people was pushing me in the wrong direction. I couldn't even move my arms to elbow my way out and the ground underfoot was so rough that I was afraid I'd lose my footing and go down. With that thought, I stumbled over a rut and fell to my knees.

A man swathed in two or three blankets and smelling strongly of drink, tobacco, and horses pulled me up again. I came up ready for trouble, but he was already moving away. I gasped my thanks. He nodded. Nothing sinister—just a disinterested act of kindness.

I was caught in a dilemma. Go with the crowd? Rely on safety in numbers? Or try for the pod again? But what if I led them to it? Or had they found it already and were just waiting for us to return?

Think, Maxwell.

They wanted me. If I led them away then at least Leon, who was still out there freezing his bits off, could reach the pod and once he was there, all things were possible. In these temperatures, if neither of us found shelter soon, we were finished anyway. At least, as their prisoner, they would be bound to warm me up a little. Unless, of course, they just killed me here and now and left my body on the ice.

I was roused from that pleasant picture by Leon seizing my arm and demanding to know, in some exasperation, why I was just standing here.

"They're everywhere," I said. "I didn't want to lead them to the pod."

"We'll make a dash for it," he said. "It's too cold to stay here any longer. Head down. Use your elbows. Get to the pod. I'll cover your back."

"Are you armed?"

"No. Go."

Head down, I barged through the crowd. The shortest distance between two points is a straight line and historians' elbows are honed by years of practice.

I heard a voice. "There! In the grey blanket!"

I braced myself again for a bullet in the back.

I was in a cathedral once. I can't remember what I was doing there—trying not to burst into flames on consecrated ground, probably. Anyway, they were getting the place ready for a TV programme and someone was checking the sound levels. At some point, the organist must have played a series of the lower notes. I hardly heard anything, but I felt the note inside my chest, rather than with my ears.

This was very similar.

The pain was sudden and savage. For a moment, I was back in the woods at Agincourt, staring at the red, wet sword protruding from my chest.

I felt my legs begin to give way. I couldn't breathe in. Sounds around me began to blend one into another, one long drone . . .

Now I knew what the hairdryer thing was. Not an EMP device. They had some sort of sonic weapon designed to neutralise people, not equipment. The effects were painful and disabling. And very unpleasant.

My lungs couldn't seem to work properly. I couldn't get a rhythm going. My heart fluttered. Beneath me, the ice swayed and tipped as I felt my head spin. Everything blurred. I couldn't get back to the pod. I'd forgotten where it was. Legs that weren't mine took two or three wobbly steps in a direction I hadn't meant to go.

All around me, I could vaguely hear women screaming. Someone crashed into me, spun me around, and I was lost all over again.

Where was I?

What was happening?

My chest was on fire. I put two clenched fists to my heart and tried to bend forward to ease the pain, but it was all internal. Nothing helped.

Sonic weapons are supposed to be less harmful than conventional types. They're not. Take my word for it—and I'm someone who knows what she's talking about.

They must have had it on a fairly narrow beam because only a few of us seemed to be really badly affected. It was the secondary effect that did the real damage.

Panic.

The Great Plague might be nearly twenty years in the past, but the nightmares were still only just beneath the surface. Londoners, seeing people drop suddenly to the ice for no good reason at all, lost their heads and panicked.

The screaming intensified. People tried to scatter away from what they supposed was infection. Maddened dogs ran through the crowds, howling and barking. They'd been affected too. Children cried. Men shouted. In fear. Or anger. Or for their families who were being swept across the ice in the panic. I heard the sounds of a stall overturning.

The worst was yet to come.

I heard a sharp crack. And then another. Beneath my feet, something trembled.

Whether because of the sonic weapon or because of the sudden concentration of people all in one spot—or maybe a combination of both—the ice was cracking.

I'd never heard of any Frost Fairs crashing through the ice, but this wasn't my world. Maybe this was the world that had suffered the dreadful Frost Fair Catastrophe of 1683 when the ice had given way and the entire fair fell into the Thames with massive loss of life. It was more than possible. That these people would be prepared to run that risk rather than let us get away was not a good sign. I remembered Leon telling me they would do anything to get the job done, whatever the cost. They were ruthless and professional and they would get what they wanted. And they wanted me.

Someone caught me from behind and lifted me off my feet. They had me.

I tried to struggle, kicking out, and flailing with my arms.

People were still clutching their heads or their chests. I could still hear screaming. Was it me? It usually was.

Someone shouted, "Door!"

I flew through the air and hit the floor hard. The universe kicked me hard in my already damaged chest and everything went black.

THREE

*J*LAY ON THE SLEEPING module, spread-eagled like a
stunned starfish under the weight of blankets. So much
of me hurt that it was probably easier to list the parts that
didn't.

No, that wasn't going to work. There weren't any.

My face throbbed with the pain of returning blood. And
my feet. And my hands. My head pounded. Even my ears hurt.
My chest was just a red-hot ball of heart-squeezing pain. I was
certain something important had been dislodged. I felt sick,
disoriented, and confused as to who and where I was. Was I
still on the ice? Did they get us?

I turned my head and immediately wished I hadn't.

And, with apologies to all the purveyors of romantic fic-
tion—bronzed, muscle-rippling heroes who can go all night
like a crazed rhino are all very well—indeed, every woman
should have at least one—but sometimes, what you need—
what you really, really need—is a quiet man with his own basin.

Afterwards, when he'd wiped my face and given me a sip of
water, I said, "Sorry."

"Not a problem. Have another sip."

"You really should get yourself a more delightful travelling
companion."

"Just what I was thinking. I'll drop you off at the next stop and look around for someone with a little more fragrance and a lot more dress sense."

I looked down at myself and groaned. "Help me sit up."

"No. This basin's not big enough for that manoeuvre. Stay where you are for the moment."

I clutched his arm.

"Leon, please tell me no one went through the ice."

"No one went through the ice."

"Really?"

"Really."

He wouldn't lie.

"You got us away safely?"

"I did. Man of the hour."

Man of every hour as far as I was concerned.

"Where and when are we?"

"Central Asian steppes."

My anxieties returned. Thousands and thousands of fierce men thundering across the steppes on thousands and thousands of fierce horses were not what we needed at the moment.

"Keep your eyes peeled for the Mongol hordes."

He leaned sideways so I could see. He'd split the screen to show all camera angles and I was worrying unnecessarily, because there was nothing out there. Nothing but windswept grass in every direction, stretching all the way to the horizon. And silver, sheeting rain. A whole reservoir was emptying itself on the empty landscape outside. I could hear it pounding on the roof. Suddenly, it felt good to be inside.

"I've set the proximity alerts for one hundred, fifty, and ten yards. We'll see anything long before they see us. We're camouflaged. I think we'll be safe for a little while. We can rest a while and then be off."

"Somewhere warm."

"Definitely somewhere warm, but not straight away. Try and sleep."

"What about you?"

"I'm fine. I'll wake you in a couple of hours. Sleep now."

WHEN I AWOKE, THE screen was on night vision. An eerie green light filled the pod. Apart from the background hum or the occasional muted beep, everything was very quiet.

Leon sat motionless at the console, arms folded, and his chin resting on his chest. Even given that green isn't the most flattering colour, he looked tired and cold. He'd turned the heating down. The lights were out. He was conserving power.

I struggled out from my blanket cocoon.

He came over to assist. "What's the problem? Bathroom break?"

"No. Well yes, actually. But it's my watch now."

"I don't think . . ."

"Well, of course you don't—you're from the Technical section. But the historian, who does this for a living, says you split these things equally. Help me up."

Once upright and once my head stopped spinning, I actually felt a little better. "Go on. Get your head down for a bit."

"I'm not sure . . ."

"Oh, for heaven's sake. I'm just going to make myself a cup of tea—after the bathroom break, obviously—and sit and watch the screen. It can't be that difficult—you seemed to be doing OK."

"My next travelling companion will be less insulting, as well. Here—take a blanket."

He settled himself down. I could tell by his breathing that he wasn't asleep, but he didn't speak.

I pottered quietly around, finally settling at the console with a much-needed mug of the amber nectar. I stared unseeingly at the screen and thought. I had a lot to think about.

First, there was the whole new life thing, which probably wasn't proceeding along the lines envisaged by Mrs. Partridge when she dumped me on Leon's carpet yesterday. Was it really only yesterday?

Then there was this Time Police thing. Who they were and what they wanted seemed fairly obvious. They wanted me—a stranger in a strange world—and, if they'd already successfully sorted out some sort of international time travelling crisis, I couldn't imagine that one small, ginger historian was going to cause them a lot of trouble. But how had they known about me? Not twenty-four hours after I'd arrived in this world, they'd come after me. I'd had less than one day in Rushford before they'd come crashing through the gate and it had been very apparent from the start that they knew who they wanted and where I was.

We'd jumped to Skaxos. We'd sat for a while, talking, and then started to set up camp. Less than an hour later, there they were again.

We'd jumped immediately—at random—and yet, a couple of hours later—they'd found us again. Spatially and temporally, bang on target. I know they were from the future and had some cool kit, but even so—this was amazing. When St. Mary's mounted search parties for lost historians, sometimes, if there were lots of people around, it could take weeks to find us, even when they knew when and where to look.

Finally, of course, there was the question of Leon and me and that was when my thoughts skidded away and shot off in all directions. I'd have to come back to that.

At some point, he fell asleep. I sat and watched the screen, listened to his slow breathing, and sipped my tea.

Perhaps because my future looked so bleak and my present so uncertain, my thoughts turned to the past. To the place where I'd always been happy. To St. Mary's. Memories crowded thick and fast. Who could forget the day when Markham set himself on fire during the Icarus Experiment? Racing across the field, frantically beating out the flames and not—being Markham—looking where he was going in any way at all, he'd run slap bang into a horse's bottom and knocked himself out cold. I could still see him, toppling slowly backwards like a felled tree, while Mr. Strong chased away old Turk, who was trying to stand on him in revenge. He survived, of course. He had to. Who wants "Fatal Impact with Horse's Arse" on their death certificate?

I looked over at Leon, still lying quietly in the corner, and heard voices from the past. A certain annual performance appraisal . . . and, for that one, I had been fairly optimistic.

"A nice programme," he said, eventually. "Well thought out, creative and, as always, imaginatively presented."

"Thank you," I said, beaming.

"Well executed and with correct adherence to protocols, but not slavishly so. Never underestimate the benefits of improvisation."

"No, Chief."

"There are still one or two areas in which you should strive for more co-ordination. Enthusiasm has its place, but remember, lower back pain is no joke."

"Yes, Chief."

"Otherwise, not bad at all. Can you pass me my trousers please?"

Or the time we had a heavy snowfall and the History department decided to stage an impromptu re-enactment of the escape of Queen Mathilda from Oxford Castle in 1142, when she and a couple of knights lowered themselves from the walls in the dark and crawled away through the snow, supposedly invisible in white nightshirts.

The party consisted of Messrs Clerk, Markham (who else?), and Roberts, and let's face it, if you lumped those three together and excavated with a JCB you still wouldn't be able to find even a single brain cell.

The plan was that they'd lower themselves from an upstairs window and wriggle through the snow down to the lake. Evans would head a small team from Security who would play the part of soldiers trying to intercept them. The whole thing would be observed and adjudicated by Professor Rapson.

What could possibly go wrong?

Well, for a start, Clerk got his knots wrong and nearly cut himself in half. They left him, dangling and blaspheming about twelve feet up in the air, and Professor Rapson, caught up in the excitement, forgot about him.

The other two idiots, gaining the safety of terra firma, immediately began worming their way through the snow in a doomed attempt to reach the lake. Undoubtedly their poor sense of direction was a factor, but what really brought the whole thing to a standstill was that, in their quest for historical accuracy, the silly asses hadn't put their drawers on.

After a great deal of wriggling through the snow on their bellies, they made the simultaneous discovery that they couldn't feel their todgers. I didn't even want to speculate on what they were doing to make that discovery, and it was at this point that they fell into the stream, where they floundered helplessly and were eventually discovered by Evans and his team who had, unfortunately for them, stopped for a mug of tea and a bacon butty.

Professor Rapson had, by this time, taken a wrong turn in the dark and was later discovered in the car park.

Roberts and Markham were rushed to Sick Bay, suffering from the effects of encasing their unprotected private parts in snow and freezing water and, when I eventually got to them, they were sitting on a table, carefully immersing their affected members in pint beer glasses filled with warm water and being supervised by a near-hysterical Nurse Hunter.

I shouted for a good twenty minutes, because if I hadn't I'd have been laughing hysterically, too. And when I'd finished,

Ian Guthrie had a go at them as well, and on this occasion, he was magnificent. They listened in a rare state of subdued obedience to his thundering denunciation of their intelligence, and their usefulness to the world in general and St. Mary's in particular. They stared at him like terrified rabbits and at one point I wouldn't have been surprised if they'd both made involuntary contributions to the contents of their glasses.

He finished by instructing Nurse Hunter for God's sake to ensure the complete destruction of the unfortunate glasses because no one would ever want to drink from them again.

"Out of respect?" enquired Markham, unwisely.

"Don't get cocky," said Hunter.

It was at this precarious moment that they suddenly remembered the unfortunately still dangling Mr. Clerk.

I lost myself in these and other happy memories, smiling for a while at my own thoughts. Inevitably, however, the comfort they brought me was tempered by sadness. The sadness of knowing that those carefree days were gone. Lost forever.

After four hours, I was cold, stiff, hungry, thirsty, bored, and determined not to wake Leon. I was shifting my position for the umpteenth time, trying to ease the pain in my chest, when he stirred.

"Max?"

"Still here."

"Everything all right?"

"Yes. Not a sign of them."

"Actually, I was enquiring after you. Did you get any rest?"

"Of course not," I said sarcastically. "You could snore for England. I would have slept better in the European Wind Tunnel. I think my ears started to bleed at some point. Do you want some tea?"

I made us both a mug and joined him on the floor. He pulled his blankets over me. Heroically, I'd left the heating off.

"How's the chest?"

"Absolutely fine," I said, uttering the traditional St. Mary's lie with the traditional St. Mary's panache.

He sipped his tea and said, "I suggest we shower, have breakfast, and then push off. The water tanks will be more than full by now."

"Somewhere warm and sunny."

"Yes, we can recharge the cells as well. Do you have anywhere particular in mind?"

I batted my eyelashes. "Actually . . ."

He sighed. "Yes?"

"Well, while your snores were rattling the ceiling, I was working out some coordinates. What do you say to Ancient Egypt? Eighteenth dynasty? Peaceful. Stable. Sunny. What do you think?"

"And?"

I put on my blindingly innocent face.

"I'm sorry?"

"You just picked Ancient Egypt at random?"

"Astonishingly, yes. It just . . . popped into my head."

"I see. Any time specific in this peaceful, sunny, stable, eighteenth dynasty?"

"Strange you should ask. I was thinking—I mean, it did cross my mind—and the coordinates were easy because we know he performed the ceremony during the third year of his reign, and it would have to take place during Akhet . . ."

"During what?"

"Akhet—the season of inundation—when the Nile floods—because no one's working in the fields then. Any other time would . . ."

"No. Stop."

"What?"

"Obviously you can remove the girl from St. Mary's, but it's less easy to remove St. Mary's from the girl."

"What are you talking about?"

"Coincidentally, that was my question, too."

"Akhenaten."

"What?"

"Not what—who. Akhenaten. The Heretic Pharaoh."

"Yes. Drawing on past experience, my finely honed instinct tells me something hugely catastrophic will happen to Akhenaten, and we, of course, we will be closely involved."

"No, no. Don't panic. Well yes, it will. But in the future. We won't be around for that. Unless you want to be, of course."

"Hardening my heart to the wistful note in your voice, I invite you to continue."

"Well, Akhenaten comes to power. He succeeds a powerful and popular father—not sure how much that's got to do with his rebellion—and immediately starts chucking sacred cats amongst the pigeons."

"Why?"

I hesitated.

"I don't think there's any clear reason why. The fact is—he's different. In every way. Deliberately so. It's almost as if he said, 'How can I overthrow the thinking of thousands of years, upset my people, antagonise the priesthood, and offend all the gods? Oh, I know! Let's abolish all the gods and have just one. Oh, and let's have a new city devoted to that one god and make people abandon the ancient city of their ancestors and live there. They won't mind. And what else? Oh, yes! Let's have a new style of realism in our art. Warts and all. Well, don't just stand there, everyone—jump to it. Nations don't just weaken themselves, you know.'"

I realised, too late, I was waving my arms around.

Leon was regarding me with a small smile.

"What are you laughing at?"

"Memories."

I let that go.

"Well, I've no doubt he came to a bad end. Is that what you want to see?"

"Oh, no. No. I'm hoping we'll see him before all of this kicks off. We know that in the third year of his reign, he celebrates the Heb Sed Festival. It's usually held in the thirtieth year of a Pharaoh's reign, but being Akhenaten, he had to be different."

"So—a festival."

"Yes."

"A happy time."

"Yes."

"No one attacks? No plagues? No earthquakes? The river will not run red with blood?"

"Probably not."

"Don't sound so disappointed."

My conscience smote me with something the same size and density as a politician's expenses claim. Was I being selfish? If the Time Police caught us, it would be the end of everything. He'd lose his pod. Maybe his life. All that risk just to see the heretic Pharaoh and his beautiful wife.

I turned to him and he smiled down at me. "I'm already looking forward to it."

WE LANDED IN A small palm grove on the banks of the Nile. There was no point in checking the proximities—the place was full of people, all picking their way around irrigation ditches or splashing through small, soggy fields, all heading for the festival and a sight of their Pharaoh.

We'd ripped up the sleeping module, taken lengths of material, folded them in half, cut a hole for our heads, and belted them firmly with another torn strip. Once again, we were wearing our bedding.

"Bet you didn't think to pick up my make-up when we left."

"Strangely, no."

I tutted. "Can you find me some soot, please?"

He actually found some, reappearing minutes later with a smooth, soot-stained stone from an old cooking fire and a complacent smirk. I mixed a paste of soot and water and applied it around his eyes.

He wasn't happy.

"Relax," I said. "No one's impugning your masculinity. All Egyptians wear make-up. Especially on the eyes. It wards off evil spirits and infections. You'll attract far more attention without it, believe me. Of course, for a complete picture, we should be shaving our heads."

"What for?"

"Lice."

"Where on earth have you brought me?"

"And that reminds me, if you cut yourself at all, tell me at once. Before you start to fester."

"This eye stuff tickles."

"I'm so sorry. I'll stop at once. Heaven forbid you should undergo any sort of discomfort."

"You can't leave me with one black eye and one pink eye."

"You underestimate me."

He sighed.

"Actually, it suits you. You should consider it for everyday use."

"Just . . . get on with it, will you."

I did my own eyes and we were set to go.

IT WAS HOT. WONDERFUL, glorious, bright, warm sunshine. Thank you, Aten. I began to see Akhenaten's point of view.

We'd argued—sorry, had a discussion—over whether to activate the camouflage system or not. Whether the uproar caused by an Egyptian inadvertently walking into an invisible pod would be a greater or lesser risk than it being discovered by the Time Police.

"Who must be at least two jumps behind us," I said. "We've got the Central Asian steppes between us and them."

"Mmm," he said, absently. "You're right. We'll leave it visible. If we have to leave in a hurry—and all past evidence indicates we will—then we'll need to find it quickly."

Not quite as reassuring as I could have hoped, but in my impatience to see the Heretic, I let it pass. I hopped from foot to foot as he made a slight adjustment to his tunic. "Yes, yes. You look very pretty."

"How's your chest?"

"What chest?" I said, because everyone knows if you ignore persistent, throbbing pain then it goes away. Like toothache. And small children. And overdrafts.

We exited the pod to find ourselves face to face with a small donkey enjoying the shade. He showed no signs of alarm, merely shifting his weight and regarding us placidly, his ears drooping in the heat. I hoped for a similar reaction from the locals.

Inundation had already occurred and the waters were retreating, although not far enough for planting to take place yet. The ground was still sodden. Walking was difficult but the feel of warm, thick, Egyptian mud oozing through my toes was actually quite pleasant. The air smelled rich and loamy. Large patches of standing water reflected the sky. There were frogs everywhere. In Biblical quantities.

To my right, the Nile glittered in the sunlight, bounded by muddy fields and the odd shaduf. If I turned my head I could see the desert and then the mountains beyond, hazy in the heat. I could even see where the fertile black land met the red desert land. The transition was quite abrupt. Washed linen was draped over bushes and hanging from tree branches. The ancient Egyptians were a very clean people. In front of us, dazzling in the bright sunshine, lay hundred-gated Thebes, the Egyptian capital.

I've been to Egypt, Greece, and Turkey, either working on archaeological sites or as a tourist visiting the ruins, and it always comes as a shock to see the buildings as they are meant to be seen. Intact. New. The crisp stonework un-eroded by the winds of time and painted in dazzlingly bright colours. I saw red, ochre, black, green, and, everywhere, that wonderful lapis-lazuli blue.

This was Egypt and so every flat wall had some sort of mural or depiction painted upon it and the combination of paint and carving was spectacular. Vivid images leaped from the walls. Giant Pharaohs trampled their fallen enemies. Horse-drawn chariots flew across the desert plain. Hunters stalked their prey through giant beds of papyrus. The gods walked among us. Jackal-headed Anubis, weighing the hearts of the dead against a feather and finding them wanting. Sobek, the crocodile-headed god, graciously accepting offerings from his acolytes. The magic eye of Horus was everywhere, watching over the city and its inhabitants.

We didn't enter the main part of the city. The festival would be held in the temple of Gem-pa-Aten. They didn't allow the peasants into the sacred enclosure, but the wide gates were thrown open and we had a good view. Akhenaten wanted everyone to witness this ceremony. His first step to dismantling the power of the god, Amun-Re, and his over-mighty priests.

I wriggled and squirmed my way through the garlic-smelling populace until we had a reasonable view.

The festival was obviously well into its ten-day cycle. Looking at the markers carefully placed around the open court, I suspected this was the day Akhenaten symbolically paced out the length and breadth of his kingdom; to assert his power and dedicate his land to the Aten. Around the courtyard, portable shrines contained other gods, invited to witness the ceremony. They all had their own retinues of priests, but Aten took precedence. No one looked very happy.

We had to wait some time. Ceremonies don't always go according to plan. Someone would have lost a sacred wreath or an important official would have gone missing, but it wasn't a problem because there was so much to look at.

It wasn't just the buildings that were adorned. Wealthy Egyptians, standing under sunshades manhandled by sweating slaves, wore wonderful golden jewellery, heavy with turquoise and lapis lazuli. Even the poorer people wore cheap beads and feathers. Their appearance was very important to them. Rich and poor alike always wanted to present themselves as young and beautiful, which made Akhenaten's strange depictions of himself even more baffling. I couldn't wait to see how accurate they were.

Hundreds, maybe thousands, of people waited quietly outside the temple for a glimpse of their Pharaoh. Their god on earth.

Actually, they were waiting very quietly. There was no buzz of anticipation. No craning of necks from people anxious for what might be their only sight of the Pharaoh in their entire lifetime. I dropped back down off tiptoe and glanced up at Leon, who was looking thoughtful.

He said quietly, "I don't like the feel of this. Is there any chance of violence?"

"I don't think so. They're not happy, but it will be years before rebellion actually occurs. They're not a spontaneous people."

We stood patiently under the warm sun. It wasn't unpleasant. I looked around me. People looked well-fed and reasonably content. Egypt was prosperous and, for the next couple of years, relatively stable. If we were looking for a long-term refuge, there were worse places to settle. I resolved to mention it to Leon when we had a moment to discuss it.

The sun was dropping in the sky when, finally, the horns sounded, and Akhenaten and Nefertiti made their appearance from the temple.

The crowd cheered but not with wild enthusiasm.

I jumped about a little. I was actually witnessing the first stages of one of the most remarkable events in Egypt's long history. Akhenaten's doomed attempts at monotheism and modernisation. I craned my neck to see him. I absolutely had to know what he looked like.

He wore the crown of Upper Egypt and a long robe of what might have been golden feathers. I wasn't close enough to see. Accompanied by his priests, he made an offering on the altar of the Aten. A priest removed this crown and another brought him the crown of Lower Egypt. He made another offering.

The crowd remained respectfully silent.

He turned from the altar and made his way down the steps to the courtyard. At the bottom, he stood quite still, arms outstretched, while attendants moved forwards to remove his robe and crown.

This was it. I was about to see . . . How deformed was Akhenaten?

Then, suddenly, I sensed a disturbance in the force.

It could be anything. This was not a happy time. Egyptians don't like change. It might simply be an unhappy, edgy, restless crowd. I tried, unobtrusively, to look around.

Leon grasped my arm. "Something's happening. Either there's about to be a riot, or our friends have turned up. Either way—time to go."

I opened my mouth to protest. To beg for another five minutes. Just until he disrobed completely. I couldn't go until I'd seen . . .

His grip tightened. "Now."

I dropped back off my toes and nodded.

Hoping it wasn't disrespectful to leave such a solemn occasion before it was finished, we began to ease backwards out of the crowd. We took our time, moving slowly, pausing every now and then to listen for sounds of pursuit. From anyone.

If the Time Police were around then they were being remarkably discreet. On the other hand, there were vast numbers of soldiers stationed around the area. These were the Medjay, the elite police force, and they didn't mess about at all. The punishment for pretty well everything is "giving on top of the stake." Impalement. There's a whole raft of historian kebab jokes that suddenly weren't that funny.

Then, quite clearly, in the silence, a man shouted, "Hey, lady, you dropped something."

The crowd gasped at such sacrilege. Around the walls, the Medjay began to move, shouldering their way through the people who shrank away from them.

The instinctive thing is to turn towards the person addressing you, especially when they speak to you in your own language. Under cover of pointing out something interesting to me, Leon gripped my arm, pointed to the ceremony, and whispered, "There's going to be trouble. Let's get out of here before it starts."

I nodded, eased my weight to my left foot, and craned my neck, as if straining for a better view. People moved around me, adjusting themselves to my new position. Little ripples spreading outwards. I eased again. And again. I wanted to run. I wanted to barge my way through the crowd and somehow gain the shelter of Thebes itself, with its narrow streets and many hiding places. But you don't do that. You slide, insinuate yourself, smile at your neighbours, ease yourself along, and watch the ceremony and you don't ever, ever do anything hasty that could attract attention, because that could be fatal.

"They're behind us," whispered Leon. "With luck, these Egyptian soldiers will give them something else to think about."

I nodded. Shouting hadn't worked for them. In fact, it had made things worse and now the hunters had become the hunted. At least, so I hoped.

We found ourselves on the fringes of the assembly, where the groups of people were thinner and smaller. Now was the really dangerous time. We had an open area to traverse and at least two sets of policemen to avoid.

And then we had a bit of luck. About bloody time. A harassed-looking woman, heavily pregnant, with a screaming child and two other infants clinging to her skirts, emerged from the edge of the crowd. She was desperately trying to hush the toddler whose cries were bouncing off the buildings. She looked hot and embarrassed, turning her head from side to side, looking for something or someone. It didn't matter. She was struggling with the kicking kid and falling over the other two under her feet. I waved as if I knew her, and before she had a chance to ask who the hell I thought I was, I'd taken the kids' hands and smiled again. Relieved of part of her burden, she nodded towards an alleyway and heaved the infant higher on her hip. We set off, slowly and openly. And very noisily. I smiled down at the kids, which probably frightened them both to death. Both were naked, as was the custom for small children at the time, and extraordinarily sticky. Their little faces were smeared with honey and snot, bless them. The infant was bellowing like an enraged bull by this time. God knows what was the matter with him. People kept turning to look at us. I crossed my fingers.

The hot sun baked the stones around us. Leon followed silently behind us, protecting our rear, but I still felt horribly exposed as we slowly walked away from the ceremony and whatever was going on behind us.

Finally, she reached a shady doorway, dragged aside a dusty curtain, and snatched her kids back. She could have them with my goodwill—one of them was nearly glued to me—and disappeared inside without a backwards glance.

I rubbed both hands down my tunic. Nope. That did no good at all, but we were out. We'd had a narrow escape and when Leon said, "Back to the pod, I think," I didn't argue.

The streets were deserted. This was good, in that it enabled us to make good speed, and, bad, because we were virtually the only people around and, therefore, horribly conspicuous.

We slunk from one shadowed doorway to the next. Leon led the way. I followed on behind and watched our backs.

How the hell did they keep finding us? Think about that later. Always deal with the now. Escape first. Questions later.

The pod was visible. Suppose they'd found it. But no—think a minute. If they'd found the pod then they wouldn't have to waste time chasing us and risking the attention of the Medjay. They could just sit in the shade and wait for us to turn up, as we were bound to do eventually. Surely, the fact they were chasing us through the streets meant they hadn't found the pod. Unless, of course, they were doing both. Herding us back through the streets to be caught just as we thought we'd made it. I thrust that thought away. Get back safely and *then* deal with whatever problem presented itself.

Chance would be a fine thing.

FOUR

E COULD JUST MAKE out the pod still snuggled in its little grove of palm trees. The donkey was facing the other way, but otherwise, everything was exactly as before. We only had to trace a path through the latticework of fields, navigate several irrigation ditches, and we were home, but not necessarily dry. Egypt at this time of year is extremely soggy.

"We'll circle around," said Leon. "Just to be on the safe side."

I thought he was being over-cautious and said so. "Besides, the Medjay will be giving them something else to think about."

"We can't afford to take any chances," he said. "We're the fugitives here. To remain free, we have to be lucky every time. To capture us, they only have to be lucky once."

Well, since he put it like that . . .

We zig-zagged our way towards the pod, skirting the big rocks that acted as boundary markers and hopping over the smaller irrigation channels. The bigger ones had rough wooden planks laid across them at irregular intervals.

We nearly made it. I was just coming to believe the Time Police were all still at the temple when, suddenly, they were right in front of us, rising up out of the empty landscape, only about a hundred yards away. Whether deliberately or not, they were between us and the pod. But just two of them. A rear guard, maybe.

"Run," said Leon, and just for once, I did exactly as I was told.

I took off around an enormous fig tree so ancient that it had pupped any number of times and now formed a small plantation all on its own. I pushed through whippy sticks and tripped over roots, emerging near a small wooden structure, purpose unknown.

The important thing was to keep something between them and us. And to deprive them of a clear shot. And to get a long way off as well. And to keep them away from the pod. There's an art to running for your life, you know. You don't just take off and hope for the best.

I hurtled out from behind the shed, and finding a nice, clear patch of dryish land ahead of me, tucked in my elbows, tried to ignore the pain in my chest, and went for it. Only to find myself confronted by The Great Drain. One of the main irrigation channels that led directly from the Nile to a series of the big reservoirs scattered around. They carried a lot of water, they were wide, and they were deep.

I turned and ran along the bank, desperately searching for some cover. We weren't far from the river itself and maybe there would be a boat . . . anything . . . I could hear Leon pounding along behind me.

A stand of dead, unharvested corn to my right offered some possibilities, but as I turned towards it, the same two black-clad figures stepped out from between the dry brown stalks, weapons raised. Still between me and the pod.

I skidded to a halt and desperately searched for a way out, but there was nowhere to go. That didn't stop me. I wasn't going to give up. They were going to have to come and get me. Veering off away from the canal, I headed directly towards the river. Maybe we could lose ourselves in the papyrus beds.

The mud was treacherous. I slipped and skidded, falling flat on my face.

I heard Leon shout a warning. Looking back, I could see him struggling with the two Time Police. He was unarmed. We had to get away now. The rest of the squad could turn up at any moment. One of them tore free from Leon and aimed his gun at me.

I tried to wriggle away, lost my footing again, and rolled down the muddy bank to fetch up only feet from the river. I should get up. I must get up.

It wasn't going to happen. I lay on my back, chest heaving. They had us.

Or perhaps they hadn't.

I heard shouting above me, and the next minute, a heaving scrum consisting of Leon and two Time Police tumbled over the bank, and came to rest in a panting, muddy heap next to me.

"Run," shouted Leon again, although where he thought I was going to go was anyone's guess.

I scrambled to my feet and prepared to break a few land speed records. Out of the corner of my eye, I saw one of them grope for his weapon and threw myself to the ground.

I don't know what happened behind me. I only know what happened in front of me.

The Nile boiled.

At least, that's what it looked like to me. A great expanse of water jumped and bubbled. Trying to disregard the stabbing, disabling pain in my chest, I stared at the bouncing water because that's not something you see every day. And while I was staring, what looked like every crocodile in Upper Egypt rose slowly to the surface, peered at us over its nostrils, and decided it was lunchtime.

The Nile crocodile. An apex predator. Aggressive. Powerful. Huge. Old males can be anything up to eighteen feet in length.

They eat pretty well everything. They're agile and they can run. Actually, they can lift themselves up and gallop. There's no point in fleeing because they'll chase you down. People are terrified of them and rightly so. They spend their days sunning on the mudflats, apparently in some sort of coma, until a person or an animal comes down to drink and then one or more will erupt from the water and drag them under.

In times of stress, male crocodiles can produce infrasonic sounds so powerful that they cause the water to vibrate and that was what I was looking at now. Vibrating water. But on this occasion, it wasn't the crocodiles. The idiot Time Police had fired their sonic weapons—on wide-beam, judging by the great expanse of dancing water.

God knows what normally goes on inside those great, ugly heads—the crocodiles' I mean, not the Time Police's—but now, at this moment, they were definitely not happy. Whether they regarded us as a challenge or lunch, a worryingly large number were starting to converge on our particular muddy bank.

"Shit," said the Time Police. In stereo.

"Shit," said Leon.

I didn't say anything. I'm a veteran. I was saving my breath for running.

You had to hand it to the Time Police. These people were dedicated. Even when it looked as if we were all the main course on today's menu, they were still trying to take us in. They both aimed their stupid weapons at us.

I heard Leon say, "I really wouldn't fire those again if I were you. Let's just call this one a score draw, shall we, and all of us get out of here."

The first of the crocodiles were lifting themselves out of the water. I stared, fascinated. They were huge and armoured, and, when they're threatened, they turn their heads and cough. A bit like a St. Mary's medical.

And then we were all running.

My wobbly legs were slipping and skidding all over the place. I was disoriented. My heart pounded and I could barely see straight. I had no idea who or what was behind me. I didn't dare take my eyes off the rough ground ahead. At any moment, I expected to be seized and dragged down into the muddy water because crocs don't bite you in half and eat you straight away. They drag you underwater, roll you over and over and over until you drown, or all your bones break and your limbs drop off, and then they wedge you under a rock or log until you're ripe and ready. *Then* they eat you.

I pushed my way through coarse, razor-sharp grass that ripped painfully at my arms and legs. Somewhere along the way, we'd shed the Time Police. I'd no idea what they were up to. Running for their lives if they had any sense. There were crocs everywhere, slithering off the mud banks, appearing out of reed beds, hauling themselves out of the water, jaws gaping. What a lot of teeth for just one animal.

Leon caught me up, seized my hand, and then we really ran. We hurdled ditches. We splashed through the mud and slipping and sliding, turned away from the Nile, dropping to a slow jog, because I was fighting for every painful breath. Egypt swam hazily around me and I couldn't get my balance. The pod was less than one hundred yards away. We were nearly there.

He stopped and looked around at the empty landscape. "You go on ahead. Check the coast is clear. I'll watch our backs, but I think we're safe now."

He turned and fell straight into the Great Drain.

Even by St. Mary's standards, we really weren't having a good day.

I'm ashamed to say my first thought was, "Well, at least it wasn't me this time," because my track record for getting from A to B without experiencing a major catastrophe at C was not so good. And then I thought it was funny.

I said, "What are you doing down there?" and got that special, exasperated look.

"I told you to get back to the pod. Don't you ever listen?"

"Sorry? What did you say?"

He was clinging to the bank, about two feet down, covered in glistening Nile mud. Even as I watched, he slid a few more inches. He scrabbled with his feet and slid a few more.

I lay on the bank, reached down for him, and that was when I realised we had a real problem because there was no way I could pull him out. The sides were too steep and his flailing feet just couldn't get a purchase. Every time he tried, he slipped that bit deeper into the ditch, and the bottom was a concoction of shallow, dirty water and thick, black, sticky mud. Once he slithered down into that, I knew he'd never get out because not too far away, a half-buried dead dog and a few rat skeletons told their own story.

He couldn't climb out and I didn't have the strength to pull him out. All I could do was just hold on and take the strain for a while.

It doesn't sound that serious, but it was, because today was a holiday and there was no one around to help.

I lay on my stomach in the warm mud. The air smelled of hot, wet earth and, apart from the frogs, everything was quiet. The landscape was empty of people. Not even the Time Police. I suppose it was too much to hope they'd been eaten. Even the donkey seemed to have pushed off.

Tomorrow would be a working day, however, and someone would open the equivalent of a sluice and the water would come roaring up—or down—the channel and he'd be whirled away. If I'd managed to hang on to him through the night.

And if the crocodiles didn't come.

I was face down, head and shoulders overhanging the edge, holding on to his wrists with both hands. He kept his head and stopped kicking and flailing around, because both he and I were muddy, and it would be so easy for his own weight to pull him through my grip. To fall into that quicksand of mud and slimy water far below.

I closed my mind to panic and lifted my head again, trying to see if there was anyone around to help. Anyone would do. Even the two sodding Time Police, whose fault all this was. Where are the bloody police when you actually need them? A part of my mind wondered if they'd been recalled to assist with the Medjay.

He lifted his head and said calmly, "I'm going to try to find some sort of foothold."

"Gently does it."

I could feel him scrabbling around but all that happened was that part of the side fell away and we were worse off than before, because now I could feel myself slipping. His weight, apart from pulling my arms from their sockets, was slowly dragging me over the edge with him, and he knew it.

He lifted his head.

"Let me go."

"No."

I felt myself slip another inch and tried to will all my weight backwards. That didn't work at all.

"Lucy, let me go."

He'd never called me that before. Leon's private name for me. My thoughts took this particularly inappropriate moment to wonder when I'd stopped thinking of him as *the other Leon*. When I'd finally accepted him as my Leon. Because that's such a useful thing to think about when you're hanging over the edge of a fatally deep ditch, looking at a prolonged and unpleasant death.

I said, "Shut up, Leon."

"Lucy . . ."

I clenched my teeth against the pain and said, "Not going to happen so just shut up."

Before he could say anything else, I lifted my head and shouted for help. I don't know why I did it—I knew everyone was at the festival, but I wasn't going to let him die and if he was going to die then I wasn't interested in the future at all. Blood was pumping into my hanging head so I probably wasn't thinking very clearly.

I slipped another inch. The edge of the ditch was crumbling. And another inch. I tried wedging my knees into the mud. That didn't work, either.

The fiery pain in my arms and shoulders was unbearable. I knew, physically, I couldn't hold on much longer.

And then the mud moved. At first, I thought I had imagined it, but no. The mud was moving. Two, no, three crocodiles were working their way up the ditch. The one in front was huge, obviously the alpha male. They didn't appear to be in any hurry, but they covered the ground deceptively quickly. Half wading, half swimming, they were heading directly for us. They didn't have to do anything. They just had to wait.

I shouted again. And again.

Someone answered.

I didn't dare try to twist around to see who it was. I didn't dare move at all. Because this was it . . . I was sliding over the edge . . . and we would both slither down to the crocodiles awaiting us at the bottom . . .

I both felt and heard running footsteps. I shouted again. I was desperate now, because I was going. . . . I could feel myself going . . . I was slipping through the mud. Leon was shouting at me to let go. I was just shouting. Because whoever was coming was going to be just half a second too late to save us . . .

An arm seized Leon. On the other side of me, another arm reached down for him. The overwhelming weight was gone. I wriggled backwards to give them room to hoist him up.

They were two slaves. Skinny but muscular. Naked apart from their loincloths. They hauled him up and out, no problem at all, and we all sat, muddy and breathless in the warm evening sun and looked at each other.

We had no money to give them. We owned nothing but the clothes that we now didn't have the strength to stand up in. We had no words with which to thank them, but there's a universal sign language. We place our hands over our hearts and bowed our heads. They smiled and bowed theirs. Then they picked up their bundles and departed. Just like that.

We helped each other up and stumbled back to the pod. To have our first argument.

FIRST THINGS FIRST, HOWEVER. We jumped. I was surprised we got away with it. We were both so coated in Egyptian mud that the computer might well have decided that we were wearing enough of Egypt to constitute a foreign object and refused to jump. However, it didn't and we jumped away.

I had no idea where to, but at least it was quiet. Or it was until we got there.

We were tired, overwrought, and hurt, so all in all, a great time for a sensible discussion in which both participants could calmly and quietly state their point of view in an atmosphere of mutual tolerance and respect.

Leon opened the batting.

"I told you to go back to the pod. Why don't you ever do as you're told?"

"Why should I? You tell me to do such stupid things."

"Hanging around to pull me out of a ditch I could perfectly easily have climbed out of is more than stupid."

"Oh, really? You could have got yourself out of that?"

"Obviously."

It was vitally important that at least one of us should stay calm. We didn't argue often, but whenever we did, Things Were Said and People Got Hurt. I should have said something conciliatory but I never got the chance.

"What is the point of me trying to keep you safe if you do stupid things like that?"

"Says the idiot who fell in a ditch."

"I didn't see it."

"It's twenty feet wide, for God's sake. Are you blind as well?"

"As well as what? No, don't bother answering that."

Just as well he said that. I had a long list prepared. I closed my mouth. Sadly, he didn't notice my restraint.

"Just tell me what on earth you thought you were doing."

"I was rescuing you."

"And while you're doing that the Time Police grab you and I lose you all over again."

"Well, I'd already lost you. You were seconds from drowning in the mud. Or being eaten by crocodiles. Or found by the Time Police. But none of that happened. *Because we pulled you out.*"

"Why can't you understand? You could have handed yourself to them on a plate. They'd have grabbed you, left me for crocodile fodder, and that would have been the end of both of us."

"No it wouldn't. I'm sneaky and resourceful. I always have a cunning plan."

"Which in this case, apparently, was to get yourself killed."

"No, I wouldn't. They keep using their sound gun thing . . ."

"Their sonic pulse weapons . . ."

"Yes—so they obviously want us alive. If they'd caught us— which they didn't—the worst that could have happened was that they would have taken us prisoner. The point I'm making is that we would have been alive and if you're alive then anything is possible. It's being dead that limits your options."

We were shouting now.

He slapped the console in frustration. "You don't know that. I could have lost you. Again. Why can't you understand?"

I was waving my arms around. "Of course I understand. Who better? Why do you think I wouldn't let go? Why can't you understand—I won't lose *you* again."

To my horror, my voice wobbled. I was going to cry. This was no good—I still had plenty to say. And I was so tired. And my chest hurt. And my arms. And my shoulders. And I'd held on to him long enough for him to be rescued. And he was yelling at me about it. And I was stuck in this new life. In this new world. And I didn't know where I belonged. And people were chasing me. That was what I was yelling about. Why didn't he know that? I leaned on the console for support and the tears just ran down my cheeks.

Of course he knew it. I really should have more faith. In fact, it was time we both had a little more faith in each other. I heard him take a deep, ragged breath.

He said quietly, "Sweetheart, don't cry."

He put his arms around me. A little awkwardly, but with luck, practice would make perfect.

"I'm sorry, Lucy. I really should look after you better. I've had you for less than two days and already you're half dead."

I sniffed into his muddy tunic. "You can't take all the credit for that. I was half dead when I got here."

"I know this wasn't what either of us expected, but we're stuck with it for the time being. I promise you, Lucy, we will get through this. We'll find somewhere safe."

I put my arms around him and closed my eyes. To have the time to stand still, just for a second . . . This wasn't about who fell in the ditch and who disobeyed whose instructions. This was about two people pitchforked into a new life together before the wounds of the old life had completely healed. Two people who were scared, exhausted, and hurt.

Actually, more hurt than they realised.

"Max, where's all this blood coming from?"

"What blood?" I stepped back and looked at my hands, sticky with blood. There were smears on the console, too.

He held me at arm's length. "Are you in any pain?".

"Yes, all over, but it's not me. I think it's you."

He pulled his tunic over his head, twisting to see his back. A huge red and purple bruise blossomed under his shoulder blade. A small cut oozed with enthusiasm.

I said. "I'd better take a look at that before it gets infected. Take a shower while I check the First Aid box."

Actually, it's not so much a First Aid box, more a First Aid cupboard. Historians can be a little accident-prone, sometimes.

He emerged, drying his hair. I washed my hands and peered at the wound.

"Can you lie down?"

"With pleasure. It's been a long day."

He stretched himself face down on the floor with a groan.

I cleaned the wound and applied antiseptic spray. He barely flinched.

"It's OK. You can be a baby if you want to."

He turned his head to the side. "I'm being a Man. Show some appreciation, will you?"

"Sorry. I'm very impressed. Just a small dressing for the cut and I have some anti-inflammation stuff that should numb the bruised area, as well. Just hold still."

I used two fingers to apply the cream in small circles, being as gentle as I could. Taking my time. The bruise was the size of a dinner plate. He must have fetched himself a real wallop when he fell.

"I never noticed," he said. "Too busy hanging on."

"Does it hurt?"

"No," he said, being Manly again.

I finished and passed him his T-shirt, but he didn't move.

"Shall I help you up?"

"Can you give me a minute?"

"What's wrong?"

"Was that supposed to reduce stiffness?"

I read the label again.

"Yes. Is there a problem?"

"I might need to write a letter of complaint."

"Why? Does it still hurt?"

A pause.

"Yes. Let's go with that, shall we?"

FIVE

*A*N HOUR LATER, WE'D indulged in the traditional St. Mary's ritual for dealing with any sort of crisis, which is to imbibe vast reservoirs of tea. People laugh, but it works. By the time the kettle has boiled, the tea made, the amount of sugar added has been silently criticised, the tea blown on and finally drunk . . . all this takes time, and if you're a member of St. Mary's with the attention-span of a privet hedge, then you've forgotten what you were arguing about in the first place.

We'd established where and when we were. In 8th-century Scandinavia. It was impossible to be more precise, and that was something else to worry about. We'd had five jumps now—one after the other in quick succession and a couple of those had been emergency extractions.

Pods need regular servicing—As, Bs, and Cs. An A service is the damage-repair every pod receives after every jump and is usually accompanied by a great deal of completely unjustified complaint and criticism from the Technical section. The B service is monthly, regardless of when it last had an A service, and the big one, the C service is twice-yearly; when the pod gets pulled out of the schedule and virtually taken apart. The established ritual is for the Technical section to sigh and shake its collective head and for the Chief Operations Officer to tear her hair out over their slowness in getting it back online.

However, our pod hadn't had any letter of the alphabet at all. I've no doubt Leon kept it in tip-top working order, but they need frequent realigning or they start to drift. This can be a bit of a bugger if you're aiming for, say, Renaissance Florence and you exit your pod preparing to view the art treasures of that period in an atmosphere of tranquil contemplation only to find you've been pitchforked into the St. Bartholomew's Eve massacre, ankle deep in blood and with Huguenot body parts lying everywhere.

We were perched on a headland. Wind buffeted the pod, although a dense wood behind us did offer some protection from the elements. The grey North Sea boomed away beneath us and a huge shining sheet of water swept away to our right. On the far side of the estuary, wooden huts clustered around several larger, more elaborately decorated halls set high up on the hillside.

Best of all, there were no longboats. It was high summer. You could tell by the way the rain was sleeting from the south. I suspected the men had taken to the longboats for a spot of rape and pillage on England's east coast. They were probably beating up Lindisfarne at this very moment.

Still, it did mean that the settlement was almost deserted. Smoke puffed half-heartedly through holes in heavily thatched roofs, but on this wet and windy day, everyone would stay inside as much as possible, which suited us just fine. Norsewomen were as ferocious as their men and with the state of us at the moment, a Viking six-year-old could probably take us with one hand behind her back.

We'd taken every precaution. We were camouflaged and the proximity alerts were set. It was now up to the god of historians to keep us safe.

I stared at the screen. The sun was struggling to break through the heavy grey clouds, sending shafts of light on to the rough water below. The effect was rather beautiful but I couldn't have cared less. Another day was beginning and I just wanted to get my head down.

Leon felt the same. "Look. We need to stop, catch our breath, and work out some sort of routine. We can't keep fleeing headlong up and down the timeline like this. We need to eat and sleep regularly, regardless of what time of day it is outside. We need to keep our own personal clocks straight or we're going to be in trouble."

He was right. At the moment, my poor old body didn't know if it was midnight or Manchester and this can be dangerous. You get tired and disoriented and then you start making mistakes.

"Let's start by having a meal."

"I'm not hungry."

Loss of appetite is one of the first symptoms. When your body hasn't a clue what's going on, it tends to shut down in self-defence.

"You must eat."

He was right. I must. No matter how little I felt like it. We had to establish a routine.

"And then a few hours' sleep, I think. How are you feeling?" He smiled. "You look terrible."

"I'm absolutely fine."

I forced down some chicken soup, a few of those tasteless, high-energy biscuits that no one ever eats so consequently there are boxes full of them in every pod, and a slice of cheese, possessed—an old joke, familiar to everyone who's ever been on compo rations.

We argued about who would sleep first and, eventually, Leon hauled out the decision-making apparatus. I called heads and then lied as the coin came down, because even though I might have looked terrible, he looked even worse.

"Wake me in four hours."

I nodded. "OK."

"No, I mean it. No sitting there until your eyeballs fall out. Four hours. Then it's your turn to sleep."

I made myself a cup of tea and found a scribble pad and pen and by the time I went to sit back at the console, he was asleep. I turned the lights and heating down and took a few moments just to stop and think about the events of the last few days.

Because that was all it was. I know I'd jumped from day to night and back again, but it still couldn't be more than two or three days at the most since I'd been injured at Agincourt. In those three days, I'd been pitchforked into another world and another life. I'd barely drawn breath before being catapulted to a small Mediterranean island, which would have been very pleasant, if I'd been allowed to enjoy it for more than an hour or so. From there to a bitterly cold 17th-century London. I'd been there for, what, two or three hours? From there to 18th-dynasty Thebes. Via the Central Asian steppes, of course. We'd managed to stay in Thebes for a whole afternoon. Now I was in 8th-century Scandinavia. For how long? How long before they found us again?

I had no way of answering that question, so I shelved it and turned my attention to things to which I did know the answer.

I watched Leon sleep for a while. He slept neatly and quietly as he always did.

You don't know that, argued a small voice inside me. *You only know that your Leon slept neatly and quietly.*

Oh, shut up.

I'm just saying . . .

I couldn't think about that. Not just at the moment.

I spent a few minutes thinking about this job Mrs. Partridge had sent me to do. I had absolutely no clues about that. For all I knew, it was something important in Thebes and I'd been so busy yanking Leon out of irrigation ditches that I'd missed it.

I didn't want to think about that, either.

I thought about the Vikings, but not for long because they weren't any of my special areas of expertise. I'm Ancient Civilisations, with British and European Medieval, and a bit of the Tudors thrown in for good measure. I tried to remember who, in my department, was the expert on Scandinavian history, couldn't, and gave that up too. That world was gone. Gone for good. I'd never see any of them again. That was something else I couldn't think about.

I stared out at the rain and doodled.

IN THE INTERESTS OF peace and harmony, I did wake him after his four hours. And I made him a cup of tea.

He sat up and rubbed his hair.

"What's happening?"

"Oh—the morning has been crowded with incidents. It stopped raining about an hour ago although we're still waiting for the sun to emerge. A small child of indeterminate sex ran out of the big hall on the left, together with a dog. A woman stood on the threshold and yelled at them. On their return, the kid got a thump round the side of the head. The dog ran off. I have to say, Viking society isn't anything like as exciting as I'd hoped. No one's been raped or pillaged at all. Quite dull, really. Do you want to use the shower? It's stopped raining. I can wait outside and we could let some fresh air in."

"No," he said, quickly, "don't open the door."

"Why not? It's a bit ripe in here—even by historian standards."

"I think you'll find it's colder than you think."

"In that case, I'm going to bed."

I curled up in the still warm blankets. The sleeping module moulded itself around me.

The last thing I saw was Leon heading into the toilet.

When I awoke, considerably more than four hours had passed.

I sat up and glared at him.

"You should have woken me."

"I tried. I couldn't get you to open your eyes. Is there a password?"

He wasn't telling the truth. Since childhood, I'm the world's lightest sleeper. On a bad day, I can make Lady Macbeth look like a raging narcoleptic.

"Anyway," he said, passing me over a mug of tea, "you'd only have been in the way. I've had the panels off the console and had a poke around inside. I can't do much because I don't have the equipment, but I've given it a bit of a tickle."

His face belied his words. He didn't look very happy at all.

"Is there a problem?"

He suddenly looked very worried and very tired.

"Leon, what's the matter?"

"I have bad news, really bad news, and catastrophic news."

I grinned at him. "Nothing new there, then. OK. Give me the bad news."

"It's not the pod they're following."

"Well, it's hard to see how they could have been, really. It's not as if we leave a vapour trail. Is that the bad news? What's the really bad news?"

"They're following us. Specifically, they're following you."

For a moment, I couldn't think. Then I couldn't speak.

Oh, my God . . .

Tiredness had drained all the colour from his face, leaving it a dreadful grey shade. God knows what colour of the spectrum I was, because now, suddenly, I'd just realised—this was all my fault.

He didn't need to tell me the really catastrophic news. I could work that out for myself. Because the really catastrophic news was that I was tagged. We all were. In case we get lost in time. No doubt, Leon, having left St. Mary's in the conventional manner, had had his tag removed—in the conventional manner. Having been bundled out of my own world without a moment's notice, I hadn't given it a thought and I should have. I know I'd been racing up and down the timeline, pursued by the forces of temporal law and order, but I really should have tumbled to it long before this. It wasn't the pod leaving a trail through time that a blind man could follow—it was me.

And with their advanced technology, the Time Police could track me wherever I went. And they were fast—so much faster than St. Mary's. And much more accurate. And we were screwed.

"I'm an idiot. A complete idiot."

"No you're not. I never realised, either."

"I should have thought . . . Why didn't I think of it?"

"Stop," he said, taking my cold hands. His hands were always so warm. "You're no more stupid than me. Neither of us realised. Let's just leave it at that, shall we?"

I stretched out my arm and looked at it, still unable to believe the depths of my own stupidity. We can be tracked. Peterson and I had once been stranded in Nineveh and even though it took them a while, Major Guthrie and the rescue teams had been able to locate us and pull us out.

"My pod is a Faraday cage. That's why the tag can't be picked up until we leave the pod. Or until we open the door."

He stopped, unable or unwilling to continue. He didn't have to. I did it for him.

"But once that happens, it's only a matter of time before they can track us down. Every time. There isn't any place or any time where we'll be safe. It might take them a while, but sooner or later, they'll always find us. And there isn't a thing we can do about it. This is all my fault."

"Before you start with the sackcloth and ashes," he said, "you've had a lot on your mind. Let's not waste time thinking about what we should have done. We need to think about what we should do now."

"But it is all my fault, Leon. I should have worked it out. Every time I step outside they're able to trace me. Us. This is bad. You know it is. Because if we can't fix this then I'm never going to be able to leave this pod again."

I stopped and looked around. Nothing had changed but everything was different. Now, far from being our little home, this pod was our prison. It was no longer small and cosy—it was cramped. No longer comfortably shabby and crowded—it was squalid and cluttered. Claustrophobic. Oppressive. Suffocating. My chest clenched. I tried not to panic. Tried not to realise I might never again feel the sun on my face or the wind in my hair.

"And it's a prison for you, too, Leon. For both of us. It doesn't matter where or when we go—we'll never be able to step outside again. Or even open the door. We won't be able to let in fresh air or get food. We'll never —"

"Stop that," he said, quite sharply. "You've no reason to think . . ."

"Yes, I do. I'm right. You know I'm right. We have to split up. You must see that."

"Not in a million years. Put that idea right out of you head."

I said gently, "I appreciate what you're saying, but you must . . ."

"I said no. Forget it."

He had that note in his voice. Arguing would not help. Time to step back and think.

"You're saying we're safe as long as we don't open the door?"

He nodded.

"OK. We're safe here, then. Why don't you get some sleep? You look worn out and so am I. We'll talk about this calmly in a few hours."

"Good idea," he said. "And from an historian, too. Who'd
have thought? Just give me a minute."

"What are you doing?"

"I'm not a complete idiot. Computer—on my mark, door
lock. Farrell voice command only. Authorisation Farrell—mike
eight three eight papa echo foxtrot. Mark."

"What are you doing?"

"I'm not waking up in four hours to find you long gone.
And don't look at me like that. You're no longer authorised to
open the door, so if anything happens to me then you're stuck
in here, forever, with my slowly rotting corpse. Killing me in
my sleep is, as they say, contra-indicated. Turn out the lights,
will you?"

I was angry. And worried. And scared. And then back to
angry again. Good job he warned me not to murder him in
his sleep because otherwise he'd be dog meat by now. I began
to devise a complicated scheme for bludgeoning him to death
with the kettle and then feeding his minced remains down the
toilet. It would have worked, I'm sure, but right in the middle of
imaginatively dismembering his corpse, I had a brilliant idea.

And it was a brilliant idea. An absolutely bloody, marvel-
lously brilliant idea.

I spent a few minutes running through it in my mind,
forming answers to his inevitable objections, and then I kicked
him awake.

"Wake up!"

"What? What's happening?"

"I've had a brilliant idea."

"I'm not opening the door. Go back to sleep."

"Open your eyes. I've had a brilliant idea."

"There is nothing you can do to me that will change my
mind."

I leaned over him.

"Is that a challenge?"

"Seriously? Do you even *know* the meaning of the word inappropriate?"

"Sit up, listen, and marvel."

"What is wrong with you? You can't sleep so no one else can either?"

"You're right, I'm being inconsiderate. Go back to sleep. I don't need you. I can do it by myself."

Five, four, three, two, one, and . . .

He sat up. "What?"

"Nothing. Go back to sleep."

I went to step over him, he seized my ankle, yanked, and down I went. He caught me and suddenly I was very close to him. I wasn't sure what to do.

"Now who's being inappropriate? You can't change my mind with sex, you know."

"Is that a challenge?"

"No. You need to conserve your strength for my brilliant idea."

He sighed. "*You've* had a brilliant idea?"

"That's what I keep saying. Will you listen?"

"Obviously sleep is something that never happens when you're around."

"No, listen. You said we can't open the door because somehow they can pick up my tag?"

He nodded.

"So, it's easy. Open the door and throw me out."

He pulled up his blanket and closed his eyes.

"I don't deserve any of this."

"Well, I put it that way for dramatic effect, but what I mean is, you drop me off . . . somewhere—" I needed to gloss over this bit, "—and then you use the opportunity to nip off to St. Mary's. You can find out what's going on, stock up on food and drink, empty the loo, recharge the cells, whatever, all of which you can do because they won't know where you are. Because

I'll be elsewhere, distracting them. Then you come and collect me again and off we go. We'll have a nice clean pod with lots to eat. We'll even be able to use the bog without getting cholera. Where's the downside?"

"And what are you doing in the meantime?"

"Nothing. That's the beauty of my brilliant idea. You can take as long as you like, replenish supplies, have a beer, have a good gossip with everyone . . . You can take days and still come back and pick me up less than thirty minutes after you left. It's not brilliant—it's genius."

"Thirty minutes may be long enough for them to find you—alone, defenceless, and in your pyjamas. Forget it."

"No. Listen, will you? You have to drop me somewhere they can't reach me. Some place where it's too dangerous for them to pursue me."

"Such as?"

I took a deep breath.

"Pompeii."

"Are you out of your mind?"

"OK. I can be reasonable. I'm not specifically wedded to Pompeii. Krakatoa will do."

"Can I refer you to my previous response?"

"Look," I said. "You're obviously tired and emotional. I'm going to sit over there for fifteen minutes. You think about things. Work your way through all the 'Oh my God, you're not doing that' nonsense—sweet, but not very helpful—and then consider, calmly, the strengths of my brilliant idea."

"But . . ."

"Not listening. Fifteen minutes."

"Will you . . . ?"

"Still not listening."

"Max . . ."

"Don't make me start la-la-la-ing."

"I'm going to smack your silly head in a minute."

"Yes, typical techie solution. If in doubt—give it a clout. You think. I'm going over there to wait for your enlightenment."

His enlightenment took about thirty seconds. Just the time it took him to struggle out of his blankets and sit up.

"What aren't you telling me?"

When you have a difficult thing to say, the secret is to hit it headlong and give it a good kicking.

"The bit you won't like."

"Yes, I thought there would be a bit I wouldn't like. Am I right in saying this relates to the tag?"

He wasn't stupid.

"Yes."

"I think you need to tell me the whole thing."

"All right. But don't start shouting until I finish. Promise."

"I don't shout."

"Well, don't start now. Here goes."

I drew a deep breath and choosing my words carefully, gave him the whole thing.

"We split up. You drop me off in Pompeii. Or Krakatoa. Or Santorini—although we don't have a specific date for Santorini and so —"

"Just get on with it."

"You jump back to St. Mary's, load up the pod with supplies, and jump straight back to Pompeii, with luck, only about thirty minutes after you left. I know it's a narrow margin, but I'm sure someone as clever as you can manage that."

This blatant flattery left him unmoved.

"I know you don't like it, but it's got to be somewhere dangerous. Somewhere they would have the same problems moving around as me. It cancels out their advantages. I thought I'd hole up in an abandoned house or shop and just keep my head down until you can pick me up. There will be ash and pumice and God knows what dropping from the sky. They'll have to take cover just like everyone else. Once I've established my presence, you nip in and pick me up. Yes, they'll lose my signal then, but we'll be in the middle of a volcanic eruption, for crying out loud. They won't be surprised."

He said nothing, so I carried on. "We go somewhere quiet—anywhere will do so long as we don't open the door—and you remove the tag. I'm sure that won't be difficult. It's only just under the skin."

"I'd feel happier if Helen did it at St. Mary's."

"We can't go there. As soon as you open the door, they'll know I'm not in Pompeii any longer. And they find us so quickly, Leon. Every time we open the door."

He shook his head, but I was right.

"We then jump back to Pompeii and chuck the tag into a heap of molten lava or whatever. As far as they're concerned, I never left and I died there under the ash, or fried in a pyroclastic flow, and then we're both free because there's no reason for them to chase you. And they won't be able to find you, anyway. We can probably go back to Rushford after a few months."

I sat back and beamed at him, not sure whether I'd get a round of applause for being so brilliant or a clip round the side of the head for being so stupid.

"I am not leaving you in the middle of a volcanic eruption."

"You have to. It has to be somewhere I could legitimately die and no one would be surprised. And where they wouldn't expect to find a body. And conditions would be too hazardous for them to investigate properly. And when they never find any further trace of my tag then it will be obvious that I'm dead."

"And you think they'll believe I went off and left you there? Come on!"

"Well, all the evidence will point to just that. I'm dodging pyroclastic flows and you're not around. They'll either think I tried to be too clever and the volcano ate me or you got fed up and dumped me. What could be more believable?"

"I'm not even going to bother answering that."

Suddenly serious, I said, "Leon. Do we have a choice? Look around us. There's condensation running down the walls and that's not good. Never mind what it will do to the pod, our clothes are damp. Our bedding is damp. We had to leave a lot of gear on Skaxos. Our food is running out. And the water. And the power. These people are relentless. They will catch us one day. And that might be the best thing that could happen to us, because, one day, the safety protocols will fail and this pod will dump us at the bottom of the sea. Or in the path of an avalanche. Or one day it just won't move at all. Then what do we do? Sit in a wet box until we die? Or make a dash for it and hope to outrun them? We haven't been very successful at that, so far. I know you don't like it, but you need to think about it. There's no point in doing it the other way around, with me going to St. Mary's instead of you. This is something only I can do. You know that."

"Setting all that aside for one moment, I don't even know how to remove a tag."

"It's only just underneath the skin. I could probably do it myself. Except I'd have to do it one-handed, but I could probably manage."

"Why not remove the tag first and throw it into Vesuvius?"

"I think they'd suspect something if it's too easy. They must see me desperately trying to escape from Pompeii. Their instruments will lose me for a while and then, suddenly, a brief flicker—and I'm gone forever."

His face changed for a moment.

I put my hand on his arm.

"Sorry."

He nodded. "I'm not a surgeon."

"You don't have to be. You're an engineer. That's almost the same thing."

"Your ignorance is frightening."

I was suddenly very tired.

"Leon. Do we actually have a choice?"

He sighed. "You look dreadful. Go and lie down."

"And you, too."

"What?"

"This is ridiculous. One of us is always exhausted while the other one is unconscious in the corner. You say we're safe with the door closed. So let's both get some sleep. And if they do turn up and catch us while we're both asleep, then at least you're spared having to hack through my arm with a rusty bread-knife."

I spread the blankets out on the floor. "Come on."

I lay down, and after a moment's hesitation, he lay down beside me. About two feet away.

I woke in the night. The pod was dark and silent. He had curled himself around me, one arm protectively over my shoulders. I could hear him breathing.

I woke again and I was lying in the crook of his arm, warm and safe.

I woke again and he was resting his head on mine. I could feel his breath in my hair.

I woke again and he was in the tiny shower.

Singing.

IT'S TRUE WHAT THEY say—things do look better after a good night's sleep.

After breakfast, we sat and talked over the plan—every aspect of it, because there would never be a second chance. We had to get it right first time. Our lives depended upon it.

Leon's plan was to land at St. Mary's and talk to Dieter, now in charge of the Technical section. While his pod was being serviced, he'd somehow sneak a word with Dr. Bairstow and load up with supplies. Whether the Time Police would have left a presence at St. Mary's, we had no way of knowing but he didn't seem overly concerned about that, because, I suspected, he was keeping all his concern for my part of the plan.

In vain did I argue that the eruption was necessary to cancel out any advantages they might have in terms of numbers and equipment. When you're fighting for your life in a pyroclastic flow, sonic weapons are about as much use as the junior party in a coalition government. In fact, I argued, as an historian, I'd have considerable advantages over the Time Police. I was commanded to state at least one. Not important right now, I said.

He sighed.

I challenged him to come up with a better plan. He sighed again. I didn't push it. Instead, I made us both a cup of tea, partly because I felt we deserved a mug to fortify us against our coming ordeals, but mostly to put off the actual moment when we would have to part.

Taking refuge in practicalities, he busied himself drawing up a servicing schedule.

I made up a shopping list of supplies and medical stuff, including industrial-strength painkillers. Understandably, he would want to be in and out as quickly as possible, but, as I kept pointing out, that was the beauty of the plan. He could spend days at St. Mary's—weeks, even—and so long as he could jump back to Pompeii soon after he left me there, it didn't matter.

"The plan can't fail," I said, ignoring such minor inconveniences as an unreliable pod, an erupting volcano, the omnipresent Time Police, a dying city, and a panicking population. "What could possibly go wrong?"

He slowly folded his lists and put them carefully away.

I shut the last locker door and there was no reason why we shouldn't get on with it. No reason at all.

So we didn't. We sat on the floor and looked at each other.

I should speak. I hadn't said anything and he hadn't said anything either, but there was a very real chance that one or both of us wouldn't get through this. His pod could whirl him off to some place there was no coming back from. I could find myself buried under the contents of Vesuvius. He could be caught at St. Mary's. I could be caught at Pompeii. This might be the last opportunity we would ever have to speak together and if it was one thing I had learned over the last year, it was never to let an opportunity pass. It might never come again.

We turned down the lights and heating to conserve power, wrapped ourselves in blankets, and we talked. We were a little hesitant at first, but there was safety in the semi-darkness. A feeling of intimacy and understanding. After a while, the words came more easily. We talked a little of our lives before St. Mary's, but not a great deal, because those weren't happy times for either of us. We talked of St. Mary's—of shared experiences, each bittersweet word recalling old memories and half-forgotten jokes.

I said, "Do you remember the day Roberts and Markham tried to get a horse upstairs?"

"Oh, yes, I'd forgotten that. They got old Turk up onto the Gallery and they couldn't get him down again. Apparently, horses can't go downstairs."

"I can't remember why they did it."

"They'd heard that Caligula slept with his horse and wanted to give it a try."

"And Dr. Bairstow turned up and told them to call the vet and tell him to be sure to bring his humane killer."

"And no one knew whether it was for the horse or for them."

I laughed. "And there was a huge argument over whether Caligula did actually sleep with his horse or his sister. Or whether that was Nero. Or Catherine the Great. And everyone was so busy shouting that they never noticed Turk wander off and they eventually caught up with him outside the kitchens, where Jenny Fields was giving him apples and Mrs. Mack had made a halter out of tea towels."

"So," he said, "can horses can walk downstairs?"

"No one saw him do it so we still don't know. It's very possible he took himself down in the heavy goods lift."

We both smiled at the memory.

"Do you remember when John Calvin called you the devil's strumpet and tried to have you run out of town?"

"No," I said, regretfully, "that didn't happen to me, but Isaac Newton did once try to have me indicted for stealing his mirror. And it was my bloody mirror in the first place. Do you remember Professor Rapson assembling a Roman tortoise and they all fell into the lake?"

He laughed. "We didn't have that, but I do remember his efforts to invent his own embalming fluid—he never said why and no one dared ask—and he had about twenty sheep's heads hanging from the trees like wind chimes. The gardens looked like something from a Tim Burton movie. Every dog in the neighbourhood was going demented trying to climb the trees to get to them."

"Do you remember Alexandria?"

"Yes. And Mary Stuart?"

"Yes."

Silence. I can't remember which of us said it.

"Do you remember Troy?"

I looked down at my hands. We should talk about Troy and Helios. We *must* talk about Troy and Helios. But what to say? I didn't want to lie to him, but no matter how much I tried to avoid it, I wouldn't be able to hide the fact that when the other Leon died, we were not together.

He said nothing, just sitting in the dark, waiting for me to speak.

In the end, I said, "At Troy—just as we were pulling out, Leon wanted to take a young boy with us. Helios. To take him to a place of safety. I refused. I made him take Helios back outside and leave him to face whatever would happen to him there."

In my mind, I saw it all again. Helios, terrified, clamped to Leon, and refusing to let go. Leon, his blue eyes bright with desperation for Helios and then cold with contempt for me. A silent pod. Just the sound of his heavy breathing. I pulled a gun on him and I would have used it. He went ahead and saved Helios anyway. Behind my back. We never spoke again. Then he died.

It tumbled out in a rush of badly chosen words and jerky sentences and when I had finished, I shut up because I was afraid of what would come next. There was no good way out of this. Would he condemn my actions? I would understand if he did because I condemned my actions. Or would he tell me the same thing had happened in this world and once again, I would have to make a choice about what to do. What to say.

I tried to take a breath, but it came out as a deep, shuddering sigh. "I went to see Helios. Joe Nelson, I should say. I told him I'd made a mistake. I apologised. It was little enough, but it was all I could do."

He nodded and then said, "What would you say if I told you I'd done the same thing here? That I had lifted Helios out of Troy and taken him to safety. That I'd done the same as your Leon. What would you say?"

There is a time in everyone's life when they wish either they had or hadn't said something. Very few people get a second chance. A chance to unsay the wrong words and replace them with the right ones. The words they should have said.

"I would say, 'I wish I had your compassion. That if it happened to me, I hope I could find the strength to do what you did. But I'm afraid I wouldn't.'"

The words hung between us. Without knowing why, I'd said something important. For a moment, I thought he might say something. I waited, but that moment passed.

A little hesitantly and not without some emotion, we talked of our deaths.

"Leon, how did I die?"

He didn't pretend to misunderstand my question.

"An accident. A stupid, stupid accident."

"You mean I didn't die on the job?"

"If you mean, was it a work-related fatality—no."

"You said they found me in my office so I assumed . . ."

"Oh. Sorry. Yes, you were at work, but not bounding around the timeline endangering life and limb. You were actually at St. Mary's, where you were supposed to be safe."

"What happened?"

"It was stupid," he said again, angrily. "A bird's nest or something fell down your chimney. And then, over the weeks, a ton of soot and rubbish accumulated on top of it and one day you switched on your gas fire . . ." He stopped.

I said nothing.

"And there was no battery in your detector. It was sitting on the window sill."

He was angry. Angry that I, of all people, should have done such a thing. I know my Leon had always chased around St. Mary's, yelling at people for disconnecting their alarms. People took them out because, they said, they kept going off and it's very irritating when you're trying to work. St. Mary's, sadly, has never made the link between the detectors going off and there actually being a reason for this happening.

Except for me. I'd always tried to show a little solidarity. Obviously, his Max hadn't and it had cost her her life. That's probably irony.

"Why didn't you return to the future?"

He and Dr. Bairstow were from the future. Sent back to found St. Mary's and—I remembered—keep it and us, safe.

"Many reasons. They would have reassigned me. You would have been even further away. I didn't want to be in a world that didn't have echoes of you bouncing around it . . ." He trailed off.

"But you didn't stay at St. Mary's."

"No. No, I didn't. I . . . We . . . I made myself the perfect life I wanted to have with you."

Something in his voice made me look up. It hurt me to look at him. His face was so unutterably sad . . .

I said softly, "Leon . . ." and he reached out for me.

We held hands in the dark, each taking and giving comfort to the other. His hands were warm and strong and rough. Just as I remembered.

I tried desperately to keep the exhaustion and fear from my voice. "Leon, how did this happen? How could it happen? Why am I here?"

"I don't know, love. I don't have the physics for this. I'm not sure anyone does."

"Try."

"You mean explain physics to an historian? I don't have any crayons."

I said nothing in a way that could clearly be understood and he relented.

"OK. Here's our two lives, running parallel to each other, sometimes similar, sometimes not, but never touching. And then—something happens. Some event somewhere—maybe you weren't supposed to die in this world, I don't know— but somehow, our two worlds touched. Just briefly. Just long enough for a door to open and for you to step across into my world."

He stopped for a moment, gripping my hands so tightly that it hurt.

Should I say anything about Mrs. Partridge? But how would that help?

He was speaking again.

"I will be forever grateful, eternally thankful that you did that. The door has closed now. I know you can't ever go back, but—if you will let me—I will devote the rest of my life to making sure that you never, ever, for one moment, regret it."

For some moments, there are no words.

And then we got going.

SIX

*P*OMPEII.

The day of the eruption.

I nearly kicked the whole thing into touch right there and then.

Vesuvius didn't suddenly erupt, right out of the blue. The eruption was preceded by a series of violent seismic tremors, which, in those days, nobody associated with imminent volcanic activity. We landed right in the middle of quite a strong one. The pod shuddered a little, but the locker doors remained closed. Nothing fell out. We sat quietly and waited for what seemed a very long time for it to be over.

All throughout the tremor, Leon very pointedly said nothing.

To make it easy for them to find me, I was wearing clothes they'd seen me in before. The first century was about to be gifted with its first sighting of yellow-and-white-spotted PJs, over which I wore my blanket, poncho style. I could use it to cover my head when things started dropping from the sky. The inhabitants of Pompeii would soon be walking around with pillows tied to their heads for protection, so I didn't have to worry too much about fashion statements.

I tucked the bottoms into my wellies, because I would soon be wading through layers of hot ash and pumice.

I half expected the tremors would cause Leon to change his mind, but he kept his attention on the screen and called me over.

"Memorise this street. This is where I'll pick you up. I can't guarantee when, but certainly not longer than a few hours. Remember, they usually turn up after an hour or so. Find somewhere safe and stay there. Be aware that as well as being pursued by the Time Police, a volcano is about to erupt, so don't concentrate on the one to the exclusion of the other."

"I'll lead them away from here, show myself, and then double back."

"At least take the pod remote. If things get bad, you can call the pod."

"No. You're taking as much of a risk as I am. I'm not going to call the pod when you might need it yourself."

He hesitated.

"It makes sense, Leon. If you're not able to come back for me then I'll die here, so the priority is to keep you safe. And we're running out of time. Just a few short hours and then our problems will be over."

"In that case, make sure you're here when I get back. Don't make me come looking for you."

There was an awkward pause, which I broke by saying, "Good luck. Don't forget the Jaffa Cakes."

He smiled and put out his hand, just as we always used to when I was setting off on assignment and we were surrounded by milling crowds of techies and historians. Memories crowded my mind. As always, his hand was warm and rough.

"Good luck. Don't forget the eruption."

He opened the door and I slipped outside into the heat of the day. I walked to the deep purple shadow of a high wall and turned back.

He had already gone.

My heart knocked against my ribs. I'd been alone before but this was the first time I had ever been alone with no way to get home. Just to cheer myself up, I reminded myself I didn't have a home any longer. If anything happened to Leon then I'd die here, along with most of the inhabitants. I was more alone than I'd ever been in my entire life. Out of my own world. Out of my own time. I've been in some dodgy situations before, but, always, St. Mary's had been in the background, somewhere. Eventually, Peterson or Guthrie or Markham or someone would explode out of the woodwork and I'd be saved. This was different.

I stared at the place where the pod had been. I'd tried to avoid thinking too much about my previous life, and thanks to the cluster-catastrophe that was our existence at the moment, I'd been largely successful. Now, typically, just when I needed to keep all my wits about me, a great surge of sadness for my loss rolled right over me. No matter what happened, there was no way I'd ever see any of my St. Mary's again.

Actually, if I didn't get a move on, I'd never see anyone again. Think cheerful thoughts, Maxwell.

We'd argued for ages over where, in a doomed city, would be the safest spot in which to land, and finally fixed on the south-east quarter—somewhere between the Porta Stabia and the Porta Nocera. Of course, the pod had its own ideas and plonked us in the north-east corner, between the amphitheatre and the palaestra. It could have been worse. Vesuvius was to the north-west and the high walls of the amphitheatre would offer some protection. I hoped.

The ground shook again, slightly. I moved into an open space and looked around. From the position of the sun, I judged it to be about noon—later than I would have liked. The first eruption—a big one—would occur in the next few hours.

However, at the moment, people were coming and going about their daily business as much as they were able. They were used to this.

This area was not residential and there were few women around. Men bustled in and out of the palaestra, looking important and talking in loud voices. My Latin returned, as it always does whenever I hear it spoken, and I listened. Three of them, the loudest and presumably the most important—in their eyes, at least—were strolling along the portico, enjoying the shade and discussing the dismal performance of their chosen chariot team—the Greens.

Few men wore togas. Tunics seemed to be the accepted garb. I saw a variety of colours—ochres, browns, some reds. One or two wore blue—next to purple, the most expensive colour there is, but sadly prone to fading.

No one paid me the slightest attention. In this world, as in any other, people don't see the bizarrely dressed, the odd ones who live outside normal society. Nobody would catch my eye in case I demanded money. I told myself I was as good as invisible.

The high, arched walls of the amphitheatre reared up in front of me. Posters advertising future events covered the lower levels. An external stone staircase led to the higher tiers. Two slaves in dingy tunics were slowly sweeping the steps. Very slowly. This was light work. They would be in no rush to finish.

The surrounding area was filled with tiny taverns and eating places. Here and there, temporary booths had been set up, to sell snacks and souvenirs to the hungry and gullible.

The ground shook again, reminding me why I was here. I needed to keep moving. I needed a crowd to get lost in and a densely built area in which to hide.

I headed west to one of the main streets, the one which ran right through town, more or less north-east to south-west. The crowds here were much more diverse and some women were present, going about normal household duties. It was still a little early for the other sort of commercial transactions. I skipped past a bakery, with its distinctive smell of hot flour and scorched bricks. I passed a wine shop. The owner, a stocky man in a dingy tunic and with an unlovely roll of fat around his neck, was still setting up his amphora. He had no idea what was about to happen. None of them did.

In twenty-four hours' time, Pompeii and its neighbour, Herculaneum, would be gone—lost under vast layers of volcanic ash. I looked at the people around me, all shouting, arguing, laughing, and haggling. All living out the last hours of their lives. This time tomorrow, they would be dead and, when the world saw them next, they would be pitiful, hollow shells, their shapes preserved over the centuries, long after their bodies had gone. I always remember the woman, trying to shelter her child, and the little dog, still chained, unable to escape, twisted in his death throes . . .

The temptation is to jump on a cart, wave your arms, and shout, "Run! Run for your lives. You still have time."

But I didn't.

I pulled myself together. I needed to get an idea of the layout. I had only about half an hour and then I was going to be running for my life.

Again.

I MADE MY WAY down to the Forum, using the stepping-stones to cross the road and jumping on and off the raised pavements. The Romans used their streets as storm drains. I could imagine the floodwaters flowing down from Vesuvius and coursing through the streets, sweeping away everything in their path. Only this time the flood would consist of volcanic debris, pumice, super-heated mudflows . . .

I mingled with the crowds outside the Forum, which was packed. Ironically, there was a great view of Vesuvius, its summit wreathed in what might be light cloud but was more probably smoke.

My wrist beeped. Leon had lent me his watch. One hour gone. The Forces of Darkness should be turning up any minute now.

The town was laid out on a grid system. I'd concentrated on the north-east corner and had the rough layout in my head. I had my route planned. I'd found two or three spots where I could conceal myself for long enough to hold them up. I couldn't do any more. All I could do now was stay alert, keep moving, and stay ahead of them. And the volcano, of course.

Another half hour passed. I stood with my back to a wall, admiring the Temple of Jupiter and watching the crowds go by.

They were late. The bastards were late. Wouldn't it be just typical if they didn't turn up at all and I was jumping around a major volcanic incident for absolutely nothing?

I sighed with frustration and then everything happened all at once.

I was cupping my hands at a street fountain when a large cart clattered by. I turned at the noise and there they were in their black cloaks, standing at the street corner. Faintly, I heard the electronic beep. They were triangulating. Time to go.

I'd just hopped down off the pavement when the world erupted in the biggest noise I've ever heard. Not a bang or a crack. Just a huge, loud, indescribable noise. My ears rang and for a moment, I thought they'd hit me with the sonic thing again and it was all over before it started.

I'd forgotten. Just for a moment, I'd forgotten about the volcano.

The sound echoed around the streets, bouncing off high walls, followed by a long, low, never-ending reverberation that found an echo in the tremors beneath our feet.

All around me, life had stopped. Some people had dropped to their knees, holding their heads. Even the mule pulling the cart had stopped dead. Everyone was staring up at the mountain, which was belching thick, black smoke high into the air.

Pliny would describe it as shaped like an umbrella pine and he was spot on.

It had begun.

I had the advantage, because I'd been expecting it. While everyone was still frozen with shock, I slipped between the cart and the wall and down a narrow, dirt alley. I turned left at the bottom, and left again, then back on to the main road. I moved slowly between groups of people still staring in stunned disbelief at the mountain. I had no time to look myself.

I'd thought long and hard about whether to stay on the streets, dodging around and making it difficult for them to get a fix, or to nip through a garden gate and find some quiet corner, stay put, and trust that Leon turned up before they found me. I decided to stay on the streets. For the time being, anyway.

In the distance, the massive column of smoke grew taller and wider. It must be all of ten miles high. Despite the dangers of falling roof tiles, more people were running out of their houses to look. Shopkeepers left their premises to join others on the street. Customers from the caupona on the corner were gathered outside, many of them still chewing. Not one of them had put down his drink. Even now, there was more curiosity than panic. People pointed, exclaimed, and chattered. I wanted to shake them because they could still escape. It wasn't yet too late for them.

I was just oozing around the wine shop when the ash started to drift down, hardly discernible first, just the odd flake here or there. If I hadn't seen it settling gently on my blanket, I might not have noticed anything.

Children ran out into the streets, dodging around, trying to catch the flakes as they drifted silently downwards and still there was no major panic or terror-stricken exodus to the gates. There was nothing I could do. Those who didn't try to get away within the next hour or so wouldn't get away at all, and now that the Time Police were here, I couldn't afford to draw attention to myself by trying to persuade people to leave.

The ground rocked again. I dropped to a crouch and waited for the tremor to subside, but this time, it didn't. The eruption had begun and the ground wouldn't stop shaking now until long after everyone was dead. I would just have to cope.

The next half hour was no fun at all. I had to make haste slowly. I checked each street before venturing forth. At all times, I had to be aware of my position in relation to our rendezvous point. I had to keep returning there to check if Leon had returned, without making it obvious that that location was in any way important. I didn't want them setting an ambush. I should be seeking shelter, but there was no chance. If I stopped moving then I was dead in the water. Or the ash.

The tremors were increasing in strength. I could hear pots toppling over and bricks or roof tiles crashing into the street. The baker had, very sensibly, doused his fires and the wine shop owner had long since stopped trying to right his toppled amphora. People were shuttering their windows against the ash and dust. It wouldn't do them the slightest bit of good. Many had returned to their homes, thinking they could wait it out as they always had in the past. There were fewer people on the streets.

The ash fluttered more thickly now and I was caked in it. It was evil stuff and I was coughing, because volcanic ash contains silicone. When it gets in the lungs, it liquefies, making it difficult and then impossible to breathe. Take it from me; covering your face doesn't help much. I had a ghastly metallic taste in my mouth. I stopped at street fountains at every opportunity, but now the tanks were full of ashy scum. With the continuing tremors, it was only a matter of time before the pipes cracked or the tall water towers came down and then there would be no fresh water at all, and they still hadn't finished repairing the water system from the last eruption.

And where the bloody hell was Leon? This is what happens when you let men go off by themselves. They don't have a bloody clue. They might be able to fold maps but they certainly can't bloody read them. I should have drawn him something in crayon, which said, "I am here." He was off enjoying a bit of a holiday while half a volcano was falling on me. I swear, when I saw him again, he was going to get the biggest ear-bashing of his life.

If you ever see him again, said the nasty little voice that always surfaces in the middle of a sleepless night. I pushed it away. If I let myself believe, even for one minute, that I'd never see Leon again, then I might as well give up now. He would be here. He would rip time apart to get to me. If he had to get out and push the bloody pod—he would come for me.

Right on cue, just as his watch beeped to tell me that I should be gone by now, the mountain blew. With a colossal roar, like a giant ripping the sky apart, the top opened right up, hurling huge amounts of smoke and volcanic material high into the air, darkening the sky. Vast clouds of smoke bubbled and boiled like giant black cauliflowers.

I found an archway under one of the external staircases on the south side of the amphitheatre and crouched with the shuddering wall at my back, telling myself this would shield me from the oncoming storm.

Walls cracked and toppled. All over the city, I could hear objects shattering. Now there was panic. People screamed. Even out here in the street, I could hear people wailing inside the buildings. Dogs barked hysterically, yanking on their chains, frantic to get away. Children cried.

The smoke streamed towards the stricken city like a huge black hand. The noise was ear bleeding. I felt the pressure change. The sun disappeared. Night came early to Pompeii. They'd had their last day.

Even worse was to come.

What goes up must come down. Now, not only were the inhabitants being bombarded with volcanic ash, but the stones, pulverised rock, and pumice that had been hurled into the heavens by the blast now started to fall back to earth.

I tied my blanket around my head as best I could. It was time to check for Leon again.

Leaving the comparative safety of my archway, I skirted the amphitheatre and caught my first glimpse of the angry mountain in the distance. Black smoke billowed, eerily lit from within by flames and lightning.

Things were not looking good.

At last, the inhabitants of Pompeii agreed with me because the streets were boiling with people desperate to escape. Most were heading down through the town towards the harbour, hoping to escape by boat.

They'd left it much too late. Both the River Sarno and the harbour would be completely clogged with banks of floating pumice. Nothing could get in and certainly, nothing could get out. Many of them would die down there.

The streets were blocked solid. All organisation had disappeared. As they always are in a crisis, people were unwilling to abandon their possessions. Men and women ran through the streets clutching as much as they could carry. Cursing drivers struggled with overloaded carts. At a major intersection, a panicking driver had failed to line up his wagon properly and the wheels were locked solidly against the stepping-stones. The pressure behind him prevented him reversing up and no one could get past him. He'd lost control of his horse and any minute now the whole lot was going to go over, spilling cherished but useless household goods across the street.

There was panic. There was confusion. There was hysteria. Families were separated. Terrified children screamed for their parents. Elderly people were knocked to the ground. People invoked their gods—with the usual amount of success.

And all the time, the ash fell, clogging everything—the streets, rooftops, people's lungs. It lay a good six inches deep now. I could feel it crunching underfoot. Everyone was coated in it. We were all turning grey.

I was so thirsty.

And Leon still wasn't here.

I uttered a curse at least as sulphuric as anything the mountain was dropping down on us and withdrew into a doorway while I considered what to do next.

Smoking rocks, fire, pumice, ash—it all rained down. The mountain rumbled and roared, the ground shook continually, buildings fell, walls cracked, and fires were breaking out all over the city. To be outside now was suicide and that applied to the Time Police as well. Volcanic debris was just as likely to fall on them as on me. They were just as likely to be trampled by the panicking citizens. Like me, they couldn't take refuge in any conveniently empty buildings, because soon the weight of ash on the roofs would cause the buildings to collapse. And, unless they had special breathing apparatus, they wouldn't be able to get around in this choking ash, either. So this part of my brilliant plan was working well.

The part where I survived the Mount Vesuvius eruption of AD79 was looking less good. I really should find somewhere safe—safe being a relative term—and wait for Leon. I decided to get back to the amphitheatre. I could hide under the arches, and then when the ash became too deep, retreat up the staircase, trusting to my innovative headgear to protect me from concussion. What could go wrong?

Well, for a start, I never got there.

The Time Police didn't find me. I found them. One of them, anyway.

Two of the temporary wooden stalls had been overturned in the panic. I didn't take a lot of notice, but, as I passed, even over all the racket going on around me, I heard a faint cry.

Peering through the murk, I could just make out a dark shape, stretched out in the ash. An officer. He was pinned underneath one of the stalls. Even as I looked, he raised an arm at me.

Cursing myself for a complete idiot, I braced myself for whatever he was about to shoot me with, but I was wrong. It was a cry for help.

Very hesitantly, and poised at any moment to run for it, I drew closer. I could smell it even through the ash and sulphur. He was burning.

A brazier had come down, spilling smouldering charcoal on his leg, burning through armour, cloth, and skin. He must have been in agony. I kicked the brazier aside, wound my blanket around my hands, scraped off the smouldering coals as best I could, and jumped back so he couldn't make a grab for me. I should leave him. No doubt he was in contact with his comrades who would—should—be on their way to pick him up. They could be here any minute now.

All the time, volcanic debris continued to fall around us. Large lumps of rock thudded into the ash, making little crater patterns. Smaller pieces of pumice and lava zinged past us, burning holes in our clothing. The backs of my hands were pitted with tiny, stinging red burns. But mostly, the ash fell, silent and deadly. He was pinned face down. At the moment, he was holding himself up on one arm, but that wouldn't save him for long. His hood had fallen back. He was very, very young.

I'm a sucker for young men. It started when I was on assignment to the Somme. Young men are so achingly vulnerable. They launch themselves into the world, thinking they're the dog's bollocks and, sometimes, the world just chews them up and spits them out. They should be spending their days messing around with cars or motor bikes. Or playing football. Or staring at girls and trying to pretend they're not terrified. They should not be hanging off barbed wire. Not lying in water-filled craters with their legs blown off. Not struggling for every agonising breath after a mustard gas attack. Not lying in front of me, crushed, burned, and fighting to keep their faces out of the suffocating ash.

There's never really any choice, is there?

The stall wasn't that heavy. People moved them all the time, trying to stay one step ahead of the authorities. He'd fallen with one arm pinned beneath him and been unable to pull himself free. I got my hands under one of the shafts and heaved. Something shifted. It might have been something important in my lower back.

I planted my feet and got a good grip. Back straight, knees bent, lift with your legs, Maxwell. I heaved again.

This time, it lifted slightly. I closed my eyes, locked my joints, and clenched my teeth against the pain. I was an invalid. I should not be doing this.

Defying the laws of physics, the stall got heavier with each passing second. My legs began to tremble. My shoulders were being pulled from their sockets. My chest was NOT HAPPY.

He grasped my ankle with his free hand and used it to pull against. I could feel him moving beneath the stall. Now he had his other arm free. He used his forearms to pull himself out.

I shouted a warning. The shaft was slipping through my fingers. We had seconds . . .

He rolled away just as it thudded down, raising another localised dust cloud.

I leaned forward to ease my aching back, put my hands on my knees, and got my breath back. If he reached for his gun now, there would be nothing I could do to save myself. I couldn't even run.

He looked at me. I looked at him.

He nodded. I nodded.

I pushed off while I still could.

When I looked back, he was still there, trying—and failing—to crawl through the ash.

Bloody bollocking hell!

Where were his people? Why weren't they combing the streets for him? What sort of organisation was this?

I should go. I should be at the rendezvous point. I shouldn't be wasting time here.

I ran back and helped him to his feet.

His leg was the problem. He could barely walk.

I got his arm around my shoulders and we limped along. Of course, just when I could have done with a glimpse of them, there was no sign of the Time Police anywhere. I was so fed up with these bloody people.

We staggered into the shelter of an archway. He went to sit down but I wouldn't let him. I'd never have the strength to get him back up again.

I had to cough and spit to clear my throat.

"Where are your people?"

"What?"

I raised my voice. "Where are you parked?"

"That big open place by the big building with the pillar things."

Obviously a potential member of the Security section.

"The Forum?"

"What?"

We were shouting to make ourselves heard.

"Do your people know where you are?"

"I tried to tell them . . ."

He broke off and shifted his weight, trying to ease the pain in his leg."

"Are they coming?"

"Don't know."

I had to get him out of here. Never mind getting him back to his people, Leon would be turning up any minute now—if he wasn't here already—and it would ruin everything if any member of the Time Police caught sight of him picking me up. It was vital everyone thought I'd died here. Looking on the bright side, that could still happen.

I decided to compromise. I'd get him away, leave him at some mid-point where he could easily be found, and leg it back here as fast as I could.

"Can you contact them?"

"Not really. The eruption is affecting our equipment." He looked at me. "We can't find you at all."

That settled it. I hoisted him more securely. "Come on,"

He could be lying, said my three-o'clock-in-the-morning voice. I told it to shut up and keep its eyes peeled.

I dragged him along as best I could. We tripped on things concealed under layers of ash and pumice. Initially, I thought it would be a good idea to keep to the walls as much as possible, for guidance and shelter, but after the third roof tile had just missed us, we moved out into the middle of the road. I could hear people in their houses and shops, barricading their windows and doorways. They would all move upstairs, thinking they'd be safer there, and so they would be until all the roofs and upper stories caved in under the weight.

I coughed and coughed. I'd been out in this stuff for hours now. My chest was on fire.

He said, "Wait," leaned against a wall and pulled out a knife.

Told you, said my nasty little voice.

He cut and ripped at his cloak and handed me a square of material. "Put that over your face."

It made very little difference, but the thought was there.

We struggled on. The heat was unbearable. I had a while to go before the pyroclastic flows killed everyone who wasn't already dead, but the heat trapped among the buildings was intense. Sweat was pouring off me, mingling with the ash. If it hardened to a crust, I'd be a statue.

I had no idea what to do with him. I couldn't march up to them and say, "Hey, is this one of yours?" I couldn't just abandon him. It had to be somewhere they could find him. We paused at a corner while I tried to think.

He solved my problem for me.

"Leave me here."

"Are you sure?"

He nodded and pulled a gun from his pocket.

A voice in my head demanded to know why I never listened.

"It's a flare. We're close enough for them to see." He hesitated. "You should go."

I was under no illusions about the magnitude of the favour he was doing me. I know I'd saved his life, but even so . . . "Thank you."

"No. Thank you."

"What's your name?"

"Officer Ellis."

"No, your real name. What does your mum call you?"

"A pain in the arse. Go."

I took two steps back and he was practically invisible. As best I could, I ran back up the street and paused on the next corner to look back. I could see a red glow, lighting the ash around and silhouetting a black figure. I hesitated, but I couldn't do any more for him. Sending up a quick request to the god of historians, I left him.

I WAS NEARLY BLIND. My eyes were stinging. Tears ran down my cheeks, mingling with the dust. I was burned, exhausted, dehydrated, and desperate. If Leon wasn't there, then I was finished. I'd left it far too late to leave the city. No one could go more than a few yards in this. If I wasn't buried alive then I'd be crushed by falling buildings and if I survived that then I'd be a very spectacular human torch for one, maybe two seconds and then that would be it. I struggled past the wine shop, now almost completely obscured under a drift of ash and rubble, and turned the corner.

The pod was there.

There are no words to describe the relief . . . the sheer, blessed relief. I vowed never to have another brilliant idea again.

He hadn't been there long—there was only a very slight covering of ash and stuff on the roof.

I staggered dramatically across the street, all ready to give him a piece of my mind.

The door opened. Someone swept me off my feet, said, "Door," and a second later, the door closed, shutting out the noise and the ash and the smell and there was silence.

He dropped me on the floor where I curled up and coughed.

"Computer, initiate jump." and the world went white.

SEVEN

THE FIRST THING I noticed was the smell of burning. Was I on fire?

I sat up and looked around. He'd obviously had nearly as bad a day as I had. The front panels were off the console. Two of the boards had been removed. One of them was a melted mess. My technical knowledge is limited to switching things on—and occasionally off—but I'm pretty sure boards shouldn't look like that.

A large number of red lights flashed angrily, demanding action of some kind.

A spent fire extinguisher lay on the floor. Powder and foam flecked the floor and walls. It looked as if a small eruption had taken place in here, as well.

I sat up, cracked my stiff hair off my face, and said, "You see—this is what happens if you let a techie drive. Did you leave the handbrake on again?"

"Don't start," he said, tersely, flicking switches like a lunatic. "It's been a lively morning."

"More or less lively than avoiding Vesuvius and the Time Police?"

"You have no idea. Just to give you a flavour of today's catastrophes—I've been trying all day to get to you. I've jumped to Pompeii yesterday, next Tuesday, last week, tomorrow, and finally, now. I've overridden every safety protocol on the board. I've fought fires, electrical failure, and a major fit of pod-sulk. Do not push me today. I am a man on the edge."

He turned as he spoke and I was shocked. He'd said he had a bit of a struggle, but that wasn't the half of it. The back of his left hand and the left side of his face were encased in medical plastic.

"You'd better let me take a look at that."

"I'm fine," he said, impatiently. "The plastic is doing its job. I'm more concerned with you. Here, drink this."

I gulped down the water he offered. I couldn't get enough. It ran down my chin and splashed onto my PJs. I was in such a state. Parts of my face and the backs of my hands were red with tiny burns. My chest hurt. My back hurt. My shoulders hurt. Everything was coated in fine dust. I shed a cloud of it every time I moved. At some point, I'd melted one of his wellies and not even noticed. I didn't even want to think about my hair. It would never be the same again.

He fingered the black square of material. "What's this?"

"My good deed for the day." I told him what had happened, expecting all sorts of scolding, but he just smiled.

"The tanks are full. Get yourself a shower. Are you hungry?"

"No. Just very, very thirsty."

"Well don't drink your shower. I don't want any historian habits here."

I staggered stiffly into the shower, throwing my ruined clothes back into the pod. The shower was wonderful. By the time I had finished shifting volcanic rubble from all my nooks and crannies, the bottom of the shower tray looked like a builder's yard.

As I turned off the water, his arm appeared around the door with a pair of shorts and a man's T-shirt.

He had a mug of tea ready for me. There should be medals struck for men who produce tea at exactly the moment it's needed. I slurped thirstily and slowly everything subsided. I was suddenly aware that I was very tired.

"Where are we?"

"England. Sometime between the last Ice Age and modern times."

"Don't you know?"

"No, and neither does the pod at the moment. All the safety protocols are down. I've had to override a lot of systems. I had real trouble getting it back to Pompeii during the eruption. As I said, I jumped to yesterday. When I tried to force it, it gave me next week. I had another go and got tomorrow. That wasn't good. We really don't want to be in Pompeii tomorrow. The heat was blood boiling. There was a . . . smallish . . . fire inside the pod and I jumped away as quickly as I could. By now, I was jumping around all over the place. I pulled the boards out, disconnected everything in sight, and gave it a strong hint as to its future if it didn't do exactly as I wanted, crossed my fingers, jumped, and there you were. Had you been waiting long?"

"Too busy consorting with the enemy," I said cheerfully, unwilling to admit, even to myself, that I'd had even the smallest doubt that I'd ever see him again. "So we're hot to trot?"

"Yes, I can fix the worst of it."

Something in his voice wasn't right.

"And?"

"And what?"

"And the bit you're not telling me. The really bad news. What's happened at St. Mary's?"

"The Time Police are there."

I stared, speechless.

"Don't panic. It wasn't a problem."

Why wasn't I reassured? "Why not?"

A long, a very long silence.

I felt my stomach shift. Something bad had happened. "Leon?"

"There were only two officers on site and they were easy to avoid."

I took a deep breath. "Because . . . ?"

"Because they were too busy looking for Helios. Max, they know."

"They know Helios is Joe Nelson?"

"No, no. They don't know Helios is Joe Nelson. They just know Helios is there. Somewhere."

"What will they do if they find him?"

"Arrest Dr. Bairstow, Peterson, Guthrie—and me, of course. You'll be all right—you're dead."

"Not funny."

"No. Sorry."

"I meant—what will they do to Helios?"

"At worst, they'll shoot him. At best, they'll take him back."

"To Troy? Right in the middle of . . . ?"

I saw it all again. The thick black smoke rising from the ruined city. The flames. Dead people everywhere. Burning bodies. Kassandra dragged from the temple. Little runty man breaking my nose. The lines of women and children on the beach waiting to be shipped as slaves. Dead babies bobbing in the surf . . .

Even though he was a grown man now, Helios would be dead in seconds, along with every other man in Troy. They would be taking him back to his death. But if he stayed, they'd shoot him as an anomaly. Certain death for Helios, whatever the Time Police did to him.

Leon was staring at his hands.

"Unless . . . ?"

He looked up. "What?"

"Unless . . . ?"

"Unless we take him back ourselves. To a time and place of our choosing. In that way, we can give him a small chance."

"Yes . . . yes, that would work. He's a man now. We could take him back to, maybe, one year on from the war. The city was never abandoned, you know. They rebuilt afterwards. It was never the same again, of course, but he would stand a chance of survival. Or from there, he could move away. It would be his decision."

He nodded. Both of us were skirting around the important issue. Finally, I said it. "Will he go?"

Because the thought of forcibly relocating him . . . dragging a struggling man into the pod, Joe Nelson from the Falconberg Arms, who'd lived all his adult life in modern times, who might be screaming and begging for his life, and then just heaving him out at the other end . . . abandoning him to the nightmare that was Troy . . .

This is what happens when historians interfere with History. Helios should have died at Troy and he didn't. I'd been surprised at the time that History hadn't sideswiped us all out of existence. Now I had a horrible feeling we were being taught a lesson. That we were being made to face the consequences of what we had done. Whatever happened to him—whether Helios died in this time or long ago, we would have this on our consciences for the rest of our lives. What was Leon thinking at this moment?

I put my hand on his arm. "This must be your decision, but whatever you decide, I'm with you all the way. To the death, if necessary. I won't leave you to face this alone. Nor Peterson, or Guthrie, or any of you. Whatever you do, you can count me in."

He reached for my hand. "I'm going to take him back. It's got to be me. St. Mary's is too closely watched."

"He won't run?"

"No. His exact words were, 'You risked yourselves for me. At the very least, I can do the same for you.'"

I swallowed. "So what's the plan?"

He was suddenly brisk. "Remove your tag and leave it at Pompeii. Stop them following us once and for all. Then we can jump back to St. Mary's, pick up Helios, and take him back to Troy."

"How will we get him away from the Time Police?"

"I've left the worst news till last. St. Mary's will arrange a diversion."

"Oh . . . dear."

HE SPENT ALL NIGHT repairing the pod. I spent all night coughing up major amounts of volcano. I drank as much water as I could and then spent the rest of the night in the toilet. The glamour of an historian's life.

When I awoke, he'd spread a cloth on the floor and laid a small meal.

"I'm going to give you painkillers in advance, so you need to eat."

I tucked in to a croissant, some cheese, and a few dried apricots while he opened locker doors so I could see. We had enough food for an army, two sleeping bags, basic medical supplies, and toiletries. Best of all, I was wearing clothes that weren't yellow and white. Life was looking up.

I cleared away the meal while he got the medical stuff together. Because now it was tag-removal time and, suddenly, I wasn't anything like as enthusiastic as I had been, but it was that or living in a box until I died. And until it was gone, we couldn't risk going back to St. Mary's, so I'd better shut up and get on with it.

I showered, tied up my still sticky hair, and lay down on the floor. He opened a sterile pack and started to lay things out. A bottle of brandy stood within easy reach. I stared resolutely at the scorch mark on the ceiling.

He picked up a syringe. "Just a little prick."

"Seriously? You're saying that to an historian?"

"Couldn't resist it. Ready?"

"Ready when you are." I closed my eyes.

He paused. "I'm sorry about all this, Max. We should have had at least a little time together."

"I'm not complaining. I can't think of anywhere I'd rather be. Or anyone else I'd rather be there with."

"Say that again in ten minutes," he said, grimly.

"It'll be easy," I said from a position of complete ignorance. "Tags are tiny. How difficult can it be?"

He swabbed my arm with something cold, and I felt the prick of the needle. He also made me swallow two painkillers. He picked up a scalpel and hesitated.

I sighed. "I'm going to have to do it myself, aren't I?"

"There's no way I'm letting an historian near a sharp implement in an enclosed space. Here we go."

To begin with, it wasn't too bad. I could feel something was happening, but so long as I didn't actually look . . . I kept my eyes on the ceiling. The scorch mark was shaped like Australia. I could see Darwin.

"Are we there yet?"

"No."

I turned my head away and counted the dents on the locker doors.

And then, suddenly, a nasty twinge. I didn't say anything because I didn't want to distract him.

"Are you unconscious?"

"I was keeping quiet out of consideration for you."

"I feel more reassured when you're talking. I don't actually listen to the words, but the drone of your voice, maundering on and on, is comforting."

"Would you like me to tell you a joke?

"I've heard historian jokes. They're either pathetic or so sick that only an historian would think they were funny. Do you actually know a joke that isn't either historically based or revolting?"

"Of course," I said, inaccurately, as a river of pain coursed up and down my arm.

He wiped the blood away and peered closely.

"I can't find it. Sometimes they . . . migrate."

"What, like geese?"

"I'm going to make the incision a little larger."

"Did I see a bottle?" I lifted my head and swallowed some brandy. "Yuk. I hate this stuff."

He tried to take the bottle away but I wasn't having any of that.

"Off you go, then. Let's hear this famous joke."

"Oh, OK. Well, there was this man . . . And he wakes up in hospital."

"A medical joke. Most appropriate. Continue."

"Nnng . . . this man . . . wakes up in hospital and the doctor says . . ."

I clenched my teeth. I really didn't want to scream and put him off, so I gritted my teeth, thought of the Battle of Salamis, and had another mouthful. Yuk.

"Is that it? Well, all right, I'll grant you it wasn't sick, but it wasn't very funny, either."

"No," I said, appreciating his efforts to distract me. "There's a bit more."

"Go on, then."

"This man wakes up in the hospital and the . . . doctor says . . . 'It's all right, mate. You've been in an accident on the Great North Road, but . . . you're all right now.'"

"Ah! There is a happy ending. That's nice. Not the usual historian style at all."

"No . . . Not finished yet. Just shut up, will you. Aagh."

"Please try and keep still."

"Sorry. It's all the excitement . . ."

"A common reaction among women whenever I'm near. You'd think I'd be used to it by now. Lousy joke, by the way."

"And the doctor says, '*But sadly, in the accident, your todger fell off.*'"

"What? Is this the historian definition of the words—happy ending? Your todger falls off?"

"And the man says . . . '*Oh no!*' and the doctor says . . . Aren't you finished yet?"

"What? I'm confused now."

"You're hacking your way through my blood vessels, muscles, capilliarilleries, and God knows what else. You'd better not be bloody confused."

"Just get on with this painfully long and unfunny joke, will you?"

"Yuk. Where was I?"

"The poor bloke's lost his todger. Not, if I might venture an opinion, a suitable subject for mirth, but I'm accustomed to you failing to meet my standards of propriety and decency."

"So the man says, '*Oh no.*' And the doctor—aaagh."

"Sorry. I'm sorry, sweetheart. I can't find it."

"Well, keep looking. Where's it going to go, for crying out loud? And the doctor says, '*Don't panic. We have the technology. We can rebuild you.*' And the man says . . . '*Thank goodness.*'"

Silence. I kept my eyes on him, grim and focused. I didn't dare look at what he was doing. Red-hot waves of pain ran up my arm with the occasional short, sharp, purple jab of agony. I took a couple of deep breaths and picked up the thread.

"And the doctor says, '*Yes, but to rebuild you will cost a thousand . . . pounds . . . a thousand . . . pounds . . .*'"

"A thousand pounds what? Despite my repugnance for this sorry tale, I have to admit to a certain grisly interest in the outcome. A thousand pounds what?"

I said, through gritted teeth, "*A thousand pounds an inch.*"

"What! Good job it's not me we're talking about. We'd need to take out a mortgage."

"Oh, please. I'm lying here . . . helpless and . . . having to listen . . . to . . . the male ego. Can it get any worse?"

Yes, was the answer to that one, and for several red and purple moments, it did. I lost all interest in the joke, the tag, the pod, the world, everything.

"Hey," he said, sharply. "Stay with me. What happens next? A thousand pounds an inch?"

"And the man thinks . . . for a bit . . . and then smiles and says, '*Oh. OK, then. Not a problem.*'"

"I still can't find it," he said, and I could hear the tension in his voice.

"Don't stop now. Make the incision bigger again. Maybe Helen inserted it lower down. Or, since I've had an exciting life, it might have come loose and be lodged somewhere in my armpit."

He stared at me. "You have no idea how these things work, do you?"

"Of course not. I'm an historian. We concentrate on the bigger picture."

He frowned. "Max, I don't know."

"You must, or we're screwed. You can do it."

"I'm hurting you."

"Not a lot. I'm just being a baby."

He began again.

I jerked. I couldn't help it. "Sorry. Sorry."

"I know, love. I think we should stop. I'm going to do some damage if I go any deeper. There are tendons and blood vessels and I haven't a clue what I'm doing."

"No, you can't stop. If you don't do this, I'll insist we split up, because you have to get back to St. Mary's."

"You'll do no such thing."

"Then get on with it and stop pissing around."

More pain. Yuk.

"So what happens after the thousand pounds an inch bit?"

"What?"

"The joke? A thousand pounds an inch?"

"The . . . the . . . doctor says, '*Look, talk to your wife about this. Any . . . radical . . . difference in the size and shape of your todger is going to come . . . as . . . a bit of a shock . . . to her.*'"

"I'll say," he said, calmly. "Imagine if I came at you waving something the same size and shape as a fire hose."

"I'd really rather not. One ordeal a day is enough."

"Against my will, I'm being drawn into this social and medical drama. What happens next?"

"The doctor calls the . . . next morning."

I had to stop for a while.

"Drink more brandy."

"Yes." I swigged a mouthful. Then another. "Oh God, I hate this stuff."

I had another mouthful to take the taste away.

Even in the dim glow of our lightstick, I could see how pale he looked. He wasn't enjoying this any more than I was.

I said, softly, "It's all right, love. You're doing just fine."

Just for a moment, we looked at each other . . .

"So, the doctor visits the next morning and says, '*Did your wife call?*' and the man says '*Yes. We discussed everything thoroughly . . . and came to a decision.*' And the doctor says, '*Great! What's it to be then?*' And the man . . . says . . . the man says . . ."

"Yes? Yes? For God's sake, I'm on the edge of my seat here."

"And the man says, '*We're having a new kitchen.*'"

Another long, pain-crowded pause.

Without looking up, he said, "I can't believe you think that's funny."

From dim and distant Brandyland, I slurred, "Of course it is. It's . . . hilarious."

"I'm not laughing."

"Sorry. Was it too difficult . . . for you? Should I have dumbed . . . it down? You know, the techie version?"

"How could you think that's funny?"

"Well, every . . . one . . . else just . . . fell . . . about. Kal . . . nearly wet herself."

"You're comparing me to that six foot blonde psychopath?"

"You . . . wouldn't . . . aaaghh . . . say . . . that if she was here."

"I wish she was here."

I said, "You're doing . . . very . . . well," and closed my eyes. Just for a second. Just for a little while.

I AWOKE SEVERAL HOURS later. Leon was lying half under the console, muttering to himself.

I smiled. "Hey."

He lifted his head.

"There you are. How are you feeling?"

My arm was on fire. My head was on fire. My chest was on fire.

"I'm never drinking brandy again."

"Hangover?"

"Mouth like the bottom of a dodo cage. Did you get it?"

He shook his head. "No."

I said, "Shit," and let my head fall back.

Now we were in trouble.

But not anything like the trouble we were going to be in.

EIGHT

$\mathcal{I}$ LOVE LEON FARRELL DEARLY. He is the still small voice of calm at the centre of my hectic, historian world. He knows me better than I know myself and doesn't allow that to put him off in any way. He knows when to agree with me. He knows when to argue. He knows when I need to be talked out of something for my own good. And best of all, he knows all this without being told. I trust his judgement more than anyone's.

So what the hell he was playing at when he let Professor Rapson organise the diversion at St. Mary's was a complete mystery to me.

We presented ourselves at the rendezvous point an hour early—a minor miracle given the condition of the pod.

We were situated just below the woods to the west of the lake. We weren't camouflaged, but outbuildings and stables would give us some cover. Helios could make his way up through the woods themselves and approach us from the rear.

Leon sat at the console, checking the systems again. Cameras and sound were turned up to the maximum. We needed to know what was happening around us.

He'd fashioned a sling to try to ease the pain in my arm and it wasn't working at all. I leaned against the chair and watched the screen.

I could see all of St. Mary's spread out before me. The old house dreamed gently in the warm summer afternoon. There were the mullioned windows winking in the sunshine, the Virginia creeper climbing the stone walls, the South Lawn, the lake with its reed beds, the straight gravel drive flanked by horse chestnuts—it was all there, the epitome of the quiet English country house. I could even hear the birds singing.

My heart thumped with the shock of recognition. There was no one around, but inside, somewhere, there would be Peterson. And Guthrie. And Mrs. Mack. And Van Owen. All of them. I wondered what they were doing. What assignments they were preparing for. Who had my job now? I gave myself a little shake and made myself focus.

Of course, this quiet, idyllic scene wasn't the whole story. I could also see the craters, the burned patches of grass, and the stumpy remains of the Clock Tower. The remnants of Professor Rapson's previous experiments lay strewn around the grounds. I did take a moment to wonder at the Time Police allowing this and whether they had any idea at all of what could—and probably would—happen. I had no clue what the diversion would entail, but it seemed safe to assume it would be fiery, spectacular, noisy—and successful.

"Right," said Leon, breaking a long silence. "We'll just run over the details. At 1400 hours, some sort of diversion will occur. God knows what. I just hope there's no major loss of life. Given the presence of the Time Police, they will probably tone it down a bit. So long as it's enough to enable Helios to get here undetected. Whatever they do will last a good thirty minutes, which should give Guthrie more than enough time to get him to us. They'll probably come through the woods and approach us from the rear. We don't open the door until he's directly in front of us. You will hide in the toilet."

"Will I?" I said, not best pleased.

"Yes. I trust Ian Guthrie with my life, but, at this stage, I'd prefer that no one, apart from Dr. Bairstow, knows about you. So no arguing. I give the word and you head for the head. Got it?"

Reluctantly, I nodded.

"You stay there until I give the all clear. The best option is to go ahead with the plan. I know we'll have to open the door to let him out, but only for a second or so. I'm pretty sure your tag won't register on their equipment. Or, if it does, it won't be long enough for them to get a fix. Understood?"

Reluctantly, I nodded.

At that moment, things began to happen and didn't stop happening for quite a long time.

Firstly, Dr. Bairstow appeared on his balcony. Two black-uniformed figures accompanied him. From this distance, it was unclear whether they were guests or gaolers. However, they seated themselves quietly enough. Dr. Bairstow's role was obviously to keep them out of the way so he'd offered them ringside seats for the afternoon's entertainment. I watched them exchanging casual remarks. They seemed amused.

Slowly, large numbers of personnel wandered from the building, clutching mugs of tea and seating themselves on a convenient wall. A black-and-yellow tape delineated a safe distance from the splash zone. This was ignored by all.

To a round of applause and cheers, three boats appeared from the other side of the lake. Two were small rowing boats, with Professor Rapson standing in the prow of one of them, rather like a Viking figurehead. He and his R & D crews had long poles with which they were attempting to guide the third boat. This was a small craft, about twelve feet long with two short, stubby masts. Two cauldrons hung suspended from these masts. Brushwood and other combustible materials were piled high in the bottom of the boat.

"Any clues?" said Leon.

"Actually, yes."

Everything inside me that was St. Mary's was singing. This was going to be good. This was going to be very, very good.

"I suspect Professor Rapson and his team are attempting to replicate part of Alexander's siege of the Island of Tyre. Alexander tried to build a causeway to reach the island and the Tyrians launched fireships to destroy it. The professor is attempting to ascertain whether they were capable of reaching the temperatures necessary to do so. It's actually a legitimate experiment. The small boat in front is stuffed full of firewood and other stuff. The cauldrons suspended from the mast will be filled with some concoction of beeswax or oil or maybe animal fat. Something that burns well, anyway. They'll light the brushwood, and then float the burning boat to the jetty over there, which probably represents the causeway. On impact, the cauldrons will swing and tip the hot mixture onto the flames. The causeway was made of stone so they'll need some pretty ferocious temperatures to do any damage. But we shall see."

He shifted uneasily. "Exactly how much are we at risk?"

"On the other side of the lake? Not at all."

You would really think I'd know better by now.

We were left in no doubt when they were ready. The professor, obviously embracing the distraction aspect of the experiment, rather than going for historical accuracy, had rigged a sound system. It seemed safe to assume the original assault was not accompanied by the ominous opening chords of "Mars, the Bringer of War." It was all very dramatic.

Making a gesture more appropriate to King Darius unleashing the Immortals at The Hot Gates, and to shouts of encouragement (and other things), the little flotilla set off, the lead boat trailing plumes of smoke from the burning brushwood. They trundled sedately and with a certain dignity across the lake.

Leon sat back and relaxed. "I don't think this is going to produce a siege-ending conflagration, do you?"

As he spoke, the little boat collided with the jetty. The impact was sufficient to tip the cauldrons and the heated mixture spilled onto the burning kindling. For a second, nothing happened. I just had time for a twinge of disappointment and then . . .

With a tremendous roar, which made birds erupt from the treetops and the horses in the paddock bolt, a huge, HUGE tongue of orange fire broiled across the surface of the lake, enveloping the jetty and sending a great oily, black cloud high into the air like a nuclear mushroom. Water seemed to have no effect on the flames, which danced higher and higher across the lake's surface. The reed beds around the south side exploded into flames. The professor and his team were blown backwards into their boats, clothes smoking and, I bet, not an eyebrow between them.

Markham appeared, shouting, "Duty fire team to the lake. All field medics with me!" Never mind field medics or fire teams, the entire unit put down its tea and set off at a run for the disaster area, obviously eager to be involved.

On Dr. Bairstow's balcony, the Time Police had stopped laughing.

Professor Rapson clambered unsteadily to his feet and beat out his smouldering lab coat. The boat wobbled violently but he remained upright. The team in the other boat slowly started to pick themselves up. No fatalities. Yet.

Suddenly, and even over the cameras I saw this quite clearly, their heads snapped around in unison, there was a moment's frozen panic and then someone screamed "Row! Row for your lives!"

They rowed like madmen. It was like that scene from *Ben Hur*. All that was missing was the fat, naked guy with the drum.

"Good God," said Leon in disbelief. "Have they let loose the Kraken?"

The R & D team reached the shore, tumbled from their boats, and shrieking incoherently, raced away from the lake, becoming entangled with Markham and his team who were racing *towards* the lake. For a few seconds everyone milled around chaotically with the professor and his team waving their arms and shouting, and Markham (whose track record rendered him perfect for the occasion) also waving his arms and shouting and considerably adding to the confusion.

I have to admit that up to that moment, I was fairly baffled. All right, the entire lake appeared to be a giant inferno, but it wasn't the first time and someone would sort it all out so what was all the panic about?

Leon pointed. Ah. That was what all the panic was about.

Swans!

Coming in at eye-height, in attack formation with necks outstretched, wings extended and some very nasty looks in their eyes, was what seemed like every swan in the county, or possibly all of England. A whole battalion of them. I had no idea we had so many. I know they can be nasty, and God knows these had good reason. Over the years St. Mary's swans have been blown up, terrorised by Plesiosaur look-alikes, had a Renault 5 engine mistakenly flung at them by a Roman trebuchet, and been dyed blue. These were swans that had had enough. Forget Nile crocodiles—suddenly, this was not the place to be.

People scattered. It didn't help. Some people assumed the traditional St. Mary's position and curled into a foetal ball until it was all over. Some headed for the hills. Some actually made it back to the main building by climbing in through the library windows. They were pursued by ten or twelve battle-crazed birds, who powered in through the open windows and proceeded to lay about them. I could hear Dr. Dowson shrieking. The fire alarms went off, adding their deafening clamour to the music bouncing off the walls, the shouts and yells of those falling victim to avian aggression, and the wail of approaching sirens. Not only could they hear us in the village, they could probably hear us in Vladivostok. There would be another letter from the parish council. Two letters, probably. And the traditional telephone call from the Chief Constable was imminent.

Markham was still trying to evacuate Professor Rapson and his crew from the shoreline while surrounded and outnumbered by what looked like millions of enraged *Cygnus Olor*, all of whom were circling the beleaguered forces rather like the Indians at Custer's Last Stand. I hoped he would have better luck than the General did. Everywhere I looked, there was chaos and carnage. The lake was still ablaze, the entire bank was burning, a thick pall of smoke hung over everything, and the sirens were very close.

Leon groaned. "The entire county must be on terrorist alert by now. There's no chance . . ."

Helen Foster appeared with her emergency medical team, shouted "What the fu . . . ?" got a swan in her face, and tumbled backwards over a low wall.

I was face down on the console, laughing.

Leon had his hands over his eyes.

"Well," I said, just to rub it in. "Thank God they toned it down a bit."

Leon groaned. "Every Time Police officer in existence is going to be here in a minute."

I turned my attention back to Dr. Bairstow who appeared to be taking a telephone call.

"Quick," I said, "Can we make out what he's saying?"

Leon fiddled for a while, enhancing one speaker and filtering out the noise from the others. Dr. Bairstow's voice, familiar but tinny, was just audible.

"Ridley, my dear fellow, how are you . . . ? And Audrey . . . ? Well, that's good news . . . No . . . No, the Siege of Tyre . . . Tyre . . . No, not the rubber product, the small island . . . No, just a tiny miscalculation . . . Yes . . . No . . . As far as I can ascertain, no fatalities at all . . . Well, no, not that astonishing really . . . No, perfectly under control . . . What noise . . . ? . . . Oh, no, just a few swans . . . No, slightly more than two . . . Yes, more than three . . . Getting warmer . . . About forty, I think . . . Well, obviously they're a little agitated . . . Ridley, I have to go now, there are a number of emergency vehicles pulling in through the gates. Quite a large number, actually. They seem very purposeful . . . Yes, Sunday evening. I haven't forgotten. Looking forward to it."

He handed the phone to someone unseen and began to usher his guests safely off the balcony. Just as they disappeared inside, he turned and looked directly at us. Obviously, I was still high on painkillers, because I could have sworn that for a moment, just for one very brief moment, he actually smiled, and then he stepped back into his office.

I grinned to myself and then the first emergency services vehicles came roaring up the drive in a cacophony of sound and strobing lights and flying gravel. Reluctantly, I turned the cameras away from all the drama and concentrated on the woods. One of our alerts pinged.

"There," said Leon, and indeed, there were two figures running swiftly towards us.

I didn't wait to be told, shooting into the toilet and closing the door behind me.

I heard a very brief murmur of voices. A pause.

And then the world went white.

I never thought I'd go back. Not after what had happened to me there. I remembered the last time I had seen Troy. Burning buildings. Drifting smoke. The smell of burned flesh. The screaming. If I closed my eyes, could I still hear . . . ?

That was in the past. A year had gone by since the Greeks had overrun the city. Not all the population had been killed or captured and the survivors would have slowly drifted back. The smoke in the wind would now be the smoke of cooking fires.

On the other side of the olive grove would be what was left of the tavern that Helios's family had run. Would he choose to stay? His father and his sister had died there. This might not have been the best place to land, but it was what he'd asked for. Because it was familiar. Because it was his home.

I cracked the door open an inch or so. Helios stood with his back to me. They were staring at the screen. Leon pointed at something and Helios nodded.

I stayed in the toilet, telling myself I didn't want to intrude. It was Leon who had risked everything to save him. They had been friends. They should have these last few minutes alone together. I know it was cowardly and I despised myself, but I was too ashamed of what we were doing to look him in the face.

Helios was barefoot and wore a simple T-shirt and shorts. On top of everything else, he couldn't bring anything with him. We weren't supposed to leave anything from our time, but I did see he was clutching a small bundle under one arm. Some food, probably, together with a knife and maybe a blanket. And if History didn't like it then that was just tough. Take it out on us. Helios was the innocent party here. And Helios was bearing the punishment.

And what of Leon? Who had fought so passionately for him? Who had sacrificed me for Helios? I thought of the quiet friendship the two of them had enjoyed over the years.

The world blurred suddenly and I had to sit down on the toilet. All of a sudden, my arm ceased to throb moderately and began to throb violently. Everything felt hot and tight. Actually, I felt hot and tight all over. Something wasn't right. I wiped sweat off my brow and waited for the two of them to finish their conversation. My arm would just have to wait.

They moved to the door and turned to face each other. I could tell from their body language that this was the final goodbye. I tried to concentrate, because Leon was going to need me. I had to hold on to the basin and wait for my head to stop spinning.

I wondered what the two least chatty men in the world would find to say to each other.

Nothing, was the answer to that one. Everything had already been said.

They shook hands. The door opened. He stepped out. The door closed.

I heaved myself to my feet and joined Leon at the screen. I watched Helios walk back through the olive grove towards the tumble of stones that had once been his home. He stopped, turned, and looked back at us. The sun was behind him and I couldn't read his face. He couldn't see me, but he knew I was there. We stared at each other. I couldn't look away and my wet eyes had nothing to do with the bright sunshine.

He turned and walked away.

It was done.

I gently touched Leon's arm. "All right?"

He nodded.

"What did he say?"

"He thanked you—us—for the extra years he never thought he'd have. Then he wished us luck. Then he said goodbye. We must go."

I turned away and sat quietly in the corner. To think. I didn't know about Leon, but I'd learned my lesson. I would never, ever interfere with History again. The rules are very clear. Don't interfere. Don't do anything to change the course of History. The price is always a life. And we'd accepted it as such. Occupational hazard. The price we paid for our jobs. But this time, the price was too high. Way too high. Because this time, it wasn't us who'd paid it.

He pulled himself together. "Computer—initiate jump."

The world went white.

HE SPENT ALL DAY working on the pod. He didn't speak at all.

I didn't know where we were. Or when. I didn't know anything at all. I slept.

Halfway through the afternoon, I wobbled to my feet and made us a cup of tea. It cost me, but I had to get up and start moving around. It was now definitely quicker and easier to list the bits of me that didn't throb unbearably.

My right foot was fine.

I was trying, one-handed, to comb my hair when he sat behind me and took the comb. "You'll hurt your arm. I'll do it."

He combed through all the tangles and braided it in a long plait, tying it neatly with a bit of bandage and finishing with a quick kiss to the top of my head.

For a moment, I couldn't speak and then cleared my throat. "Not bad."

"No, it's not, is it?" he said, modestly. "I must say when I was younger I spent many hours trying to choose between a career in engineering or hairdressing."

"When do you think you'll finally make the decision?"

And because he was so close, and because everything hurt so much, I allowed myself the luxury of leaning against him.

I closed my eyes. Only for a minute . . .

DARK DREAMS. DREAMS I hadn't had for years. A relentless procession of my past. And no matter how I ran, or twisted and turned, there was no escape. There hadn't been then and there wasn't now. Nothing goes away. It all lies dormant, waits until you're too sick to contain it any longer, and then it explodes in unstoppable thoughts and pictures. Every detail is presented for inspection. Every memory. Every fear. That's the problem with locking things away—they never get used. So when they do finally burst forth, every tiny, fear-enhanced fact is perfectly remembered. All the colours are bright and shiny. Every picture is sharp and detailed. As if it happened only last week. Or yesterday. Or now . . .

Then the past blends into the present. Faces change. What was comforting and safe suddenly is not comforting and safe any longer. The past is here, submerging me. There is no escape. There never was. It is here. Now. Leaning over me as I sleep . . .

"Max. Wake up!"

I shuddered. This was not right. I was drenched in sweat. My arm throbbed. Shadows swirled. Was I awake? The past swooped again, seeking to carry me away to somewhere I didn't want to go.

"Max. Wake up. Wake up now."

I opened my eyes and the world resolved itself back into one small pod. "Why are you shouting at me?"

"Because you're frightening me."

I said, feebly. "No need. I'm fine," and he swore. Really, really swore, which he didn't usually.

"Let me see your arm."

He twitched away the blanket and even I could see that someone had stolen my arm in the night and replaced it with a purple, shiny sausage. A throbbing, purple, shiny sausage.

"Is that my arm?"

I know, but cut me some slack here.

He didn't answer, gently peeling off the dressing to see the damage. I'm a qualified Field Medic and I'm damned sure it shouldn't look like that.

He rummaged in our first aid kit, pulling out a syringe.

"What's that?"

"Antibiotics. A lot of antibiotics. Hold still."

"Not in this arm," I said, being a baby.

"Don't worry. I'm going to make a start on the other arm, now."

He disposed of the empty syringe and sat back.

"I'll get you some water."

"I'm not thirsty."

"You must drink. Just sip it."

I did as I was told. A bit of a first, but I really didn't feel that good.

"Would you like some tea?"

No, actually, I wouldn't, but if I said so then he'd really start to worry, so I nodded. I would just forget to drink it.

He brought it over and it was perfect. He'd remembered to get fresh lemons, so there were two slices of lemon, just the way I liked it. He sat down alongside and helped me hold the mug.

"Just a sip."

I did try.

"And another."

Apparently satisfied, he took the mug off me. I closed my eyes.

"No. Don't go to sleep."

He was right. Sleeping was a bad idea. I didn't want those dreams again. Not with a witness, anyway.

He'd turned the lights down very low. The pod was silent. Even the little background electronic noises had ceased.

He took my one working hand and gently rubbed his thumb across my knuckles.

"So who's Bear?"

Oh, shit. I'd been talking about Bear.

I said nothing for a long time. He didn't repeat the question, but it didn't go away, either.

So who was Bear?

I wondered how much he knew. Wondered if my past life here was the same as my past life there. With my luck, it would be worse.

I don't know if it was the infection floating around my system, the fever, the knowledge I might be dying, or a combination of all of these. It might even be that something in my head decided, after years of silence, it was time to tell the story of Bear.

I spoke into the cold darkness.

"I'd always had Bear. I don't know where he came from or who gave him to me, but I'd always had him. And no, he wasn't the traditional teddy, all grubby, with bare patches and one eye missing. I looked after him. He was my best friend. We had adventures together. We flew to the moon and found it was made of cheese. We rode the waves with the mermaids. We lived in imaginary kingdoms." I stopped suddenly. "I . . . loved my Bear."

There was no sound in the darkness.

When I could, I continued.

"On my ninth birthday, we had a party. Afterwards, I was in my room, about to get ready for bed and telling Bear all about it."

I paused again.

"My mother wouldn't let me wear my Captain Spaceman pyjamas. She laid out a long white nightie. It was very pretty, with flowers and birds embroidered all over. I preferred Captain Spaceman, but I didn't argue. She said I'd like it. She said I looked like a princess. And Bear said I looked like a princess, too. She combed my hair and tied it up in long white ribbons. I asked her why and she said my father wanted to see me in his study and I should look pretty because it was my birthday. She spent ages getting the bows even. She said it was important. Even Bear got a white bow around his neck.

"I was excited because I liked his study. He had a skeleton called William—and if I could name five bones, I won half a crown. Sometimes he would take down a book and show me pictures. He was teaching me to play chess. So I was pleased and excited. I picked up Bear and tucked him under my arm, she took my hand, and we walked down the stairs to his study. She wouldn't let me wear slippers and the floors were cold."

I stopped. My heart was hammering away and I could feel the sweat running down my back. Just say it, Maxwell.

"She opened the door. She didn't look at me. She said, 'In you go, then. He's waiting for you.' Then she walked away."

I took two or three deep breaths, but it was too late to stop now.

"I never saw Bear again."

Silence.

"I don't know what happened to him."

More silence.

"He's out there, somewhere. Lost in the dark. We both were. I never found him. No one helped me. My mother bought me another teddy and I threw it away. She kept telling me to stop crying because my father liked his little girl to smile, that I should always smile for him . . . because that's what he liked . . . but I never would. I cried for my Bear and it made him angry. Everyone was angry with me. Just because I'd lost my Bear and wouldn't smile . . .

I broke off, because in the darkness, I heard a tiny crack.

"What was that?"

"Stupid mug," he said, lightly. "The handle just fell off."

"Did you hurt yourself?"

"No."

We both sat in the darkness. Now what?

I said quietly, "You're angry too, aren't you?"

"Yes. Yes, I am."

I sat silent in the darkness, regretting every word. Telling people things is never a good idea. A trouble shared is a trouble quadrupled.

"But not with you, sweetheart. I'm not angry with you. I'm angry for you."

"You won't tell anyone about . . ."

"No. I'll never tell anyone about . . . Bear."

"When I was little, I used to hope that someone nice had found him and that he was happy even if that meant he'd forgotten me. But that was OK, if he was happy. When I got older I realised that, afterwards, my father had just picked him up off the floor and tossed him into the bin." I smiled in the dark. "I was a lot angrier and a lot less trusting by then."

"Are you angry now?"

"No. Not usually. My teacher at school—you remember Mrs. De Winter?—she showed me how to use it. To focus. She helped me to get to Thirsk University and then on to St. Mary's. Maybe losing Bear was the price I had to pay for a better life."

His voice was bitter in the darkness.

"A better life? You're lying in a broken pod in the middle of nowhere, pursued by people who will probably put you down like a dog."

"Hey, stop that. It could be worse."

"How? How could it possibly be worse?"

"Well, I could be kneeling by your body, feeling my heart crack wide open and knowing I'll never, ever see you again. I know that whatever happens to me, nothing—nothing—will ever be that bad again."

I stopped, exhausted.

"Are you all right? Can I get you anything?"

"I'm absolutely fine."

"You never complain, do you?"

"Are you kidding? Deep down inside, it's just one long, perpetual whinge."

"It really will be OK. I promise you we'll get out of this."

I patted his hand. "I know. Don't worry about me."

"But I do."

"There's no need."

"I should look after you better."

"I look after myself."

"Yeah? How's that working out for you at the moment?"

"Work in progress."

I could feel waves of heat rising. In a minute or so, I'd be off in my own world again. I shifted slightly and was aware I was drenched in sweat.

I felt him stand up. A click and the lights came on. Well, one light. We were still conserving power.

He sat at the console and began to fire things up.

"What are you doing?"

"Taking you somewhere safe."

"There is nowhere safe. Not while I've still got this stupid thing in my arm."

"I've had an idea."

"You're not going to chop it off, are you? I'm prepared to take one for the team, but that's a bit above and beyond the call . . ."

"No, I'm not going to chop your arm off. You are not the only one around here who has brilliant ideas. Now, it's my turn."

I said, doubtfully, "You've had a brilliant idea?"

"Yes. You're not the only one. I can do it, too."

"Really? I thought you worked in the Technical section."

"We have more than our fair share. Shut up and listen. I'm going to take you back to St. Mary's."

I struggled to sit up. "No."

"I'm taking you back for medical treatment. You might die if I do, but you'll certainly die if I don't."

"And that's your brilliant idea? There's no point. They'll know where we are as soon as you open the door."

"No, my brilliant idea is that we land inside the big transport pod—TB2."

"Why?"

He sighed. "I'll keep it simple for the History department. I land inside TB2 and exit this pod, closing the door behind me. I am now inside TB2 and can open that door because this pod door is shut. It will be like an airlock. So long as one door is always closed, the Time Police won't be able to track you. I get Helen to remove your tag—properly, this time. I'll take the tag and drop it inside the volcano as discussed. They'll think you perished in the eruption as we planned. We'll both be free and clear. Now, hush. I have to do this manually. Let the master work."

I snorted and then found I did want the rest of my tea after all.

THE INTENDED DISCREET TOUCHDOWN at St. Mary's went about as well as everything else had up until now. He'd done his best, but he hadn't got it quite right, and we materialised about a foot off the ground, dropping with a bone juddering crash onto the floor of the big transport pod, TB2.

A sympathetic and supportive companion, aware of what a cracking job he'd done under difficult circumstances, and of how tired and stressed he was, would have chirped reassuringly from her nest of blankets and then kept her mouth shut.

"Am I the only person in this unit who can land a bloody pod properly?"

He was shutting things down. "Are we on fire? Have we cartwheeled across the hangar? Are we upside down? No. By your standards, that was a perfect touchdown. How's the arm?"

"Fine. What now?"

"Well, at least I won't have to go and look for Dieter. Half of St. Mary's will be outside by now."

With sudden anxiety, I said, "Take care, Leon. The Time Police might still be here."

"I'll turn the screen so you can see what's going on. Back in a minute. Do not open that door."

He disappeared. And reappeared.

"Don't say anything. To anyone. You're too sick to speak— understand?"

"Yes."

He sighed in exasperation. "What did I just say?"

"How should I know? I wasn't listening."

He disappeared again.

TB2 was our big pod. Designed to carry large numbers of people or specialised equipment, it was easily able to accommodate one small pod. There was enough light to enable me to make him out. I watched him walk to the doors. He looked back once, to check the pod door was still closed, let down the ramp, and disappeared. The ramp came up again and I was on my own.

Our pod was suddenly very empty.

I lay for what seemed like a very long time with no clue as to what was happening out there. Had he been arrested? Had the Time Police pounced as soon as he exited TB2?

"*No,*" said a rarely heard voice of reason. "*Otherwise they'd have been in here and shot you by now.*"

True.

I didn't dare take my eyes off the screen. I could feel waves of hot, dark pain washing over me and I knew that, in a few minutes, I'd be walking in shadows again, and I couldn't afford that. I had to stay alert. I stared at the screen as if my life depended upon it, which it might, and tried not to worry. I concentrated on lying still because the least movement sent ripples of red-hot pain surging up my arm.

Come on, Leon.

I felt sweat run down my back. My scalp prickled with it. I was drenched again. I jerked open my eyes.

Come on, Leon.

I swear I never took my eyes off the screen, but suddenly, the pod was full of people.

I saw Dr. Foster. She had short hair. It suited her. I saw Nurse Hunter, a little plumper than the one I remembered, but she still smelled of baby powder. I had forgotten that. Dieter was there, as well, big and blond, arms folded, guarding the door.

Outside in TB2, two other medics were setting up some sort of temporary hospital area. I looked at Leon. I couldn't leave. Had he forgotten?

No, of course he hadn't.

Hunter began to unpack her kit. Helen knelt beside me. "My name is Dr. Foster. I'm just going to take a look."

I flinched. I couldn't help it.

She carefully folded back the blanket. The dressing fell off by itself and we all stared at my arm.

No one spoke.

Helen broke the spell.

She smiled reassuringly at me. She was being kind. Now I knew I was in another world. Or dying. "It's a bit of a mess, but we'll get it cleaned up and make you feel more comfortable."

I'd never heard her speak so quietly. She seemed very . . . restrained.

She turned to Hunter, issuing instructions, still in the same level tones. I searched for Leon, who stood nearby.

She stood up stiffly and moved towards Leon who drew closer to listen.

She belted him. She fetched him a wallop that I myself would have been proud of. He actually staggered.

"Ow!"

She hit him again.

I tried to lift my head.

She was incandescent. She was absolutely furious. For one moment, she seemed to struggle for words. But only for a moment.

"You imbecile! You cretinous, moronic imbecile! Of all the idiotic, half-witted, brainless, irresponsible . . . I used to think that apart from me, you were the only person in this entire establishment who had more than one brain cell. What the hell did you think you were playing at? Let me make it simple. I'm the doctor. You're the engineer. I'm the one with all the years at medical school. You're not. Do I ever swan down here to Hawking, rip the front off a console, and go at it with a 5lb lump hammer and a bent paperclip?"

Wisely, he made no attempt to reply, but she swept on, regardless.

"No—I do not. Because I don't know the first thing about electronics and you don't know the first thing about medicine. Do you? Did you seriously think you could get away with surgery in this . . . this . . . ?" She waved an arm. "Look at the state of this pod. This place is Ground Zero for every infection in the universe. Did you think you could pick up a copy of *Surgery for Dummies* and blindly undertake what amounted to a major procedure? How stupid are you? Look what you've done. A tag is the size of a grain of rice, for God's sake. Was it really necessary to open her arm from elbow to wrist?"

She had to stop for breath.

"I couldn't find it," he said, defensively, keeping his distance.

There was the same sort of pause you get before a major volcanic event. And I should know.

She struggled for calm, speaking with a restraint that was terrifying.

"Of course you couldn't bloody find it! Because it's not bloody there! You operated on the wrong bloody arm!"

Her word reverberated round the tiny space. I made a huge effort, but there was no chance. Laughter bubbled inside me, as unstoppable as a greased elephant on a helter-skelter. I curled into a ball and couldn't stop. It was so funny. His face. Her face. All that effort. All that pain. All that blood. And it was the wrong bloody arm!

I was still laughing uncontrollably when something cold slid into the back of my hand.

I AWOKE SOME TIME later, blinked a little, and looked around me. I lay in a little pool of light. An oasis in the dark, echoing space that was TB2. As far as I could see, I was alone. I couldn't see either Leon or his pod, but that didn't mean they weren't here somewhere. I hoped.

My right arm was hugely bandaged and resting on a pillow. The other arm had a tiny red mark on the inside, just below my elbow. I could barely see it. Actually, I could barely see anything. I floated, warm and comfortable on a pink, fluffy cloud of peace and security. There was no pain. This was more like it. Things were looking up. The complete absence of any sort of threat was a very welcome change.

There was also a complete absence of Leon. I had no idea what time it was. Or what day it was. Or even what year it was. Where was he? Surely it wouldn't take that long to make the return jump to Pompeii, open the door, toss out a successfully removed tag, and jump back again. Minutes? Seconds? He must be here, somewhere.

Hard on that thought, I heard the ramp coming down. He was back.

I was quite unprepared for the great wave of—something— that left me breathless. I heard Dr. Foster say, "Just a few minutes," and then he stepped into my little pool of light.

At some point, he'd had a shower, shit, and shave, and picked up some clean clothes, so he looked reasonably presentable. And exhausted.

We stared at each other. I remembered my instructions and didn't say a word. Which was good, because I couldn't think of anything to say, anyway. I tried to smile, but it was a very poor effort. His was even worse.

He turned abruptly, wandering aimlessly around the pod before finally fetching up at the foot of my bed, picking up Helen's scratchpad, and pretending to read her notes.

Finally, he said, still not looking at me, "I thought I'd lost you. Again."

I said nothing.

"Helen says you'll be up and about soon. At the moment, you're stuffed full of some very serious medication."

I nodded, even though he couldn't see me.

He finally looked up. I noticed his burns were healing. At some point Helen had renewed his plastic.

"The tag is gone. As is Pompeii. Dieter and I patched my pod as best we could, and I jumped back. There were bodies everywhere. The heat was unbearable. The mountain was still belching muck into the atmosphere. I threw the tag out into the street and it was covered almost immediately. I don't know if the Time Police were still there. I don't know if they would have been able to pick up the signal, but your plan will still hold. They tracked you there. They saw you there. There was a violent explosion. Your signal was gone. Whether they believe you're dead or not, they can't track you any longer. No one knows you're here but the medical staff, Dieter, and Dr. Bairstow. You have your life back."

Yes, I did. And what was I going to do with it?

I held out the one hand that still worked and he came and sat on the bed. It was nice to have him so close again.

"Anyway, what I wanted to say, Max, is that you're safe now. They don't know you're here. In a day or two, we can go wherever we like."

He smiled, and his was as wobbly as mine. "It was quite a ride, wasn't it? Just like old times."

I nodded. Just like old times.

"I wanted to say . . . I know we haven't known each other long and we agreed to take things very slowly . . . but I wanted to say . . ."

God, he was hopeless.

I lifted his hand to my cheek and held it there and it was almost too much for both of us.

"Lucy . . ."

He stroked my cheek and, leaning forward, kissed me gently.

My world rocked. I hoped it wasn't anything to do with the medication.

"I have a lot to say to you, but all that's for later. The main thing is that you're safe now and they will never find you again."

The ramp came down. Fast. I heard running footsteps. Dr. Foster was pushed backwards into the TB2. Somewhere, I could hear Hunter shouting.

Two black-clad figures strode forwards, their weapons at shoulder height, covering the pod.

Hunter was hustled in, struggling in the grip of another one. Even as I looked, she kicked out viciously. He yelped and back-handed her to the ground. She scrambled to her feet, furious and ready to tear him apart. He pulled a pistol, pushed her against the wall, and held it to one eye. The message was unmistakable.

Silence fell. I could hear her panting for breath. Even Helen had stopped shouting. For a few seconds, no one moved at all and then I could hear footsteps coming up the ramp.

Another black figure walked slowly into the pod and looked around him.

Dr. Foster surged forwards and was immediately restrained. That didn't stop her. "I protest. This is an emergency medical area. There are sick people here. Dr. Bairstow —"

"Is under arrest," he said quietly. "St. Mary's is under my jurisdiction now."

His gaze travelled around the pod.

"A merry dance," he said. "But I have you at last."

I stiffened, ready to resist to the best of my ability. I was tethered to the bed by tubes, wires, and other medical stuff. Even so, I wasn't going to go quietly.

Leon jumped to his feet, ready to defend me but we'd got it all wrong. It wasn't me they wanted.

Words fell into the silence.

"Leon Farrell, you are under arrest for . . ."

He got no further.

Leon took three long strides across the pod, shouted, "Door', and literally vanished.

I couldn't help myself. I don't know what sort of weapons they were wielding, but very little hardware responds well to having a jug of water thrown at it. Especially if you follow up with the jug itself. It only bounced harmlessly off his helmet, but it gave Leon a valuable second or two. I felt the pressure change as his pod jumped.

Given their current record, I was surprised they didn't shoot me where I lay.

Both Dr. Foster and Nurse Hunter tore free of their captors and literally hurled themselves between them and me. For a second or so, it all hung in the balance, but the Time Police had more important things to do.

The officer who had tried to arrest Leon barked a series of orders into some sort of com device. His men scattered. I could hear running footsteps and then everything went very quiet. I could hear him breathing. He stared at me. For a very long time. I braced myself for what was to come. His com squawked and after a long moment, he strode from the pod.

I realised I'd been holding my breath.

THEY SEARCHED ALL NIGHT for Leon, ransacking St. Mary's from top to bottom. Initially, I wondered why, but when three guards turned up, two outside and one inside, I realised they expected him to come back for me. I was a hostage.

Obviously, they didn't find him. I would have been surprised if they had. Even if he had still been here—which he wasn't—St. Mary's would have placed every obstacle possible in the path of his pursuers. Doors would have been inadvertently locked. No one would know the keypad combinations. People would have blocked corridors and been slow to move out of the way.

I lay all night, listening to shouted instructions up and down the building and then outside in the grounds. Dawn came and they hadn't found him. Of course they hadn't. He was long gone and they had no way of tracking him. They'd never catch him now. I wondered where he would go.

I wondered if he'd ever come back.

NINE

$\mathcal{I}$ SUPPOSE I'D BEEN LULLED by the familiarity of this world. There really seemed very little difference between this one and my own. Yes, obviously in this world, they had the Time Police. And yes, in this world, I was dead, but apart from that, everything seemed normal. The History was pretty much the same, along with the language, the food, the clothes . . . And then, suddenly, everything was different.

I won't go so far as to say I thought I could just pick things up from where I left off, but I was unprepared, completely unprepared, for the suspicion and the downright hostility which I encountered at St. Mary's and it hurt. Far more than the physical pain I'd encountered so far, this rejection cut me to the core. It shouldn't have, but it did. I was more vulnerable than I knew.

And I was alone. Leon was gone and I had to meet it on my own.

I AWOKE TO SUNLIGHT and shadows. They'd moved me. I was in Sick Bay. It doesn't matter in which world I lived—some things never change. I was still waking up in Sick Bay. The walls were cream instead of green, but it still smelled just the

same—disinfectant, the burnt paper smell from the incinera-
tor, floor polish . . . I turned my head. They'd put me in Isolation. Possibly because it was more comfortable, being designed
for long-stay patients who might be incubating something
unpleasant, but more likely because they could lock the door.

I lay very still and listened. I could hear breathing and the
odd rustle of clothing. Once, a chair scraped. Of course, they'd
left a guard. I was their only link with Leon Farrell. They were
waiting for him to come back for me. Although if he ever did
anything that stupid, the Time Police would be the least of his
problems.

I opened my eyes.

An officer sat on a chair by the door, his leg stretched stiffly
in front of him.

He'd made it. He'd survived Pompeii. Officer Ellis. The
one with the burned leg. Of course, it made good sense. He
could barely walk, so shove him on guard duty. And since he's
injured, shove him on guard duty in Sick Bay.

His helmet lay on the floor by his chair. There was no sign
of the big sonic rifle, just a neat handgun on a sticky patch on
his thigh. I tried to find that reassuring. He sat, arms folded,
looking out of the window. He had the sort of face that really
didn't lend itself to the brutal crew-cut inflicted upon him by
his job. Instead of threatening and sinister, he just looked like
a little boy. The ears didn't help. What on earth was he doing in
an outfit like the Time Police?

He turned his head and caught me looking.

Neither of us said anything. I closed my eyes and he
resumed his stare out of the window.

HUNTER ROUSED ME TO have a bath. Apparently, I had to have
one or there would be no breakfast.

She turned to the guard.

"Wait outside."

He shook his head. "No. She can undress in the bathroom. Leave the door open."

She glared at him. He was unmoved. Maybe he wasn't in the wrong job after all.

She disconnected me from everything, which took a while, and I hobbled into the bathroom.

I'd been a little surprised that, so far, no one actually seemed to recognise me. Granted, only Dr. Foster, Hunter, and Dieter had seen me, but they all knew me very well and no one had said a word.

When I saw myself in the mirror, I could understand why.

The face that stared back at me was not my own. For a start, my hair was stained dark with sweat, grease, and dirt. My face had lost all colour—even my lips were bloodless. The dark shadows of strain changed the colour of my eyes and I'd lost so much weight that the shape of my face had altered.

No wonder no one recognised me. I didn't recognise me.

The bath was wonderful. Hunter washed my hair. It took three goes before the water ran clear.

When I emerged, pink and wrinkled, Officer Ellis was still sitting quietly in his chair, but if he hadn't taken the opportunity to check around my bed space and under my pillow for anything incriminating, he was the most useless officer in existence. Good luck to him anyway, because, in this world, I didn't even own the clothes I stood up in. In which I stood up. Whatever. I wondered what would happen if Leon never came back.

HUNTER HAD COMBED OUT my hair and plaited it for me. When she came to take away the breakfast stuff, it was almost dry. This was when they realised they were harbouring a ginger. She stared for a while, said nothing, picked up the tray, and left.

Here we go.

Dr. Foster came in, aimlessly checked a few readings, bashed something into her scratchpad, stared at me, and went away again.

I wasn't left in peace for long. I expected to be interrogated—which wouldn't do them the slightest bit of good since I was determined to carry out Leon's instructions and say nothing. Silence is always the best defence.

I expected the Time Police—two or three of them, maybe. Good cop, bad cop, and one to wield the telephone directories. The door opened and I braced myself. But not anything like enough, because my visitor was Bitchface Barclay.

I'd forgotten all about her. In the all too brief time we'd had together, Leon had said she was my friend. A remark that had gone straight over my head at the time.

She stood in the doorway. Here was another one who stared. Good job I was getting used to it. I kept my face very carefully neutral. No surprise. No welcome. No hostility. No fear. And especially—no guilt. Because, in my world, I'd murdered Isabella Barclay. Not in a fair fight or in self-defence; I'd shot her in the back and then I'd shot her in the head. My only defence is that she was on her way to murder Leon as he lay unconscious and helpless. But I could have, maybe should have, given her a chance. I could have called out or challenged her, but I did none of that. Before you feel too sorry for her, she'd once left four men to die in the Cretaceous period. She'd sided with that bastard Clive Ronan when he invaded St. Mary's. She probably hadn't actually killed anyone herself, but she'd certainly connived at the murder, rape, and torture of St. Mary's personnel.

So I shot her dead.

Now, she was standing here, her face a little puzzled, but perfectly pleasant. Like me, she wore her red hair in a plait over one shoulder. Historian wannabe. I waited to see what would happen next.

She jerked her head at Officer Ellis, who got up and limped out of the room. Well, that was interesting, but I didn't have time to think about it. She pulled up his chair and sat down. Apart from her expression, she looked no different. Instead of her usual sneer, she looked quite pleasant.

We began well.

"Hello. Do you know me?"

Not prepared to commit myself either way, I made no sign.

She smiled uncertainly and tried again.

"My name is Isabella Barclay. Do you remember me at all?"

Receiving no response, she soldiered on. She never had any trouble listening to the sound of her own voice.

"You're at the St. Mary's Institute of Historical Research, just outside of Rushford. I'm Head of IT here and Deputy to Dr. Bairstow, the Director. He sends his apologies for not being here. He is currently—indisposed."

What did that mean? Was he dead? If he was—indisposed— then discounting the Time Police, that left her in charge, which was not good news. Not good news at all.

She continued. "I'm sorry. I don't mean to stare. You have to excuse me. You look very much like a friend of mine who died recently, and I'm still a little . . . what did you say your name was?"

When it became apparent I wasn't going to reply, she said, "Do you understand me? Do you speak English?" Repeating herself in French, German, and Spanish.

I remained silent in many languages.

She didn't give up.

"Can you tell me how you came by your injuries?"

Nope.

"We don't often have visitors here at St. Mary's. I hope they have made you comfortable?"

Silence.

"You've received treatment here and we're certainly happy for you to stay until you have recovered. However, there are some people who are anxious to speak to you about the man you were with—Leon Farrell? I wondered, if you're still not feeling very well, would you prefer to speak to me?"

Not bloody likely.

She looked at me, expectantly.

I said nothing.

Suddenly, she leaned forwards and put her hand on my good one.

"Please—tell me. Are you Max? Are you my friend? Why wouldn't you tell me?"

Well, this was a bit of a turn-up. My identity was causing her some anxiety. In my world, Bitchface Barclay would have danced on my grave.

I'd like to be able to say that that was the moment when I had my first inkling, but I can't. I was so confused by this new Barclay that my thoughts were flinging themselves all over the place. I held on to the one certainty in this new St. Mary's. Leon had told me to say nothing, so I said nothing.

"Max? Please, please talk to me. Rumours are flying around St. Mary's. Everyone wants to know. Are you Madeleine Maxwell? Just nod."

Again—not bloody likely.

She bit her lip. "Look, I've brought you something. I've brought you some chocolate. Your favourite."

She placed two giant bars of chocolate in my lap.

This is how you're trapped. The instinct is to say thank you. It's hard-wired into most of us. We're taught to respond appropriately. I so very nearly opened my mouth and said, "Thank you." I actually took the breath to speak but I lifted my eyes just that little bit too soon and, just for a moment, her face . . .

A second later and it was gone. I might have imagined it. I might have been allowing a bone-deep prejudice to get the better of me. She might simply have been screwing up her eyes against the bright sun. But she wasn't. I'd seen it and she knew I'd seen it. This was no act of kindness. This was a trap. We regarded each other. No words were spoken. I had no idea of what sort of relationship she'd had with the other Maxwell, but I knew exactly how this one was going to go . . .

She smiled and leaned forwards. "You don't look very comfortable at all. Let me rearrange your pillows."

She stood up and pulled out a pillow from behind my head, holding it in both hands.

Hunter stuck her head around the door. "Anything?"

She plumped up the pillow, slipping it gently behind my head. "No. She can't or won't speak to me. Has she said anything at all to you?"

"No, not a word. Not to anyone. Perhaps she can't speak English."

Barclay finished with the pillows, straightened, and said, "There. Is that more comfortable for you?"

They both looked at me. I could almost feel them willing me to speak.

Still not going to happen.

I turned my head and closed my eyes, hoping everyone would go away.

I heard the door close and opened them again.

Barclay still stood at the foot of the bed, full of sympathy and concern.

"Remember, I'm never very far away."

The guard came in as she went out.

I should think through what I'd just heard. This was not my world. I must not approach people and situations with preconceptions. It was important not to judge people by the standards of my own world. And that was another mistake because I must remember that this was my world now.

So far, I wasn't enjoying it that much.

I SPENT THE REST of the day with my eyes closed. I wasn't asleep—just keeping the world at bay. I blessed Leon and his instructions to say nothing. It made life easy. I didn't have to think of lies and then remember them (always a problem for me). I didn't have to say anything.

It couldn't last, of course. That evening, the Time Police turned up. Three of them. My guard left. I wasn't happy to see him go.

Two stood by the door, casually menacing.

The third, the one who had tried to arrest Leon, pulled up a chair and sat down.

I've always had a problem with authority—parents, school, uni, Barclay, everyone. Up to this moment, I'd never before appreciated how skilfully Dr. Bairstow managed not only me, but also all the other social misfits and eccentrics at St. Mary's.

This man was no Dr. Bairstow. I prepared to be difficult.

He let the silence build so that I would be properly intimidated and, actually, I was. Barclay was easy—I'd been getting up her nose for years—but this man was different. My heart knocked against my ribs. I hoped he couldn't hear it.

He was small, slightly built, and had eyes the colour of the North Sea on a raw day.

"My name is Colonel Albay. I am a member of the Time Police and I am currently in charge of this establishment. To save us both a very great deal of time and trouble, I will tell you now that I recognise your big-eyed innocent act for the sham it is. Innocent people do not attack my officers with water jugs. I shall ask you three questions. Failure to answer them promptly and fully will result in my pursuing a more direct route to the truth. It is traditional, in these circumstances, to say that neither of us will enjoy that. This statement is untrue. You will not enjoy it. I could not care less. We shall begin. What is your name?"

Counting is good. Apparently, the brain gives this task priority. It's a useful way of keeping calm. When they say, "Count to ten," it really is a good idea. I fixed my gaze on my hands and slowly began to count.

At fifteen, he said, "Where did you meet Leon Farrell?"

I restarted at one.

Precisely fifteen seconds later, he said, "Where has Leon Farrell gone?"

I went back to one.

At fifteen, he started again. "What is your name?"

He showed no emotion. He was remorseless. Like a machine. Every fifteen seconds he asked a question. The same three questions, over and over and over again.

My heart was thumping. I could feel sweat running down the small of my back. The compulsion to speak was over-whelming. I don't know how he was doing it—he never raised his voice or made any threatening moves, but I was very, very frightened.

I honestly thought about telling him everything. Anything to get away from this. The implied violence. The two guards standing motionless by the door. Just waiting for the word. The knowledge that no one knew I was here. No one in the entire world knew I was here. He could do with me as he pleased. I knew it. He knew I knew it.

Without any change in his voice, he sent for Dr. Foster. She appeared immediately. I guessed she had been waiting outside. Without a word, she crossed to the bed and took my pulse. It must have been racing, but she said nothing.

"It's not my style to beat up my suspects, Doctor. My methods are more subtle. I require you to carry out a medical procedure."

He held up a syringe.

Oh, shit! Shit, shit, shit!

He turned to me. "Your time is running out."

Dr. Foster shook her head. "That won't work. She has so many drugs in her system, she doesn't even know who she is, let alone where and when, and what's been happening."

Didn't I?

"We can always use the cuff."

I didn't like the sound of that. What cuff?

"Again—she won't know what she's saying. And we still don't know if she can talk."

"Has she spoken at all?"

"No, not one word. We're not even sure she understands English."

"Oh, she understands every word."

"Well, her body chemistry is skewed. The cuff probably won't work. She still has periods of delirium."

This was news to me. I lay back and tried to look delirious. It was surprisingly easy.

"How long before she can be interrogated more thoroughly?"

"Seven days."

"You have three."

He swept from the room. You had to hand it to him, he really did like dramatic entrances and exits.

TWO DAYS LATER, I was told to get up. They brought me a set of greys to wear. Most St. Mary's personnel wear jump suits. The History department wears blue, IT wears black, the Security section is in green, and the Technical section wears convict orange. The Admin people wear whatever they like and the nutters in R & D wear white coats, armour, fireproof suits, lifejackets, or any combination thereof, depending on their current project. Dr. Dowson, our librarian and archivist, and who has the misfortune to work directly underneath R & D, usually wears a jacket with leather patches, and either a sou'wester, a hard hat, or a gas mask, according to what's coming through his ceiling at the time.

Only trainees, the lowest of the low, wear grey.

I was a little reluctant to leave the comparative safety of Sick Bay and the faint protection of Dr. Foster, but I couldn't stay forever. I had to face this new world sometime. Besides, I might hear something useful.

Trailing my appendage, or Officer Ellis, as he would probably prefer to be known, I left the ward.

I did remember to turn the wrong way to get to the stairs, hoping my hesitation would get back to Colonel Albay. I had to unremember everything I knew of St. Mary's—its layout and its people. I had no shared experiences with anyone here. No common memories of triumphs or disasters. I had to see everything with new eyes—the eyes of a stranger.

St. Mary's is shabby and battered. As are the inhabitants, although at the moment, none was more shabby and battered than me. There's very little paint below shoulder level. The lovely oak panelling is gouged and scraped. People have carved their names all over it. The parquet floors are scuffed and loose. Not many windows have both curtains of the same colour. The whole place smells of floor polish, disinfectant, and damp stone, with occasional top-notes of whatever R & D are brewing up that day.

Ellis nudged me and I set off.

I was halfway down the stairs when it suddenly dawned on me. There was one person in this building who knew perfectly well I could speak. I stopped dead and Ellis walked straight past me, realised he'd lost me and turned back. I was two stairs above him, which made us eye to eye.

"Took you long enough," he said, gruffly, and motioned me to continue.

I didn't allow myself to consider him an ally. He was simply repaying a debt and now it was paid. I couldn't count on any more favours.

At the bottom of the stairs, I went to turn right to Hawking Hangar, where we keep the pods. I knew he wouldn't let me, but it did no harm to try. He pointed me left instead, and we set off down the long corridor that joined Hawking to the main building.

The sun was shining through the windows, laying long patches of bright sunshine on the floor. As always, I had the sensation of passing from one world to another. From light to dark. From warm to cool. From then to now.

I stopped at the end of the corridor. The Great Hall lay ahead, with the kitchen and dining room off to the left. The Hall would be full of historians, preparing for their next assignments, writing up their reports, shouting, squabbling, and generally getting through their working day. I felt suddenly . . . afraid. This had been my world. I had been head of this department. I had been their Chief Operations Officer. And now? What was I now? Prisoner? Outcast? Suspect? Freak?

Why was I here?

Because I had a job to do and I still didn't know what it was.

No. Why was I *here now?*

Because the colonel wanted to see what I would do. How I would behave. How people would behave towards me. Which just went to show that he was a bloody sight cleverer than I was, because I screwed everything up in the first ten minutes.

I didn't recognise him at first, which wasn't my fault because I'd never actually seen him standing up. I hadn't realised how tall he had been. I'd only ever known him hunched in his wheelchair, with his bony shoulders and elbows. But his eyes were unchanged. The same bright eyes.

Even as I stared at him, I heard him say, "Hey, Prentiss. Knock-knock."

It was David Sands.

He'd been involved in a car crash that left him paralysed. He'd become my assistant and died shortly afterwards. He died in my arms, fighting for breath and still trying to tell me some stupid knock-knock joke. And here he was, right in front of me. Uninjured, glowing with health, and enjoying his life.

He was wearing civilian clothes and dangling a set of car keys. He was about to drive into Rushford. I heard him say, "No, I can't stop. I'm late already."

He was in a hurry. He was going to Rushford. Was this the day he had his accident? Was this why I was here? Mrs. Partridge had been very fond of David Sands. She was distressed when he died. Had she brought me here to prevent his accident?

I looked around for her, but she wasn't there. I stared at the stone floor, the battered panelling around the walls, and the old oak staircase at one end. The stair carpet was dark red instead of green, but all of it was identical to the Hall I had known. The only exception was that here, at some point, they'd overcome the problem of bad lighting by installing a large glass lantern in the roof. I could see the sky, which was nice, but didn't solve my immediate problem.

What should I do about David Sands?

The answer to that was—nothing. If I spoke now then I ruined everything and placed God knows how many people in jeopardy. I should let him go. This might not be the day that changed his life for ever. It probably wasn't the day that changed his life for ever, but could I take that chance? If it was and I said nothing—in a year's time, he would be dead and I might have been able to prevent it. This wasn't changing History. It hadn't happened yet. And I might be able to prevent it ever happening at all.

I looked around again for Mrs. Partridge.

Nothing. She wasn't here. I felt very alone. Even the familiar frosty stare would have been welcome.

I took a step forwards and Ellis pulled me back.

"Where are you going?"

Sands was threading his way through groups of historians, heading towards the doors. I had only seconds. What should I do? Could I live with myself if I did nothing? If today was the day . . . ?

I'm an historian. Well, I used to be. I'm trained to make decisions. It's easy. In a crisis—deal with the now. Sort out the future later.

I struggled feebly with Ellis, but he had hold of my arm and wasn't going to let go. David Sands was almost at the door. I couldn't possibly get to him in time. In a few seconds, he would be gone. If I was going to do anything, it had to be now.

Was I going to do anything? Was I going to take the risk?

Of course I was.

I took a deep breath.

"David Sands. Don't go into Rushford this afternoon."

The words rang around the Hall far more loudly than I intended and everyone stopped talking.

Heads turned in the sudden silence.

Sands took two or three paces back into the Hall, his face puzzled.

"What? Who said that?"

It was too late for me. I'd burned my boats, but I might as well do the job properly.

I pulled free of Ellis and said more quietly, "Don't go into Rushford today."

"But I must. Why not?"

I said nothing.

"Why not?"

I still said nothing.

I saw the challenge in his eyes.

"Who are you?"

"The person telling you not to drive into Rushford today."

Now, everyone was staring at me. Heads appeared round doors. I saw shock, surprise, disbelief, anger, but no welcome.

No one moved for what seemed like a very long time. He looked back towards the front doors. Undecided.

I said nothing.

He said again, "Who are you?"

I said nothing.

He turned and walked back towards the vestibule doors. I felt a kind of sick despair. I'd buggered it all up for nothing.

He reached the doors, went to push them open, paused, and looked back.

I held his gaze.

Nothing happened, apart from my heart trying to break out of my chest and then, slowly, he put his keys back in his pocket. The huge surge of relief made my legs go weak.

He stared at me. Everyone was staring at me.

Something made me look up.

Colonel Albay was looking down from the Gallery. Smiling.

THE DINING ROOM WAS full. St. Mary's always sounds like feeding time at the zoo. Some of the animals might have better manners and smaller appetites, but otherwise, there's not a great difference.

I stood in the doorway and the noise died away. It's a shame there was no piano to stop playing. Everyone was looking at me. For lack of anything better to do, I stared back.

I saw Dieter with Polly Perkins from IT, sitting together, both of them peering at a printout while they ate. Not a flicker of emotion crossed their faces. My stomach clenched. Schiller and Van Owen sat with Roberts and Clerk. Over in the corner, the Security section had pushed three tables together. People twisted in their chairs to look at me. There were faces I didn't recognise, but the familiar ones were all there. Except for Peterson and Guthrie who were still, presumably, under arrest along with Dr. Bairstow.

I very nearly bolted. Just for a second, I nearly turned and ran away. Then Ellis nudged me towards the food.

I struggled, one-handed with my tray. Toad in the Hole— must be Wednesday. I helped myself to a good portion. Mrs. Mack, kitchen supremo, watched me in silence and then took my plate from me and began to load up a pile of vegetables. I watched in horror. No good ever comes of eating green food.

"Doctor's orders," she said, handing me back my plate.

I sat with Ellis at a quiet table by the window and watched them all ignore me. No one came over to enquire how I was. Or even ask who I was. I faced a wall of blank hostility. I blinked back tears and concentrated on my food. This was really not my world.

Who was I kidding? This was exactly my world—because even as I ate my way carefully around the vegetables, someone shouted a warning outside, and I heard the sound of furiously galloping hooves.

Mr. Markham on horseback was a strange enough sight. He didn't enjoy a happy relationship with the animal world.

Mr. Markham on board Turk was an even stranger sight. He steered clear of horses, especially since, whenever he was near, they tended to form an outward-facing huddle and bare enormous yellow teeth at him. Whether they'd had some sort of temporary reconciliation, I had no idea. Maybe that had only happened in my world.

I reminded myself again that this was my world now.

Anyway, the two of them were galloping headlong across Mr. Strong's cherished South Lawn. Old Turk was going full tilt, bony head outstretched, snorting like a dragon, and obviously not intending to stop any time soon. His huge hooves threw great clods of turf up into the air. A distraught Mr. Strong ran behind, calling down blood-curdling curses upon the pair of them, and waving his arms.

The thing that lifted this one from the realms of the comparatively normal (for St. Mary's, that is), was that Markham, not, in the scheme of things a natural horseman anyway, was facing backwards—a position that gave him no control over Turk whatsoever. He lay face down across his rump, grimly clutching his (Turk's, I mean) tail with both hands and calling piteously for assistance. Being St. Mary's, no one moved, although as a tribute, one or two people did stop eating.

Turk, who liked having his tail pulled as little as any horse, increased his speed. Markham increased his wailing. Behind them, Mr. Strong fell grimly silent. He was obviously in it for the long haul.

The trio Dopplered across the lawn and were last seen heading west where, presumably, they would all eventually fall into the sea. Or hit Ireland.

The Security section began to lay bets on whether any of them would ever be seen again.

Officer Ellis sat frozen, his mug of tea halfway between table and face.

"What . . . ?"

"Parthians," I said, helpfully.

He refused to defrost so I tried again.

"The Parthians. Great horsemen. Best known for their tactical retreats. They would apparently flee the battlefield and then, when the enemy chased after them, without slowing down at all, they'd turn themselves around on their horses, face backwards, and unleash a hail of arrows upon their luckless pursuers. Hence the expression, "Parthian shot." Of course, for it to be effective, the riders had to have a level of skill possibly not possessed by our Mr. Markham. And the cooperation of their horses as well, of course. Something definitely not possessed by our Mr. Markham."

He said, seemingly casual, "How did you know his name was Markham?"

"Nurse Hunter's boyfriend."

"Really? That pretty blonde girl?"

"'Fraid so."

"Will they come back, do you think?" he asked, craning his neck for a final, disbelieving glimpse.

"Oh yes. Soon as he gets hungry," I said, and which one of them I was talking about was anyone's guess.

AFTER A WHILE, THE buzz of conversation started again, slowly at first, and then two minutes later, you couldn't hear yourself think. Just another working day at St. Mary's.

It was easier to look out of the window, so I did. Like many things here, the grounds were similar but not identical. Beeches fringed the South Lawn rather than cedars, and they'd planted rose beds under the terrace, but otherwise, things were pretty much the same. Apart, of course, from the huge area of devastation around the lake. Most of the reed beds were just blackened stumps. The entire bank looked as if it had been on the wrong end of Lord Kitchener's scorched earth policy. The jetty was just a memory. The sad remains of black-and-yellow safety tape fluttered in the breeze and there wasn't a swan in sight. God knows where they were now. Still in the library, maybe? On the roof? India?

I was just finishing my lunch when Isabella Barclay made her entrance.

She'd once accused me of having stolen her life. That everything I had should have been hers. Well if that was the case, she certainly had it all back again. It was my turn to sit, sullen and resentful, watching her talking and laughing as she made her way across the dining room, exchanging insults and jokes with those around her. She'd certainly stepped into my empty shoes quickly enough.

I tried again to clear my mind of preconceptions.

She hadn't come to eat. She had a folder in her hands. The dreaded St. Mary's paperwork. She'd come for me.

To put off the moment, I got up and made myself a pot of tea. When I returned to the table, Ellis had gone.

Seemingly unaware of the deathly silence around us, she opened the folder.

I busied myself pouring my tea, using the time to decide what to say and do. I would have to say something. They all knew I could talk. If I said nothing, they would stick needles in me and I'd have no control over anything I said, or even remember afterwards what I'd said, and I couldn't afford for that to happen.

I added sugar and stirred, desperately trying to see a way out of this, but the only thing in my head was a picture of Markham and Turk. That was typical of St. Mary's. Even though they were in the midst of a crisis, with their senior staff under house arrest, St. Mary's did things their own way. Maybe . . . so should I. Perhaps now was the time to go on the offensive. I could do that. For some reason, she'd chosen to do this in front of everyone. Was she trying to expose me in public? Of course she was. Perhaps it was time I sent a message.

She sat across from me, smiling pleasantly. I remembered her leaning over me in Sick Bay. I didn't care what the rest of St. Mary's thought about her. She was trouble. She always had been. In every time. In every world.

"I have a little paperwork to complete so if you could let me have a few details, please, just for our records . . ."

She let the sentence die away.

Well, I'd already screwed up once this morning. Let's see if I could do it again. Maybe this was the time to declare myself. In fact—let's really give them something to worry about. It occurred to me that if they concentrated on me, here at St. Mary's, maybe Leon would have a chance out there. Wherever he was. Whatever he was doing. I felt again the blast of hot air in my face. When he jumped away. When he left me . . .

Her voice brought me back. "Can I have your name, please?"

"Maxwell."

I didn't raise my voice. People listen harder if you talk quietly.

Her hand jolted. I heard her swallow.

"And your first name?"

"Doctor."

I was back at school again. Defying authority and digging myself a deeper hole with every word uttered. My own worst enemy and about to enjoy every minute.

"Indeed?" she said in polite disbelief. She looked me up and down, taking in my still very bedraggled appearance. I'm sure they all thought I was just some scruffy, ginger bint Leon had picked up from somewhere—which wasn't that far from the truth when you think about it.

Somewhere, someone laughed. I grew very cold.

"Well," she said, politely disbelieving. She was still smiling so everyone could see how nice she was, but her eyes were telling me a different story. "Let's see if you are able to verify that statement, shall we? Perhaps you can give me some personal details. What about qualifications? Do you actually have any? At all?"

I took a deep breath and said in Latin, "Graduated from Thirsk University. L'Espec College—Northallerton campus. Doctorate in Ancient Civilisations. Post-graduate qualifications in Archaeology and Anthropology. Fluent in German, French, and Latin. Passable in Middle English and Greek. A smattering of Spanish, Italian, and Turkish. Fully qualified Field Medic with hospital experience. Reasonable with a quarterstaff, good with a bow, and bloody good with a handgun. Current in self-defence and side-saddle." I put down my cup. "I can make a weapon out of anything you care to put in front of me and should any proof be required, I'll happily kill you with this teaspoon."

My words rang around the room. I could hear whispers as people translated for those without Latin. I'd done everything except come right out and say I had been Chief Operations Officer. I knew Barclay didn't speak Latin, but I was willing to bet she had a very good idea of what I'd just said. She kept her head, however, and rather than be seen to sit there, at a loss, she gathered up her paperwork and left the room.

I was shaking with rage. And fear. I sat quietly, staring out of the window, holding my tea with a trembling hand, wondering if I'd made things better or worse.

Gradually, the room emptied as everyone went back to work and I was alone.

What about me? Where should I go? Even my guard had left me. I pushed my chair back and slowly walked from the room.

I had no idea where I was going or what I was going to do when I got there.

Nothing new there then.

I MADE MY WAY through the Hall. It was a familiar scene; groups of historians clustered around data tables or whiteboards, arguing, discussing, waving their arms. I caught snatches of conversation. Van Owen, who was probably in charge now, was saying, "My compliments to Professor Rapson. War budgies—yes. War goldfish—yes. War elephants? Not in a million years."

Some things never change.

Something caught my eye and I came to a sudden halt, taking two steps backwards to stare at a whiteboard headed Battle of Shrewsbury—1403.

I studied the bullet points listing the aims and objectives and tapped the board. "There's a legend that the road nearby is named Featherbed Lane because that's where the women dragged out their featherbeds for the wounded to rest on. You might want to check that out," I said, and passed on before anyone could comment.

I made for the shelter of the library. I needed some peace and quiet before I fell apart altogether.

The high-ceilinged, sunny room was exactly as I remembered it. Apart from the strong chemical cleaning smell that

was possibly not unrelated to the recent invasion by a dozen or
so angry but loose-bowelled swans leaving ankle-deep calling
cards with malicious intent.

Ignoring the siren call of Leick on Mesopotamia, I thought
I would catch up on some old favourites. Since there weren't
any out there, I needed the comfort of familiar friends in here.

I pulled down *Jane Eyre*, *Pride and Prejudice*, a book of Sher-
lock Holmes short stories, the first *Harry Potter*, and finished
off with Tom Holland's *Persian Fire*. That should keep me
quiet until teatime. I avoided Thomas Hardy because everyone
should, and anyway, I was depressed enough. And Dickens.
I've never liked Dickens. I laughed like mad when Little Nell
died.

I found a comfortable chair, dropped the books on the floor
around me, and curled up with the Bennett sisters.

It was a measure, I think, of how seriously my mind was
disturbed. I'd read this story so many times but now, for some
reason, I saw so much wrong with it.

There was Mr. Bennett, quietly comical, along with his
wife, the extremely silly Mrs. Bennett—except that she wasn't,
was she?

We're supposed to laugh at Mr. Bennett's dry wit and gently humorous comments, but this is the man who has so mis-
managed his family's affairs that, on his death, his wife and
daughters will be homeless and almost penniless. In an age
when there was no mechanism for gently born women to earn
their own living, how would they survive?

The answer to that almost certainly kept Mrs. Bennett
awake at night and, knowing this, who could criticise her
frantic efforts to get all her daughters safely married, their
future well-being taken care of, while Mr. Bennett amusingly
uncaring, reads in his library? Poor Mrs. Bennett. Laughed
at by generations of readers. I wondered about Jane Austen's
contemporaries who would, like Mrs. Bennett, have been

only too aware of the likely fate of the Bennett girls—had they laughed too?

Bloody hell, I was a right little ray of sunshine today.

I let Elizabeth Bennett slide to the floor and picked up *Jane Eyre*. The library was very quiet. I could hear Dr. Dowson moving around the shelves, but otherwise, the place was empty. There was no sign of my guard. Obviously, I didn't need one any longer because I'm an idiot and I'd told them everything they needed to know.

I sighed, turned another page, and someone coughed at my elbow. Looking up, I saw Dr. Dowson. He took off his spectacles and polished them.

"I was wondering . . . we usually have some tea around about this time. Would you care to join us?"

This unexpected gesture of kindness brought a lump to my throat.

I swallowed. "Yes, I would. Thank you."

"Please, come this way."

I picked up my books and followed him to his office, a small room between the library and the archive.

Professor Rapson was already there. Just as I remembered him, with his shock of Einstein hair and his beaky nose. His eyebrows hadn't yet grown back after the fireship trauma. Today he wore a white coat with a huge scorch-mark just over his heart. Heaven knows what had been going on there.

Dr. Dowson ushered me into their cosy room. "Andrew, break out the crumpets! We have a guest."

"Excellent. Excellent. Welcome, my dear. Come and sit down."

"You'd better have the chair by the fire," said Dr. Dowson. "Try to make sure the old fool doesn't ignite the furniture, again."

"You can't count that time, Octavius. The chair merely smouldered. It doesn't count unless there is an actual flame, you know."

He impaled a crumpet on a long fork and held it in front of the hissing gas fire. "I'll toast. You butter."

I nodded.

Dr. Dowson made the tea.

At some point, the sun had disappeared and now rain splattered the windows. It was extremely pleasant to be in here, snug and warm, toasting crumpets with two old friends. Of course, any minute now, the professor could explode the sugar bowl.

I watched them moving around in this small space. Cups, saucers, and plates were all handed around. I buttered enough crumpets for a small country. It was all very peaceful. The sound of them bickering amiably was oddly soothing and familiar. This, at least, had not changed.

Eventually, we each had a small table, a plate of crumpets, and a napkin.

Professor Rapson handed me my tea and said, without looking at me, "Should they ever find him, Leon Farrell will be charged with removing a contemporary from his own time, the sentence for which is death. Dr. Peterson and Major Guthrie will be charged as accomplices. Dr. Bairstow, as the person ultimately responsible for everything has, only temporarily we hope, been removed from his position as Director of St. Mary's.

"As mission controller, Dr. Maxwell would have been charged as well, but she died. At this stage, we're not sure if the colonel believes that or not. If he thinks you are Max, you'll be shot. If he thinks you're not Max, they might shoot you anyway. A no-win situation for you, I'm afraid. One lump or two?"

"Three, please," I said, calmly, hoping my face showed nothing.

Old sins have long shadows. We'd taken Helios back and we still weren't safe. Would we ever escape the consequences of that day?

I looked up from dark memories, to find the pair of them watching me. Gone were the familiar bickering academics.

That was just the face they chose to present to the world. Neither of them was the bumbling buffoon they appeared. I suspected the charade gave them a great deal of quiet amusement.

Professor Rapson continued. "You are in a difficult position, but your ringing declaration in the dining-room may not be the catastrophe you think it is. You are Maxwell. Of that I have no doubt."

He twinkled at me, and suddenly the world was not such an unfriendly place. "Of course, which Maxwell is another matter completely. If you will accept a friendly word of advice, stick with that. News of your possible identity has caused a considerable amount of consternation in the right quarters, which I am certain you will know how to exploit. Our Miss Barclay, for example, was most taken aback, don't you think? One would have thought that the return of someone for whom she always professed great affection would be a cause for joy. One would have thought. And yet . . ."

He petered out, peering thoughtfully into his cup.

"I am certain Dr. Bairstow will be busy weaving this revelation into his plans even as we speak."

"Plans?"

Dr. Dowson helped himself to another crumpet. "Oh yes. I've never known Edward not to have a plan of some kind."

Without any change in his voice, he continued, "Oh, for heaven's sake, Andrew, look what you're doing, will you? You'll have that chair up in flames if you're not careful."

He lunged forwards, upsetting the teapot. The table went over and they launched themselves into an ocean of recrimination and abuse, and Officer Ellis, who had been standing unseen in the doorway, informed me that the colonel wished to see me.

TEN

WHATEVER I'D BEEN EXPECTING, it hadn't been this. I'd never given it a thought . . . It had never occurred to me . . . The shock nearly knocked me over. The world blurred again and I would have gone down with a terrible crash if Ellis hadn't seized my good arm and pushed me into a nearby chair. Things whirled sickeningly, and for one moment I hung helplessly over an abyss. I gulped for air, desperately struggling against the overwhelming panic. I'd never thought . . . Why would I . . . ?

There was no Mrs. Partridge.

I stared in disbelief. I'd fretted over just about everything else, but the one thing I'd never, ever considered, not even for a moment, was that there would be no Mrs. Partridge in this world. To guide me. To give me some sort of clue. To give me her familiar exasperated stare.

Her desk was occupied by Rosie Lee and, trust me, an unexpected encounter with Miss Lee should not be on any invalid's list of Things To Do Today.

She stared curiously. She wasn't tall and her hair waved around her head like Medusa's snakes. The tailored suit was unfamiliar but the intimidating attitude was spot on.

"Dr. Bairstow is not available at the moment."

"Got a message to see Colonel Albay," said Ellis, trying to step past her. I could have told him he was wasting his time.

"Why?"

He seemed confused. I was guessing this was their first encounter. "Why what?"

"Why does the colonel want to see you?"

"How should I know? I'd like to find out, though."

Silence.

He shifted impatiently. "Should we go in?"

"How should I know? I work for Dr. Bairstow."

"For the time being."

She snorted. He was going to have to do better than that.

I don't know whether she'd done it intentionally, but their brief interchange had given me the time I needed. I sat up and stared around.

The battered furniture was the same. Everything was the same except for the sign on the wall behind her.

Lack of planning on your part does not constitute an emergency on my part.

That figured.

A light flashed on her phone.

She made no move.

I watched, cutting my eyes from one to the other, waiting to see what would happen next.

The silence dragged on. Miss Lee had once been my assistant. I'd actually found our daily battle of wills quite stimulating, but it was fun to see someone else on the receiving end for once.

Ellis caved first. "Should we go in?"

She smirked with satisfaction. "Obviously."

I heaved myself to my feet and followed him in.

Dr. Bairstow's room was as I always remembered it. There was the scuffed parquet floor and the square of faded carpet. The colours had once been red and gold, but now the pattern was only discernible around the very edges.

The only difference was that his desk was now occupied by that sensitive and sympathetic people person, Colonel Albay, while the Boss himself sat at his briefing table, a little way off. Under arrest he might be, but the colonel was wisely keeping him under observation.

Ellis took my arm as we marched in. It was a little late for the tough-guy treatment but I could appreciate he would want to give the right impression, so I staggered a little and did my best to look brutalised.

Albay was busy flipping through a file, doing the "I'm too busy to deal with you at the moment even though I've just sent for you" routine so beloved of senior managers everywhere. He was wasting his time. I was flouting authority before he was born.

I peeled off and walked over to Dr. Bairstow, who stood up, as he always did, because even in a crisis, he was never less than courteous.

He leaned on his cane and extended a hand. "How do you do."

Which told me everything I wanted to know. I returned the greeting. "How do you do."

He was not going to commit himself over my identity and neither should I.

He indicated a chair opposite. "Please sit down."

Colonel Albay realised, too late, that control of the interview had just passed out of his hands.

"I am Edward Bairstow. I trust my people have made you comfortable."

"Very, thank you."

"Have you completely recovered from your injuries?"

"Just about. I —"

We were interrupted. Albay had realised that unless he wanted to shout from all the way over there, he would have to join us. Some people think it's the big desk that confers the power, but there are people like Dr. Bairstow who could sit on an orange box and still be the most powerful person in the room.

Albay pressed his intercom.

A voice squawked, "What?"

I caught Dr. Bairstow's eye, just for a very brief moment, and then he looked away.

"Tea."

"What?"

"Tea."

"Tea what?"

He gritted his teeth. "I would like a cup of tea."

"I would like a cup of tea what?"

"I would like a cup of tea *now*," and wisely closed the connection before she could reply.

I hid a smile and then gave Colonel Albay my full attention because although he was a pillock, he was a dangerous pillock.

"So, you can speak?"

I said nothing, just to annoy him.

"What is your name?"

I said nothing.

He turned to Dr. Bairstow. "Who is this woman?"

He shrugged his shoulders and said clearly, "I have no idea. We have only just met."

"She claims she is Dr. Maxwell."

"So I heard."

"Dr. Maxwell is dead."

"Quite so."

"So who is this woman?"

"Asked and answered."

He turned to me.

"Last chance. Are you Maxwell?"

"You just said she was dead."

He stared for a moment and then shrugged.

"I summoned you to tell you a hearing to determine your true identity and to advise you of possible charges against you will be held tomorrow at 4 p.m. You will prepare yourself to jump to a destination of my choosing."

Dr. Bairstow stirred. "No. That will not happen. The Charter clearly states that all investigations should be carried out in their own time. You yourself said this is only a preliminary hearing to ascertain this person's identity and decide whether or not to press charges. No useful purpose can be served by removing her from her own time." He smiled nastily. "After all, isn't that what this is all about?"

For a second, it all hung in the balance. The silence lengthened as they stared each other out. I sat as still as a mouse and then . . .

The door crashed open and Miss Lee entered, complete with tea tray. If I required any more proof that this was not my world, this was it. She'd never brought me tea in my life. If anything, it had been the other way around.

She dumped the tray on the desk and began to pour. Dr. Bairstow received a cup and saucer. I recognised the best china. A mug reflected my social standing. Colonel Albay's tea remained in the pot.

She handed Dr. Bairstow a folded note and turned to go.

He unfolded it and glanced at the colonel who was pouring his own tea.

In large, red letters, she'd printed:

DO NOT DRINK THE TEA.

I watched him spirit the note away and struggle. The chances were that she'd only spat in it. On the other hand, this was Rosie Lee, and who was to say she hadn't purloined something from Professor Rapson's skull and crossbones cabinet. Two sips and the colonel might be stretched out, lifeless, on the carpet. Would Dr. Bairstow take the chance? And what could he possibly say?

He sighed. "I wouldn't drink that if I were you, Colonel. Miss Lee, while possessing many admirable qualities," his tone led us to believe he hoped, one day, to discover one, "does not always allow the kettle to boil quite sufficiently. I believe this to be one of those occasions."

The colonel wasn't stupid. He pushed the tea away from him and said to me, "You will present yourself tomorrow at sixteen hundred hours. I advise you to give some thought to your defence. Officer, you may remove this person."

I spent the evening in Sick Bay, ostensibly deep in *Jane Eyre*, while I thought things through. Occasionally, I remembered to turn a page.

That night, I slept just long enough to experience a dream that drove me not only from my bed, but out of the room and downstairs as well. If this was to be my last day then I intended to get my money's worth out of it. Starting with an early breakfast.

Time Police patrolled the corridors, but no one challenged me.

Mrs. Mack was on the early shift and bustling around. I paused. I'd hoped for gentle Jenny Fields who would let me make myself a bacon buttie.

She saw me standing in the doorway and maybe the remains of my nightmare were still written on my face because she stared for a while and then said, "Come in, if you're coming."

I stepped into the kitchen and looked around.

She said, in a voice that brooked no argument, "Cocoa," and suddenly I knew that was what I wanted above everything else. A huge mug of frothy cocoa. Thick and sweet. A bit like me, really.

She nodded at her office.

"I'll bring it in."

Her office was small and cluttered. The centrepiece was a huge, hairy cat, slumbering heavily on a copy of *The*

Flour Handling Regulations. Another difference. My Dr. Bairstow always maintained that an organisation possessing Mr.
Markham should not additionally burden itself with pets.

I made myself comfortable and passed the time by reading
those parts of the Regulations not currently covered in cat.

"Vortigern," announced Mrs. Mack, dumping a tray on the
desk. Two steaming mugs and a silver pot for top-ups. It always
pays to stay on the good side of the kitchen staff.

I assumed Vortigern was the cat. Rip Van Winkle might
have been more appropriate.

I blew the steam away and sipped. It tasted the way cocoa
should. Hot, rich, and chocolatey.

We sat in silence while the building creaked around us.
Faintly in the distance, I could hear footsteps and voices. The
guard was changing.

I waited for the question du jour—who are you?—but it
never came.

I warmed my hands around the mug and licked off my
chocolate moustache.

Not looking at me, she said, "I don't know who you are but
I'll tell you this. If you're not Maxwell then you'd better learn to
be, because if it's one thing this unit needs at the moment, it's
a Maxwell of some kind."

Startled, I stared at her.

Having said that, she finished her cocoa in silence.

As did I.

I SHOULD HAVE SPENT the day quietly preparing for the hearing. Running through likely questions and rehearsing my
answers. A bit like a job interview—although an unsuccessful
applicant usually just gets a polite letter—not a bullet in the
brain.

That's what I should have done. It didn't work out like that.
Not at all.

THE FIRST THING THAT happened was that Barclay turned up. "I've allocated you a room if you want to come and have a look."

"Is it worth the effort? I'll probably be dead by this time tomorrow."

Her eyelids flickered. "Come and see, anyway."

I never expected to go back to my old room in the main building. I wondered who had it now. I expected to be allocated one of the trainees' rooms on the first floor of the Staff Block. They were OK—a bit small but so was I, and it wasn't as if I had any possessions to clutter up the place.

I'd underestimated her.

There are a number of small rooms on the ground floor. They're not very pleasant, the tiny windows are barred, and they offer a panoramic view of the wheelie bins and the car park. Mr. Strong had commandeered most of them as storerooms.

She'd excelled herself.

This one was at the end of a long narrow corridor and smelled strongly of the floor cleaner that had undoubtedly been kept in there. A narrow metal bed was pushed against one wall. A battered chest of drawers occupied another. An old-fashioned strip light hummed and flickered. The floor and ceiling were of concrete. The bathroom was on the floor above. The horses were better housed.

Now I knew why she'd put herself to the trouble. Revenge for yesterday. Well, at least we wouldn't have to pretend to be friends.

"I'll leave you to get settled in."

That wouldn't take long. I looked around. I never thought I'd say this, but I really missed Sick Bay. And Dr. Foster's invisible but very real protection. I never thought I'd say that, either. It struck me that, as well as being thoroughly unpleasant, this room was horribly isolated. Anything could happen at the end of this corridor. Fire, for instance. And all the windows were barred. I might not even live long enough for the hearing.

Well, I had nothing to lose.

"Why did you do it, Izzie?"

I'd touched some sort of nerve. Her face froze and for a moment, she was somewhere else completely. But only for a moment.

"We couldn't leave you in Sick Bay indefinitely, could we?"

"No, I mean, why did you grass up Leon Farrell?"

She loved him. I was sure of it. She'd always loved him. She must have been over the moon when I died. Then he moved to Rushford and she had him isolated and alone and vulnerable. She'd been poised to make her move. Then I came back and wrecked everything.

She stared at me and I could see her lip lifting in the familiar sneer. This was more like it. I *knew* that underneath that smiling face—

"You don't know, do you? You really have no idea."

I shouldn't have asked. I should have just walked away.

"Know what?"

Above our heads, the light flickered again. Shadows came and went.

"I didn't report Leon Farrell. I reported Madeleine Maxwell. It was Madeleine Maxwell who should have been arrested, not Leon. He just covered for you. They all did."

"Why? What did I do?"

Gone now was any pretence. With no witnesses present, she really let rip. Spit flew from her mouth with the violence of her words.

"You don't get it, do you? The great Maxwell. Except you're not. You're not great and you're certainly not Maxwell. You're just a rather silly girl who's completely out of her depth."

I felt myself begin to grow cold, but I'd come too far now. With an assumption of ease I was far from feeling, I said, "Talking rubbish as usual, Izzie. What don't I get?"

This was her moment and she seized it, spitting the words she knew would destroy my world.

"It wasn't Leon, you stupid cow. It wasn't Leon who lifted that contemporary from Troy. Only one person would ever do anything that stupid."

My world slid away from me but I had to ask anyway.

"Who was it then?"

"It was you. Her. Maxwell. Maxwell did it. You did it because you're arrogant and conceited and full of yourself and you think you're wonderful and you can do anything you want. And everyone covered for you. And then you died so it didn't matter any longer and I thought we were safe. And he was getting over you. One day he would have seen me. And then you turned up and ruined everything. And now we're all at risk. Again. Do you wonder people hate you?"

We all have our own self-image. A picture of ourselves as we hope we appear to others. Mine was based on my work. I saw myself as I hoped others saw me—professional, hard-working, dedicated, competent—all the usual stuff. To have that blasted away in an instant . . . To know that I had committed a crime so terrible . . . to know that it was me. It was me who had done it. I had endangered the timeline, St. Mary's, my colleagues . . . Had Leon run away? From me? My world crashed down around my head.

I felt as if I had plunged into a bath of icy water. The shock took my breath away. She'd kicked away the foundations of my world and suddenly, I wasn't the person I thought I was. The last thing I owned in this world—my sense of self—had been stripped from me.

I didn't know what to do. I really didn't know what to do. How to feel. What to say. No wonder Leon had told me to say nothing. This was the reason Leon had hidden me in the toilet. So that I couldn't talk to Helios. So that I wouldn't find out. That in this world it hadn't been Leon. It had been me. The person who had threatened the timeline, risked everything, had been me.

It was a measure of how much I identified now with this life I had taken over—I felt every bit as frightened and ashamed and horrified as if I had done it myself. Maybe I should hand myself over to the Time Police—admit my crime and take my punishment. Was that why I was here? To provide the Time Police with a scapegoat? But no, that wouldn't save Peterson or Guthrie or the Boss. Far from it. Because if I was guilty then so were they.

What was I going to do?

What could I do?

I DON'T KNOW HOW long I stood, lost in thought and panic, but when I looked up, she was gone.

I sat heavily on the little bed. The springs chinked beneath me. I tried to think, but the same three words ran through my mind. "It was you. It was you. It was you." I don't know for how long I sat there. The overhead light flickered. Shadows danced. Time passed. I should be preparing for this hearing. Preparing my defence. Except I didn't have one. If I were Maxwell then they'd shoot me. And Guthrie and Peterson and the Boss. And Leon if they ever found him.

And even if I weren't Maxwell—would that save anyone? Who would believe I was from another world? I couldn't prove it. And they couldn't dig up a body because I'd been cremated and my ashes scattered. No mouldy earth for me. Just a small stone with my name.

I didn't care about me. Knowing what I'd done, I wasn't even sure I wanted to survive. If I hadn't come here . . .

I was so completely in my own dark world that I never heard the quiet footsteps in the passage. When she spoke, I nearly had a heart attack.

"Good afternoon, Dr. Maxwell."

The voice had the majesty of millennia.

I wasn't in the mood.

"Push off, Mrs. Partridge."

Perhaps I could goad her into finishing me off now.

"I can see that you are considerably distressed, but there really is no need for discourtesy."

She was in full battledress, her dark hair looped around her head and held in place with silver pins. A long, gracefully draped robe fell around her sandaled feet. She held a scroll in one hand. This was obviously a formal occasion.

I pushed myself to my feet. To confront her. My voice shook with emotion, although which emotion, I couldn't have told you. I felt like a pressure cooker—ready to explode at any minute and bring half the building down with me.

"Is this why you brought me here? To take the blame and get the Time Police off your backs? Am I to be sacrificed for something I didn't do? I was dying at Agincourt, so you thought you'd bring me here and I'd be so grateful for a couple of extra weeks of life that I'd put my hand up for anything? Well, I tell you now, Mrs. Partridge, I am not your puppet. I don't care what you want me to do—I won't do it. You'll have to get another Maxwell from somewhere. It shouldn't be a problem—you seem to have an inexhaustible supply."

I had much more to say but it never happened. The overhead light flickered wildly. Shadows flew around the room. I'd finally done it. I'd finally made Mrs. Partridge angry.

We stared at each other. I would not back down. She could whistle up storms and portents and shake the earth and it wouldn't do her the slightest bit of good, because in this world, I'd done something so terrible that I couldn't live with it, and if she wiped me off the face of the earth now, she would be doing everyone a favour.

"Go on," I shouted. "Go on. I defy you. Do your worst and do it now because I'm finished with you."

I hadn't realised she was so tall. She regarded me long enough for my first faint stirrings of fear to register. Then everything was still.

"Dear me," she said lightly. "I do think we should sit down, don't you?"

I had no memory of moving, nor had I intended to, but there I was, sitting on the bed, listening to the birds singing outside on a lovely afternoon.

"I think we need to update each other. Shall I begin?"

I didn't want to do this. "I'm facing a hearing at four o'clock. I need to concentrate on that."

"Well, you have an hour or so yet."

"I need to prepare some sort of defence."

"I'm sure you'll successfully wing it, just as you always do."

I gave it up. And it would be nice to get some answers. "All right. You begin."

"The Time Police must be stopped. If they are not—if St. Mary's cannot prove its innocence, then people will die. Dr. Bairstow, Peterson, Guthrie, you—all the people on whom St. Mary's depends. Their removal will pave the way for a new director to be appointed—we both know who—and the events you worked so hard to prevent in your own world will occur here because there is no one to prevent them."

"But," I said, "how can we stop them? We are guilty. I'm guilty."

Once again, I stood on the precipice of panic.

"No," she said, slightly exasperated, "you're not."

"But I can't prove it. No one's going to believe me. I as good as admitted who I was. In public. In front of everyone. Everyone thinks I'm Maxwell."

Now she was really exasperated. "You *are* Maxwell."

I was back to being confused again. Only a short journey for me.

"But how does that help? If I'm Maxwell they'll shoot me because of Helios. If I'm not Maxwell, they'll shoot me because I'm an anomaly."

"I am sure that if you take the time to think carefully, every-thing will become clear."

I was bloody sure it wouldn't.

"If I give myself up—will they let the others go?"

"I doubt it."

"Then why am I here? Am I to be sacrificed to get the Time Police off your backs?

"Certainly not. Where do you get these ideas?"

"Oh, I don't know. In between being sick, chased, frozen, shot, chased again, shot again, covered in mud, covered in ash, sick again . . . A crowded schedule but still leaving room for the odd existential query—why am I bloody here? For God's sake, Mrs. Partridge, what do you want me to do? Give me some sort of clue."

"I cannot. You must choose your own path."

"What path?"

Silence.

"Perhaps," I said bitterly, "I should just let them shoot me."

"You have died once in this world. Try not to do so again."

"Aren't I supposed to die? Isn't that why I'm here? I'm to be executed to get the Time Police off your back."

"On the contrary, you are to do your very best to remain alive."

"Why?

"To tell the truth."

"You mean admit to being Maxwell."

She said again. "You *are* Maxwell."

True.

She continued. "You are making this far more difficult than it needs to be. I am sure, if you think about it carefully, you will see the wisdom of admitting who you are."

I doubted that. A thought occurred to me.

"Did you kill me? As a punishment for what I did with Helios?"

She smiled, but not with amusement. "I did not get the chance."

I sat back, overwhelmed.

"Perhaps this will help. Drink this."

What she gave me really was the worst thing I'd ever drunk and I'd once got blitzed on Babycham. Eventually. It took about four crates but I got there in the end. And subsequently wished I hadn't. I took a huge glug of something that nearly blew my head off. I took a while to recover and when my eyes stopped watering, she was on her way out of the door.

I disregarded instructions and panicked.

"Wait. You haven't told me what I must do."

She turned back.

"Remember—we can't change the past. But we can change the future."

Then she was gone and Officer Ellis was there, telling me it was time.

ELEVEN

A PERIOD OF CALM REFLECTION would have been nice. A period in which I would be able just to stop and think for a moment. To consider what I had been told. To think about what I was going to do. What I was going to say.

Fat bloody chance.

I don't know what was in that drink she gave me. I only know that as I followed Ellis back into the building, I felt as if I could have conquered the world. Forget Hercules—I could have completed all twelve labours before lunchtime and then taken on the Minotaur. While standing on my head and whistling *God Save the King*.

My feeling of invincibility lasted all the way through the building and finally into the Great Hall itself. The place was packed, which was a bit of a surprise because I'd been expecting something in a cellar. With electrodes and no witnesses. On the other hand, the silence that fell as we entered was neither friendly nor welcoming. Neither was the layout.

An unknown woman sat alone at a table with her back to the stairway, facing the main doors. She wore the black Time Police uniform, which was not reassuring. She was about Dr. Bairstow's age and the sun streaming through the glass lantern overhead picked out the silver in her hair. She didn't look up as we entered, continuing to write, her hand moving slowly but steadily across the page.

To her right, Colonel Albay and an officer unfamiliar to me sat at a smaller table heaped with electronic equipment.

Dr. Bairstow, Peterson, and Guthrie sat alone in the first row, flanked by guards, with the rest of St. Mary's seated in rows behind them. Miss Lee sat off to one side, scratchpad laid on the table in front of her. She would be keeping the record.

Most ominously, a solitary chair stood isolated in the middle of the room, directly under the glass lantern. Well, at least they were going to let me sit down.

Ellis gave me a little nudge. "Go on."

I walked slowly down the Hall. How many times had I been in here—working, arguing, presenting, giving and receiving briefings? I never thought it would come to this.

"You may sit," said Albay, so, just to annoy him, I took my time, moving the chair slightly out of position, gazing around me, noting the position of familiar faces, smoothing my clothes and making myself comfortable. I didn't make the mistake of looking for encouragement or support. Ellis took up a position behind me.

Silence fell. The woman continued to write. We hadn't even started yet. What on earth could she possibly be writing?

The coughs and scuffling noises slowly died away into complete silence. A bit of a first for an historians' working area. I stared at my feet. As far as I was concerned, they could take as long as they liked.

Eventually, she laid aside her pen and looked up.

"Good afternoon. Let's get the introductions out of the way. My name is not important. I have agreed to preside over this hearing, the purpose of which, as I understand it, is to establish the identity of the person before us.

"Allow me to present my own credentials. I worked for St. Mary's for many years before transferring out and taking up a position with the Time Police. It was felt that these qualifications would give me a foot in both camps and allay any possible uneasiness over bias or prejudice. Should anyone have any reservations over my suitability, please speak up now. Silence will be taken for unopposed consent."

She stared around the room. Silence. Good God, she was a female Dr. Bairstow. I wondered in which particular incarnation of St. Mary's she had served and was just grateful it wasn't mine.

"To my right is Colonel Albay who will be leading the hearing this afternoon. As I understand it, this hearing is part of a larger investigation into the alleged removal of a contemporary from his own time?"

He nodded.

"Yes, Madam President."

"I believe any witnesses to be called are already present?"

"Yes, ma'am."

"To my left is the subject of this enquiry. Good afternoon. I understand you are not yet completely recovered from recent ill health. Are you quite comfortable?"

"Yes, thank you, Madam President."

"Colonel, you will remember the witness's state of health and adjust your questioning accordingly."

He stood.

"Ma'am, I intend . . ."

"I am sure you do, Colonel. I am simply warning you not to provide grounds for any subsequent appeals."

That shut him up.

"I am grateful, ma'am."

She picked up her pen and started writing again.

"You may begin."

Here we go.

"Madam President, this witness has shown herself to be hostile and uncooperative. I am advised that administering any kind of drug is contra-indicated and therefore, unless you have any objection, I intend to use the truth-cuff."

This bloody cuff again. I deliberately hadn't asked Ellis about it because I didn't want to know.

The unknown officer approached, carrying a box, from which he extracted a metal cuff, about six inches long, with an LED display built in. A number of lights flashed yellow.

"Please state the nature of this device for the record."

"Madam President, this is a truth-cuff. It cannot lie. In-built sensors monitor the body's reactions to questions asked. Untruthful answers will cause the lights to flash red. Prolonged untruthful answers will cause the cuff to react in such a way as to discourage any subsequent untruthful answers."

Bloody hell!

A stir ran around the room, but no one actually stood up and said, "You can't do this."

I resolved that should Leon ever return, he and I would be having a quiet word about this. For an hour or so. Possibly longer.

Colonel Albay rose. He had no papers in front of him. Clasping his hands behind his back, he turned to me.

My mind was all over the place. I needed to focus. Concentrate Maxwell. What are you going to say? Did I admit to not being from this world? Would that be enough to free those accused of this crime along with me? I doubted it and who would believe me, anyway?

Or did I try to convince them I was indeed Maxwell? What could that possibly gain?

I really, really wished I hadn't given up silence as an option. Then I looked at David Sands in the third row back, alive and unharmed, sitting between Schiller and Roberts, and didn't regret a thing. I'd think of something. A voice in the back of my mind told me I'd better make it quick, because he was off.

"Madam President, this is a simple matter. There are currently three people accused of assisting in the removal of a contemporary from his own timeline. A fourth has evaded custody and is not present today. However, if, as I suspect, this is Madeleine Maxwell, then she was the instigator and the person chiefly responsible."

"I understood Madeleine Maxwell was dead."

"I suspect that is not, in fact, the case. I believe I can prove this person is Dr. Maxwell. If that is so, then the court must hear her testimony."

"This is not a court, Colonel."

He made a dismissive gesture. It didn't matter. And he was right. Once he established my identity, we were all for the short walk and even shorter goodbye.

"Well, this seems an easy matter to resolve, Colonel. I assume DNA samples are available."

"They are, ma'am."

"And the result?"

He hesitated.

"Close. Very close."

"How close?"

"Very close."

"Close enough?"

He hesitated again.

"I ask again. Close enough?"

"The results are inconclusive."

"How so?"

"They neither prove nor disprove whether she is Madeleine Maxwell. The samples are not identical. They are, however, a very close match."

"Are you saying she is not quite Madeleine Maxwell?"

"I'm saying that she is and that somehow the samples have been tampered with and the results skewed just sufficiently to raise doubt."

Helen bristled angrily. I didn't give much for his chances if
he ever found himself alone with her.

"How can they have been skewed? Your own people verified the results."

"I don't know how—I just know they were."

"That is not good enough, Colonel."

"I am convinced, ma'am, that this woman standing here
today is Madeleine Maxwell. She was heard to admit it herself."

"Then prove it, Colonel, and stop wasting our time."

At a nod from Albay, his officer slipped the cuff over my
right forearm. He struggled to get it closed. The swelling had
not yet completely gone down. He tried to squeeze it shut and
it hurt. I laughed. Because I'm stupid, and antagonising someone already causing you pain is such a good idea.

She didn't even bother looking up.

"Use the other arm, Colonel."

"Ma'am, the results are more accurate . . ."

"Then wait until her arm is healed. I can adjourn the hearing."

He set his jaw and nodded.

The cuff slipped easily over the other arm. He clicked it
closed. It was very heavy. And very cold.

I'd like to say I had some sort of plan. That I'd thought
everything through thoroughly and come up with a carefully
crafted course of action that would ensure a successful outcome. Yes, I'd really like to be able to say that.

On the other hand, Mrs. Partridge had told me to wing it
and who was I to disobey?

Someone was talking to me.

"Sorry, miles away. Say that again."

He frowned and said sarcastically, "Should I speak up, perhaps?"

"No. No need. Sometimes I just don't listen."

Lights on the cuff glowed green. Someone laughed.

"I shall begin by asking you a few simple questions, the purpose of which is to calibrate the cuff."

I gestured airily. "Take your time. I'm quite comfortable."

There was some of muttering at the table. The unnamed officer made a few adjustments to his equipment and finally, off we went.

"Please could you answer this question untruthfully."

"My pleasure."

"How old are you?"

"One hundred and eight."

Rather worryingly, it took the red light a second or two to show.

"Thank you. What colour is your hair? Please answer truthfully.

"Flame-flecked auburn."

The red light flashed.

I sighed. "Ginger."

Green.

Madam President looked up. "The cuff appears to be working perfectly, Colonel. You may proceed."

I waited with trepidation, memories of my last interrogation still fresh in my mind.

He leaped straight in.

"Did you remove a contemporary while you were on assignment at Troy?"

Something snapped into place inside my head and I stopped feeling sorry for myself and concentrated. Suddenly, I thought I could see my way through all this. In the matter of identity, I was on very rocky ground, but in the matter of removing contemporaries, I could actually display a pure and shining innocence. Because, of course, I hadn't. It wasn't me. Suddenly, there was a possibility I could get the whole show over with right now. Today. Because, sure as eggs is eggs, I couldn't afford a trial. If I was drugged then

God knows what I might say. Here, today, I did at least have some control.

However, if I answered too easily, he might become suspicious. I needed to keep him focused on the removal of a contemporary and hope, in the excitement of the chase, he forgot about establishing exactly who I was. Piece of cake. I could still feel Mrs. Partridge's liquid fire coursing through my veins.

"Last warning, Colonel."

"I beg your pardon, ma'am. I merely wished to save the court some time."

"The hearing reminds you again that this is not a court."

"Very well. Your name, please."

I didn't want to get into a pissing contest with Colonel Albay, so I addressed my responses to Dr. Bairstow in the front row. As far as I was concerned, he was the one in charge here. And I could see that it annoyed the colonel, so no downside there.

"Maxwell."

We all looked at the green light.

He allowed the silence to become heavy. When I shifted my position slightly, I could feel my T-shirt drenched in sweat.

"Are you Madeleine Maxwell?"

"No."

Red. Pure, solid, unblinking red.

And three seconds later—a sharp pain. Not for long. Not savage. But it could be if I didn't start telling the truth.

I said, "Ow," and looked indignantly at the colonel. "That hurt."

"It was supposed to. Are you Madeleine Maxwell?"

I shook my head, thinking it might be safer. It wasn't. The pain was a little sharper this time. I couldn't prevent an indrawn hiss of breath. And these bastards had wanted to attach it to my damaged arm . . .

I looked across at Dr. Bairstow, whose face was of stone. "You torture people here?"

He said, with careful emphasis, "*We* don't, no."

"The witness will confine her remarks to the hearing," said Albay.

"The witness is pretty pissed off at the moment."

"The witness will remember this is a formal hearing."

"The witness is unlikely to be allowed to forget it."

"May we continue, please, Colonel."

"Of course, ma'am. You are Madeleine Maxwell?"

"No."

Red.

A short sharp jab. I could not help jumping in my seat. I was hanging on to my temper by a thread. I'd have his bollocks for this.

"Do you now or have you ever worked at St. Mary's."

"Yes."

Green.

There was, as they say, a sensation in the court.

"Might it not be easier, Colonel, to allow the witness to make a statement and then question her as to the contents. We appear to be going nowhere, at the moment."

I couldn't help glancing over at Dr. Bairstow whose face, suddenly, had a "welcome to my world" expression. He caught me looking and immediately rearranged his features.

I shifted position on my chair.

"My name is Maxwell. I was living in Rushford with the man known as Leon Farrell. One day, from nowhere, a group of armed men attacked us. They did not, at any point, identify themselves or offer any explanation. We escaped and ever since, we have been pursued by a group of incompetent thugs whose disregard for the safety of the timeline and the contemporaries therein has been breathtaking."

I took a deep breath. Irrepressible anger roiled inside me. I stood up and faced him, because you can't do this sort of thing sitting down.

"You fired a sonic weapon indiscriminately while standing on a frozen river. You cracked the ice, you morons. That you didn't cause the Great Frost Fair Catastrophe of 1683 was a miracle. There were hundreds of people on the ice. Men, women, children, and you put them all at risk. If they'd gone into the water, they would have died in seconds. You could have irrevocably changed History.

"And then again in Thebes. Your sonic vibrations woke up every crocodile within a radius of five miles. Don't you know that's how they communicate? You were fortunate everyone was at the festival. If the banks had been full of fishermen, families, people drawing water, people bathing, livestock drinking, there could have been massive loss of life that again would have been entirely due to your reckless irresponsibility."

I said nothing about Pompeii. There was no point getting Ellis into trouble.

"Ma'am, if asked my opinion, and I hope very much that one day I will be, I would say that the damage done by these officers as they ran riot up and down the timeline is far greater than the crime they are supposed to be investigating. A crime, I might add, that is vigorously denied by everyone charged, and for which no evidence exists outside of the imagination of the Time Police. Why have they not produced this contemporary? Where is she? Or he?"

I looked artistically around the Hall. "Oh! That's right! Not here! How strange! The one piece of evidence that would prove the case beyond a shadow of doubt and they can't produce it. Because it doesn't exist.

"Madam President, I would like the record to show that in my opinion, their behaviour has been appalling. Abominable. Unprofessional. Careless. Stupid. By seeking to punish those whom they consider responsible for a non-existent misdemeanour, they have rampaged through History, endangering the timeline and countless lives along with it. The Time Police are a disgrace, Madam President, and I call for them to suffer the strongest censure possible."

I fell back into my seat. Someone at the back started to clap and slowly, it was taken up around the Hall.

I tried not to show the satisfaction I was feeling. Because I could deny I was Maxwell until I was blue in the face and no one was ever going to believe me after an outburst like that.

At a gesture from Colonel Albay, members of the Time Police unshouldered their weapons and made their wishes clearly known. St. Mary's slowly subsided, but something had changed.

Colonel Albay stood, slightly flushed with what I hoped was triumph, his mouth set in a grim line. I hoped—I really hoped—that my outburst had given him all the ammunition he thought he needed to finish me.

I turned to look at Madam President. Who was still writing. I was battling for my life—and those of Guthrie, Peterson, and the Boss—and she was still writing. She turned her head, caught me looking. She said, quite calmly and with no inflexion whatsoever, "The witness will now tell the truth."

I nodded. The witness would indeed tell the truth. Because, finally—at long last—our Colonel Albay had allowed triumph to get the better of his judgement. He was about to make a mistake. He was some distance away, but even from here, I could feel his sudden excitement. He thought he had seen his way clear.

"Ma'am, I think it is obvious now to everyone in this room that this is Madeleine Maxwell. Her familiarity with St. Mary's and its functions make this very clear. They think that by claiming Madeleine Maxwell is dead and conveniently cremated that, somehow, they can escape the consequences of her actions, but I will not have it. Ma'am, I am prepared to state—on oath, if necessary—that this woman here today is Madeleine Maxwell."

"You are absolutely certain?"

"Yes, ma'am. I am. Without doubt, this is Madeleine Maxwell. This is the woman who, while on assignment to Troy, removed a contemporary from his own time. The penalty for which is death."

She turned to me. The silence was absolute. The only things moving were the dust particles, swirling in the sunlight shafting through the lantern.

I could feel the sweat running down my back. My arm throbbed. My chest throbbed. I had a splitting headache. I suspected Mrs. Partridge's witch's brew was wearing off. I was going to crash any minute now.

The witness had been told to tell the truth.

She said clearly, "Please state your name."

"Madeleine Maxwell."

Green.

No one moved.

"You will take some time to consider your answer to this question and you will answer truthfully. Did you, last year, while on assignment at Troy, remove anyone, anyone at all, from their own timeline?"

I held up the cuff where everyone could see it and let my voice ring around the Hall.

"No, I did not. My name is Madeleine Maxwell. I was Chief Operations Officer at St. Mary's and I have never, ever removed anyone from their own time."

Green. Right across the board. Every light showed green.

A huge cheer rang out.

She waited for the noise to subside.

"Has anyone, to your knowledge, ever removed a contemporary from their timeline?"

Shit. She'd asked the wrong question. Because in my world, yes, Leon had done that very thing. Was I, at this late stage, going to blow everything?

I took a deep breath and held up the cuff again. My head was pounding. "To my sure and certain knowledge, no one present today has ever witnessed me removing a contemporary from their timeline."

This wasn't quite what she had asked, but no one seemed to notice.

The cuff showed green and another cheer rang out.

"Have Major Guthrie or Dr. Peterson ever assisted with, or connived at, or been involved in any way with the removal of a contemporary from their own timeline?"

Shit! Shit, shit, shit! How to put this?

"Neither Major Guthrie nor Dr. Peterson have ever assisted me in the removal of a contemporary from their own timeline."

Green. Eventually. No one seemed to notice the delay. Don't ask about Leon. Don't ask about Leon. Don't ask about Leon.

"To your knowledge, has Chief Farrell ever assisted, or connived at, or been involved in any way with the removal of a contemporary from their own timeline?"

And the answer to that, of course, was yes.

Think, Maxwell.

"To save time, Madam President, I state here and now—not only have I have never removed anyone from their own timeline, but no one from this unit has ever assisted me, or connived with me, or been involved in any way with me doing so."

A bit convoluted, but the cuff got the gist.

Green.

The noise was immense.

Colonel Albay stood amongst the chaos, head bent in thought.

She stood up and silence fell.

"This hearing is concluded. The witness is released."

He was bewildered. "Madam President? No. There are charges to answer."

"Colonel, there are no charges to answer. You clearly stated you believed this witness to be Dr. Madeleine Maxwell. And she has admitted she is. You believed this witness to have committed a capital offense, and sought to bring her to justice. You charged three colleagues and the current Director with complicity. She has clearly established her innocence. And if she is innocent then so are her colleagues. The cuff does not lie, Colonel Albay. You said so yourself. Clearly, a mistake has been made. I proffer my apologies to those involved. This hearing is concluded."

"No," he said furiously. "I know that this crime did take place. I don't know how they've done it, Madam President, but we have been deceived. I insist this matter be pursued."

"Colonel, you can't keep charging people with the same crime until they give up and plead guilty. It's not lawful."

"Nevertheless, ma'am, I insist."

He turned to me. "If you are so innocent, why did you run?"

"We ran from whatever you were going to do to us. You didn't identify yourselves. You could have been anyone. We just saw men with guns, firing wildly in all directions and causing chaos wherever they went."

"You could have spoken. In Sick Bay—you could have explained."

"Too sick to speak," said Dr. Foster, shouldering her way through the crowd. "I did tell you. On several occasions. You wouldn't listen."

He kept looking around. He'd been had. He knew he'd been had. He just didn't know how.

"Give it up, Colonel. Someone here . . ." and I did not look at Barclay, "has used you for their own ends. You've been deceived. You should concentrate your efforts on finding the person responsible for wasting your time."

I paused, in case he wanted to take this opportunity to shoot Barclay, but sadly, no.

Albay wasn't going down without a fight. "We are the Time Police and you are subject to . . ."

Dr. Bairstow intervened.

"The Time Police have shown themselves to be easily manipulated, reckless in their actions, and careless of the consequences. They have destroyed any credibility they had within this organisation. The consequences are about to be serious. Madam President, if you would, please . . ."

She stood in front of the hearing. Every eye was on her.

"Seven Directors of St. Mary's established the Time Police and according to the charter it will take seven Directors to disestablish them. Since the death of Dr. Maxwell, St. Mary's has not been able to assemble seven Directors, but now that you have stated—clearly and before witnesses—that this is, beyond doubt, Madeleine Maxwell, the problem is solved."

Wheels within wheels. This wasn't about me. It wasn't even about Helios. It was all about the dissolution of the Time Police. Mrs. Partridge wasn't the only person using me for her own ends.

"Are you Madeleine Maxwell?"

"Yes," I said, wearily. "I am."

"The cuff shows she is telling the truth. The cuff you yourself introduced, Colonel."

Always be wary of people who go white with rage. It's never a good sign. He was white now. "I will not allow it. I will not allow these criminals to escape punishment. The Time Police . . ."

"Are finished." She flourished her papers. "This document is the new Charter. You will be signed out of existence as soon as we can assemble all seven Directors."

"You don't have—and will never have—seven Directors in one place. It will never happen. And while you inch your way towards failure, I have a job to do here. The prisoners will be removed for a more thorough investigation. Sergeant, take them to the pods."

It wasn't over yet. I tensed my tired muscles. I don't know what on earth I thought I was going to do.

From the corner of my eye, I saw Markham give a signal and our own Security team stepped up. And they weren't the only ones. All of St. Mary's stood up.

Colonel Albay smiled unpleasantly. "You are all unarmed."

Dr. Bairstow's smile was even more unpleasant. "How little you know my unit."

All around the Hall, people produced their own private arsenals. The Security team had Tasers. Mrs. Mack flourished her battle ladle. I reached up for my hair pins. One of those in each eye would slow anyone down. As the saying goes—it's not much, but it's the thought that counts.

Dr. Bairstow's voice cracked like a whip. "Leave my unit and take your thugs with you."

For a second . . . it all hung in the balance. They were outnumbered but they were armed. Would they make a fight of it? If they did, people would die.

Softly, into the silence, Madam President said, "It's over, Colonel. Accept you have overstepped your authority. Go while you can."

"It is not over. I will fight this. You will, all of you, be brought to account."

"Colonel, there was never anything here. You have searched—thoroughly—and found nothing. It seems obvious that you have acted on information that was not only incorrect, but also personally motivated. There will certainly be an investigation into its source. You have allowed yourself to be used. You overstepped your remit. Accept it and move on."

He looked around the Hall. I knew who he was looking for. I may not have looked good, but I bet I didn't look half as sick as Isabella Barclay.

He said quietly, "We'll be back," and it wasn't clear to which of us he was speaking.

TWELVE

ONCE, I WOULD HAVE celebrated in the bar, just like everyone else. I would possibly have had a drink or six, probably exchanged a great deal of less-than-witty but very noisy banter with my colleagues, and almost certainly would have had to be helped to bed later. We would have woken the next morning, partaken of a very gentle breakfast, and then got on with the day.

Now, however, with blurred vision and legs that would hardly support me, I made for my bed. I just had enough strength to pull the foot of the bed across the door to deter any nocturnal visitors and fell sound asleep.

I woke well into the next day, enjoyed a careful shower, and headed for breakfast. Or lunch—I'm quite flexible about what I call my meals.

I made myself a pot of tea, picked up an egg and bacon buttie, and made my way to the same table as yesterday. Someone had left a copy of the local paper, folded back to display a report of a road traffic accident two days before, on the Rushford by-pass. Apparently, it was a miracle that no one had been seriously injured.

Someone had scribbled something underneath.
Knock-knock.

Who's there?
Ivanna.
Ivanna who?
Ivanna say thank you . . .
I stroked the page and smiled.

AFTER I'D EATEN, AND somewhat curious to see what would happen next, I wandered into the library. I was pretty sure Dr. Bairstow would want to see me sooner or later. My plan was to return to Rushford. I had concerns for Leon's flat and workshop after the Time Police had rampaged through everything. I just hoped Dr. Bairstow would lend me half a crown for the bus fare.

The library was deserted this morning. Judging from the distant thunder, all the historians were working in the Hall. Dr. Dowson bustled in and out, giving me a cheery wave every now and then. It was all very peaceful and pleasant.

I was staring out of the window, wondering what would become of me and not thinking about Leon in any way, when Miss Lee turned up and announced that Dr. Bairstow would like to see me. Her tone led me to believe it was a toss-up between me and leprosy and I'd won by only the narrowest majority.

I followed her to Dr. Bairstow's office.

He greeted me politely but neutrally, and we sat down.

"You look a little pale this morning, Dr. Maxwell. Are you feeling quite well after yesterday?"

"Yes, very well, thank you. A little tired, but nothing to speak of."

He realigned the files on his desk. I decided to take the initiative.

"I'm really very grateful for your hospitality, Dr. Bairstow, but I think I should return to Rushford as soon as possible. I'm anxious about Leon's flat."

"I don't think that would be a wise move, Dr. Maxwell. I'm certain we haven't seen the last of them and, thanks to their efforts, your flat is not, at this moment, habitable. I'm sorry."

I sat, dismayed. So just to recap, no home, no possessions, no identity, no job, no money, no Leon . . . Normal people reaching my age have usually acquired houses, mortgages, jobs, cars, families, pets—I had nothing. I had even less than I started with all those years ago. I didn't even own the clothes I was currently sitting in.

"I have a proposal for you, instead. We recently received an assignment I think might interest you. 14th-century London. Southwark, to be precise. The Tabard Inn. An in-depth investigation into medieval pilgrims journeying to Canterbury. You might even catch a sight of Chaucer himself. You and Dr. Peterson. Would you be interested?"

I smiled. "This is a test, isn't it? After I shot my mouth off in the dining-room the other day. You want me to put my money where my mouth is."

"If you wouldn't mind, yes."

"And will I come back?"

"I'm sorry, I don't understand."

But he did. He knew exactly what I was saying.

"Well, it's all over now, isn't it? Everyone's pretty well off the hook. And if you can get rid of me then even if they do come back, their star suspect is dead in an unfortunate accident in the 14th century. How sad. Still, probably a blessing in disguise, don't you think? Of course, Leon will take it badly, but he must be getting used to it by now."

Oh my God, did I just say that? I wondered if, perhaps, I was becoming a little unhinged.

Time ticked on. As it does. I could hear a motor mower outside. That would be Mr. Strong giving the South Lawn a Brazilian. The lovely smell of fresh-cut grass floated in through the window and still we stared at each other. It crossed my mind again that I really should have died at Agincourt.

"I am sorry you feel that way. It has not been my intention ..." He stopped. "Perhaps it is time we all put our cards on the table. As a mark of good faith, I shall go first. You are obviously aware of the Time Police and their function. Leon will have told you. You will know that Leon and I are from the future. That we were sent back to set up and then oversee St. Mary's. To keep it safe."

I nodded.

"The Time Police are formed a long time in the future. To combat a very real threat. They presented themselves at various incarnations of St. Mary's, all of whom voluntarily signed the Charter. We did not, initially, foresee any problem with them. Then. But when the threat disappeared, the Time Police did not. And then they became the threat. You know all this, I believe?"

I nodded again.

"I have sent Leon to visit every incarnation of St. Mary's. It is difficult and it is dangerous. I don't know for how long he will be gone. His mission is to persuade every Director to reject the presence of the Time Police in their unit. Even to foster rebellion if he has to. I hope that, up and down the timeline, the Time Police are being evicted from every St. Mary's even as we speak. Some will be easier than others, of course. And by now he will have a price on his head."

He hadn't left me. He hadn't run away and left me. The dreadful black fear living inside me, the one I hadn't acknowledged, even to myself, shrivelled and died. For a moment, just for a moment, my heart soared. And then crashed back to earth again.

He stared out of the window.

"It is very possible he will not return."

"He might already be dead?"

"He might be, yes."

"And we'll never know."

"If the Time Police ever do return here, then we will know that he failed. We will be preparing for that event. In the meantime, after discussion with my senior staff, we are all of the opinion that you might, for a while, be safer in the 14th century than here at St. Mary's. However, this is a genuine assignment with a genuine purpose. I hope very much that you will accept it."

Outside, the motor mower roared past again. We were talking about Leon dying and the end of St. Mary's and outside, life carried on as normal.

It was my turn to speak.

"My name really is Madeleine Maxwell, but I'm not your Madeleine Maxwell. I really did work at St. Mary's, but not your St. Mary's. I was appointed Deputy Director and chose Agincourt for my last jump. It all went wrong and I received a fatal chest wound, as I'm sure Dr. Foster has reported. I fell and when I opened my eyes, I was bleeding on Leon's carpet, in Rushford."

My voice wobbled and to my horror, I found I was going to cry in front of Dr. Bairstow. I struggled on. "I don't know why I'm here. Or how I got here. I don't know what's going on. I . . ."

My voice died away. I could not continue, but he was Dr. Bairstow and Dr. Bairstow always understood.

"You are here, alone, in a place that's both familiar and hostile at the same time. You have been running for your life. You are exhausted and hurt. You did not get a chance to say goodbye to Leon and you've just learned that you may never see him again. I can only imagine how very isolated and afraid you must feel at this moment. Please allow me to assist you."

He handed me a box of tissues and tactfully retired to the window while I disgraced myself.

Fifteen minutes later, I accepted the assignment.

THERE'S NOTHING GOOD ABOUT the 14th century. It opens with the Battle of Bannockburn, Edward II's humiliating defeat at the hands of the Scots. After a disastrous reign, he was overthrown by his wife. Serves him right. What sort of idiot marries a woman known as The She-Wolf of France?

The country was right in the middle of the Hundred Years' War with France. As usual, England had started well and then failed to follow through. Edward III dissolved into senility. His grandson, the erratic Richard II, embarked on a long minority rule and was eventually overthrown. The century closed with his imprisonment and murder.

In the middle of all this, the country suffered repeated occurrences of the Black Death, which resulted in over 20 million deaths throughout Europe. A third of the population died. Whole villages were wiped out by the plague and were lost from all knowledge until the arrival of aerial photography revealed their sad outlines under the soil.

The huge decrease in population meant there weren't enough people to work the land, no matter how much they were paid. The price of bread rocketed and more riots broke out. Unable to stand the strain, the feudal system began to crumble. Peasants defied their lords and left the lands worked by their forefathers or commuted their labour for money. The faint beginnings of tenant farmers were born.

This social upheaval led to the Peasants' Revolt and Wat Tyler. A feeling that God had abandoned them contributed to religious turmoil. Even the weather was dire.

It was definitely not a good time to be alive.

Guess where we were going?

I WAS KITTED OUT in Wardrobe. They gave me a long, linen shift with loose sleeves, a thick, brown woollen dress, with another lighter and shorter surcoat to be worn over the top. I eased my feet into soft leather shoes. There was none of the usual banter.

Mrs. Enderby handed me a square of linen and they all watched in silence to see what I would do with it.

I sighed. Everything was a test.

I'd already plaited my hair and pinned it up. I twisted the square and tied it tightly around my hair, tucking in the ends. No mirror and all achieved in about five seconds flat.

Normally, I'd be squirreling away the traditional historian's arsenal of stun gun and pepper, but not on this assignment. I shrugged my shoulders a couple of times to let everything settle, walked a few paces to check the shoes were comfortable, tied a battered leather scrip to my belt, checked myself in the mirror by the door, said, "Thank you, everyone," as I always did, and left them to make what they could of that.

Peterson met me outside Pod Three. He also wore brown. He carried a cloak, a staff, and a wide-brimmed pilgrim's hat.

I looked up at the gantry. A row of silent people stared down at us. There were no insults, no unhelpful advice, and no jokes that were only funny if you worked at St. Mary's.

We looked at each other in silence. I would not allow myself to think of the last time Tim Peterson and I went out together.

He folded his cloak over his arm.

"Anything I should know?"

"Such as?"

"Well, which language will we be speaking?"

Sometimes, I'm my own worst enemy.

"Oh, that's easy. At street level, it's Middle English. The clergy speak Latin. Your social superiors will speak Middle French. Remember that most words have a final e, which you should pronounce if the following word begins with a consonant. Except when that consonant is h, w, or y, of course. If the following word begins with a vowel, then that e is silent. Every letter in a word should be pronounced. If in any doubt, remember the ph in banana is always silent. Any questions?"

Dieter broke a fairly unfriendly silence by telling us to get a move on.

"In your own time," said Peterson, indicating the console and stowing his gear.

I was strongly reminded of my first assignment, when we'd jumped to London, to Westminster Abbey. On that occasion, I'd done everything while he apparently fell asleep. This felt very similar, although I was prepared to bet he wouldn't be taking his eyes off me this time.

This was just as much a test, but I wouldn't let him rush me. I sat slowly at the console and scanned the read-outs. Everything seemed more or less in the right place. I flicked a few switches and nothing blew up.

Dieter handed me the coordinates and taking my time, I laid them in. They both watched my every move. The silence was unnerving. When I'd finished, I sat back and let them check it over.

They looked at each other and nodded.

"You can't initiate the jump," said Peterson. "You're not authorised for this pod. Or any pod. So you'd better make damn sure nothing happens to me, because, if I'm dead, you won't even be able to get back inside again. Remember that."

I refused to be intimidated. "The last time I went out with you, you nearly lost an arm. Try to take a little more care this time. It took ages to wash your blood out of my hair."

I like to think that shut him up for a bit.

Dieter scowled at us both impartially and left.

"Computer—initiate jump."

The world went white.

Southwark. A red-light district. Over the river from London. Home of thieves, rogues, actors, prostitutes, and politicians. And now, historians. Yep—all low life was here.

We parked somewhere in the triangle between the Gryne Dragon, St. Savyor's Church, and The Bolles Hede, strolled through Chayne Gate and out into the heaving High Street.

And heaving it was.

Peterson stood stock-still like a trainee, so it was obviously up to me.

I said sourly, "You should have brought a clipboard," and drew him back against a wall so we could get our bearings.

To our left, the High Street led to London Bridge. The year was 1383. Exactly three hundred years in the future, I would be just a couple of hundred yards upstream, dodging Time Police, and freezing my arse off. Today, however, was summer. The sun streamed down from a cloudless sky. This might actually be quite a pleasant assignment.

To my right, the road widened and became St. Margaret's Hill. Directly in front of me stood the pillory. Mercifully empty. On the other hand, of course, that left plenty of room for an erring historian.

The market was just a little way up the road. People pushed past us, laden with baskets of produce. Two men pulled a hand-cart filled with cow's heads and hooves. A cloud of flies hovered above them. Just a little way off, a man was extolling the virtues of his cooking pots at the top of his voice and vigorously banging one with a wooden spoon, just in case anyone was in any doubt. Coils of rope lay on the ground outside a chandler's, neatly stacked for inspection. A chicken ran past, squawking madly, closely pursued by two laughing children.

The road was thick with dust, scraps of vegetables, and dung—animal and human. A pack of dogs squabbled over something purple and wobbly that had been tossed into the gutter.

The smell was—robust.

This was the Dover road, running south through Canterbury, so it would have been busy, anyway. And it was market day. Add in the hundreds of people setting off for, and returning from, their pilgrimage to the tomb of St. Thomas; thirsty sailors on leave from their ships anchored not so far away;

young bloods in search of a good time and finding it in the many inns and taverns lining the road; ladies who probably charged by the minute—it was just chaos. Every now and then, a group of drinkers would lurch from one of the many hostelries and stagger through the crowds, singing and shouting and making things even worse.

You couldn't hear yourself speak. You couldn't even hear yourself think. People shrieked in each other's faces. Livestock bellowed, bayed, and clucked at the top of their voices. Somewhere, I could hear the ring of an anvil. A horse neighed and another answered.

The Tabard, favoured starting place for the pilgrimage to Canterbury, was up the road and on the left.

I pointed and mouthed, "This way," to Peterson, who nodded, and we set off.

We never reached The Tabard.

We never did see Geoffrey Chaucer.

Peterson and I had a major argument in the middle of the street and then he got the plague.

Apart from that, the assignment was a huge success.

He caught my arm.

"Just one warning. I meant what I said about access to the pod. You don't have any. So if you had any thoughts of making a run for it and abandoning me here, forget them."

I was so fed up with this. "What a coincidence—I was about to say the same to you."

"What?"

"Well, isn't that why I'm here? Oh, I acquit you of outright murder—you're not actually going to kill me, are you? But in a minute, I'll look round and you'll be gone and I'll go back to the pod and that'll be gone too, and when Leon turns up you'll all look sad and tell him there was a tragic accident. Isn't that the plan? There's really not much to choose between you and the Time Police, is there?"

I have no idea what thoughts ran through his head. His face showed nothing. However, the strength of his grip on my arm told its own story. He pushed me back against the wall, and right in the middle of an assignment, before we'd got our bearings, when we were at our most vulnerable, and with most of the 14th century cursing as they tried to get past us, we had it out. There and then.

"What's that supposed to mean?"

Words fell from my mouth. All the things I never meant to say. All the things that should not be said.

"Weren't those your instructions? A tidy end to an untidy problem. And no blood shed. Let's face it, if you walked away from me now, there wouldn't be anything I could do about it, would there? I don't understand why you didn't save yourself the effort and just open the door and throw me out."

I didn't actually believe any of it, but I was so fed up with all of this. This was Tim Peterson, for crying out loud. I had a sudden, aching vision of the last time I saw him . . .

"Is that what you think? You think that I would . . . ? You're not Maxwell. I don't care what you say. She would never think . . . never believe . . ."

I knocked his arm away.

"Well, there you go then. I'm not Maxwell. Happy now? Just walk away, Peterson. Go on. Look, I'll even turn my back and make it easy for you. Don't worry—I'm not tagged. No one will ever find me. You can tell whatever story you like."

I turned and walked away, so buoyed up with rage that I had no idea where I was going. I shouldered my way through the crowds, back the way we'd come, until I suddenly realised that instinctively I was heading towards the pod. Without thinking, I wheeled right and found myself in a narrow alleyway running between two inns.

Suddenly, the street noises disappeared. This place never saw the sun. It was cooler here and the stones were damp.

Green patches showed on the walls, even in the height of summer. I could hear my own footsteps. I felt very much alone.

What the hell was I doing? Of all the stupid, irresponsible . . .

I wheeled about and trotted back down the alleyway, hoping at every moment to catch a glimpse of Peterson. He was tall enough to show above the crowd. Especially in that hat. I gazed up and down the High Street. Surely, he'd be around somewhere. He hadn't really gone back to the pod and left me. I was the stupid one, not him.

There he was. I caught a brief glimpse of him, conspicuous in his pilgrim's hat, exiting The King's Head. Wisely, since he was looking for an historian, he was starting with places purveying alcoholic refreshments. I could see him staring anxiously up and down the street. I shouted his name, but my words were lost amongst the day-to-day noises of 14th-century Southwark.

I had some difficulty getting across the street, but eventually emerged, breathless and tousled on the other side, and headed down a passageway after him.

It all happened so quickly.

I opened my mouth to call his name. Two figures stepped out of the shadows. One raised a cudgel. There was a sickening noise and Peterson went down like a tree. They bent over him.

I shouted, "Hey," and went down that alleyway like a rocket. If they'd stood their ground there would have been two of us unconscious, but they didn't. They grabbed his scrip—much good it would do them, being as empty as mine—and ran off.

I hurled myself to my knees beside him, terrified of what I might find, praying desperately to the god of historians that he wasn't dead. That he couldn't be dead. Not Tim Peterson. I think it's to my credit that my first thoughts were for him. It was only much later I realised what a problem I would have had if he had been dead.

He wasn't.

Not yet, anyway. He had a lump on the back of his head, but when I probed gently, nothing moved. His skull was intact. However, his face was white and his breathing ragged and heavy. I tried not to panic. Raising my voice, I shouted for help. And again. And again.

I don't know why I did that. Surely, no one was ever going to hear over the clamour of the street, but someone did hear. A small figure clutching a basket of greens appeared at the other end of the alley.

I picked up Peterson's staff and stood up, ready for anything, but it wasn't needed.

A shabby Augustinian monk, with the sad remnants of a soft, brown tonsure and an even sadder, softer, brown face, put down his basket and knelt to take a look.

He probed the wound, as I had done, listened to his breathing, as I had done, and then stood up.

"My child, can you understand me?"

He spoke in heavily accented English that I could barely make out. I had an idea.

I said, in Latin, "Yes, brother. I beseech you for aid."

If he was surprised, he hid it well. "Wait here. I will return. Do not worry—they will not come back."

I gripped my staff. "They had better not."

He scurried away, leaving his basket behind.

I made sure Peterson's airways were clear and checked him over for any further injuries. I'd only seen the one blow, but he might have broken an arm or collarbone as he fell.

The monk turned up only a few minutes later, pulling a flat handcart, and together we lifted Peterson onto it. He pulled—I pushed. We trundled down the alley, emerging seconds later into a wide sunny space, at the end of which was what looked like a church.

I felt a sudden excitement. I knew what this was. This was the famous St. Thomas's Hospital, named for Thomas Becket.

It would be clean and safe. Just for once, we had fallen, figuratively speaking, on our feet.

No we hadn't.

It's hard for us today to understand the importance of religion to the medieval mind. Doubly so for heathens like me. I never gave it a thought.

They wouldn't let him in.

They were very nice about it and I was reassured that as soon as he was able to confess, he would be admitted immediately.

In vain did I recklessly commit Peterson to the Catholic faith and promise he would confess as soon as he was actually conscious. In the same way that a modern hospital fears the contamination of superbugs, so did medieval hospitals fear the contamination of sin. In their world, the body and the soul were linked, with the soul taking precedence. Cleanse the soul and the body would follow. The first step was confession. They were very sorry, but they couldn't take him in until he confessed. I begged and pleaded. I even cried a little. They were sympathetic but unmoveable. And while all this was going on, Peterson lay white-faced on the handcart and never moved.

I was frantic. What could I do with him? I had nowhere to take him. There were no relatives who could render assistance. I couldn't even get him back to the pod because it wouldn't let me in. I'd be stuck outside with an unconscious man on my hands and trust me, when night fell, this would not be a good place for either of us to be. And jolting him around in a handcart wouldn't do him any good, either.

The little plump monk found an acceptable compromise.

There was an old shed behind the kitchen gardens, empty at present. He would bring a mattress and blankets. There was a well. He would see some food was sent over.

Everyone breathed a sigh of relief. I wiped my nose on my sleeve and we bumped Peterson through rows of beans and peas to an old wooden shack next to three magnificent compost heaps.

The little monk was as good as his word. We laid Peterson out on an old straw palliasse and covered him with coarse brown blankets.

He lay like the dead. I tried not to panic.

The little monk smiled at me.

"I am Brother Anselm, child. What is your name?"

If in doubt, always take the name of the ruling king or queen. The year was 1383. Edward III was king and his wife had been Philippa of Hainault.

"I am Philippa. Philippa of Rushford. This is my husband, Thomas."

He smiled. "A fortunate name. Fear not, he will be admitted as soon as he wakes, which will be soon, I am sure. Rest and quiet are all he needs for the present. There is a well, over there, by the wall. I will return after Vespers, when, I am sure, with God's help, he will be waking."

I nodded.

"Thank you, brother."

"Do not thank me, child. Thank God who saw your need and guided my steps to you."

"I will, brother."

Left alone, I took Peterson's pulse, checked his breathing, tucked the blankets around him, and sat in the open doorway, looking out to the big, grey stone building across the kitchen garden.

This was the famous St. Thomas's Hospital, named after the martyr, Thomas Becket, who was murdered in Canterbury Cathedral more than two hundred years ago. And I should know—I was there. And so was Peterson.

If I could have got him into the hospital, he would have had a bed, clean linen, good food, and a safe place until he regained consciousness. Instead, he was lying on the ground in someone's garden shed which smelled of earth, dung, and wet sacks, and there would probably be rats.

He hadn't moved at all. Or made a sound. I checked him again, but there was nothing I could do except wait for him to regain consciousness.

The afternoon shadows lengthened. The hour of Vespers was upon us. Through the open door, I could hear the chanting, drifting across the garden in the late afternoon sunshine.

I thought he might send a servant, or a sister, but Brother Anselm came himself, bearing a bowl of thick vegetable broth and a heel of bread. I ate while he examined Peterson again.

"Has he moved at all?"

"A little. About an hour ago. And his breathing is better."

"Yes, it is. Tomorrow, I will bring a poultice. He may well be awake by then."

"With God's good will," I said, getting into the swing of things.

"Indeed."

He sat himself down on the dirt floor, and looked at me. I hoped he was only waiting for the bowl back, but I knew he was curious. Like a bird. Indeed, his bright eyes, coupled with his habit of asking a question and then waiting for the answer with his head on one side reminded me of a small, brown sparrow, except he was clothed in shabby Augustinian black. He smelled strongly of musty cloth, earth, and incense.

"You speak in Latin, my child?"

I nodded, and taking care to make a few simple mistakes, said. "My father had dealings with the monks of the Great Hospital in Norwich. He taught me so that I was able to assist him when my brother died. And after my father died, I helped my husband."

"Ah. You can read, then?"

I shook my head. I wasn't going to be dragged into the deep waters of women's education. "But," I said, proudly, "I can write my name."

"Why that is excellent, my child. Your husband—he is a pilgrim?"

"Yes." I mopped up the broth and swallowed the last of the bread. "He will journey to the shrine of St. Thomas to ask him to intercede for us. These last years have not been good for us. Always, the plague comes back."

"It does indeed, child. But God and the saints hear every prayer. Place your trust in them and all will be well."

I nodded, vigorously. His simple faith shone from him like a beacon and, for a moment, even I believed all would be well.

"You will be safe here, tonight. The gates are locked at dusk. No one will approach. I will come back tomorrow, at Lauds, when, no doubt, your husband will be awake. I must caution you, however, it will be some time before he will be well enough for his pilgrimage. You would do better to return to Rushford and wait until he is recovered."

"I understand, brother. I thank you for the food and shelter. And God, of course," I added.

"Amen," he said, and went away.

I ALWAYS THINK THAT being an historian is very similar to asking Rosie Lee to do something. Both are examples of optimism triumphing over bitter experience. I settled down for the night in reasonable comfort, content to lie alongside Peterson in the pungent darkness, and savour the peace, grateful for the opportunity to mull over the chaos, confusion, and catastrophe that was my life at the moment.

It didn't last.

For the first hour, all was well, but as the moon sailed across the sky, and owls hooted nearby, he grew more restless. To begin with, it was nothing more than a break in his breathing. Then it happened again. I sat up and listened to his breathing growing uneven and ragged. I touched his forehead and he was hot. I removed the blankets and bathed his face with water I'd drawn from the well. I wrapped his forehead in a damp cloth. Nothing worked, and as dawn approached, he grew worse. I know that fevers are always worse as the sun rises and sets and I was hoping his would disappear with the new day. That he would open his eyes, have a bit of a curse, sleep for a while, and then, with luck, be well enough to let me guide him back to the pod and to safety at St. Mary's.

Like most of my plans, it didn't work out that way at all.

As the sun rose, I got a better look at him. He was flushed with fever and muttering to himself. I thought I would wash his face and hands in cool water, to try to make him more comfortable and that was when I saw them. Around his left wrist and a little way up his forearm—small, red fleabites.

I stared, aghast.

That bloody mattress! That bloody, bloody straw mattress! Home to every form of insect wildlife going, especially fleas. And this close to the river—infected fleas. Bound to be. Infected fleas from infected rats. How could I be so bloody stupid? Why hadn't I chucked that stupid mattress out of the door as soon as their backs were turned? And the sodding blankets, too.

Peterson would have been bitten half to death in the night. What were the chances he would get the plague? Stop panicking, Maxwell, and think clearly.

He would be up to date with all his vaccinations. At St. Mary's, rarely a month goes by without them sticking us with something. Bubonic plague was not so threatening to the modern world, although every year a small number of people did still die of it. Antibiotics usually sorted it out and we had antibiotics. Stacks of them. In the bloody pod. Which I couldn't access.

Calm down. He was a fit, healthy, reasonably normal modern man, strong enough to overcome infection. No, he wasn't. He was a man with a head wound and a fever.

Stop that. These fleas might not be infected. Yes, they were. This was the 14th century. The plague was everyone's constant companion. And this was a hospital. There was a more than good chance that someone plaguey had already died on this very mattress. Not understanding the causes of infection, they would just use it for the next patient, which was Peterson.

Well, there were things I could do.

I rolled Peterson over and pulled the mattress out from underneath him. I took it outside and dropped it a good long way off.

I undressed him, right down to his shorts, took his clothes outside, and shook them vigorously, and then checked him all over. He had more bites around his ankles. Struck by a sudden thought, I checked myself. Yep. Two or three around my right ankle. Don't scratch, Maxwell.

I went over every inch of him—and I do mean every inch, checking his body for those small, deadly signs of plague—the sinister black marks of gangrene that gave the Black Death its name.

Finding nothing, I sat back on my heels with a sigh of relief. No gangrene, no skin lesions of any kind, and, most importantly, no signs of swelling in his armpits or groin. This might be just a simple fever associated with a blow to the head. We might be that lucky.

I'd just talked myself into this state of completely unjustified optimism when Peterson awoke.

He opened unfocused eyes, blinked, and closed them again.

I sat quietly and a few minutes later, he opened them again. This time, they stayed open. I said quietly, "Hey."

He made a sound.

I dipped my fingers in the water and gently touched his lips. He licked the water, thirstily. His eyes wandered around the little shed, rested on me a moment, and then closed again, but I was satisfied. He'd woken up.

Brother Anselm would be here soon. I went to the door to wait for him, looking out over the green gardens. The air smelled of recently turned earth. Rows of onions, peas, and beans ran from left to right. Here and there, I could see a bent, black back hoeing slowly in the sunshine. Away to the left, two lines of washing flapped gently in the sunlight. Three sisters were laying mattresses out to air in the sun because they genuinely believed that cleanliness was next to godliness. Everyone here was fulfilling their purpose in an atmosphere of calm tranquillity. Even the little brown sparrows, hopping over the freshly turned earth, sang sweetly. The monks had done their best to recreate the world they believed God had intended for us. I could see the attraction of spending the next few days here in perfect safety, but I couldn't leave Peterson untreated. If he woke again and could be safely moved, then by this time tomorrow, I could have him back at St. Mary's.

I sat in the sunshine and fretted.

THIRTEEN

*I*T CAME ON UNBELIEVABLY quickly. I'd read reports of people who were going about their business in the morning and were dead by tea-time. People dropped in the streets and died where they fell. Most people died within twenty-four hours. With the plague, the longer you survived, the longer you were likely to survive.

I don't know how long I'd been sitting there when I heard a sound behind me, and turned from the tranquil scene to confront something from my worst nightmares.

Peterson lay, tossing and turning, red with heat and sweat. His hair was plastered to his head. His entire body shook with fever. His arms and legs flailed wildly. He seemed to have no control over them and it was plain to see that every movement caused him great pain. Every time I covered him with the blankets, he threw them off again, becoming increasingly violent with every minute. His eyes were open, but jerking wildly from side to side. He had no idea who I was. I don't think he even saw me.

Our luck had run out.

With a wildly beating heart, I checked each of his armpits. They were clear. No swellings of any kind.

Then I checked his groin. And there it was. In the crease at the top of his leg. The bubo. Still quite small, but already it looked tight and angry.

My heart stopped. I felt the world recede. Oh God, Peterson had bubonic plague. The Black Death. The one that swept across Europe, killing almost everyone in its path. The plague had arrived in England around 1348, liked what it saw, and wouldn't leave for hundreds of years.

A sound at the door made me turn. Brother Anselm stood there, dark against the sun.

I stood up and held out my hands, palms towards him. "Do not enter, brother," I said, quickly. "You must not come in."

He ignored me, stepping forward for a closer look, his experienced eyes taking it all in. He said quietly, "How long?"

"About an hour."

I could see the pity in his eyes.

"You must pray for him, my child."

I nodded. I would. It would probably be more effective than forcing him to drink his own urine or cutting live pigeons in half and tying them to the infected parts of his body. I was cold with fear because in this world, the cures were as horrific as the diseases and I was helpless. I couldn't do a single thing for him.

I pulled myself together. Yes, I could. There's always something you can do. Even if it was just ensuring everyone stayed away from him. That should give him a fighting chance.

"Brother, you should go. You can do nothing. God will decide what happens here."

I was right, but he still hesitated in the doorway. He was a good man.

"You understand, I must close the door."

"I understand."

"And lock the door."

"I understand."

I was on my own. They wouldn't take him into the hospital now.

"I will come every day."

He would. I knew instinctively that he would.

"I will pray for his soul."

"Thank you."

"And yours."

Well, about time someone did.

"Thank you, brother."

He stepped back and pulled the door to behind him. I heard the bar being pulled across.

I was on my own.

The little shed was pleasantly dim. Enough sunlight filtered through the rough plank walls to give a reasonable light. Chinks of light shone through the roof. If it rained, I would have a problem.

I studied my resources. A few gardening implements leaned against one wall. Piles of empty sacks were stacked in one corner, together with some lengths of twine that had been rolled into a big ball. Peterson's discarded clothing, neatly folded, lay nearby. I had his two blankets, his boots and hat, his staff, and the small knife he kept in his boot. A hidden pocket in his cloak revealed some waterproof matches, a compass, and a small pepper spray.

There was a bucket of water by the door and a small wooden bowl. I suddenly realised Brother Anselm hadn't left us anything to eat. We could both be dead in a few hours. Perhaps they wouldn't bother feeding us.

Not that I had time to eat. I spent all my time trying to keep him cool. On the one occasion I tried to get him to drink something, he knocked the bowl from my hand. Shortly afterwards, he seemed to fall asleep. I didn't know whether to let him sleep or whether to keep him conscious. Since he was in such pain, I left him, just trying to keep his head and hands cool and watching the swelling get bigger. I couldn't believe how fast it swelled. If I took my eyes off it even for a second, it seemed to have grown again when I looked back. It looked angry and painful. I knew that if it burst, there was a chance of recovery. And he only had the one bubo. And he would have been vaccinated against just about everything under the sun. And he was strong. I told myself he could survive this . . .

He was caught in a vicious circle. The fever kept him restless. Every move was agony. The pain inflamed the swelling, which increased the fever. And so it went on.

Hours passed. I sat beside him, wetting his lips with water and considered my options.

When he started to scream, I made the decision.

I stood up and undressed, laying the linen shift aside and redressing in my dress and surcoat. Using his knife, I cut and ripped my shift into strips for bandages. I filled up the bowl with water and had it ready. I took a sack, cut that up as well, and mixed it with a little twine. Both sack and twine had been waterproofed with something that smelled like creosote and which I hoped would burn well.

I sat back on my heels and rehearsed everything in my head, going over it all several times, making sure I had everything I needed close to hand, because once I started there would be no going back.

I made a little fire, gently puffing the flames into life, and adding small strips of sacking. I didn't want a massive conflagration, just a small flame. Just enough to sterilise a knife and burn the soiled dressings.

All this took time and when I looked at him again, he appeared to have lapsed into deep unconsciousness. I wasn't sure if this was a good sign or not. Hoping to God that I hadn't left it too late, I pulled off his shorts and set them to one side.

Here we go.

I held the knife in the flame for a few seconds, commended us to every god I could think of, and gently pulled his leg away from his body.

The swelling was huge and ugly. The size of a golf ball, it nestled in his groin. In the last few minutes, it had turned from red to purple. I could almost see it throb. Peterson had grown ominously silent. Dried saliva caked the corners of his mouth, dark with blood where he'd bitten his lips in pain. His breathing was all over the place. I was gripped with a sudden urge. Do it now. Before it was too late.

Still not knowing if I was doing the right thing or not, I carefully placed the tip of the knife in the centre of the bubo. He jerked and I nearly dropped it. Do it quickly, Maxwell. Do it now.

I sank the knife into the swelling. He shrieked and a huge fountain of hot, thick, yellow-brown pus erupted out over my hand. I discarded the knife, picked up the first bandage from my pile, and began to clear away the matter, glancing anxiously at Peterson as I did so. After that initial shout, he'd fallen worryingly quiet. But he still had a pulse and that was good enough for me.

I squeezed and mopped and squeezed and mopped. The stench was awful. The discharge colour darkened to brown. Streaks of blood began to appear. I kept at it because there was no going back now. I remembered Hunter once telling me that the secret with any infected wound was to keep at it until the blood flowed. Then you could be almost certain everything was cleared out.

On the other hand, this was Peterson's groin and there were some major arteries in this area—to say nothing of various bits of equipment he appeared to set great store by—so definitely no more knife work.

I worked away, mopping and swabbing, throwing the soiled linen into the fire. I was beginning to worry I'd run out of dressings, when I saw it. A nasty, stringy clot of blood and pus.

My eyes stung with sweat. I blinked hard to clear my vision, because I couldn't afford any accidents now. I took the knife and using just the point, gently teased it free. It came out quite easily, and suddenly, there was blood. Bright red blood.

The relief was overwhelming. I took a clean pad and pressed hard with both hands. He murmured and shifted, but I wouldn't let go. He was just going to have to lump it.

Finally, I took my hands away, gently removed the dressing, and looked. A small trickle of blood oozed gently, but nothing to worry about. I replaced the dressing with a clean one and bandaged it in place as best I could. It's an awkward area on a bloke—too many knobbly bits.

Then I sat back on my heels, carefully washed my hands, and got my breath back.

PETERSON LAY LIKE A stunned ox for the rest of the day. I left him to sleep, and when I could force my aching back and legs to move, I cleaned up the obvious signs of my butchery, washed myself all over as best I could, had a long drink of water, and watched him like a politician studying his popularity ratings.

I was awoken by the sounds of the bar being removed and Brother Anselm telling me there was food outside.

I cautiously opened the door and looked out. He stood some ten feet away.

"How is your husband?"

"Better."

He looked a little surprised. I think he thought I was making it up so I could escape. Or that I was deluding myself.

"No, brother, the bubo has burst and his fever gone. He is sleeping now."

"God be praised, that is good news, indeed. But you must watch him."

"I will, brother. Thank you for the food."

"And you, my child, how are you?"

"Well, so far, thanks to God."

"You know I cannot let you go."

"I understand."

"It is almost certain that you will contract the disease."

"I may not, brother. My parents both died of the plague when I was young and I did not contract it then, either."

He nodded. "I have heard that survival when young sometimes ensures survival later in life. Your parents' misfortune may be your salvation." He paused. "I am praying for you."

I smiled. "Thank you."

I meant it. It was so good to have someone on my side, for once.

EVEN THOUGH I WAS stranded in the 14th century with a plague-ridden Peterson, targeted by the Time Police, and worried out of my mind for Leon, it was the most peaceful evening I'd had for a long time. Nothing erupted. There were no crocodiles. The weather was pleasant. No one came close enough to shoot me.

I finished the bread and cheese he had left me, chewing carefully because medieval bread is full of medieval grit and I didn't need a broken tooth on top of everything else.

I sat next to Peterson with my back against the wall. He wasn't out of the woods yet. The fever had gone, leaving him semi-conscious and very weak. He could still succumb to infection or any of the other unpleasant diseases rife in the 14th century. I tried to get him to sip a little water, lifting his head to help him drink. His eyes were open but he didn't recognise me, or anything around him. He could still die. He probably would. Once again, I was an historian watching someone die.

While there was still enough light to see by, I checked him over again. There were no other swellings that I could discover.

His body was much cooler to the touch and his pulse slower and stronger. I peeled off his dressing, peered closely at the wound. It looked fine, but just to be on the safe side, I lowered my head and sniffed.

A feeble voice demanded to know what the hell I thought I was doing.

For a moment, I couldn't speak properly. I cleared my throat. "Checking for infection. Close your eyes if it bothers you."

"They are closed . . . Makes no difference. I can still hear you . . . snorting away like a pig . . . rooting for truffles."

"Trust me—if I find one down here it's all yours."

There was no reply. He seemed asleep.

I followed his example.

It had been another long day.

WE BOTH WOKE SEVERAL times in the night. I helped him sip a little water. This led to problem number two. Well, number one, actually.

"I'll get the bowl."

He was too feeble to do it for himself. I helped a little. Despite my best efforts, he managed to pee on me. Not for the first time. We both stared at the ceiling. I sought for something to say. "Have you had your holidays yet?" seemed a little inappropriate.

With the air of one making polite conversation, he said, "How's your arm now?"

"Fine. I'd forgotten all about it. How's your head?"

"Fine. I'd forgotten all about it."

It was like draining a reservoir and took about the same amount of time.

Finally, he said, in a tired thread of a voice, "You shouldn't have to do this for me."

"You should be grateful you don't have to do it for me. We don't all have outside plumbing. Imagine the difficulties involved with aim and flow control."

"Oh . . . gross."

"Exactly. Your problem is that you don't know when you're well off."

He averted his gaze from my ham-fisted assistance. "You're right."

I tidied him away afterwards and picked up the bowl and got to my feet.

"Where are you going?" he said, in sudden alarm.

"Just taking the piss."

HE WAS AWAKE WHEN Brother Anselm knocked the next morning.

I called out and he cautiously opened the door.

A great shaft of sunlight flooded the little shed. Peterson blinked in the sudden brightness and tried to put up a hand to shade his eyes.

I said quickly, "Husband, this is Brother Anselm; to whose goodness we owe our lives. And to God, of course."

He stood in the doorway, beaming. "Praise God for his goodness. This is a miracle indeed. And you, my child, you are well?"

"Yes, indeed, brother."

"And the swelling?"

"It has gone. The fever dropped immediately. I have kept the wound clean."

"Let me see."

He knelt beside Peterson, who once again suffered the indignity of crotch sniffing.

"Everything seems as it should be." He hesitated. "You understand that because there is still a risk . . ."

Yes, I was still a plague risk, myself. Besides, the last thing we needed now was for Peterson to be admitted to hospital. If he continued to improve, I would ask for the cart tomorrow and get him back to St. Mary's for proper treatment. They would quarantine us in the pod and treat us there, but that wouldn't be a problem.

I nodded, solemnly.

Brother Anselm disappeared to bring food and clean bandages.

Peterson slept for most of the day.

Brother Anselm visited regularly, each time asking after me. I think my stubborn refusal to develop the disease caused him some puzzlement. It puzzled me, as well. The only explanation I could find was that, after my infected arm, I was so stuffed full of antibiotics that my body had been able to fight off the nasty medieval plague germs and, as each hour passed, it seemed less likely that I would get it. Not that that would save me from ruthless quarantine when I got back.

That evening, Peterson swallowed a little soup, which stayed put. You can't keep a good historian down for long. He insisted on feeding himself, so I guided the spoon and mopped him up afterwards, grumbling about his poor aim. He grumbled about my abysmal nursing skills.

We settled down for our third night.

The question came out of the dark.

"Who are you? Really?"

I sighed and sat up. "Well, I'll tell you because you might still die, and it will save me killing you later. I'm Max, but I'm not your Max. That's how I was able to tell the truth to the Time Police. I was about to die on my last assignment and woke up here. I'm not an imposter or a substitute or a copy. I'm me. And you're not my Peterson. And it's not my St. Mary's. And this isn't my 14th century. And I don't know what's going on most of the time. And Leon's not here. But apart from all that, everything's fine."

I struggled again with a dizzying panic that was akin to feelings of vertigo.

He pulled my skirt. "Hey. Come back."

"Sorry."

"What was your last assignment?"

"Agincourt."

A pause. "Was I there?"

"Yes."

"So tell me . . . what happened?"

In as few words as possible, I told him about the attack on the baggage camp, his wound, and my struggle to get him back to the pod. I described how I'd hit him on the head, rolled him under a bush, and drawn off our pursuers. It was a bald, factual account, recounted with difficulty, and afterwards, there was a long silence.

Eventually, he said, "I don't know what to say."

I shrugged in the dark.

I was about to lay back down again when he said, "I found you, you know."

At first, I didn't understand. Then I did.

"I thought Leon found me."

"No. He telephoned you. He said afterwards that he knew something was wrong. He rang me in my office and asked me to nip along and make sure you were on your way to meet him. I walked in through the door . . . and you were on the floor." He tried to laugh. "You still had the Famous Assassinations assignment in your hand."

I said nothing. He needed to say this.

"Your face was bright red. I knew at once . . . carbon monoxide . . . I dragged you out into the corridor. Markham was walking past. We did everything we could. Helen arrived. She did everything she could. Everyone knew it was far too late and that it was all useless but we did it anyway. Then Leon arrived."

He stopped. I wondered if I should stop him talking. He was so weak, but he needed to say this.

"It was bad for us, but for him . . . His life just stopped. You could see it in his face. For him, everything just stopped dead.

And it never started up again. Oh, he went through the motions, but when you went away, a large part of him went with you. He wasn't the only one. Dr. Bairstow was devastated. Both Mrs. Mack and Mrs. Enderby cried. And as for Kal . . . It was a terrible time for everyone." He tried to laugh. "Especially you, of course."

I tried to laugh, too. "In my world, it was Leon who died."

"Tell me . . ."

So I did. In fact, apart from Mrs. Partridge's role in all this, I told him everything. Right up to the hearing.

Another long silence. I helped him to more water.

"We didn't treat you very well, did we?"

"Well, what were you to think? You saw me dead. Everyone was bound to think that I was some sort of imposter. Or that Leon had lost his mind and picked up some bint who just happened to look like me. I don't hold any grudges."

Except maybe for one.

"But even so, Max . . ."

"Well, you're right, my life is not good at the moment. But every time I feel like giving way, I remember the day I walked into a pod and saw Leon Farrell stretched dead on the floor, and I know that however bad things are, they'll never be that bad again." I grinned in the dark. "Plus, every time you see me, like it or not, you'll remember that you're only alive today because of me. Because I'm absolutely bloody wonderful."

"And let's not forget modest either."

"As if you'll ever get the chance."

So we talked. And slept. And talked again. A lot was said although not all of it was spoken.

I woke early. At some point in the night, he'd reached out his hand and grasped a fold of my dress.

I wondered who was comforting whom.

MY ESTIMATE OF TWO days for Peterson to be strong enough to get back to the pod proved to be wildly over-optimistic. Brother

Anselm refused to bring the handcart and even I had to admit that Peterson was nowhere near well enough to be moved. The fever had gone, the swelling had disappeared and his wound was healing, but he was frighteningly weak. He had lost an enormous amount of weight and he'd been skinny to begin with. I could clearly see his cheekbones showing under yellow skin that seemed stretched too tightly across his face.

He slept a great deal and although he did his best, forcing down a few mouthfuls of every meal, he could not disguise his lack of appetite and lethargy. I told myself there was no point in dragging him back to St. Mary's for proper medical treatment if the journey killed him.

Brother Anselm continued his fascination with Peterson's recovery, visiting two or three times a day to question me closely about his treatment. In the end, I told him I'd seen a horse with a swollen leg treated in a similar manner and just copied what I'd seen. He seemed amused. Peterson wasn't.

After four days, however, he agreed to bring the handcart. I told him we had a small hut behind The Bolles Hede and once he realised I wasn't going to drag Peterson back to Rushford there and then, he nodded.

Part of me was sorry to leave. It was quiet, peaceful, the food was good and plentiful, and I liked Brother Anselm, but deep down, I worried that Peterson might still die. That he might take a turn for the worse, or pick up the pox or something. He was my responsibility. If this was a normal assignment, I'd have stuffed him full of antibiotics and had him back to St. Mary's. They would have confined us to the pod, but getting him back would have been the sensible thing to do.

I said this to Peterson who laughed and said if I was talking about the sensible option he now knew I couldn't possibly be the real Maxwell.

He indignantly refused to lie down in the cart, and so we heaved him, sitting bolt upright like Patience on her monument, through the gardens, down the passageway, and out into the dusty High Street.

We halted outside the pod. Peterson slithered off the cart and leaned against the door for support.

We all looked at each other.

Peterson stretched out his hand. "Thank you, Brother. I am sorry I have no money left to pay for my care. But when I return to Rushford, I will make a donation to the poor in gratitude."

And he did. He never made a big thing of it, but he sent off a generous cheque to the free clinic in St. Stephen's Street.

Brother Anselm nodded, apparently well satisfied.

I looked at the plump little figure standing in front of me, arms thrust into the sleeves of his carefully darned habit. Quietly doing his best every day. Invincible in a faith I could not understand. Doing battle for his God. Winning some. Losing most. I felt a gentle regret at leaving him.

Peterson tactfully turned away.

"I read great trouble in you, my child. Your life is burdened with doubt and fear. I say to you, place your trust in the God who loves you and all will be well. Do not waste the time given you in fretting over events you cannot control. If you only let him, God will amend all. Have just a little faith."

I swallowed hard and nodded. Just for a moment, I couldn't find any words.

Suddenly brisk, he said, "I have duties to perform. Call on me when you return to make your pilgrimage."

"We will," I said, knowing we wouldn't ever see him again.

"God's blessing be upon you both, my children."

"Amen," said Peterson.

We watched him trundle his cart back into the High Street and be swallowed up in the crowd.

I like to think he lived a long and useful life, happy in the service of the God in whom he believed so implicitly, but there's no record of him anywhere, either of his life or his death. I know, because I looked.

THE FAMILIAR POD SMELL greeted us—hot electrics, damp carpet, stale air, the toilet, and cabbage. Even in this world, they had the cabbage smell.

Peterson looked too weak for a seat, so I lowered him gently to the floor and crossed to the console. "The jump's all laid in. All you have to do is initiate."

He nodded. "Just a minute."

"What's the problem?"

He fidgeted. "I just wanted to say . . ."

"There's really no need. If you could do the honours, please."

We landed as lightly as thistledown in a soft summer breeze if you listened to Peterson. Or like a plummeting pachyderm if you believed me.

"You've got the pox," I said, checking the screen. "What would you know?"

"Plague! I have the plague! For God's sake, do not go around telling people I have the pox. Please tell me you know the difference."

"Well, I treated you for pox and you got better. Ergo—you had the pox."

"You mean—all that crawling around between my legs and you hadn't got a bloody clue what you were doing?"

"Listen, ingrate. My ministrations, ungentle as they were, will be as nothing once Doctor Foster gets hold of you. She's going to stick you with every antibiotic known to man—and probably a few still in the experimental stages. Are you ready for decon? I'm going to do it at least twice."

He nodded and I operated the decontamination system. The cold, blue light flickered and I could feel the hairs on my arms stirring.

"And again."

The lamp hummed.

"Do it once more," he said. "The more we suffer in here, the less we suffer out there."

"I think you're underestimating the medical section," but I operated the lamp again anyway.

Three times in such short succession left us both feeling a little sick, but it was necessary. We decontaminated after every assignment. Dr. Bairstow's procedures were rigorous. There was no way we would ever bring something unpleasant back from the past. Apart from each other, of course.

"OK," I said. "Let's put the cat amongst the pigeons." I activated the comm. "Attention please. Code Blue. Code Blue. Code Blue. This is Pod Three declaring a Code Blue. Authorisation Maxwell. Five zero alpha nine eight zero four bravo. I say again, Code Blue. Code Blue. Code Blue. This is not a drill."

I had no authorisation here, but they would get the message. I left the mike on and switched on the internal cameras so they could see what was happening in here and went and sat alongside Peterson who was still on the floor.

"How do you feel?"

"Not too bad, despite being irradiated by that bloody lamp."

"Yes, I gave you a good blast. You're almost certainly sterile by now."

"What?"

"When the two of you are finished," said Dr. Foster's voice, "please state the nature of the contamination."

I gestured to Peterson. He was the patient.

"Pox," he said.

"What?"

"Plague! I mean plague! I've got the plague! Stop laughing, Max."

THE NEXT HOUR WAS busy. Priority was given to ridding ourselves of the infected fleas we had almost certainly brought back with us.

On Dr. Foster's instructions, I helped Peterson undress and shoved him into the shower. While he was in there, I found his knife and, not without some misgivings, sawed away. After a few minutes, two long red plaits fell to the floor.

"Oh my God," said Peterson, emerging. "I can't believe you've done that. Dr. Bairstow will go ballistic."

"Not with me. I'm going to tell him you made me do it."

Following procedures, I incinerated everything—my hair, our clothes, everything, and then took a shower myself, letting the warm water run through my traumatised hair.

Five minutes later, I was back, enveloped in a towel.

Outside, Hawking was deserted. Dieter would have had them all out of the hangar like greased lightning. I could see a ring of armed guards in hazmat suits setting themselves up. Their job would be to shoot anything that tried to leave the pod without medical supervision.

We waited.

"Been anytime nice this year?" said Peterson, arranging his towel primly across his lap.

"Let's see. A London Frost Fair. A quick glimpse of Akhenaten. Pompeii was good."

"Really? We're scheduled for Pompeii later this year."

"Well, if you see me, give me a wave."

They zipped us up in plastic suits, carted us off to Sick Bay, and I was back in the isolation ward.

"Nice," said Peterson, looking around him.

"Better than the sock-smelling den of squalor that is the men's ward, yes. I'm definitely not going in there. God knows what I'd come out with."

Both Hunter and Dr. Foster were engrossed with Peterson's groin.

"A man can never have too much of that," he said with a grin, which disappeared when they outlined the programme of vaccinations they had planned for him.

It was wiped from mine as well when I discovered I was in line, too. In vain did I protest I hadn't actually had the pox. Plague! Dammit! Plague!

WE WEREN'T ALLOWED VISITORS, but people lined up to peer through the viewing window and point and laugh. They could at least have thrown peanuts.

Someone pasted up a list of famous people who had suffered from syphilis:

Hitler

Mussolini

Ivan the Terrible

Bonaparte

Cesare Borgia

Casanova

Lord Darnley

Chief Operations Officer Peterson

I laughed, but was a little hurt that my own name wasn't up there. Relations were better, but we weren't yet on familiar terms. When your name appears on the pox printout, you know you've been accepted.

We wrote our reports and sent them off to Dr. Bairstow, who presented himself punctually at 0930 every morning to stare at us. It was beyond his nature to smile and encourage, so we could only assume he was there to intimidate any lingering plague germs. He certainly intimidated us.

I didn't develop anything. I don't think anyone expected me to, but it was a wonderful excuse to lock me up for a couple of days. I wasn't bothered and Peterson, when he didn't have people peering at his nether regions, was good company. I advised him that if this kept up, to start charging a viewing fee.

"I could be the next national monument," he said enthusiastically. "Open on Sunday afternoons. Cream teas for half a crown."

I said nastily, "There's nothing monumental about you, Tiny Tim," and left him spluttering indignantly.

ONE NIGHT, I COULDN'T sleep. The relief and elation I felt at having got Peterson back more or less intact had worn off, and fears for the future now crowded my mind.

I lay in the dark and stared up at the ceiling. Peterson snored gently in the corner. I contemplated getting out of bed and giving him a poke, but just as I pushed back the covers he grunted, snorted, and turned over.

In the blessed silence, I thought I heard a faint sound outside my door. The dark shape that appeared in the window was too tall for Hunter. Even as I raised myself on one elbow, the door opened a little way; a dark figure slid through the gap and closed it silently.

I reached for the tried and trusty water jug and prepared to sell my life dearly.

A whisper in the dark. "Don't switch on the light."

"*Leon?*"

"Shh. Don't wake Peterson."

I said, exasperated, "Have you ever *tried* to wake Peterson? What are you doing here?"

"Just a minute . . ."

He drew back the curtains and a little moonlight fell into the room. He groped his way to the bed and sat heavily. "Ouch. What's that?"

"My feet. Where have you been?"

"With Edward."

"No, I mean . . ."

"I know what you mean. I can't tell you. I've jumped back to report and receive fresh instructions. I can't stay long. I shouldn't be here at all."

"What's going on?"

"I can't say."

"Then why are you here?"

"I wanted to see you."

"We're in the dark," I said, exasperated.

I felt him move, the little bed light clicked on, and there he was—drawn and haggard, with a half-healed cut over the bridge of his nose that was going to leave a scar. He wore light body armour, had a blaster slung over his shoulder, and two handguns on a sticky patch on one thigh. He looked tough, competent, and completely worn out. Once again, I had the feeling that big things were happening and I was only a very small cog.

We looked at each other and I said, accusingly, "You went off with all the Jaffa Cakes."

"The word on the street is that you've been rummaging in Peterson's groin."

"If it makes you feel better, neither of us enjoyed it very much."

"You can't have been doing it properly. Didn't you used to have hair?"

"It's the new post-plague look. Talk to me."

"I've been back to the future. Things to do. People to see. I should be there now."

My throat closed. With some difficulty, I said, "Will you stay there?"

He put his hand over mine. "Nothing will keep me from coming back to you."

I blinked to clear my eyes.

"How long can you stay?"

"I shouldn't be here at all."

"It's . . . good to see you."

"You too." He cleared his throat. "I . . . um . . . I brought you something."

He passed me a small cardboard box. It was very light.

"What is it?"

"It's for you. Now I must go." He stood up.

"Wait. Please. Stay a little longer . . ."

"I can't."

"Just while I open . . ."

I pulled open the flaps and peered inside.

I couldn't move. Not a finger. I think I forgot to breathe.

A small, brown face smiled up at me.

I lifted him out so very gently. I know that these days, teddy bears are designed to survive the attentions of small children—or a thermo-nuclear blast; the two are not dissimilar in terms of destruction—but I was terrified of breaking this precious object.

I remembered the circumstances under which I last saw my Bear . . .

And Leon, who knew it all, and to whom none of it was important, said softly, "This is Bear 2.0. A gift to you. From me. No more looking back, Lucy."

I stroked the velvety fur. Touched his soft leather paws. His smile tore at my heart.

I mumbled, "I don't know what to say."

"You don't have to say anything."

"Thank you."

"It's an honour and a privilege."

"No. No, it shouldn't be. When I think of what I've done . . . the mistakes I've made. I condemned when I should have shown compassion. I wiped Leon out of my life for what he did. I can't help thinking—would he still be alive if I hadn't . . . ? Did he literally die of a broken heart?"

"No. You can't die of a broken heart. Trust me."

"When we talked about Helios—that night in the pod—you were going to say something."

He hesitated. "You know, don't you, what the other Max did?"

"I do now." I didn't mention it was Barclay who told me.

"Did you blame your Max—as I blamed my Leon?"

"No, of course I didn't blame her. Nobody did. No one was safe in Troy. Terrible things would have happened to that little boy and, when he was no more use to anyone, the Greeks would have cut his throat and moved on. She saved him from that and I loved her for it. I will never forget that you forgave me freely when you thought I'd done it, and I forgave her, too."

I nodded, though he could barely see me in the dark.

"Will the Time Police come here?"

"Not if I have anything to do with it."

"Can you keep them out?"

"I'm trying. Many people are trying. And knowing that you're here . . . Believe me, if they come here, it will be over my dead body. But that won't happen."

"Why are you here?"

"To report to Dr. Bairstow and get further instructions."

"Report what?"

He hesitated.

"Leon?"

"The date."

"What date?"

"The date they have scheduled their attack."

"So they do come here?"

"Not if I can prevent it."

I reached for him in sudden panic.

"Leon . . . you must take care. Nothing must happen to you."

His hands covered mine. "Sweetheart, I have to say this. I know we agreed to take things slowly—to get to know each other, but time has run out for us. So I'm telling you now, in case we never . . . in case anything happens to either of us. I know we said . . . but I can't bear the thought you might never know how I feel. About you. About us. It's all right—you don't have to say anything. If you don't . . . I mean, I understand . . . '

I couldn't stop crying.

"Leon . . . take me with you. Let me fight with you. If we fall, we fall together."

"I can't do that, sweetheart. But it won't come to that. I'll keep them out, I promise. I promise you'll be safe."

I pushed back the bedcovers and stood up.

"Leon . . ."

I put my arms around him.

He stood motionless for a moment and then I was not just held, but crushed against him. His armour was painful. There would be bruises to explain away in the morning, but none of that mattered now. There didn't seem anything to say so we didn't. Time was short and I don't think either of us could bear to waste it saying goodbye. We stood together a long time. The window-shaped patch of light travelled slowly across the room and neither of us noticed. Neither of us moved. Or wanted to. I breathed him in. He rubbed his hand gently up and down my back. I reached up and touched his cheek. He kissed my palm and folded my fingers over to keep it safe.

"I must go," he said, softly. "Try not to lose any more hair."

"Bring Jaffa Cakes next time."

Something feather light brushed my cheek and then he was gone.

I switched off the light and sat in the dark, trying desperately not to wake Peterson and I was completely unsuccessful, because I heard him move and the next minute, he was sitting beside me on the bed.

He said, "Hey," and put his arm around me.

I struggled not to make foghorn noises.

After a while, I wiped my nose and said thickly, "Do you think Leon will come back?"

"God, I hope not. I'm practically in bed with you. I'm wearing nothing but a pair of shorts. You're only wearing a T-shirt and you're decent by less than an inch."

I opened my mouth to reply but at that moment, Hunter came in to see what all the noise was about. We had to endure another of her all-purpose bollockings, and after that, I curled myself around Bear 2.0 and tried to sleep.

FOURTEEN

T HE NEXT DAY WE were allowed visitors. Markham, Schiller, Van Owen, and Roberts were the first through the door, bearing gifts. I wasn't forgotten—they'd brought chocolate, which was kind of them.

They wanted to hear everything. Schiller and Van Owen sat on Peterson's bed. Roberts bagged the only chair and Markham leaned against the foot of my bed.

"So, tell us how you got the pox."

"Plague," shouted Peterson. "It was the bloody plague, I tell you. I've never had the pox in my life."

No one was listening.

"Did Max really have to chop off one of your testicles? Which one was it?"

"The one nearest the window—what do you think?"

"Don't tease him," said Schiller. "He's faced great peril."

"You don't know the half of it," said Peterson, rummaging in the box of goodies they had brought him. "Trust me—you don't know what peril is until you've had Maxwell come at your groin with a Swiss Army knife and that look in her eye."

They all looked at me.

"Well, there's gratitude for you. Next time you get a swelling in your groin, you can handle it yourself."

There was a thoughtful silence.

"Yes," said Markham. "The other Maxwell never knew when to shut up, either."

WE WERE RELEASED BACK into captivity a couple of days later. Peterson was white and wobbly, but plague free. And pox free, too. Hunter had done him a certificate to that effect, which he proudly displayed to everyone who asked. And everyone who didn't.

I think they gave up waiting for me to fall sick. As usual, I'd completely failed to live up to people's expectations.

On our last morning, they brought our clothes. I came out of the bathroom to find a complete set of blues laid out on my bed. Not greys—real, proper, historian blues. I touched them gently.

Peterson stood behind me, saying, quietly, "Have I thanked . . . ?"

I turned and smiled at him. "An honour and a privilege, Dr. Peterson."

He stretched out his hand. "Tim," he said. "The name's Tim."

My heart sang. I was as proud then as the day when I was awarded my first set of blues, back in that other world.

They gave us a round of applause when we went for lunch. Tim proudly flourished his certificate.

"Pox-free, ladies. Please form an orderly queue. No pushing."

I sat with him and Dieter for lunch, and we were just finishing when someone said Dr. Bairstow wanted to see me.

I sighed. Now what?

AND FINALLY, THERE SHE was, sitting demurely behind the desk in Dr. Bairstow's outer office. Just when I'd given up all hope of ever seeing her again.

I stopped dead. Peterson walked into the back of me.

I said cautiously, "Good afternoon."

She inclined her head, regally. "Good afternoon."

I stared. She continued calmly to stack assignment files.

"Um, I believe Dr. Bairstow wanted to see us . . ."

At that moment, the Boss himself opened his door.

"Ah. Good afternoon to you both. May I introduce Mrs. Partridge, my new PA?"

"Oh my God," said Peterson. "Did Colonel Albay shoot Miss Lee on his way out?"

A very real possibility.

"Miss Lee is to return to her old position as assistant to the Chief Operations Officer."

The Chief Operations Officer paled. "What?"

I felt a twinge of sympathy for him. Been there—done that—got the scars.

"All this is for later discussion. Mrs. Partridge, may I introduce Doctors Maxwell and Peterson."

"Hello," said Peterson, who had obviously never been brought up not to talk to strangers. "I'm Peterson." He held out his hand.

She rose gracefully. Her manicure was exquisite. "How do you do. I am Mrs. Partridge."

"Nice to meet you, Mrs. Partridge. Welcome to St. Mary's."

"Thank you," she said, smiling at him. Everyone smiles at Peterson. He beamed back.

She looked at me.

Sometimes I just can't help myself.

"Yes. Welcome to St. Mary's. Nice to meet you, Mrs. Peacock."

"Partridge," she said, expressionlessly.

"Really? Are you sure?"

"Almost certain, yes."

"Partridge?"

"Yes."

"Not Peacock?"

"No."

"I could have sworn . . ."

"No."

"Oh. Well. Nice to meet you, Mrs. . . . Partridge."

"And you too, Dr. Murphy."

I opened my mouth, but Dr. Bairstow had disappeared back into his office and Peterson pushed me in after him. Mrs. Partridge followed us in and shut the door behind her.

We seated ourselves at his briefing table. Major Guthrie, Professor Rapson and Dr. Dowson, Dieter, and Dr. Foster were already present.

No Barclay.

Just for a moment, I wondered . . .

"Miss Barclay is not attending this afternoon's meeting?"

"Miss Barclay has been called away today, but she is already fully integrated into all my plans for the future."

We sat down.

"Dr. Peterson, how are you now?"

"Refreshingly plague-free, sir."

"Remain so."

"Yes, sir."

He regarded me.

"The 14th century having proved inadequate for our purposes, Dr. Maxwell, I propose to keep you here for the foreseeable future."

"For how long will that be, sir?"

His face set grimly.

"Not for very long, I fear. However . . ." he sat up straighter and rearranged his papers, "we are not finished yet. According to information received from a reliable source," (he meant Leon), "the situation is not good. St. Mary's is under attack. Every version—every incarnation. We must defend ourselves, too. Possibly to the death. I know we have expected this. That we have been preparing for it for some time, but now the moment has arrived. An armed force will attempt to take control of St. Mary's in the very near future."

"But they're a police force," I said, sounding stupid even to myself. "Aren't there guidelines they have to adhere to?"

"Once, yes, but this is a fight to the finish. Only one organisation will survive. They're being attacked up and down the timeline. They will defend themselves. If they're not stopped—sooner or later, they will get to us."

I said, "Surely they can't kill us, sir. To them, we're contemporaries."

He smiled sadly. "It might already be written that we were all killed in the famous Battle of St. Mary's, and therefore they would have no choice."

"Sir, I think I should give myself up."

"Oh, I don't think I can allow that, Dr. Maxwell. Of everyone here, you're the only person who didn't actually connive at removing a contemporary from his own time. Besides, surrendering you, or any of us, will not serve our long-term purpose, which is to dismantle the Time Police. Colonel Albay is an unpleasant and ruthless man who lets nothing stand in his way when executing his duties, and those who come after him will certainly be even more ruthless and unpleasant. It is the duty of all of us to prevent that ever being allowed to happen."

"But, sir . . ." I said. When had I started calling him "sir"?

"At various moments in the future, St. Mary's is fighting to throw off Time Police control. Fighting for its independence. Fighting for its existence. The least this unit can do is put up a good show. For Leon."

I caught my breath suddenly, remembering what he had said. If the Time Police came back, then Leon was dead.

"Yes, this is about more than us, Max. If they do turn up then we don't stand a chance. But we'll go down fighting." He sighed. "They'll have to rename the unit, of course, because it won't be St. Mary's any longer."

We sat silently around the table. He roused himself.

"We all have important roles in this. After our people and our pods, knowledge is our most important asset. Professor, please work with Doctor Dowson. Start packing everything up. Absolutely everything. If this goes south, I'm not leaving anything behind for these people and we can't send anything to Thirsk. That's the first place they'll look. Therefore, everything is to be stored in the pods and the pods themselves will be sent to our remote site with two or three caretakers. I want this place cleared in a week.

"All non-essential personnel will be evacuated. I have a high regard for every member of this unit. I will not risk them unnecessarily. They are to be removed to a place of safety.

"The building is to be fortified and made defendable. Major Guthrie, you have plans for just such a contingency, I believe. Please let me see them after this meeting. Doctor Foster, I imagine I don't have to tell you what arrangements to make. Requisition whatever you need. Mrs. Partridge, there will be an all-staff briefing tomorrow at eleven. Everyone is to attend. Any questions, anyone?"

WE DO OUR BEST, but it's fair to say things don't always go according to plan. We all assembled promptly for the briefing the next day. The Boss made his appearance to total silence. A bit of a first.

He went through everything, slowly and clearly. I looked around. People's faces were serious. There was no fidgeting. He had everyone's attention. When he started issuing instructions to pack up, there was much activity with scratchpads, but when he moved on to evacuation instructions, it was immediately apparent that he had lost his audience.

He started on specifics and that was when he faced his first mutiny. Frankly, I always thought it would be me, but this came right out of the blue. He was working his way down the list of names to evacuate, when little Mrs. Enderby from Wardrobe stood up and the whole thing crashed to the ground.

"No," she said.

He actually read two more names before it registered. "What did you say?"

"I said, no."

"No what?"

"No, I won't go."

He rallied valiantly. "I'm sorry if I inadvertently gave the impression this was a discussion."

"I won't go."

He seemed dumbfounded for a moment and I'm guessing this was another first. "Mrs. Enderby ..."

"I'm sorry, Dr. Bairstow, but I won't go. St. Mary's is my home. I have lived here for as long as you. I was one of the founder members. I won't go off and leave St. Mary's and you to face whatever is coming. I believe in what we do here and I will fight for it with all my might."

There was a breathless silence.

A chair creaked. Mrs. Mack stood up. "I won't go either. And before you say anything, I was in Cardiff in July and August of '68, and I fought in the Monmouth Riots two years later. I've almost certainly seen more combat action than some of Major Guthrie's young saplings over there and I'm very sorry to defy you like this, sir, but I won't go."

Wow! And before I could get my head round that, Jenny Fields stood up and, gripping the chair in front of her, said breathlessly, "I'm not very brave and I've never shot anyone, but I'm not leaving either."

Both Dr. Dowson and Professor Rapson, each attempting to be first on their feet, became entangled, glared at each other, and said simultaneously, "Nor I."

The professor added, "Sorry, Edward."

It must have been the most polite mutiny in history.

Dr. Bairstow visibly pulled himself together.

"Major Guthrie!"

"No, sorry, sir, but I'm *definitely* not going!"

The laughter relieved the tension.

"Major, please ensure that any member of St. Mary's who volunteers to remain is fully incorporated into your plans."

"My pleasure, sir."

The Boss stood for a long time, looking at his feet. The silence lengthened. I watched the dust dancing in the shafts of sunshine streaming through the lantern.

Finally, he spoke. "St. Mary's thanks you for your service. As do I."

They sat down.

"I must tell you, however, there is very little chance we will survive this." He smiled faintly. "It's not Mafeking. No one will relieve us. We are completely alone. We dare not ask for support from other incarnations of St. Mary's who will also have their hands full. Or from the army or the government. It is imperative that no one ever knows that things go so badly wrong in the future. St. Mary's would be disestablished overnight. Therefore, we cannot risk outside involvement. There is only us. You are my friends. Some of you have been my friends for many years. I would be wrong to lead you into this without making you aware of our very slim chances of survival."

Mrs. Mack stood up again. "When can I draw my weapon?"

IN THE END, ONLY three people elected not to stay. They left that night. Another four volunteered to go with the pods as caretakers.

For me, the next three days were a bit of a blur. Peterson went with Professor Rapson to assist with clearing out Wardrobe, R & D, and all the workrooms along that corridor. I was seconded to the library and archive. The trained staff did all the packing and stacking and I lugged flatbed after flatbed down the long (and rapidly getting longer) corridor to Hawking, where the archive boxes were carefully stowed in their designated pods.

Techies were swarming over everything like orange ants. The IT people were backing up and shutting down, which was a long business. I could see Barclay striding around, barking instructions.

I sat on my flatbed, ostensibly for a glug of water, and studied her. As always, her face gave nothing away. She appeared to be concentrating all her efforts on shutting down our IT systems safely. She moved from group to group, occasionally pointing at a screen or offering a word of advice. She had a clipboard and a serious expression. She never once looked in my direction.

There were lighter moments amongst the gloom. We were standing around the Boss's data table working out deployments when, with barely a knock, Mrs. Mack swept in—a woman with a mission—closely followed by Jenny Fields, who was burdened with a cardboard box and an embarrassed expression.

The Boss straightened up, faintly surprised. "Good morning. Can I help you?"

"Oh good, you're all here. Yes, you can all help. I need condoms, please. As many as possible."

We stared at her.

She said, sharply, "Now, please, if you would be so good."

We stared at her.

"I know at least some of you must have some and I need as many as I can get."

We stared at her.

Peterson jerked himself back to reality. "Um . . . I think there are machines in the . . ."

"I have all those," she said, jerking her head in the direction of Jenny and her box. "I need more. These may not be enough."

We stared at her.

You would not believe the pictures cartwheeling through my mind.

After a long moment, Dieter pulled out his wallet and tossed two onto the table. "Two," he said.

Peterson grinned. "I'll see your two and raise you one," laid down three, appeared to be struck by a sudden thought and snatched two back. Mrs. Mack glared at him and he reluctantly let them go again.

Markham rummaged endlessly through pockets and wallet and produced a great handful. A great, multi-coloured, ribbed handful. "Way to go, Mr. Markham," said Peterson in admiration.

After a brief pause that actually seemed to go on for quite a long time, the Boss laid down two. A more than respectful silence fell. Nobody caught anybody's eye. Mrs. Mack departed.

I heard the Boss murmur, "I sometimes wonder what goes on in that kitchen," and we continued with the briefing.

SAYING GOODBYE TO THE pods was hard for everyone. They were to jump to our remote site, the location of which was a closely guarded secret. The Boss tried to make Dr. Dowson go with them, ostensibly because he was our archivist but also because he was nearly seventy. He refused to leave, and in the end, the Boss relented.

The whole unit assembled in Hawking. I stood on the gantry with the rest of St. Mary's and watched them disappear, silently, one by one, taking my memories with them. Eventually, the vast hangar was empty. Dieter looked as if he'd lost his entire family, which, I suppose, he had. Polly Perkins was in tears. I wondered whether I would ever see them again. Whether any of us would ever see them again.

WE WERE DIVIDED INTO teams.

I was in Markham's team, along with Professor Rapson and Dr. Dowson (presumably so we could argue the enemy to death), Peterson, and Mrs. Partridge. Our position was at the foot of the stairs. From there, we could cover the entrance to the long corridor to Hawking and the front doors.

Weller, Evans, and Clerk covered our rear from the half landing. Major Guthrie's teams were ranged around the Gallery. Dieter's team was stationed outside Hawking. Helen was covering Sick Bay and the civilian staff were deployed around the building as reserves.

Everything was locked, shuttered, bolted, barred, barricaded, booby-trapped, and anything else we could think of. Unless they brought heavy explosives, the only ways in were through Hawking or the main entrance, and we reckoned they wouldn't want to risk damaging Hawking, so the main door was where we were concentrated.

"Remember," said Guthrie, at our briefing, "you are only responsible for your particular area. Be aware of what goes on around you, but if you look around, you will see each team is covered by the others. Check your range and designated target areas. Fire only along your lines of sight. Don't go waving your weapons around from left to right. Trust your colleagues on either side of you. Trust those behind you."

We spent hours on the ranges. At first, it was chaos and we were in more danger standing behind some of our volunteers than in front of them, but it settled down. We didn't go for anything fancy—just aim for the centre of the body and pull the trigger. Single shots. Those of us with more experience did our best to pass it on. We held drills, stripping down weapons and re-assembling them with our eyes shut. Ditto re-loading. Mrs. Partridge was our designated re-loader. She was quick, clean, and dexterous. I felt reassured, knowing she would be nearby.

Gradually, it began to gel. A feeling of optimism was encouraged, although I could see this wasn't shared by Guthrie, or Markham, or anyone with any sort of combat experience. We were on our own. We would be pitted against better-armed, ruthless, professional troops who had already demonstrated their complete disregard for anything or anyone who got in their way. We were going to die.

But we're St. Mary's and we weren't dead yet.

I SAT ON THE stairs, looking down into the Hall. It had been another long day. Night had fallen. Only a few lights burned. Guards were posted and most people were getting their heads down. The slightest sound echoed eerily around the empty building.

I don't know for how long I'd been sitting there, alone with my thoughts, but even the hard wooden stairs were more comfortable than my cramped little concrete cell, and, quite honestly, I was too tired and unhappy to move.

I heard uneven footsteps approaching and when I looked up, Dr. Bairstow stood before me. Scrambling stiffly to my feet, I said, "Good evening, Dr. Bairstow."

He looked at me for a while and then said, "I wondered if you would care to join me for a moment."

Mystified, I followed him back to his empty office.

He pulled open a drawer and brought out a bottle and two glasses. He poured generously and passed me one.

He stood, in the dark, his back to me, looking out of the window.

His first words surprised me. "We can't win this. I am presiding over the end of St. Mary's as we know it. No matter what they say, I should send everyone away."

"If I might argue with you briefly, sir . . ."

"The word *briefly* never applies to any of your arguments, Dr. Maxwell. The word *interminable* is a far more apt description."

"Well, actually, sir, the word *compelling* best describes my arguments, but, be that as it may, you should consider this. Everyone here is a volunteer. You heard Mrs. Enderby. She said she believed in what we do here. We all believe in what we do here, sir. Some of us think it an honour and a privilege to be offered the opportunity to defend something as important as St. Mary's. Personally, sir, I count myself in good company."

"As do I, Dr. Maxwell, the very best company. With one or two notable exceptions, I could not have asked for better people around me, which makes it all even more of a waste, I think. When I consider the planning, the effort, and the sacrifices made . . . and not just by this unit."

"Sir, if it was easy then everyone would be doing it. It's no fun if it's not difficult."

He turned from the window to look at me through the gloom. I still couldn't see his face.

I sat quietly, facing him. The light from Mrs. Partridge's office was behind me so he couldn't see my face, either.

I thought about what this meant to him. This was his unit, his world. This was the culmination of everything he'd worked for. He'd built it up from scratch. He'd sacrificed his future to jump back and found St. Mary's. He'd fought the good fight up and down the timeline. He wouldn't allow anyone to take it from him. He wouldn't go quietly into the night. He would fight to his last breath.

And so would we.

I said nothing. Around us, St. Mary's settled and the last noises died away. The silence was very heavy.

When I had control of my voice, I said, "When Leon was here, what did he say?"

"According to Leon . . . the day after tomorrow. The attack is scheduled for the day after tomorrow at about five o'clock in the morning." His face was still in shadow. "If they come . . ."

"This is about much more than Helios, isn't it?"

"Yes. I'm sorry you've been caught up in this, Max. You and Leon deserved . . ."

"Don't be, sir. Perhaps some things are just never meant to be."

He drew a breath and topped up my glass.

I changed the subject. "Sir, I haven't thanked you for taking me in."

He said gently, "I think that between such old friends as us, Max, thanks are not needed."

I took a painful breath. "Will they come?"

I looked directly at him and he paid me the compliment of looking directly back.

"Yes. I'm sorry, but I think they will come."

I knew what he was saying. If they came, it was because Leon had failed. It would mean all the other St. Mary's Institutes had been unable to hold them back and that Leon was dead.

FIFTEEN

MIDNIGHT.

Team Markham assembled at the foot of the stairs, behind the big barricade. We checked each other over, tightening straps and slapping helmets. Mrs. Partridge stacked her spare ammo. I inspected my weapons—two 9 mm semi-automatics taking 30 round clips, and a wide beam blaster, fully charged. Never having envisaged a situation where all of St. Mary's would be in the firing line, Major Guthrie didn't have enough equipment for everyone and priority, obviously, went to the Security section. I had some armour and a helmet, but no night vision.

I stood at the foot of the stairs, got my bearings, and noted who was where. I verified my allocated target areas and the range. Beside me, Peterson was making sure his weapons pulled free from his sticky patches without snagging or catching on anything.

When we were satisfied, we sat down and made ourselves comfortable.

Then we waited.

Would they come?

I could hear breathing and the occasional rustle of clothing as someone shifted position nearby. Around us, the building creaked and settled.

We sat quietly, watching the hours pass. Every hour they didn't come meant that Leon was still alive. That he was still out there somewhere. We made it through the small hours. Then 3 a.m. Then 4 a.m.

Around me, people dozed. Markham snored. I didn't dare close my eyes. Peterson sat motionless alongside me. Earlier, I'd seen him take the opportunity to exchange a few words with Helen Foster. They'd stood a little apart, not speaking. He held her hands. I'd caught a glimpse of their faces and had to turn my head away.

Around four-thirty, the sun began to think about joining us and they still hadn't turned up. I told myself it would be light soon and surely they wouldn't risk a daylight attack. That they weren't coming after all. That Leon had been successful.

There was an occasional murmur or someone rearranged their equipment, but otherwise we waited in silence. I checked myself for the umpteenth time.

Mrs. Partridge waited slightly behind us with stocks of spare ammo. Dr. Dowson and Professor Rapson were off to one side of me, whispering indignantly to each other in the dark.

I wriggled round, hissed, "What?" and stopped and stared in disbelief at their miscellaneous weapons of mass destruction. I saw what looked like a flame-thrower apparently made of an old milk churn and some industrial hosing, caltrops, a homemade crossbow, half a dozen Molotov cocktails, and what looked like a Vickers gun from WWI.

"What is all that?"

"Back-up," said Professor Rapson and I wondered if it was too late to request a transfer to another team. There seemed every indication this one would fall victim to friendly fire.

"Last resort," I said warningly, wondering if we were in more danger from behind than in front.

"Got it," they said gleefully. Markham rolled his eyes.

Peterson turned to me. "Bet you wish you'd stayed at Agincourt, now."

"I'm prepared to admit it might have had attractions that I overlooked at the time. How about you? Any regrets?"

"Well, I always wanted Carthage. And Waterloo. Thermopylae would have been good, too. I'm sorry to have missed that."

"Yes, me too. Well, if we ever get out of this, maybe you and I could . . . ?"

"Good idea. We'll take a picnic. Now there's a good title for a book. *Picnic at Thermopylae.*"

There was a pause.

"I'm glad we're in this together, Tim."

"That's us. Always together. Through thick and thin."

"Sick and sin."

"Loss and win."

In my mind, I saw another Sick Bay. Another Tim.

I smiled, sadly. "One last adventure . . ."

They were brave words, but we really didn't stand a chance. This wasn't Thermopylae where a thousand stout hearts could hold off overwhelming odds. Or Agincourt, where brilliant tactics and iron nerve won the day. This was St. Mary's. A handful of people, inadequately armed, defending a dilapidated old building. A couple of well-placed mortars would bring the roof down, then it would just be a case of them mopping up the survivors, installing their own people, and then their victory would be complete. They would have it all.

If they came.

And if they did come, it was because Leon had failed. Somewhere, in some far-off time I'd never know, he'd gone down in a hail of fire . . . dying for what he believed in and the bright, brilliant flame that had been St. Mary's . . .

No. Stop that.

I thought of Leonidas of Sparta. He didn't know the future of the western world rested on his shoulders but that didn't stop him drawing his sword, planting his feet, and defying the entire Persian Empire.

Our forebears at the Gates of Grief didn't know they were the direct ancestors of nearly everyone on the planet—they just built their little rafts, climbed aboard, and struck out for the unknown.

History glitters with the tales of men and women who, with no thought of reward or glory, make their stand and quietly do their duty. I wasn't going to be a lesser person than my ancestors.

We crouched in the dark and waited for them.

If they came.

THEY CAME.

ALL THE HEATH ROBINSON devices installed around the building sounded off simultaneously, signifying the arrival outside of the Forces of Darkness.

My world stopped and for a moment, I just couldn't move at all. Because I'd lost him. Again. Our second chance was never going to happen. All our plans . . . All those whispered conversations in a cold, dark pod . . . When we'd allowed ourselves to hope . . .

I looked down at the gun in my hand and felt everything begin to drift away. Peterson, who knew what this meant to me, briefly touched my shoulder, bringing me back.

I nodded and swallowed something huge and painful in my throat.

Then it was down to business.

In the absence of Major Guthrie, Markham spoke a few rallying words to the troops.

"OK people, listen up. This is it. We all know what to do. If we remember our training then we'll be fine. Our job is to hold the front doors and stairs for as long as possible. There will be noise and chaos and you'll be scared, but that's OK because we're St. Mary's and no one does noise and chaos as well as us. Major Guthrie estimates we'll be outnumbered about six to one . . ."

Around me, heads bobbed up sharply and Peterson said, "Um . . ."

"So what I'm saying is, the first one to shoot their six nips back and puts the kettle on."

There was a startled silence, then someone laughed and Mrs. Partridge (wonderful woman) raised her arm and said, "Milk and two sugars, please." There was more laughter and then, suddenly, this was it.

An amplified voice boomed from outside.

"Dr. Bairstow. This is the Time Police. You are no longer in control of this unit. Please instruct your people to lay down their weapons and surrender."

My com crackled. Dr. Bairstow was broadcasting to all of us.

"Good morning. This is Dr. Bairstow. Our pods and archive have been removed. You will get nothing from us. You should leave now, while you still can."

"Members of St. Mary's. We understand that you are acting on the instructions of your Director. Do not allow him to imperil your lives. Lay down your weapons and exit the building. We wish you no harm."

Silence.

"Dr. Bairstow, you are outgunned and outnumbered. There is no other option other than to surrender immediately."

There was a long pause and then Dr. Bairstow said, "Very well, I am willing to discuss terms of surrender."

A murmur ran around the building.

"There are no terms. Simply lay down your weapons, exit the building, and await instructions."

"I'm terribly sorry; I seem, quite inadvertently, to have given you the wrong impression. It was your surrender I wished to discuss."

Hardly had the words left his mouth than the whole world exploded. The front doors imploded. Someone, Guthrie, I think, bellowed, "Enemy at the gates! Good luck, everyone." This was it.

We crouched behind our barricades and opened fire. Everyone performed perfectly. We laid down a continuous barrage and nothing got through the shattered doors. I kept firing until empty, passed for reloading, picked up my second weapon, and did it again. And again. And again. And again.

Guthrie yelled, "Cease fire!" and silence dropped like a lead weight.

I shook my head to clear the ringing in my ears.

I could hear shots firing outside and around Hawking. We took advantage of the pause and shifted our position slightly. Mrs. Partridge passed me two fully loaded weapons. I checked my unused blaster was still within reach and flexed my fingers, arms, and shoulders.

Markham turned his head and whispered, "Everyone all right?"

"Yes."

"Yes."

"I think so."

"Don't say it like that, Andrew. This is a military situation. You must strive to convey your information with the utmost speed and accuracy. Like me."

I said, "So, you're OK then, Dr. Dowson?"

"Oh, yes, yes, my dear. Never better."

I avoided Markham's eye.

WE COULDN'T HOLD THEM back. I don't know why we ever thought we could. Dieter's team fell back from Hawking and into the Hall in good order. Markham and I moved forward to give them as much cover as we could while the other teams covered us.

I fired until my head ached with the noise of it. My hands were burning. Occasionally, Mrs. Partridge would hand me a reloaded weapon. I hadn't realised she had moved forward with us. Thinking about it, I would have been more surprised if she hadn't.

I could hear fragments of chatter in my ears.

"Evans! To your right! To your right!"

"Ritter's down!"

"Cover me! Moving forward!"

"Pull him back! Pull him back!"

Slowly but surely, Dieter got his people away. I caught a brief glimpse of him, supporting someone whose face I couldn't see.

Markham tapped me on the shoulder and indicated I should withdraw. Mrs. Partridge was already gone. The barricades were opened and Dieter and his team were dragging their wounded through. The other teams upstairs continued to lay down fire so I turned, and keeping low, ran back towards the stairs. Throwing myself through the gap, I was seized by Professor Rapson and hauled in. Dr. Dowson replaced the barricade.

Mrs. Partridge was crouched over Ritter, her hands pressed hard over a horrifying chest wound. Her hands, bloodied to the elbows, were inside his chest. I couldn't even see if he was still alive. She shouted, "Medics!" and we got him away. The rest of the team dispersed to join the others around the Gallery and on the floor above.

I turned back, found my line of sight, and the next minute they were appearing in the shattered doorway, firing as they came. I know fear increases numbers but it struck me we were outnumbered a good deal more than six to one. I wouldn't be getting my cup of tea anytime soon.

My gun was so hot I could barely keep my grip. Sweat ran down into my eyes and blurred my vision. Despite my best efforts, my wrists and forearms trembled with the effort. My mouth was so dry I could barely swallow. Casings flew around me, pinging off the floor.

After what seemed like an entire ice age, the firing ceased. I craned my head to see why. Yes, we'd held them, but they had only to keep pressing their advantage. It was surely only a matter of time. I looked at Mrs. Partridge's seriously depleted stock of ammo. She shook her head.

I checked my weapons. Both were empty. My blaster was still charged, but that wouldn't last long.

For some reason the Time Police had withdrawn back through the doors again. Had they retreated? Surely, it couldn't be that easy?

The Hall was littered with casings, pieces of barricade, lumps of plaster, and splintered wood. Thick, blue smoke stung my eyes and rasped my throat. The whole world smelled of cordite, burning wood, and dust. I was desperately thirsty.

I rolled over and lay on my back to catch my breath, staring up through the lantern at the dawning day. We'd been at this less than an hour. It felt like years.

Then, suddenly, they were back. I heard Guthrie's voice raised in warning.

"Incoming!"

A hail of something ripped across the Hall. Plaster cracked and was instantly vaporised into dust. The lovely old wooden bannisters disintegrated. Lethal splinters of wood ricocheted across the Gallery. The noise was ear bleeding. I had no idea what sort of weapon it was, but whatever it was pointed at just flew apart in a shower of death and destruction. Around the Gallery, people couldn't move. Like me, they were completely pinned down. There was nothing we could do.

"Heavy fire! Heavy fire! Take cover!"

It wasn't just here in the Hall. Beneath me, I felt the building shudder. The blast doors were opening. Hawking was breached.

I was conscious of huge disappointment. I thought we would have lasted longer than this. We'd tried so hard. But, although I personally wouldn't care to tangle with a bunch of tea-crazed historians, there was no getting around the fact that we were amateurs. They were about to roll straight over the top of us just as the Persians eventually rolled over the Spartans, all thanks to that treacherous bastard Ephialtes.

Why did I keep thinking of the Spartans?

I became aware that the sounds of gunfire were dying away. I risked a quick look around. Were we out of ammunition?

"Attention," said Major Guthrie, in my ear. "All civilian staff withdraw. This is not a suggestion. Hand over any weapons and ammo remaining and get yourselves to safety. That's an order."

I felt, rather than saw movement around me. They were reluctant to go and I didn't blame them. They were being cleared out of the way for the final act. I wouldn't have gone, myself, and I was surprised they took it so quietly. I expected at least a murmur of protest from Professor Rapson, but one at a time they pulled back into the shadows and disappeared.

Guthrie spoke again. "We can wait to be cut to pieces, or we can take as many as possible with us. Load up. We move in thirty seconds."

St. Mary's' last charge.

I thought back to the day I first walked up the drive of that other St. Mary's, all those years ago. I never thought I'd end my days here, in a strange world, caught up in someone else's war, about to die with my boots on.

Beside me, Markham rammed home his last clip and grinned at me. I turned my head to Peterson. "Still no regrets?"

"No," he said, checking his stun gun was still on his belt. "You?"

I did not think of Leon. If he was dead then nothing mattered very much anyway. "No," and left it at that.

The barricade was in splinters. There was nothing to stop them getting in and we'd never hold them. The best we could do was a final all-out blaze of glory. Typical St. Mary's. When the chips are down we don't whine and we don't run—we do some damage.

"Right," said Guthrie. "On my mark. Straight down the stairs—fan out to each side of the Hall, and nail the bastards as they come through the vestibule. Everyone set?"

Peterson slapped my helmet and I slapped Markham's. I picked up my blaster. We rose to a crouch—ready to go.

"Steady," said Guthrie. "Mark!"

I leaped to my feet, took one pace forward, and crashed heavily to the ground as someone grabbed my ankle. At least two people ran straight over the top of me. What the hell . . . ?

I rolled over and very nearly blew Mrs. Partridge's head off. Why was she still here? Why was she hanging on to my ankle?

We glared at each other as people ran past.

I tried to pull my leg away, desperate to be with the others in their last moments. "Let me go."

She shook her head and pointed down the Gallery.

I saw just the slightest flicker of movement in the gloom on the other side of the Gallery. Bitchface Barclay. I hadn't given her a thought. What was she up to? Could be anything. She could be taking a message. Or going for fresh ammo. Or looking for a better position. Even running away.

No, she wasn't doing any of those things. Now I knew why I kept thinking of the Spartans and betrayal. She was making sure that whatever happened to anyone else, she came out a winner.

I hesitated.

Below, down in the Hall, I heard the battle roar—"St. Mary's!"

Ian Guthrie led the charge, firing as he went. Markham was at his shoulder. Peterson, Van Owen, Dieter, they were all there.

No one held back. My heart broke with pride and grief. The noise was overwhelming. Like the Thunderchild, St. Mary's was going down with all guns blazing. I should be down there with them. It wouldn't make the slightest bit of difference, but that wasn't the point.

I kicked out again. "Let me go."

I must have hurt her, but she wouldn't release me.

I heard her clearly over all the racket. "You wanted to know why you are here. You are here for Justice." I could hear the capital letter.

Now? Now she tells me . . . ?

She relinquished her hold and crawled away into the shadows before I could say anything. Her calm assumption that I would abandon my colleagues and friends to do her bidding was breathtaking. Who did she think I was?

I was the person who would sort out Isabella Barclay, that's who she thought I was.

I handed my blaster to Prentiss as she ran past, because her need was greater than mine. She grabbed it and was gone.

I moved around the Gallery, hugging the wall, crunching over the remains of the banisters, shattered doors, and lumps of plaster. Glancing down into the Hall, I could see there was nothing I could do. My presence would not have made the slightest difference.

The Time Police were pouring in through the vestibule.

I saw something arc through the air and with a clap that hurt my ears, Ian Guthrie was blown backwards. He hit the wall with tremendous impact and lay very still. The same blast flattened Evans who disappeared under a pile of rubble.

On the other side of the room, Markham, who had escaped the worst of it, flung himself at an enormous black figure. He was casually batted aside. The last I saw of him, three more Time Police were converging on him.

Peterson got the furthest, nearly reaching the doors before a hail of something spun him around, and he fell to the floor.

I had to move. I could do nothing for anyone down there, but up here . . .

Trying to combine speed and invisibility, I slipped into R & D. Some of the wounded had been brought in here. Hunter was working on someone and shouting instructions to someone else at the same time. She saw me, paled, and said, "Markham?"

I couldn't find any words, so I just nodded. She'd find out soon enough.

All these old rooms had connecting doors. I worked my way through Wardrobe, finally emerging in the short corridor that led to the Boss's office.

Below me, I could hear gunfire, people shouting, and the crump of another explosion. I hesitated, still feeling I should be back there, standing with the rest of St. Mary's and defending my unit as they went down one by one.

"You are defending your unit," said the stupid voice in my head. "Something's not right. Stop pissing about and find out what it is."

Mrs. Partridge's office was still empty. Bare shelves, bare tables. With typical Mrs. Partridge thoroughness, she'd even emptied the waste bin. Moving as silently as I could, I eased around the door. Barclay was talking. Of course she was talking. She was always bloody talking.

Dr. Bairstow stood at his desk in front of the window. Sounds of battle came up through the floor. Why was he here instead of with his unit?

One of the big blasters was propped against the wall behind him, just out of his reach. He was in full battle kit and by the expression on his face, in no mood to take prisoners.

I slid further into the room, desperate to see what was going on and hidden, I hoped, in shadow.

Another explosion brought part of the ceiling down somewhere behind me. I heard lumps of plaster clatter to the floor but I didn't dare take my eyes from the scene in front of me.

She held a gun on him. Behind her, the safe door stood ajar. Whatever was going on here, I was too late.

As I watched, she reached into the safe and twisted something. Behind her, on the wall, a small panel snicked open. She moved carefully across the room, trying to cover him and retrieve whatever was in there at the same time.

He stood perfectly still. I saw his eyes drift towards his blaster. She saw it too, saying sharply, "No. Put both your hands flat on the desk."

"What are you doing, Miss Barclay?"

"Oh, for heaven's sake! What does it look as if I'm doing?"

"It looks as if you are taking advantage of the situation to make your long-planned move to assume control of this unit."

"Well done. And?"

"And what?"

"Aren't you going to say 'Over my dead body' or something equally ludicrous and dramatic?"

"No."

"Shame," she said. "Come in, Maxwell."

I didn't move.

"Come in—or I shoot him now instead of later."

I walked slowly into the room. I had nothing—no weapon and no plan, but I wasn't going to leave Dr. Bairstow to face this alone. If, somehow, I could buy him a few vital moments, I would do it gladly. I couldn't care less what happened to me, but I did care what happened to Dr. Bairstow and to St. Mary's. If, somehow, I could take this bitch with me . . .

"Gun on the floor."

"I'm not armed," I said, regretting now that I'd given my blaster away and holding up my hands.

"Stand over there. Right over there. By the window."

I complied.

"Now," she said. "I'm going to remove the data stick. You cannot prevent this. The only thing I have to do then is decide whether I shoot you both now, or later."

Not at all would be my first choice.

"Give it up, Izzie. You'll never get out of the building alive."

"I don't intend to get out of the building at all. While everyone is battling it out downstairs, I'm up here heroically defending Dr. Bairstow from assassination. I find you trying to steal vital data concerning our remote site. Bravely, I intervene. We will struggle. The gun will go off, tragically killing Dr. Bairstow. I wrest it from you, and in the struggle, I shoot you dead. Who will blame me? I shall be a heroine. Should the Time Police prevail, possession of this information will render me more than acceptable to them. Should St. Mary's win, I fought to defend Dr. Bairstow from someone half the unit still considers an imposter. In either case, I shall be appointed Director of St. Mary's. Which will be very pleasant, but not half as pleasant as killing both of you."

Dr. Bairstow raised his head.

"Whatever did we do to you, Isabella? As far as I know, we welcomed you here. You were one of us and yet you've been selling us out for years. You're how they knew that Maxwell had returned to St. Mary's."

Her face twisted. Deliberately or not, he'd touched a nerve.

"She's not Maxwell. Maxwell is dead. Why can't any of you believe that? We all saw the body, for God's sake. She's dead, I tell you."

The gun swivelled to me. "I don't know who you are, but you're not Maxwell. You're just some tramp Leon picked up from somewhere, when he should have been looking at me."

Below us, the sounds of battle redoubled. I had to finish this quickly. People were dying out there. I needed to provoke her into doing something stupid and then when she shot me, with luck, Dr. Bairstow could shoot her. Not my favourite plan, but better than nothing.

I said wearily, "Oh, we're not back to that again, are we? He's not interested, Izzie. You said it yourself. He'd rather be with some tramp off the street than with you. Anyone would."

I really must try for a career in the Peace Corps.

She was too angry to speak. In her world, I should be begging for my life and I wasn't. I swept on.

"You're wasting your time. He never even sees you if I'm in the room. You could drape yourself naked at his feet and he'd still step over you to get to me."

"Shut up!"

"She's right, Isabella," said Dr. Bairstow, quite calmly for a man trapped in a room between two snarling redheads. "In fact, St. Mary's doesn't want you, either. You may consider your employment at an end."

Her gun came up and her eyes flashed dangerously. "We'll see about that. You are about to be caught in an unfortunate accident and she's going down with her face blown off."

"And you're going to be Director of St. Mary's and Leon is going to fall into your arms," I interrupted. "And no one will ever know what a two-faced, scum-sucking, piss-boilingly treacherous bitch you really are. And always have been."

"I would not, if I were you, Isabella, assume that the Time Police will welcome you back into their fold. They didn't seem too pleased with you the last time they were here."

"They'll come round when I give them this."

She flourished the stick. The location of our remote site. With our pods. And our archive. Everything they needed to start again. They could just wipe us out and start elsewhere.

"It's encrypted," I said, desperately.

She smirked. "And I'm Head of IT. Without this—without your pods and your archive, St. Mary's does not exist. We take

this and re-establish elsewhere. Under the leadership of someone who appreciates the true potential of time travel."

She really shouldn't have used those words. They're like a
red rag to Dr. Bairstow's bull. He made an involuntary movement.

She jumped and fired, frightening herself as much as
everyone else and at that range, even she couldn't miss.

He crumpled to the floor.

I should have leaped there and then, but for one fatal
moment, I was so shocked I couldn't move at all.

She shot Dr. Bairstow!

He lay on his side, with his bad leg twisted beneath him,
still gripping his stick.

I couldn't believe what she'd done. I couldn't believe she
would shoot Dr. Bairstow.

Neither, it seemed, could she, standing open-mouthed,
staring at the still body at her feet, eyes wide with shock.

I tried to press home the advantage, saying gently, "Yes, it's
not so easy to kill someone close up, is it, Izzie? Much easier
to do it from a distance." I looked around the room. "Shame
there's no gas fire."

She dragged her gaze from the unmoving Dr. Bairstow.
"What?"

"You know—a gas fire. You light them and they give off
heat."

She stared at me.

"Or, in some cases, you light them and they give off carbon
monoxide. Not normally, of course. You usually have to shove
a bird's nest down the chimney first and then top it up with
a bucket full of twigs and gravel and soot. Having done that,
you sit back, wait until the cooler weather, and practise your
grief-stricken expression. Oh—and remove the battery from
the detector, of course. It's all a bit of a waste of time if you
forget to do that."

If she'd been white before, she was grey, now. The hand holding her gun was vibrating uncontrollably. Was I about to have my face blown off by accident?

Even over all the clamour downstairs, I could hear her whisper. "Who are you? For God's sake, who are you?"

A voice that wasn't my own said, "I am Justice and I have come for you."

She stepped back and then made a desperate attempt to recover, dragging her eyes from Dr. Bairstow, swallowing hard, and standing straighter.

"I don't know what you're talking about. I didn't do anything."

"Yes, you did. And I'm not the only one who knows, either."

She was getting herself under control again.

"Oh, really? You're going to try to buy your life by saying that if anything happens to you then this other person will go to the authorities? Good luck with that. You have no proof. There is no proof."

"Oh, God, Izzie, concentrate, will you? This is me. I don't care about the bloody authorities. And I certainly don't care about proof. And neither does the other person. So know this. If anything happens to me, she will come for you. Silently. Out of the dark. And you'll never see it coming. And you'll never know anything about it."

The words jerked out between cold, stiff lips. Quiet, deadly, little words in a quiet, deadly, little voice that was, nevertheless, perfectly audible above the noise below.

She backed up until she was a good, safe distance away from me. She had the winning hand and she knew it.

The data she carried was priceless. She could bargain her way out of any situation and she would. Beginning with the demand to be the new Director of the new St. Mary's. The first steps on the road to God knew what. This was no longer about Leon. Or me. Or the other Maxwell. Or even the Time Police. She had to be stopped.

Below us, the Battle of St. Mary's raged on. Occasional muffled booms shook the building beneath my feet.

I said, "Let me see to Dr. Bairstow," and moved slowly toward him. She raised her gun. "Stop right there."

I don't often do as I'm told, but I was alongside his desk, which was where I wanted to be. From here , there was just the faintest chance I could reach her.

We stared at each other. Everything else slowly receded into the background.

I took a deep breath to calm down. I had to get this right.

"So, Izzie—what now?"

"For you? Nothing."

At that moment, with a final explosion that shook the room, all sounds of battle ceased. The silence was deafening. And terrifying. I could think of only one reason why everything should stop.

St. Mary's was finished.

SIXTEEN

THEY SAY THAT JUST before you die, your whole life flashes in front of your eyes, but since I was too busy concentrating on Barclay, I missed it.

"Take off your helmet."

I blinked. "Why? What for?"

"I want to watch your brains splatter all over that wall. I want to watch your face blow apart. I want to see that stupid, smug, self-satisfied smile wiped off your face. For ever. So take off your helmet."

She quite literally shook with fury. Or fear, maybe. She should turn and walk out of the room. Now. I'd be too busy with Dr. Bairstow to prevent her. She should go now. That was what she should do. But she was going to take a moment for personal revenge and that's always a mistake. I've said it before. Don't gloat—just shoot.

I reached up slowly and fumbled to get my helmet off. I pulled it away from my head, took a moment to sigh with relief, wiped my forearm across my sweaty forehead, turned slightly to lay it on the desk, pivoted on my heels, and threw it at her.

And missed.

She fired at the same moment and her bullet thunked into the wall beside me. I felt the wind of its passing on my cheek. Bloody hell! If I'd known she was that good a shot . . .

I leaped for her.

I was far too far away. I would never have made it. I should have died there and then, knowing that I'd lost everything.

Dr. Bairstow swung his stick and caught her behind the knees. She sagged forwards, instinctively catching at the table to save herself, dropping the gun. I threw myself on her. We both crashed to the ground and fought for our lives.

I'd once killed her. She'd once killed me. A score draw so far. Now we were into extra time.

I drove my fist hard into her face, feeling bones shatter. Hers and mine. She was jabbing below my ribs—short, hard blows, every one precision-delivered in exactly the same place. I felt pain shooting through my kidneys, around my back . . .

She bucked suddenly and I flew through the air, rolled, and staggered painfully to my feet. I couldn't stand straight, but she couldn't see properly. Blood streamed from her nose and mouth. Already, her eyes were swelling.

My hand was a ball of throbbing fire.

Face to face really wasn't her style at all. She was looking past me for a way out. No, she wasn't—she was looking for her gun. We both saw it at the same moment.

She tried to scramble for it and I fell on top of her, which must have driven the breath from her body, because she suddenly went limp. I seized a great lump of her stupid red hair and banged her battered face into the parquet. Hard. She screamed in pain. I put my knee on the back of her neck, leaned forwards, removed the gun from her fist, and slapped it on my sticky patch.

Rolling off her, I stood shakily.

"Get up."

She moaned something indistinguishable and I kicked her hard on her knee.

"Get up."

She was crying. Great bloody bubbles frothed from her nose. Blood ran down her chin. Her jaw looked the wrong shape. I'd done some real damage there.

I wasn't much better myself. My hand looked and felt like a purple, puffy football. A belt of fire encircled my waist. Every time I breathed, a sharp pain stabbed my ribs.

I left her for a minute and bent painfully over Dr. Bairstow.

"Sir?"

He was very white. I stared anxiously, but couldn't see any blood. Kevlar does its best, but he'd been shot at close range. At the very least, his ribs were broken.

His eyes flickered open.

"Buy . . . me . . . time."

"I will, sir."

I picked up the precious data stick and placed it in his hand. His fingers curled around it and a little colour came back into his face.

I placed the blaster within his reach and left him.

Time to find out what was happening elsewhere.

And buy him some time.

I HAD TO HELP her up. I wasn't very gentle, but as far as I could see, her weakness was genuine. I heaved her out of the door, and with the gun rammed into the back of her neck, we took the short walk to the Gallery and looked down.

The Battle of St. Mary's was over.

People lay where they had fallen. My heart clenched. They couldn't all be dead, surely? I forgot Barclay, forgot everything. I stood on the Gallery and stared down at the ruins of St. Mary's.

The Hall was wrecked. Small fires burned. Scorch marks bloomed up the walls. The plaster was pockmarked and scored from flying shrapnel. Splintered wood lay in heaps. Most of the banisters around the Gallery had just—gone.

Bodies sprawled everywhere. I forgot this was another St. Mary's. These were people I'd known. People I'd worked with. People I'd loved.

If I turned my head, I could see Ian Guthrie, slumped against the wall like a broken doll, his chin resting on his chest, looking curiously vulnerable.

Dieter lay where he'd fallen. His eyes were open but I was certain he didn't know where he was. Markham was partially buried under a pile of rubble and broken glass. What I could see of his face was just a mask of blood.

There was so much blood. Great arcs of it sprayed up the walls and pooled across the floor. People had walked through it and bloody footprints criss-crossed the floor.

Professor Rapson and Dr. Dowson lay as they'd fought—together. The professor still clutched the remains of his home-made crossbow. By the looks of things, he'd run out of bolts and been using it as a club. Dr. Dowson's blood-stained morningstar had fallen from his grasp and lay nearby. Even now, he was making feeble moves to pick it up.

Our caretaker, Mr. Strong, lay nearby. He'd disobeyed the order for the civilian staff to retreat. His glorious comb-over was in disarray. Long strands of grey hair flopped over his face. He lay very still. He was an old man and he had pinned on his medals and turned out to fight for St. Mary's. He lay very still as dust floated downwards, slowly covering the brightly coloured ribbons on his chest. It looked as if he'd been defending St. Mary's with some kind of garden implement.

A dirty and furious Dr. Foster was supervising the removal of the wounded. Hunter knelt over someone I couldn't see, packing a wound, and calling over her shoulder for more dressings.

A figure I thought might be Peterson lay in a heap. Not moving.

I saw Perkins, Clerk, and Prentiss, their helmets off, being pushed against a wall and made to kneel. Dirty, defeated, and angry.

All the courage. All the spirit. All the bloody-mindedness. All gone.

The Time Police were kicking open doors and pulling out people who had their hands in the air. Everyone was shunted down into the Hall. All those not actually unconscious were kicked into a kneeling position, their hands behind their heads.

Something was missing.

Even as I stared, Colonel Albay, helmet off, his face streaked with sweat and dirt, glanced up.

"Dr. Maxwell! Please join us. Is that a hostage? How kind, but it's not a bring your own, you know."

I preferred him before he had a sense of humour.

"Please take care on the stairs."

He wasn't joking. Lack of ammunition had not been a problem. We're St. Mary's. We can fashion a heat-seeking missile out of two toilet rolls and an elastic band. I remembered the tangle of equipment behind Dr. Dowson and Professor Rapson. They had been letting rip with medieval anti-personnel devices, and with some success, it appeared. The stairs glistened with oil. An old medieval trick, oiling the staircases and ramps. Simple, but effective. Judging by the smears on their uniforms, quite a few of the Time Police must have come crashing down.

Two of them were kicking homemade caltrops to one side of the Hall. Caltrops are two or more nails, twisted together in such a way that one wicked spike always points upwards. Not something you want to fall on if you've just slipped on a patch of oil.

And the third part of their unholy trinity—sand. You heat buckets of sand—something with which St. Mary's was always liberally provided in the form of fire buckets—and tip it over the battlements onto the attackers below. As anyone who's ever eaten a sandwich on the beach knows, sand gets everywhere. In your hair, down your neck, inside your armour . . . and hot sand, baking-hot sand, is no different. And it retains its heat. And it doesn't shift. It gets into all your nooks and crannies, and even when it cools, it's still chafing away, driving the victims insane. I sometimes wonder if Professor Rapson did his training in one of the circles of hell.

I felt a momentary surge of pride. We'd taken on a superior force and we'd given them a run for their money. They knew they'd been in a fight. We'd fought with every last weapon at our disposal. I suspected the professor had even had a plan to prise up the stone flags and throw those as well.

But we'd been defeated . . .

It was a measure of the completeness of his victory that Albay didn't even bother to send an escort for me. There was nothing in the world I could do that would threaten him in any way. If I resisted, he'd simply have someone shot.

Since I had no choice, I pushed Barclay ahead of me. Given her recent history with the Time Police, she was probably as reluctant to go down there as I was, because, somewhat dramatically, as we reached the top of the stairs, she collapsed.

I sighed. Nothing but trouble.

My foot, never a limb over which I'd had a lot of control, made one of those inadvertent nudges and she fell down the stairs. She came to rest on the half landing, and since she'd come so far, it seemed unkind not to help her the rest of the way. Her head hit every single stair with a kind of thudding, booming noise. Her arms and legs whirled limply. I thought I heard something crack. She lay in a tangle at the foot of the stairs. If she hadn't been unconscious at the top, she certainly was at the bottom.

Slowly, I followed her down and was relieved of my weapon.

"And where is Dr. Bairstow?"

I said, dully, "Here, somewhere," and looked vaguely around.

"Do I really have to tell you what will happen if you lie to me again?"

"She shot him."

He nodded and two officers peeled off towards his office. Good luck to them. He had a blaster.

The occupiers were clearing rooms and gathering weapons. Over in the corner of the Hall, someone was setting up a series of portable lights.

I wondered how Hawking looked and whether there was anything left. I wondered if Dr. Bairstow had managed to get away. I hoped to God that he had because I really didn't want him seeing this. I looked around at a defeated St. Mary's and had to blink hard to keep back the tears.

The lights came on, illuminating the Hall but leaving everywhere else in deep shadow. I looked around at the groups of people being herded together and realised what was missing. Or rather—who. Where were the civilian staff? Oh, my God. Had they already been removed? I had a sudden dreadful picture of them being shoved into some closed vehicle, shocked and hurt, and driven—where? And for what purpose?

I stared hard at the stone flags, impotent rage and despair boiling inside me, forbidding myself to cry.

It started to snow.

I know! That's what I thought! But I swear, it started to snow. The air was full of a fine white powder, drifting gently across the Hall to fall silently on every horizontal surface. I peered upwards into the gloom. I could see dark figures up high, leaning precariously over what was left of the Gallery, shaking white dust over everything.

And while I was getting my head around that, something sailed out of the dark, fell at my feet and burst. And another one over there. And there. I looked up. Above our heads, Mrs. Mack was hurling scores of fat condoms down into the Hall, and, believe me, that is not a phrase anyone should ever expect to use. Intimate rubber items plopped around us, splitting on impact, and diffusing even more clouds of white dust.

Colonel Albay and I, united for once, stared at them in disbelief. I looked down at myself, lightly dusted with flour.

Flour? Were we going to bake them to death?

Then my mind flew back to the day I sat in Mrs. Mack's office, watching the cat, Vortigern, slumbering heavily on a hairy copy of *The Flour Handling Regulations* and I knew what was going to happen next. Flour dust is one of the most explosive substances around. More explosive even than coal dust.

Guthrie had led the conventional defence. When that was finished, the professor had done what he knew best and improvised. And when he was done, the civilian staff had stepped up. Surreptitiously, I looked around for somewhere safe to hide.

Around me, The Forces of Darkness had stopped rounding up personnel and were looking around in puzzlement. I saw one raise a com device. "I think it's flour. No, no idea, sir. Yes, copy that." He motioned his men forward. There were a good number of them in the Hall now. They were all looking around, watching the flour fall.

I edged slowly backwards.

Because Mrs. Partridge stood motionless at the top of the stairs. She was dirty and smoke-streaked. Her arms were bloody to the elbows and her hair was falling down. I thought suddenly of The Furies, those remorseless, merciless goddesses of retribution, who pursue their victims to the grave and beyond. She stood under the glass lantern, holding something cylindrical. Not a scroll, this time. She was holding a fizzer.

Around the Hall, everything stopped. Half a hundred Time Police stared in disbelief and then the penny dropped for everyone.

Beside me, Colonel Albay raised his gun. I grabbed for his arm, pulled it down with all my might, and shouted at her. "Do it. Do it now."

She pulled the tag.

Time does slow down when you're about to die. I saw the flash as it ignited. I watched her draw back her arm and hurl it high into the air. It rose in a graceful arc, turning end over end and then, at the height of its trajectory, exploding into a brilliant red ball of flame, just as it was designed to do.

I pushed the colonel away and dropped. Around me, those of St. Mary's who weren't already on the ground were hurling themselves there and covering their heads. I ignored my complaining ribs and curled into a tight ball that I hoped would expose as little of me as possible and waited for flour power.

Nothing happened for long enough for me to worry it hadn't worked.

A long second passed. The building seemed to inhale and then exhale.

And then it was the end of the world.

I THOUGHT I'D GONE blind. My eyes hurt. Even to blink was painful. And I couldn't see. Just an after-image of dirty swirls. No—I could see. I wasn't blind after all. The dirty swirls were thick clouds of heavy dust hanging around. Through them, high above my head, I could see a tiny patch of beautiful blue sky. Clever Mrs. Partridge. The Hall, with its thick walls and glass lantern, was built like a fireworks factory and the main force of the blast had obviously gone straight up, taking the lantern with it. I could see the remains of the metal framework silhouetted against the sky.

Lifting my head one painful inch, I found I was covered in dust, dirt, and shards of broken glass. Lumps of rubble and debris were still settling around me. Everything smelled of toast. And singed hair. Mine.

Everyone was down—Time Police, St. Mary's, everyone. Bodies were scattered everywhere. The only thing still moving was the dirty smoke rising lazily out through the hole in the roof.

I don't know for how long I lay there. Time ceased to have any meaning. I would have been quite happy to stay there for ever, but a little voice at the back of my mind was screaming at me to get up. Because the first people on their feet would have won and it had to be St. Mary's. Mrs. Partridge had bought us another chance, but at what cost to herself? If I could just get up . . .

It wasn't going to happen.

All right, if I could just move an arm . . . Start with that and work up . . .

No. Still not going to happen.

Get up, Maxwell. For God's sake, you have to get up.

I turned my head. Colonel Albay lay on his side, facing me, bleeding badly from a deep gash across his cheekbone. He focused on me and smiled. I blinked to clear my eyes of the stinging dust, but he definitely smiled. I saw him make the effort to move. He began to pull himself towards me. Old memories came flooding back. When something bad was about to happen . . . and I was paralysed. Unable even to close my eyes. When something evil crushed me with its weight and I couldn't move even a muscle to prevent it and there was no one to help. There was never anyone to help.

Using his forearms, he dragged himself towards me. There was no escape. I could barely move my eyes, let alone anything else. Unable to move, I watched him crawl over rubble and glass, leaving a bloody trail in his wake.

I never realised what large hands he had.

He placed one hand carefully over my mouth, as if to prevent me calling for help, although I couldn't have, even if I wanted to. I had no voice. And who would have heard me?

Slowly, gently almost, he adjusted the position of his hand until it seemed he had it positioned to his complete satisfaction.

He was still smiling.

Then, using his thumb and forefinger, he pinched my nostrils closed.

Suddenly, I couldn't breathe. I couldn't breathe. At all.

I tried to twist my head from side to side. To dislodge his grip. To suck in some desperately needed air. I could hear my own pulse throbbing inside my head. I tried to get a hand free. I tried to drum my heels. It hurt. Everything hurt. My chest was exploding in pain. My lips were smashed against my teeth. Even my poor nose hurt.

And all the time—he smiled.

Something moved. From the corner of my eye, I caught a movement. And so, it seemed, did Colonel Albay.

Dark shadows moved in the swirling dust. I could see a little red dot jumping and jerking its way across the hall. Then another and another, then a whole bunch of them. Ruler straight lines of red light cut through the murk, others bloomed in the swirling dust.

Bloody hell, no wonder he was smiling. Reinforcements. Even more of them this time. These people had endless resources and we had nothing left. We'd given our all and, finally, we were finished. I was too tired to feel despair. Silly little thoughts danced through my mind on their way to oblivion. That the red lights in the swirling dust clouds were really rather pretty. That in all the worlds out there, somewhere, surely there was one where Leon and I managed to be both alive and together. That, somewhere, we had a future.

Albay looked down at me. I was the last thing he ever saw. He was still smiling when he died.

I heard a sound. Above me, I felt him convulse. Blood trickled from his mouth onto my face. His lips moved, although his eyes were unfocused. The pressure eased. His hand slipped away—thank God—and I heaved in great lungfuls of air.

He fell slowly to one side. His limbs twitched uncontrollably. I smelled the sharp tang of urine. And then he died.

Behind him, a helmetless officer with a brutal haircut, barely able to support himself on one elbow, his face creased in pain, let his gun fall, closed his eyes, and fell back on the rubble.

The red beams continued to track their way across the Hall. There was no one to stop them. They fanned out, searching. One found me. I could see the little red dot bouncing on my chest. Something armoured followed along behind it and stood, looking down at me.

He turned his head and called, "Here!"

No. I wasn't going quietly. I found my last strength from somewhere and heaved myself upwards. I was aiming for his throat but sadly got only as far as his knee. I clamped myself around his lower leg and bit him.

He was wearing armour. I'm really not bright.

I waited for the bullet that would end my life, or for my head to be clubbed in, because unless he was prepared to spend the rest of his life with an historian clinging to his leg, it would be the only way to get rid of me.

My hearing must be coming back, because I thought I heard a faint voice.

"Sir, this one's trying to bite my leg."

And even more faintly, "Does she have red hair?"

They'd found me.

Things blurred and became unimportant.

Nothing mattered any longer.

I BECAME AWARE OF people around me and panicked, flailing around like a maniac. I couldn't see very well, but I know I hit someone because a voice said, "Bloody hell, that hurt."

Another voice said, "Well, at least she's not biting you," and I slid away again.

WHEN I FINALLY WOKE properly, I was in the female ward. A strange man in medical scrubs stared at me. I stared back, swallowed, and found a tiny croak.

"Friend or foe?"

"Friend," he said hastily. "For God's sake don't bite anyone else."

I stared suspiciously, formulating plans to throttle him with a bed sheet.

"How are you feeling, Dr. Maxwell?"

"Who are you? Why are you here?"

"We're from the future. We're the people who came through the door yesterday. After the explosion. Remember? The red lights? The laser sights?"

I saw again the ruin of St. Mary's. The blood. All the broken people . . .

I could summon up only a hoarse whisper, but it would do. "You couldn't have intervened an hour earlier? Half an hour even? What did you do? Wait outside until you knew it was safe to come in? After we'd done all the hard work for you? We sort out your problem and you can't even be bothered to turn up on time!" I tried to bat his arm away. "Don't touch me. Where's Dr. Foster? I want a proper doctor!"

"Dr. Foster is injured. You can see her later today."

"What's happening? Where are the Time Police? Where's Dr. Bairstow?"

"St. Mary's has regained control of the unit. That's all you need to know for the moment."

"No, it's not. What happened? Tell me'

He sighed. "I'll bring someone to talk to you. Just wait a moment."

He disappeared.

I looked around again. I was in the female ward and it was packed. Machines beeped faintly. Mrs. Partridge was directly opposite me. One arm and the side of her face were badly burned and covered in medical plastic. Fizzers are not meant to be hand held.

Mrs. Mack lay in the corner bed, one arm in a sling and a large dressing on her face. Prentiss, Polly Perkins, and Van Owen were on mattresses on the floor. We were going to need a bigger Sick Bay.

When I opened my eyes again, Helen was sitting on my bed—something that would mean instant annihilation for anyone else. I looked at her. She looked at me.

"Who are these people—good or bad? Do you want me to get out of bed and deal with them?"

"Can't you behave, just for once? You're frightening our rescuers."

"We have rescuers?"

"Don't you remember what happened?"

Memories came crashing back.

"Dr. Bairstow? I had to leave him. Did he survive?"

"Yes. He's on his feet."

"Peterson? Guthrie? Dieter?"

"At the moment, if you added them all together you wouldn't have enough for a working human being."

"So no change there, then."

"Nothing that won't scab over. They're all next door. I think Dr. Bairstow wants a word with you."

"Familiar words. Can you find me a dressing gown?"

"Idiot. He's coming to you."

There was a tap on the open door. "Ladies, may I come in?"

He wore unfamiliar sports sweats and looked very pale. For the first time ever, I thought he looked his age. He was moving with some difficulty and he limped badly. On the other hand, of course, he was limping when I first met him.

While Helen helped me sit up, he went to talk to Mrs. Mack. I heard him say, "Theresa, my dear, how are you?"

I looked away.

After a few words, he went over to Mrs. Partridge. He sat on her bed and took her unburned hand. They talked quietly for a while.

I stared out of the window.

Everyone else was asleep, so I was next on the list. Helen put a chair for him. He briefly placed a gentle hand on her shoulder. She nodded and walked away.

We stared at each other for a while. Someone should say something.

"Never thought I'd see the day when you had more hair than me, sir."

Was there a very faint sound from the bed opposite?

He countered.

"Dr. Maxwell, I hear you brought the house down."

I looked over at Mrs. Partridge who was a picture of smug innocence. "You give me too much credit, sir. I merely cushioned its fall."

He smiled slightly. "I need you again, Max. It is important to me that we remain on good terms with these people, who are our rescuers, after all. Their commander is anxious for a word with you. I would take it as a personal favour if you could at least be civil."

"Sir . . ."

"I know, Max, but nevertheless, they did their best and at the end of the day, they were here just when we needed them. Remember that when you meet him."

He was right. We'd blown up the Time Police, but we'd blown ourselves up too. When they recovered, they would have walked around and shot us like fish in a barrel. If the future St. Mary's hadn't walked through the door at that moment, we'd all be dead, and if they'd come any sooner they'd have been caught in the blast too. I should give credit where it was due.

I felt suddenly tired. I just wanted to sleep. "You're right, sir," and we both blinked a little at my actually having uttered those words. "I can let it go."

He smiled gently and I felt a lump in my throat. "You never let me down, Max."

There was a long pause while we both geared ourselves up for what was coming next.

He sighed.

"Normally, this duty falls to the Director. I do not, at present, occupy that position, but it takes the weight off other shoulders and I thought you should hear it from me."

I grew very cold. I knew what I was going to hear. Had to hear. Didn't want to hear.

"Tell me, sir. Who didn't make it?"

With a great effort, he said, "Miss Fields."

Gentle Jenny Fields. Gentle and brave. She'd volunteered to stay and now she would never leave. I looked past him to Mrs. Mack. She turned her head away.

"She was caught in the crossfire outside the library."

I took a moment to remember her, unusually pugnacious, telling everyone she'd never shot anyone before, but she wanted to stay.

I knew there was more.

"Who else?"

"Weller and Ritter. From the Security section. Ritter fell and Weller went back for him."

Of course he did. The three of them, Ritter, Weller, and Evans had been together for as long as I could remember. And now, only Evans was left. How did he feel today?

"Esterhazy from IT. She died outside Hawking. Caught in the blast."

I hadn't known her, but I grieved all the same.

"Four Time Police officers also lost their lives. Eight dead, altogether."

"And what of the wounded, sir?"

He said with some difficulty, "Mr. Markham was caught by a blaster and appears to be blind."

"Permanently?"

"It is, as yet, too soon to say. Mr. Sands was crushed by falling masonry. He has lost the lower part of his left leg, thus giving rise to an immortal exchange of words between him and Mr. Roberts. Upon Mr. Sands exclaiming that he appeared to have lost his foot, Mr. Roberts attempted to reassure him with the words, 'No you haven't. It's over here!'"

I choked, but with what emotion, even I couldn't have told you.

"And Mr. Stone, sir?" I saw again his faded medal ribbons.

"He will recover. A broken arm and shoulder. He is already conscious. And it's not just Mr. Stone. All the kitchen staff . . . And Mrs. Enderby, apparently, led a valiant effort to defend the upper stairs. She has a concussion and is, at the moment, quite unaware of what is happening around her."

He saw me looking around the ward.

"She is lodged in one of the treatment rooms. Dr. Foster has utilised every facility. We have people sleeping on the floor, in treatment rooms, along the corridor . . . The main part of the building is quite uninhabitable at present."

"What on earth are we telling people about this?"

"A World War II re-enactment, coupled with an unfortunate gas explosion."

"Do we even have gas out here in the country?"

"The bottled variety is, I believe, sufficiently volatile to add realism to our story. Apparently, the word in the village is that those mad bastards at St. Mary's have finally managed to blow themselves sky-high."

I could feel my eyelids droop.

"What next, sir?"

"What next, Max, is a punitive visit from our friends at SPOHB—the Society for the Protection of Historical Buildings. I fear they will find much to deplore. However, we have a week or so before that horror confronts us."

I had more to ask, but I must have dropped off in front of him because I don't remember him leaving. In fact, I slept most of the day. I opened my eyes to find the other doctor adjusting the machines and staring at me.

I said, "What? No chair and whip?"

He patted his pocket. "Pepper spray."

"You won't need it. I'm sorry."

"It's understandable. How do you feel?"

"Don't you know?"

"I'm a doctor. I know everything."

"So how am I?"

"Well, you've broken your hand, cracked some ribs, been involved in an explosion, and the lantern fell in on you. I was going to make a clever joke about the glass ceiling but I'm now so intimidated that I've forgotten it. Have you eaten anything?"

"I've only been awake for two minutes, for God's sake. When would I get the chance?"

"Difficult and uncooperative patient," he said slowly, writing on the chart. "When did you last open your bowels?"

"February. What happened to the Forces of Darkness? Are they still here?

He put the chart down. "No, they've all been removed. Dead, living, wounded, the lot."

"Where to?"

"Where they belong."

Did I want any more details? I decided not.

"Dr. Bairstow is on the sick list, so St. Mary's has a temporary caretaker director. He'd like a word, if you feel up to it. And if you promise to behave yourself."

I said hopefully, "Surely I'm too ill to see anyone."

He snorted.

HE WORE THE CONVICT orange of the Technical section. He looked desperately tired and there was more silver in his hair than I remembered, but his blue eyes were as bright as ever.

Something inside me soared.

He pulled up a chair and sat down. "Well, then."

I waited, but that seemed to be it. About par for the course. Of course, the ward was packed full of people, all of whom were desperately pretending to be asleep.

I had a medical glove on my broken hand, and the other hand was on the far side of the bed with tubes and other medical paraphernalia, so not a lot of me was accessible. He briefly touched my forearm and then drew back.

"What happened to your hair? Again."

I said, with dignity, "There was an explosion."

"Why weren't you wearing a helmet?"

"I took it off to make it easier for Barclay to shoot me."

He smiled, but it was an effort.

I looked at his worn face. "For how long have you been gone? In real time?"

"About six months. I gather it's been about three weeks here."

I nodded. He'd seen some wear and tear in those missing months. I was no longer the one with the most scar tissue. But he was here now.

There was so much to say. Too much. But sometimes, you don't need words.

I reached out my gloved hand and he took it between his own, cradling it like a broken bird. We said nothing. There was no need. Someone's tear plopped down onto the glove. He gently wiped it away with his thumb.

The door opened and someone called his name.

Without looking taking his eyes from me, he said, "On my way."

The door closed. Silence fell again.

Without opening her eyes, Mrs. Mack said, "Oh, for God's sake, just give the girl a kiss, will you."

I ASKED TO SEE Peterson and was trundled into the other ward the next afternoon. I had to take a couple of breaths to steady myself. Dieter was in the bad bed nearest the door, but it had to have been a toss-up between him, Peterson, and Guthrie. I've never seen so many wound dressings in so few square feet. As in the female ward, there weren't enough beds. Sands and Roberts reclined on mattresses on the floor, trying to play cards. Markham lay nearby, his eyes and face heavily bandaged.

My heart broke for him. If he was blind, there was no future for him here. I noticed how Guthrie watched him without seeming to. They all did. Even as they scoffed at his efforts to find his water jug, one of them would gently slide it within his grasp.

I told Markham he looked like the invisible man.

Roberts said, "If only . . ."

Leon offered me his chair, but I preferred to sit heavily on Peterson's bed, which served the dual function of breaking Sick Bay rules and crushing his feet at the same time.

"How come you're up and about?" said Guthrie. "Were you hiding at the back? Typical bloody historian."

"We always stand the Security section at the front," I said. "Cannon fodder."

"Have you noticed," said Markham, plaintively, "only senior officers get beds? The true heroes have to pig it on the floor."

"It's disgraceful," I said. "Why don't you come back to the female ward with me?"

He cheered up immediately.

"Oh, yes. You've no idea how I suffer, Max. The snoring. The grunting. The farting. The smell of feet."

"Don't worry—we can supply all of that. And you can have my bed."

"Great." His little battered face brightened hopefully through his bandages. "Will you be in it?"

"No," said Leon, severely. "She will not." He turned to Guthrie. "He's in your crew. Why don't you do something about him?"

Guthrie closed his eyes. "So long as he's not in bed with me, I don't really care."

SEVENTEEN

OR SOME REASON, THE ceremonial signing of the Charter was to be held at our St. Mary's. Ours had been the final battle, apparently, therefore, ours was to be the honour—the honour of signing the Time Police out of existence. We'd survived SPOHB—a feat in itself. The main building was shored up with scaffolding and wreathed in plastic. St. Mary's wasn't beautiful but it was safe—a statement that could not have been truthfully uttered at any point during our occupancy.

Most of us had been medically discharged, but I still lived in Sick Bay. Anywhere was better than the concrete room to which Barclay had assigned me.

Now, over the next few days, strange faces appeared and disappeared. Conferences were held. There was a great deal of noise and bustle and commotion.

And then everything stopped. We wondered why.

"Getting things done at St. Mary's is a bit like elephants mating," explained Peterson. A remark that caused some mystification.

"You know—there's frantic activity at high level. There's screaming and stamping. A lot of dust is raised. Nothing happens for two years and then you're crushed by the result."

THREE LONG TABLES HAD been pushed together in the Great Hall. There were seven seats down one side for the Time Police and eight down the other for representatives of St. Mary's. I couldn't help laughing. All that effort and they hadn't needed me after all. Now that Leon was Caretaker/Director, they actually had their seven directors.

I said as much to Mrs. Partridge.

She gave me a very strange look. "You should not underestimate the importance of your presence here today, Dr. Maxwell," and with that typically enigmatic statement, slipped away before I could ask.

Pods and people arrived all that day. People whose social skills far exceeded my own tactfully kept Time Police and St. Mary's apart.

The only thing that kept us on even moderately polite terms with them was that everyone was recovering fast. No one dared to die of their injuries, which was a tribute to the fear in which Dr. Foster was held.

The other piece of good news was that Mr. Markham could see—a fact which had led to an astonishing explosion of wrath from Hunter that easily dwarfed all her previous efforts, impressive though these had been. For some time it looked as if his Time Police-related injuries were the least of his worries as she sought him up and down the corridors of St. Mary's, terrifying in her rage.

It transpired he'd actually recovered his sight fairly early on, but caught up in the earthly delights of bed baths and other personal treatments the like of which he had hitherto only dreamed, he had somehow neglected to mention this to Nurse Hunter. This situation lasted for nearly a whole day, until Helen turned up to give him a routine check and blew his cover. With the entirely inappropriate relish of one with many scores to settle, she had conveyed this news to Nurse Hunter, with the result that Markham was now being hunted the length and breadth of St. Mary's. So far, she had been unsuccessful in locating him. Popular opinion said he was on a tramp steamer to Tristan da Cunha and never coming back.

BEFORE THE SIGNING, HOWEVER, we had a small ceremony of our own.

We assembled in the echoing Hall. Everyone who was medically fit was there, together with quite a few who weren't.

Dr. Bairstow and Chief Farrell faced each other on the half landing and complete silence fell.

"Director, you are relieved."

"Director, I stand relieved."

They shook hands to enthusiastic applause.

WE ARRANGED OURSELVES DOWN opposite sides of the tables with the careful politeness of two groups of people who really don't like each other very much. Madam President sat at the head. In a tactful and conciliatory move, she wore civilian clothing.

Dr. Bairstow sat opposite a young woman with a prematurely aged face. I wondered if she had sustained some sort of temporal accident. It can happen, apparently.

My opposite number was a very young officer, recently promoted by the looks of him. His brutal crewcut had grown out. I grinned discreetly at Lt Ellis. He grinned discreetly back again.

Apart from Ellis, I knew no one on the other side of the table. Arranged down my side were Dr. Bairstow, Chief Farrell, and Pinkie, who was an old friend from the future. I would try for a word with her before she left. There was also an elderly man, fiercely bright-eyed, whom I guessed was Dr. Bairstow's director—the man who would send him here all those years ago. All the others were strangers to me, but all of us were, or had been, directors of St. Mary's.

History was being made today and just for once, instead of merely observing and documenting, we were part of it. A nice change for us.

Madam President stood and addressed the assembly.

"Some time ago—in the future—the organisation known as the Time Police was formed to counter a very real threat. Their response to this threat was everything that could have been wished and I would like to place on record, here today, our grateful thanks for this response. Their task was not easy and involved considerable sacrifice on their part. Members of the Time Police—St. Mary's thanks you for your service."

A polite ripple of applause ran through the room.

A movement caught my eye. Mrs. Partridge was edging her way politely along the second row. Just as she sat down, she caught my eye and all the doubts and uncertainties that had, for days, been whirling around what passes for my brain suddenly coalesced and became clear. I stared at the table and wished I was somewhere else.

Madam President continued. "However, as we are all aware, circumstances change. The threat has been removed and the time has come to disband the organisation formed to deal with it. Delegates from the Time Police, together with everyone who has ever served as Director of St. Mary's have gathered today to do just that."

I leaned back in my chair and looked along the table to my left.

Pinkie was staring at me.

Madam President gestured to the pile of documents before her and smiled ruefully.

"This could take some time."

She was right. It did. It took longer than anyone expected because it never happened.

Because I refused to sign.

I PUT IT THAT way for dramatic effect, but actually, I wasn't the only one.

I watched one set of documents travelling down the other side of the table, each delegate signing the copy in front of him or her, and then passing it along for the next signature.

I watched the same thing happen on the St. Mary's side with growing unease. I really wasn't sure about this. And I wasn't the only one.

We had a bottleneck. A pile of unsigned documents was growing in front of Pinkie. She made no move to pick up her pen.

I was conscious of a faint murmuring around the Hall. Lt Ellis signed the last of the Time Police copies, stacked it neatly with the others, and waited for ours to be passed over.

He never got them.

Madam President said, "Is there some problem, Director?" and everyone looked at Pinkie. Personally, it would have intimidated the hell out of me but she was made of tough stuff. To dignify today's occasion, she'd put up her sandy hair, which only made her look more stubborn and more pugnacious than usual. She stared belligerently around the Hall, daring anyone to disagree.

She spoke. "I know, Madam President, that many sacrifices have been made to get us to the table today. I know that many at St. Mary's have worked long and hard to achieve this. Perhaps I should have spoken before, but if I had done so, events might have turned out differently and we would not be negotiating from today's position of strength.

"And we are, Madam President. Today we are in a position of great strength but we should not let that lead us in what I think might be the wrong direction. The Time Police were formed to counter a terrible danger. We cannot close our eyes to that fact. Knowledge about time travel is out there, and I'm certain a time will come when they will be needed again. It will happen. And on that occasion it may be too late for them to be reformed. I'm sorry, Madam President, Directors, members of St. Mary's, but I am not at all convinced that by signing them out of existence today, we are taking the right step."

There was a rather nasty silence. I suspected both sides were thinking of those who weren't here today and wondering, in that case, what the bloody hell it had all been about. A very valid point. But, today, we had the chance of a new beginning. Not something that could have happened if Colonel Albay had still been in command.

The silence lengthened until a rather shaken-looking Madam President said, "Does anyone else here agree? Or is Madam Director alone in her thinking?"

"No," I said, getting up. "She is not."

I didn't dare look at anyone. God knows what St. Mary's would do to me now. "The Director is perfectly correct. One day we will wake up to find it's all happening again and if we've disestablished the Time Police then we'll be in no position to deal with any future threats. I think we should take the time to remember the catastrophes that can occur when others use time travel so indiscriminately. Neither must we forget the purposes for which it could be used by the unscrupulous. I believe we need the Time Police. Surely, there must be some way in which we can all work together? A system of checks and balances that allows each of us to operate successfully?"

Silence.

I tried to keep my voice steady, but it wasn't easy. Not when I looked around the Hall for faces that weren't there. Would never be there again.

I persevered. "We have fought each other to a standstill. People have died. I think we should all take a step back and reconsider why we are here today."

Absolute silence. No applause. On the other hand, no heckling.

Somewhat sheepishly, I sat down. I looked for Mrs. Partridge but she'd gone. Perhaps to fetch her flaming sword. Again, I wished I was a million miles away.

Eventually, the old/young woman broke the silence. Almost as if she was thinking aloud, she said, "The integrity of the timeline must always be maintained."

Dr. Bairstow looked at Team St. Mary's ranged on either side of him and then said, "We agree."

"Perhaps a Code of Conduct . . . ?"

"That could certainly be addressed."

Silence.

A Director I didn't know cleared his throat and said, "St. Mary's would require the freedom to pursue our research without let or hindrance."

She said, "We agree."

"No permission need be sought?"

She said, carefully, "There should be an understanding perhaps, that permission could be withheld, but probably will never need to be."

More silence as most of St. Mary's worked that out on their fingers.

Dr. Bairstow nodded. "We agree."

"The Time Police reserve the right to advise, consult, and warn."

"We agree. St. Mary's reserves the right to implement its own plans and strategies."

"Subject to the Code of Conduct, yes."

"Such Code to be the subject of mutual agreement."

She nodded. "We agree."

He grew stern. "The purpose of the Time Police will be clearly defined. You will protect and defend the timeline. That is all. You cannot be the judicial system as well. You are not our masters. We will regulate ourselves. I can, however, envisage occasions when we would be glad of your assistance or advice. I hope you will make it easy for us to ask for it."

"We agree."

Silence fell again. Everyone looked at everyone else.

"Does anyone else have anything to add?" asked Madam President in tones guaranteed to dissuade anyone else from doing any such thing.

No one had. Apparently, we'd all decided to quit while we were ahead.

"Did anyone think to write all that down?" enquired Madam President, hopefully.

An excited Professor Rapson shot to his feet. "Yes, yes. I've got all that." He tore a leaf out of a battered notebook. "If someone could just make some copies, please."

And so the historic Treaty of St. Mary's was scribbled in red felt-tip on a page torn from a battered notebook, photocopied, signed by all, and distributed with the reverence of Magna Carta. Which, in its own way, it was.

That done, everyone relaxed for a moment. They would be serving tea soon.

Ellis and I, duty done, stood, stretched, and stepped away from the table.

I checked no one was listening and said quietly, "You saved my life. Thank you."

He looked over his shoulder to check no one was listening. "One good turn . . ."

There was no need to say any more.

"How's the leg?"

"Fine. How's the arm?"

"Fine."

He looked around the room.

"I see she's not here today."

I was baffled for a moment and then realised he meant Barclay. I'd more or less forgotten all about her. How stupid am I?

He continued. "It would have been interesting to watch her try to twist this situation to her advantage."

"Yes, a Time Police/St. Mary's coalition would be the last thing she wanted. I wish I could see her face when you tell her."

He turned his head, suddenly intent. "When *I* tell her?"

I've had the ground shift beneath my feet on several occasions, but never with as big a shock as now. And for him, too. I could see it in his face. We thought they had her and they thought we had her. We'd all taken our eyes off the ball.

I saw Dr. Bairstow's head snap round. He never missed a thing.

"You don't have her, Lieutenant?"

"No, sir. Don't you?"

"Why should we have her? We thought she'd been arrested by the Time Police because of that business with Maxwell."

"We thought you had taken her into custody, sir, and were dealing with her yourselves."

"So where is she?"

A very good question.

I knew I should have shot her.

Sometime in between me accidentally kicking her downstairs—twice—and Leon leading the rescue, against all the odds, she'd got up and got away. Probably just after the explosion when everyone was on their backs wondering what the hell had happened. Somehow, she'd escaped.

It was a blow. I'd been happily imagining her availing herself of all those very uncomfortable facilities unique to the Time Police and they obviously thought we'd spirited her away for purposes of our own. But no. She'd got away and it was far too late now. I tried to push it to the back of my mind.

And succeeded for nearly thirty minutes.

AFTER HALF AN HOUR, people started to drift away. I'd chatted briefly with Pinkie and been introduced to Dr. Bairstow's Director, but that had been it. I hadn't been able to exchange even a single word with Leon, whom everyone wanted to talk to.

While I waited for him, I thought I could collect my few belongings from my room and bring them back with me.

I slipped quietly from the Hall and made my way through the safety tape and polythene sheeting to the staff block. I was thinking about Leon, so when I pushed open the door to my room, it took a few minutes for the full realisation of what I saw to impact upon me.

My first thought was that there had been some sort of blizzard in here. Small, white, fluffy lumps of something lay everywhere. I couldn't think what it could possibly be. Then I saw the sagging remains of Bear 2.0, skewered to the wall with a knife through one eye. His little body had been ripped open from top to bottom and his white filling scattered around the room.

Bear 2.0, a gift from Leon, who had taken time out from saving the world to bring him to me, and I'd left him in this horrible room, to be torn apart in a fit of spiteful rage by Bitchface Barclay. I felt that I had let him down. That somehow, I had let both him and Leon down.

I stepped into the room on legs that were suddenly weak with shock. She'd been in here. At some point, she'd been in here. Attached to the knife was a note.

Your turn next—

Followed by a really nasty word. You know the one I mean. The state of the handwriting and the number of blood-stained fingerprints on the note told me she'd been badly hurt when she wrote it. She must have been desperate to get away before someone found her, or before she succumbed to her injuries. And yet, despite her haste, she'd taken the time to come down here, destroy my one precious thing, Leon's gift to me, and leave a very tangible threat. How much she must hate me.

And where was she now?

I spun around in sudden panic, which was stupid because, of course, she was long gone.

But she could be anywhere out there. Watching me. Waiting for her chance. A quick shove as I waited to cross the road. A little something added to an unattended cup of tea. A bullet literally out of the blue as I walked in the afternoon sunshine. I would never be safe again.

My mind skidded this way and that. I actually wondered, if I ran now, how far could I get, when, thankfully, my eyes fell on the real victim in all this. I reached up and pulled the knife out of his eye, crumpled the note and threw it away. I laid him gently on the pillow. Then I crawled painfully all over the room, groping under the bed, pulling the furniture around until I had every last piece of him collected. I put it all very carefully in the cardboard box and went to see Mrs. Enderby, still pale, but very much recovered. She was sitting quietly in one of the window seats in Wardrobe with a cup of tea beside her.

"Max." She seemed genuinely pleased to see me.

We asked each other how we were and then I passed her the box. She peered inside.

"Can you do anything, Mrs. Enderby?"

She took out poor Bear and laid him in her lap. She smoothed him out, assembled his little leather paws, checked the stuffing in the box, and said, "Yes, I think so. Come back in a few days."

I said, "Thank you," and for no reason at all, the tears started to fall.

"What a dreadful girl she was," she said, mildly, tactfully ignoring my struggles. I had to laugh. So much for throwing the note away. She'd guessed immediately who would do something like this. "You're not going to let this upset you, are you?"

"Not at all," I said firmly.

"Very wise," she said. "Come back for him on Wednesday."

That was when I made the decision. Mrs. Enderby was right. Yes, Barclay was out there somewhere and I would see her again one day, no doubt of that. When that happened, I'd deal with it. But, until that moment, if I did anything other than live my life normally then she'd won without even lifting a finger, and there was no way I'd ever let that happen. I'd fought too long and too hard to give up now. Because, finally, I had a future. I had a future and I had Leon.

Speaking of whom . . .

EIGHTEEN

I SNAGGED A CLIPBOARD AND some paper from Admin and waited in Leon's room. It was very quiet up here and I was able to work away without interruption.

He appeared about half an hour later, closing the door behind him. I thought again how tired he looked. He was certainly in need of some R & R.

I smiled. "There you are. I thought you'd got lost without me around to keep an eye on you."

"What are you doing?"

"Sitting on your bed."

"I mean, what's all this paper? Are you writing a book?"

"Of course I'm not. When does anything exciting ever happen to me?"

"So, what is all this, then?"

"Nothing for you to worry your pretty little head about. Just a few simple questions. Now then," I cleared my throat and raised my pen. "Do you have any pre-existing medical conditions?"

"What?"

"Any lower back pain?"

"What?"

"Any favourite sexual positions?"

"All of them. What is this about?"

"Foreplay."

He sighed. "I worry about you, sometimes."

"Look," I said, quite patiently, I thought. "This is us. Any minute now, some shady organisation will attack. Or Clive Ronan will kick the door down and kidnap you. Or Professor Rapson will unleash some toxic substance that will kill us all where we stand. Or Markham will reappear and the wrath of Nurse Hunter will bring down the rest of the building. Therefore, I thought I'd save us some time, because any minute now I'm going to be in your trousers like a frenzied ferret. I'm just getting the preliminaries out of the way. Now, do you have or have you ever had . . . ?"

He seized my clipboard and threw it out of the window.

"Well, that was a little unnecessary."

"Stop talking."

"There's a whole section on sexually transmitted diseases to work through yet."

"Let's move things on a little, shall we? Because I've spent months not allowing myself to think of you in any way and I warn you—I am so wound up I can barely function. If I can't touch you within the next few seconds, I *will* burst into flames. I am almost blind with desire for you. So, please, stop talking."

I pulled my T-shirt over my head.

"Does that help?"

"Not . . . noticeably."

"How about if I remove your T-shirt?"

He stepped back. "If you touch me I will explode."

I threw my bra across the room.

"Then touch me instead."

It took him three goes to get the door locked. When he turned back, my shorts had gone the same way as the bra. He stood very still. I don't think he was even breathing. His eyes were very dark. There was no blue. He walked slowly across the room, like a man wading through water. I reached for him, but he caught my wrists. "Please. You have to give me a minute. I wasn't kidding about exploding."

"No. No minutes. I wasn't kidding about something or someone getting in the way. If it's one thing I've learned, it's to seize my opportunities while I can. So now, Leon. Right here, right now. No more minutes."

There were no preliminaries.

The table went over with a crash that probably brought half the ceiling down on the unfortunate occupant of the room downstairs, and then he was right there in front of me, blocking the light, shoving me backwards against the cold wall. I could feel him against me. Every inch of him. He kissed me. Hard. I could taste him. I kissed him back, feeling everything inside me slide south.

I tore at his clothes while he kicked off his shoes and then, finally, he stood in front of me. We took a moment, just to look at each other. The only sounds in the universe were his uneven breathing and my thumping heart. He stepped forwards and slowly, very slowly, reached out for me. There was that never-to-be-repeated moment when skin touches skin for the very first time. I trembled against him.

He touched my face, very gently. As if he didn't trust himself to do more. "I am drowning in you . . ."

I groaned and melted against him because I had forgotten . . . oh God, I had forgotten . . . I stretched myself against him. His hands were all over me. Urgent but gentle. A deadly combination. For me, anyway.

He said, "Lucy," just once, in a voice that took my breath away. He lifted me up and then he was there. Hot and hard inside me. I could feel him. Feel his need. Pushing himself into me.

I wouldn't let him leave me behind. I pushed back. Matching his movements. Matching his breathing. I couldn't see—I couldn't hear. There was only a thick, heavy rhythm that found an echo in my blood as he pushed himself harder and higher with every movement. I wrapped my legs around him, wanting him—desperate for him. Now I knew how it felt to have a man lose all control and all thought. To lose himself in joy and love. To lose himself in me. To sweep me away in the flood of his own desire. His skin burned under my hands. I could feel his muscles moving. Hear his jagged breathing.

The wall was cold and hard behind my back. I found a moment to hope the room on the other side was empty because, any minute now, we could be coming through the wall. The bedside lamp toppled over. Something fell off the wall. I heard glass shatter. One of us knocked the alarm clock onto the floor and the alarm went off. God, it was loud. Although not as loud as us. I hoped the entire landing was empty. Because he was unstoppable. Relentless. Suppose we brought the building down. Again.

I caught a sob in my throat for the things I thought I'd lost and hadn't. Neither of us had. Finally, we were here. Now. Together.

I began to fall into hot, dark places . . . and still he moved inside me . . . picking up speed . . . great, glorious waves of pleasure . . . Oh God . . . I was lost . . . I cried out . . . and then all the anxiety, the fear, the uncertainty, everything washed away in surges of light and colour . . . and he must have been waiting for me, because with one, final, massive push, he exploded . . . and I could feel him inside me, pulsing, endlessly it seemed, on and on, carrying me with him, until, finally, he was still.

We slithered down the wall and lay in a tangle on the floor. He reached over and seized the still shrieking alarm clock, which went the same way as the clipboard. Silence fell. He pulled the duvet off the bed.

I lay, safe and warm, in his arms. "There's a perfectly good bed over there. Why are we sleeping on your bedroom floor?"

He tucked the duvet around us and said drowsily, "Would you prefer to sleep on someone else's bedroom floor?"

He closed his eyes.

I watched him sleep for a while. He was battered and scarred, his hair was turning grey, and for me, he was the most precious thing in this world. In any world.

I cried for him. I couldn't help it. And maybe I cried a little for myself as well.

DR. BAIRSTOW SENT FOR me. I knew what this would be about. It was time to make a decision. I'd honestly tried to give the future some thought and every time my mind had just shied away like a nervous horse. I didn't know what I wanted. I didn't know what Leon wanted either. We really were going to have to stop hurling ourselves at each other and sit down and talk about it. And soon.

Dr. Bairstow was in his office, at his desk. Mrs. Partridge was seated behind him, scratchpad in hand. I don't know why, but seeing her there caused a bit of a lump in my throat. I swallowed it down because this was not the moment to go all wobbly.

Initially, he wanted to talk about the memorial service. I hesitated because I still wasn't that sure of my position at St. Mary's.

"You should attend," he said. "I think it would be appreciated. And it will give you a chance to grieve for your own St. Mary's and the friends you will never see again."

I couldn't speak for a moment.

"There are no words, Max, to thank you for the sacrifice you have made."

"It wasn't really a sacrifice, sir. I would have died, otherwise."

"Then we should both be thankful you are here. Which leads me to my next question. Will you stay?"

"I don't know."

"Do you miss St. Mary's?"

"Yes, very much. But just recently, there's been so much death . . ."

"Yes, far too much death. But we're historians and it's part of the package."

"And after what she . . . Maxwell . . . did . . . at Troy . . ."

"It wasn't you. You didn't do it. You must remember that. I know you identify very closely with the other Max and it's not surprising that you should do so, but she wasn't you and you're not her."

He moved some files on his desk.

"Now, Dr. Dowson and I have put our heads together and come up with the following, which we hope you will approve.

"We can't have two Madeleine Maxwells, so you are Lucy Maxwell. You are some sort of cousin to Madeleine Maxwell. You never met her so you're not sure of the precise relationship. You studied at Thirsk, reading History, and have postgraduate qualifications in Archaeology and Anthropology.

"You worked at various archaeological sites around the eastern Mediterranean. I leave it to you to decide how and when you met Chief Farrell. I leave it to you to decide how much to tell people, although I suspect no one will ask. And I leave it to you to decide your future, as well."

He pushed an envelope across the desk. Inside, I saw a passport, a driving licence (didn't they know I was the world's worst driver?), an ID card, an NI number, credit and debit cards. A completely new identity. A completely new life.

I looked up, startled—and suspicious.

He smiled. "Let me make it clear. None of this is contingent upon you remaining at St. Mary's. This—all this—is yours to keep, whatever decision you make. I make no secret—I would like the both of you to return to St. Mary's and resume your lives here. However, I do accept that that is up to you and if you do decide to leave, my best wishes for your new life go with you."

He paused and lined up the files on his desk again.

"Let me help you come to a decision. If you do decide to remain here, I shall appoint you Chief Operations Officer. In fact, if you do leave, I shall have a problem, because Dr. Peterson has already requested to return to his former position as Training Officer."

I wondered whether that was anything to do with his new assistant, Miss Lee. Whom Dr. Bairstow had reassigned. Had he foreseen Peterson's request? I remembered Dr. Dowson saying that Dr. Bairstow always had a plan.

"Furthermore, to mark your return, you may select whatever assignment you please. Your choice. Your team. Your mission. Take that away and think about it."

"As a reward?"

"Good heavens, no. Please be perfectly clear about this, Dr. Maxwell. It is a bribe."

I looked at him. "Anything?"

He visibly braced himself. "That is what I said."

Half a dozen crazy ideas flashed through my head, and then I remembered Helios and the price he paid for what we had done, and the lessons learned, and swallowed what I had been about to say.

Behind Dr. Bairstow, Mrs. Partridge lifted her eyes from her scratchpad, smiled in rare approval, and continued to take notes.

I remembered a recent conversation. Me, Tim, and a picnic . . . at Thermopylae.

"Can I get back to you about that, sir?"

"Of course."

I REALLY THOUGHT I deserved a drink. Apparently, so did the rest of St. Mary's. Think that they deserved a drink, I mean. The bar was packed and noisy.

I got myself a tonic water and lime and looked for somewhere to sit. Time to test the waters. Not without a little trepidation, I joined the group by the window. Nobody made a big thing of it, but everyone moved up to make room. I was accepted.

Just as the other St. Mary's had taken in that lost, lonely girl all those years ago, so had this one done the same. And, all right, the new colour scheme in this room was disgusting, and the toilets were further away, but, whatever the minor differences, the characters of the people here were exactly the same and what a relief that was. To have something familiar to cling to. To know that, in this St. Mary's, Tim was still his own gentle self. That Dr. Bairstow could still freeze your blood at twenty paces. That Markham was still engaged in his unending quest for Hunter's affections. That Mrs. Partridge would still look up from her scratchpad with that expression of resigned exasperation . . .

I resurfaced to find they were discussing Prentiss's love life. Or lack thereof.

"It's quite easy, really," Hunter was saying. "You just talk to them. These days, men can understand even quite complicated words. Watch."

She turned to Markham, who had recently returned to the orbit of her affection like an erratic comet, and smiled dazzlingly at him. As always, whenever she was near, he sat up and looked like an expectant spaniel.

She dropped her voice an octave or two. "Well, hello there, big boy. And how tall are you?"

He swallowed hard. "Five foot six."

"Well, let's forget about the five feet and talk about the six inches, shall we?"

I thought he was going to faint. He made the faint gobbling noises of one whose blood has fled south for the winter.

Hunter regarded him complacently and then turned back to Prentiss.

"See? Easy. Give it a go."

"I will."

She looked around. Major Guthrie was just walking past.

"Good afternoon, Major. How tall are you?"

"Um, six feet and half an inch," he said, and stood bewildered, as, to a man, St. Mary's slid to the floor and laughed its head off.

"What on earth . . . ?" said Leon, turning up half a minute later and surveying the scene.

I wiped my eyes. "Tell you later. Did you want me?"

"Yes. Have you got a minute?"

I got up to go and paused. It would have taken a better woman than me to resist the temptation.

"Leon, how tall are you?"

"Five foot ten inches."

What can you say?

WE SAT OUTSIDE AT one of the tables overlooking the gardens. The sun shone. Birds sang. In a few minutes, they'd start the institutionally approved violence known as football, when the Technical and Security sections relieved the week's tensions by kicking the living shit out of each other in the name of sport. But just at the moment, all was peace and tranquillity.

We sat in the warm sunshine for a while and then he said, "I think the time has come to talk."

I nodded. It had. I looked at him. He was wearing the old jeans and sweater from when the Time Police had first turned up and disrupted our lives. I was in historian blues. I wondered if that meant anything.

"I think we need to talk about what we want to do. If you like, I'll go first."

I nodded again.

He reached over and took my hand. Right in front of anyone who cared to look. He turned to look at me and his blue eyes were very bright.

"If there's one thing I've learned, it's that this is too important to mess about with. We're too important. So no more of this, Max. I'm going to say what I want. Then you can do the same. Then we'll talk about how to achieve it. We'll talk honestly and say the things we really feel. All right?"

I nodded again.

"Here goes, then. I don't care. I don't care whether we live here at St. Mary's, or whether we go back to Rushford. I really don't care. So long as I'm with you, I'll live in a box in Tesco's car park, if that's what you want. I've learned that happiness is too fragile and fleeting to be messed around with. You have to grab it while you can. So, you say what you want to do and I'll happily go along with it. Just so long as you want to do it with me."

I looked at his battered hand holding mine. I thought about life here at St. Mary's. A unit to put back together again. I thought about Peterson and Markham and Guthrie. I thought about the noise, the arguments, the solid feeling of good friends. I thought about how I felt every time the pod door opened and I stepped out into the unknown.

Then I thought about his little flat. I thought about sitting at the kitchen table, watching him cook while I sipped wine and just enjoyed being with him. I thought about the paintings I could produce. I thought about all the pictures in my head that might never see the light of day if I stayed here. I thought about staying in bed with him on Sunday mornings, reading the papers and getting toast crumbs everywhere. I thought about waking up every morning and he would be there, beside me, smiling.

I looked across at the football pitch and the battle lines being drawn up there. "I don't mind, either. I just want to be with you. But happiness is like grains of sand. The more tightly you clench your fist, the more it just slips through your fingers. I think that if we just come to rest somewhere and wait quietly, then one day we'll look up and it'll be there. So, like you, I don't care. Whatever you want to do, I'll do it with you."

"Well, we're a hopeless pair, aren't we? It looks as if I'm going to have to deploy the decision-making apparatus again."

He delved in his pocket, pulling out half a crown.

"Heads we stay. Tails we go."

"Fine with me."

He tossed the coin. I watched it fly up into the air, catching the light as it spun. He caught it neatly, slapped it down on the table. We both leaned forwards to look. And then we both leaned back.

"Well," he said, reaching for his coffee. "That's that sorted."

THE END

No Time Like the Past

In *No Time Like the Past*, St. Mary's has been rebuilt, and it's nearly back to business as usual for the history department. Except for the visit to St. Paul's Cathedral with a seventeenth-century ghost that only Mr. Markham can see. And getting trapped in the Great Fire of London. And an unfortunately-timed vacation at Thermopylae that leaves the fate of the western world hanging in the balance.

Actually, that sounds quite like business as usual for Max and the gang.

$12.99 paperback
978-1-59780-872-9

EXCERPT FROM
NO TIME LIKE THE PAST

*A*NOTHER ALL-STAFF BRIEFING FROM Dr. Bairstow. The first since our unpleasantness with the Time Police last summer. However, they'd gone—we were still here—most of the building had been restored, and St. Mary's was open for business.

We work for the Institute of Historical Research at St. Mary's Priory. We investigate major historical events in contemporary time. For God's sake—*do not* call it time travel. The last person to do that had her head thumped and then was inadvertently caused to fall down the stairs.

Anyway, the building had recovered from its wounds—we'd recovered from ours—and here we all were, slowly suffocating in the smell of new wood, damp plaster, and fresh paint. Not the best smells in the world, but still a big improvement on cordite, blood, and defeat.

Tim Peterson and I sat in the front row and assumed expressions of near-terminal enthusiasm and commitment. Once we would have sat at the back and played Battleships, but senior staff have to sit at the front and show willing. It makes the destruction of the enemy fleet that much more difficult, but we were willing to rise to the challenge.

Here came the Boss, limping to the half-landing and standing in his usual position, leaning heavily on his stick. The cold winter sunshine streamed through the newly restored glass lantern above him as he surveyed his unit with the expression of an impatient vulture waiting for a dying wildebeest to get a move on.

"Good morning, everyone. Thank you for coming."

As if we had any choice.

"As you can see, with effect from 10 a.m. this morning, St. Mary's is up and running."

There was a polite smattering of applause. Most of us had been working our socks off for the last three weeks, restoring the Library and Archive, and generally helping to put the building back together, so whether St. Mary's was open or not actually made very little difference to us.

"There are a few staff changes to announce. If you care to consult the organisational charts distributed at the beginning of this meeting by Mrs. Partridge . . ." He paused for the traditional panic from those who had lost theirs already. Peterson and I were using ours to record the disposition of our respective armadas.

"Firstly, I would like to confirm Dr. Maxwell in her position of Chief Operations Officer."

He paused again. I fixed my attention on my imperilled destroyers and mentally crossed my fingers. There was a small round of applause and I breathed a sigh of relief. There had been that episode last Christmas, when Dr. Bairstow had returned from a rare night of carousing in Rushford to find he had mysteriously acquired two additional historians. He'd taken it very well, all things considered. They were off now, reorienting and acclimatising themselves at Thirsk University—a necessary procedure after such a long absence. They'd been missing for ten years. And Ian Guthrie, to whom one of the missing historians was very special indeed, had caught me in the corridor one day, held my hand very tightly, said, "I owe you, Max," and then walked away before either of us displayed any unseemly emotion.

Dr. Bairstow was forging on. "Dr. Peterson assumes his original position of Chief Training Officer. Chief Farrell returns as joint head of the Technical Section, alongside Mr. Dieter. Miss Perkins is appointed Head of IT, replacing Miss Barclay who has left us."

Yes, she bloody had. She'd escaped in the confusion arising from the kitchen staff blowing up the building with flour-filled condoms. Long story. Still, a wrecked building was a small price to pay for ridding ourselves of Bitchface Barclay. Sadly, she hadn't gone for good. She was out there, somewhere. It was only a matter of time before we met again. She'd left me a note to that effect.

He continued. "I would like to congratulate Mr. Markham on his promotion to second in charge of the Security Section."

No, I didn't think he'd be able to bring himself to utter the words, *Number Two* and *Mr. Markham* in the same sentence. It would be asking for trouble. Markham sat up and beamed amiably at him. His hair, as usual, stuck up in irregular clumps. He looked like someone being treated for mange. And not for the first time, either.

"Mrs. Partridge is confirmed as my PA and Miss Lee will return to her former position as admin assistant to the History Department."

The History Department sighed. As did I. Yes, there she was, two rows along, her short dark hair waving around her head, just like Medusa's snakes, but slightly more intimidating. She turned her Gorgon stare upon the History Department who promptly shut up.

"I would also particularly like to welcome back our caretaker, Mr. Strong."

This time, the round of applause was enthusiastic and genuine. He was an old man and last year he'd disobeyed instructions, pinned on his medals, and stepped up to fight for St. Mary's. He'd been injured—we all had. Some of us had died. The Boss had tried to send him away to convalesce and he'd respectfully refused to go and spent his time stumping around the ruins of the Great Hall, telling the builders where they were going wrong and infuriating the Society for the Protection of Historical Buildings, who were supposed to be overseeing the repairs. They'd complained and Dr. Bairstow, in a few well-chosen words that echoed around St. Mary's, had given them to understand that Mr. Strong was one of his most valued employees and his long years at St. Mary's made him a leading authority on the building and everything in it. They got the message. Mr. Strong had, however, in the interests of good will, consented to a two-week visit to see his grandchildren.

"Mr. Strong has asked me to remind you that this building is in better condition now than at any time during its long history—and certainly since we moved in—and he would be grateful if you could all use your best endeavours to keep it that way. As would I."

He paused for this to sink in as Peterson whispered, "B6."

"Miss!"

"Normal service is to resume as soon as possible. The History Department will let me have their schedule of upcoming assignments and recommendations by tomorrow."

"B7."

"Bollocks!"

"Dr. Foster, please confirm all personnel are medically fit to return to duty. Or at least as fit as they are ever likely to be."

"B8."

"You're cheating, aren't you?"

"The Technical Section is to confirm that all pods are serviceable."

"B9."

"Sunk."

"Dr. Peterson? Do we possess any trainees at this moment, or did they all run for the hills during our summer unpleasantness?"

"No and no, sir. We didn't have any trainees before the summer unpleasantness, let alone afterwards. Our last recruiting drive was . . . ineffective."

He sighed, impatiently. "I cannot understand why St. Mary's finds it so difficult to recruit and retain staff."

In my mind's eye, I saw the broken bodies, half-buried under the rubble, the blood, heard the thump of explosions . . .

"Please draw up ideas and suggestions for recruiting and, most importantly, retaining suitable personnel. Please do not construe this instruction as permission to roam the streets with nets and ropes, offering people the King's Shilling. Attempts to retain future trainees by nailing them to their own desks will be discouraged."

"You are imposing unreasonable restrictions, sir, but I shall do my best."

He started on about something else, but I'd discovered Peterson's cruisers, cunningly clustered together in the top left-hand corner of his A4 ocean. In the subsequent orgy of destruction, I completely missed what he said next, and was roused only by his traditional, "Are there any questions?" which is Dr. Bairstow-speak for "I've told you what to do—now get on with it." He had once been forced to attend a "Caring Management" seminar, during which someone had courageously informed him that staff are more productive if they feel included and valued. Clearly, he hadn't believed a word of it. There were never any questions.

"Dr. Maxwell, if you could spare me a moment, please? Thank you everyone. That will be all."

Back in his office, he didn't waste any time.

"I'll leave you to set the date, Dr. Maxwell. I think you'll agree that sometime during the coming summer seems most convenient—good weather and so on. There will be an enormous amount of work, of course, but farm it out as you think appropriate. I shall want weekly updates, but just a quick progress report will be sufficient. Draft in whomever you need. I'll be able to let you have details of the budget sometime over the next few days."

I hadn't the faintest idea what he was talking about.

Behind him, Mrs. Partridge smirked unhelpfully.

"I'm sorry, sir?"

"Mrs. Partridge will handle the admin side—licenses, permits, insurance, etc. Pass all the details to her."

"Um . . ."

He handed me an already bulging file and dismissed me. "Thank you, Dr. Maxwell."

My finely honed historian senses told me I'd missed something. And he knew it. There was no escape.

"I'm sorry, sir—perhaps you could elaborate a little?"

He sighed, and as one addressing an idiot, said, "The Open Day."

"What Open Day?"

"St. Mary's Open Day."

"What? When?"

"Whenever you select the date. St. Mary's is to hold an Open Day and you are to organise it."

"Am I? When was all this announced?"

"About twenty minutes ago. Just as you destroyed Dr. Peterson's second submarine."

I WAS BACK IN my newly refurbished office. The windows had been heaved open, but even so, the stench of paint was making my eyes water. The smell reminded me of the polyurethane poisoning I'd had as a student, when I'd painted my room one weekend and had only a very rudimentary understanding of the words "adequate ventilation."

In reverse order of importance, I had something ergonomic in the way of a desk, a new, posh chair, and a new kettle. Sadly, I also had Miss Lee, who was peering at her screen and possibly frying a few circuits with her Gorgon glare.

I dropped the folder onto my desk with a thud and was about to request a cup of tea from Miss Lee—yet another example of blind optimism over experience—when Markham burst into the room.

"Max! Quick! Someone's fallen off the roof!"

I shot to my feet and followed him out. We ran down the corridor to the second window from the end. Unlike the others along the corridor, it was open. He thrust out his head and shoulders, leaning precariously over the low sill.

"It was here!"

I grabbed a handful of his green jumpsuit and yanked him back.

"Steady on or there'll be two of you stretched out on the gravel . . ."

There was nothing there.

I looked left and right but there was nothing there. The bare-stemmed Virginia creeper covered the walls, but other than that, there was no plant life for yards around. A wide gravel path ran along this, the eastern side of St. Mary's. There was just the path and the frosty grass sloping down to the lake. The only sign of life was a few of our less traumatised swans, stumping up and down on the far side of the lake. Other than that—there was nothing.

I pulled my head in.

"Where?"

"Here. I saw it. They fell past this window. But when I looked, there was no one there."

I didn't bother asking, "Are you sure?" This was Markham. To be sure, he was small, grubby, and accident prone, but he was also virtually indestructible and very, very tough. Yet here he was, standing in front of me now, so pale that I could see the blue veins in his temples. There was no doubt he thought he'd seen something.

He stuck his own head back out of the window, presumably in case the body had magically reappeared.

"Perhaps they weren't hurt—or not hurt very badly," he said, "and they got up and went for help."

"Good thought." I opened my com link and called Dr. Foster. "Helen—has anyone reported to you at any time in the last ten minutes?"

"No. Why?"

"There's a possibility someone may have fallen off the roof."

"Check around. Especially those idiots in R & D. Sounds like the sort of thing they might do. I'll let you know if anyone turns up."

She closed the link.

Markham was as near angry as I'd ever seen him. "There's no 'possibility' about it. I know what I saw."

"What did you see? Tell me every detail."

"I was standing just here."

He pushed me aside and stood where I had been.

"I was walking towards your office."

He mimed walking, just in case I was having some difficulty grasping the concept.

"The window was on my left. Just as I drew level, something black fell past. I was so surprised I couldn't move for a second."

He mimed a level of surprise and horror that would lead anyone else to believe he'd just witnessed an asteroid wipe out the dinosaurs.

"Then I heaved up the window, leaned out, and . . . and there was nothing there."

"Is there a possibility they got up and ran away before you had a chance to see?"

"I don't know. It took me a while to get the window open, but you've seen for yourself—there's no cover. All right, they might not be dead since they only fell on gravel, but it's three floors up—they'd have broken a bone or two at least. And why would they hide? It doesn't make sense."

He looked genuinely agitated, which was a first for him.

"I think," I said slowly, "that someone's pulling your plonker. Someone's up on the roof—they push off an old dummy and in between the time you see it and struggle to get the window up and look out, someone's leaned out of a downstairs window and pulled it in. I bet they're down there now, laughing their heads off and waiting for you to appear at any minute and start dashing about looking for bodies."

His face cleared. "Of course. Bastards! Good trick though. Talk about shitting bricks—I nearly evacuated a monolith. Thanks, Max."

He strolled off, presumably to bring down retribution on persons unknown, and I wandered back to my office.

The next day, he was back again and this time he wasn't alone.

They burst through my door, Peterson escorting Markham who looked—not to put too fine a point on it—as if he'd seen a ghost.

"It did it again," he said, not very coherently for someone brought up in the Major Guthrie tradition of concise reporting.

First things first. I opened my mouth to instruct Miss Lee to make him a cup of much-needed tea but she was already ahead of the game, gathering up two or three files at random and heading for the door, announcing she had to catch the post, which indeed, would be collected in about four hours' time.

Peterson made us all a cup of tea. I contemplated adding something comforting from my bottom drawer, but Markham was incoherent enough.

"I saw it again, Max," he announced. "A black figure falling past the window and when I looked out there was nothing there. Again. Dr. Peterson was there. He saw it."

"I saw you see something," corrected Peterson. "I didn't see anything fall, but I can confirm there was nothing there when we looked."

"But you must have," objected Markham. "A black figure, silhouetted against the sky. I saw arms and legs. Just for a moment, true, but you can't mistake a falling body."

I had a thought. "What did you hear?"

He sat quietly, running through things in his mind. "Nothing."

"Nothing? No cry? No sound of impact?"

He looked suddenly thoughtful. "No. There was no sound of impact. And if those buggers from R & D were playing silly devils and chucking things off the roof then you'd hear something, wouldn't you?"

Yes, you would. I looked at him again. I'd seen him wounded; I'd seen him running for his life; I'd even seen him in drag, but I'd never seen him like this before. I couldn't dismiss this lightly.

I stood up. "Tim, can you check out R & D? Tactfully, please."

He nodded. "What are you going to do?"

"I'm going to talk to Dr. Dowson." I looked at Markham. "You all right?"

"Yes. What shall I do?"

"Nothing for the minute. If someone is playing a trick on you then the best thing you can do is ignore it. We'll meet back here at half past three."

Dr. Dowson was our librarian and archivist. In most organisations, this means spending the day in an atmosphere of tranquil serenity. Books don't usually give you a lot of grief. Today, he was standing on his desk, pounding the ceiling with a broom handle and shouting curses. In Latin, Greek, and possibly Morse code, by the sound of it.

He broke off to greet me with a smile. "Ah, Max. Can I help you?"

I knew better than to ask what was going on. He and Professor Rapson from R & D were old friends, which apparently was sufficient grounds for mutual abuse and recrimination at every opportunity. R & D occupied the rooms directly overhead and possibly inadvertently, but probably not, had done something to incur his wrath.

I helped him down off his desk and told him the story and feeling a little foolish said, "Is it possible, is it just possible, that we have a ghost we didn't know about?"

He stood still for a moment, polishing his spectacles, lost in thought, and then disappeared briefly, returning with an old book, two modern pamphlets, and a file of loose photocopies.

He laid them on a table and we sat down.

"Right." he said. "A potted history of St. Mary's.

"The first building, the original Priory of St. Mary's, was raised by Augustinian monks towards the end of the 13th century. That building stood for more or less a hundred years. I think the location was too remote, however, and over the years, the monks just drifted away. St. Mary's, the village, and all the land with it were eventually acquired—it doesn't say how—by Henry of Grosmont, 4th Earl of Lancaster. He did nothing with it, other than collect the rents, but his son-in-law, John of Gaunt, Duke of Lancaster, bestowed the manor upon Henry of Rushford, a comrade in arms, for services rendered during the 1386 campaign in Castile.

"This next bit is interesting. There was, apparently, a bit of a skirmish during the confusion of 1399. While Richard II and Henry Bolingbroke jostled for supremacy, it would appear another branch of the Rushford family took advantage of the confusion and attacked St. Mary's. Despite a spirited defence, the attackers did gain entry, but were foiled when, in a last desperate effort, the defenders, led by Henry's granddaughter, attempted to burn the place down to cover their escape to Rushford. Exciting days, eh?

"Matters were obviously resolved satisfactorily, but St. Mary's passed out of the Rushford family's hands a generation or so afterwards. No heir, as is frequently the case, I'm afraid. I really don't know why these things are always passed down through the male line—girl children are much more robust than their brothers, and let's face it, Max—while there may always be doubt about the identity of the father, most people are usually fairly clear about who the mother is."

He brooded for a while on this unsatisfactory state of affairs, and who was I to disagree?

"Anyway, St. Mary's had any number of owners, all of whom apparently lived perfectly peacefully, even during troubled times. The estate survived the Wars of the Roses, religious strife under the Tudors, and then, in the late 16th century, the Laceys of Gloucestershire moved in."

He opened the book. "The Civil War split them down the middle, with half of them supporting the King and the other half lining up for Cromwell. In 1643, a contingent of Parliamentary forces, led by Captain Edmund Lacey, left Gloucester for some reason, and rode here. Accounts are jumbled, and there are several versions of events, but they all agree that the Great Hall was torched and Margaret Lacey and her elder son, Charles, perished in the blaze. The younger son, James, who was only a very young boy at the time, escaped to the roof, was rescued by a servant, and taken safely to the village. Captain Lacey disappeared, was tried, and found guilty of murder in his absence and was never seen again. The Hall was rebuilt by James and is largely as we see it today. With the exception of the glass lantern, of course.

"St. Mary's continued to change hands, shedding land as it went, until it fell empty in the late 19th century. It was too big for a family house and since there was no longer any land left to support it, it became a bit of a white elephant, I'm afraid. It was used as a convalescent home for soldiers during and after World War I, and then was a school, briefly and disastrously. Apparently, someone left a tap running and the ceiling came down in what is now Wardrobe. It was used as a hospital again during World War II. And that's it until we moved in, my goodness, some years ago now." He tapped the documents. "It's all here. And much more besides."

I said slowly, "Thank you, Doctor, but I think might I have what I need."

He nodded. "1643?"

"Yes, I think so. The little boy ran up to the roof. He survived, but maybe someone did fall. Captain Lacey, maybe. Perhaps that's why he was never seen again. Because he died. Either in the fire or in the fall. Can you get me more details?"

He smiled. "I expect so. Give me an hour."

WE RECONVENED. THERE BEING no sign of Miss Lee, I made the tea this time.

"You can't be doing it right," said Peterson, smugly. "My Mrs. Shaw brings me chocolate biscuits as well."

I ignored him.

"There seem to be two candidates for Mr. Markham's falling body. In 1399, there was a minor skirmish over ownership. I suppose it's perfectly possible someone could have fallen from the roof."

"Or possibly, someone had a mad wife and she jumped, like Mrs. Rochester," added Markham, never one to choose the obvious option. "And she dashed her brains out on the flags below."

"When did you ever read *Jane Eyre*?" demanded Peterson, easily distracted.

"I broke my ankle."

We waited, but that seemed to be it.

"Or," I said, firmly dragging them back on track, "in 1643, during the Civil War, the Roundheads arrived, threatened, and possibly murdered a woman and child. But, and this is the interesting bit, a second child sought refuge on the roof. Describe the body again."

"There's nothing to describe. A black shape with arms and legs."

"Could it have been a child?"

"It could, I suppose. It didn't look very big, but . . ." He sounded doubtful. "I don't know. And anyway, the kid survived, didn't he? It's a bit of a mystery."

Silence. We slurped our tea.

"Well," said Peterson. "Now what? All very interesting, but what has this to do with us?"

There being no good answer to that one, we finished our tea and stood up. I walked with them to the door and out into the corridor.

"Sorry, mate," said Peterson to Markham. "There's just too little to go on. Apart from your daily hallucinations, we just don't have any—"

Markham stiffened, pointed, and cried, "There! Oh, my God! Again!"

We stood paralysed, because we're highly trained professionals, and then rushed to the window. Peterson heaved it up and stuck out his head. I elbowed myself some room and did the same. Markham, realising he stood no chance, ran to another window and looked out.

The sun shone down on the frosty gravel. We looked to the north. We looked to the south. Markham thought to hang even further out of the window, twist himself around, and look up.

Nothing.

"Come on," he said, and we headed for the roof, emerging through a tiny door in the north-east corner. Despite the frost,

the roof was a bit of a suntrap and pleasantly warm. In the
old days, it had been gabled and tiled, but at some point in its
history, the roof had been replaced and flattened. Groups of
tall chimneys stood around. The big glass lantern, which let
some much-needed light into the Hall, was over there. Over
to the right, we could look down on lower roof levels. There
was even a fire escape, which Markham headed towards. We
watched him go.

"What do you think?" said Peterson. "It's astounding, isn't it?"

"I know. I'm still gobsmacked. Jane Eyre!"

"Are we going to check this out?"

"Are you kidding?"

"We'll never get permission."

"Leave that to me. I've had a brilliant idea."

He groaned.

Markham returned and crossed to the parapet, which was
just above waist height and looked down. We joined him.

"Bloody hell," said Peterson, stepping back.

"You all right?"

"Fine," he said, averting his eyes and stepping four or five
paces back. "Just tell me what you see."

"Nothing. There's nothing."

"And nothing's been up here today," added Markham.

He was right. Our footprints were clearly visible on the
frosty roof. And only ours. Unless someone had come up here
barefoot . . .

We looked around, our breath frosty in the cold, sharp air.

I looked at Markham. "Are you up for this?"

"How can you even ask?"

I SPENT THE REST of the day putting things together and just
as the lights were coming on and people beginning to drift
towards the dining-room, I went to see Dr. Bairstow. Who
looked about as pleased to see me as he usually did.

"Dr. Maxwell. Can I assume you will bring me details of your progress organising our Open Day?"

"All in hand, sir," I said, with massive confidence and even more massive untruthfulness.

"Then you are here because . . .?"

"I'd like to claim my jump, sir. If you please."

At the end of our unpleasantness last year, as an outright bribe, he'd offered me the assignment of my choice. At the time, I'd considered Thermopylae, but now . . .

"Really? Where and when did you have in mind?"

"St. Mary's. 1643."

He finished stacking his files and straightened, slowly.

"An interesting choice. May I ask why?"

"Ghost-hunting, sir."

He looked at me sharply. "There is no ghost at St. Mary's."

"We may have recently acquired one, sir."

"How?"

I considered my options, remembered no good ever came of lying to the Boss, and said, "On three occasions now, Mr. Markham has seen someone fall off the roof. When we go to check it out, there's never anything there."

"1643? That would be the dastardly Captain Lacey?"

"That's the one, sir."

He moved the files around.

"Do we have a working pod?"

"I'm sure Chief Farrell will have one tucked away somewhere, sir."

I waited. There was no need to remind him of his promise.

"Do not let the fact that I have pre-approved this assignment lead you to believe I will not wish to see the usual mission plan, Dr. Maxwell."

"Of course not, sir."

"Or that the usual parameters will not apply."

"No, sir."

"And your team will consist of . . .?"

"Me, Dr. Peterson, and Mr. Markham."

"Ah. The usual suspects. Why Mr. Markham?"

"It's his ghost, sir," I said, more accurately than anyone realised at the time.

"Well, I suppose Mr. Markham's absence from St. Mary's is always a cause for celebration."

"Well, not really, sir. He'll still be here—just four hundred years ago."

He sighed. "I don't really think that will be long enough."

ABOUT THE AUTHOR

*J*ODI TAYLOR (WHO ALSO writes as Isabella Barclay) is, and always has been, a History Nut. Her disinclination to get out of bed for anything after 1485 can only be overcome by massive amounts of chocolate, and sometimes, if it's raining, not even then.

She wanted to write a book about time travel that was a little different, and not having a clue how difficult this would make her book to classify, went ahead and slung in elements of history, adventure, comedy, romance, tragedy, and anything else she could think of. Her advice to booksellers is to buy huge numbers of her books and just put one on every shelf.

The result is the story of the St. Mary's Institute of Historical Research and the nutters who work there.